ANDREW RATHWELL

Whispers of the Uncharted Green

First published by Rathwell Books 2025

First edition

ISBN: 9798262620050

This book was professionally typeset on Reedsy.
Find out more at reedsy.com

To my wife, Shelby, whom I love more than I can put into words.

Contents

Preface

I am proud to present Whispers of the Uncharted Green. This book originated from the simple idea of sailing on a seemingly endless sea of grass. The imagery of that concept has been rattling around in my head for over eleven years. There were a million things that came together to make this book a reality, including the desire to write a stand-alone story, an unhealthy obsession with a particular series of fantasy RPGs that blend magic and technology, and, of course, my very heartfelt belief that love is the single most important thing you can do with your life. Despite it taking nearly a decade, it all began with a teenager's dream to write a story about an ocean of grass, and I think that really demonstrates the tremendous power of a small idea if you refuse to give up on it. I hope you enjoy it, and as always, thank you for giving this book a chance.

I

The Verdant Sea

1

The Verdant Sea

Nothing could have prepared Sylus for his first real sight of the Verdant Sea.

Growing up in an isolated mountain village above the cloud layer meant that most days, the vast grass oceans weren't visible. Even on clear days, the surrounding peaks only offered the occasional glimpse of green in the world below.

Sylus knew what grass looked like, of course. Even high in the mountains, it grew in patchy bursts, small tufts of green breaking up the monotonous grays and browns of his childhood home of Hearthhallow. Sylus had often used those patches for imaginary play, "sailing" his wooden airships across them as he imagined a life on the blades.

Now twenty-three, Sylus stepped through the cloud layer for the first time and entered the world he'd longed to join his entire life, stumbling to a stop as the world opened up beneath him.

Shades of swaying green stretched as far as the eye could see, surrounding his island of Altaris. Vibrant emeralds faded into duller, darker colors of forest and brightened again into paler greens, swaying as the winds of the Whispering Reach occasionally threw up darker splashes that saw the sun less often. Even more shocking was the horizon, where the green grasses of the Verdant Sea met the blue and white sky in a striking line, separating the earth from the heavens.

There were no more islands visible in that vast expanse. Islands were few and far between, for they were not truly islands at all, but mountain ranges. Mountains were the only lands tall enough to escape the spread of the ever-expanding grasses that dominated the lower ranges of the world.

Out in the blades, Sylus could see the colorful sails of countless ships, the vibrant colors easy to spot in the Green, by design. Sylus could not help but wonder if one of those ships was the one he was looking for. He patted his coat pocket, searching for the letter his mother had written. It was his key to a new life away from the small village he'd grown to hate. It was still there, as he knew it was, for he checked it nervously every ten minutes.

A gust of wind ruffled his messy brown hair, bringing with it an earthy, sweet scent. Suddenly filled with a desire to get close enough to see the blades of the Verdant Sea up close, Sylus stopped staring and started walking. He needed to be close enough to touch the blades, close enough to hear the sound of the wind rustling through the fields.

The journey down the mountain took several days, but growing up in the peaks did have its benefits. While he was only moderately tall for his age and wiry in build, the daily effort of life and chores in the rocky terrain had made him as strong and resilient as the woody plants that clung stubbornly to the rocks, and a several-day hike was easy for him.

His destination sprawled out beneath him; the port town of Windmoor stuck out like a sore thumb on the edge of the blades, its stone walls and straight lines easily visible against the rocky shoreline now that he was below the clouds. Sylus could see the docks stretching out behind the port, reaching into the green to provide a launching point for the airships that moved to and fro.

One of those ships was Sylus's way off the island of Altaris, or at least he hoped it was. There was no guarantee that his uncle would be there. As far as Sylus knew, his mother had not heard from her brother in over twenty years, following a falling out. She never left the mountain village of Hearthhallow, and the man certainly never came to visit them. His mother would never tell him what the falling out was about, only that the man had endangered everyone around him by sailing the Verdant Sea in search of Thaumatech, and she refused to have anything to do with Thaumatech after his father's death.

That was why she lived as far away from the Verdant Sea and civilization as possible. Her fear of Thaumatech meant they shivered in the winters and boiled in the summers. Up among the clouds, they lived in poverty and hardship while the rest of the world moved on without them. Ultimately, it was the reason she died.

Sylus immediately felt guilty at the thought. It wasn't her fault. Reclaimed had killed his father before he was born, and most of his mother's family. It was Thaumatech that created Reclaimed, if you weren't careful with it. The technology of the old world was both dangerous and extremely valuable. Plus, it was true. A Thaumatechne could have saved his mother's life if only she'd let the town send someone to Windmoor to fetch one.

Whatever her reasons, Sylus had brushed his mother's constant warnings on the dangers of Thaumatech aside. He'd spent his youth dreaming and preparing for the day he would be old enough to leave the mountains and seek his fortune on the Verdant Sea. It was why he'd spent most of his free time sneaking away from his mother to listen to old Galleon, an old sailor who'd somehow wound up in the mountains and lived upon his old airship. Sylus's questions about the ships that sailed the Verdant Sea quickly turned to practical lessons, and he'd learned everything he could so that when he went to Windmoor, he'd be ready.

With his mother's letter of introduction - her final gift - Sylus was ready. Or at least, as prepared as he could be. Now all Sylus needed to do was find his uncle, a man he'd never met, and convince him to take Sylus onto his crew.

Sylus swallowed the nervousness that wormed its way up his throat with the thought. He steeled himself against the crushing weight of possibility. He couldn't entertain the idea of failure, not with the walls of Windmoor rising before him, and his dream finally within his grasp. He would find his uncle and convince him. He would not go through life scared of the world, fading into obscurity. He would sail the Verdant Sea and make a name for himself, or die trying.

2

Windmoor

Sylus eventually drew close enough to Windmoor to see the roads. They led down the coast in either direction from the small city, winding into the port through gates he could not see, and faded into the distance, to towns he did not know.

His village didn't have much in the way of maps, and Altaris was one of the smallest island nations in the Whispering Reach. Sylus looked down at the path beneath his feet, if it could even be called a path. It was more like a goat trail. Hearthhallow didn't get a road. Why would it? The villages up in the mountains held nothing of interest to anybody, except the occasional Technepriest from the Church of the Binary Gods, hoping for easy converts.

Sylus could see a small gate into the city facing in this direction, though he found it baffling why they bothered. People mostly traveled along the main road, riding wagons or walking, but nobody was on this path. In the distance, Sylus saw a caravan of wagons kicking up dust as they headed toward the port. He wasn't sure if Altaris produced anything of value, but it must, or else there wouldn't be a port. He knew there were towns of similar size to Windmoor elsewhere on Altaris, but he did not even know their names.

Strangely, his ignorance about his own home country only fueled him onward. Sylus began to feel a strange excitement growing with every step that brought him closer to the port; a thrill at everything he was about to discover. Everything his mother tried to keep from him, everything he ever wanted to learn about, was right in front of him, waiting to be explored.

The gate was near enough now to see a single soldier guarding the entrance, watching the empty goat trail, looking shocked to see him. Since there was nothing out this way except the mountains, Sylus thought it must be a dull shift, but he watched the soldier with equal interest as he approached. There were no soldiers in Hearthhallow, because there was no crime, and there was no crime, because nobody possessed anything of value.

Sylus's eyes moved hungrily over the soldier, lingering on the swords strapped to the man's waist. His armor was simple steel, plain and well-worn, adorned only with a colored shoulder tassel attached at the front of the shoulder and hung over the back. Sylus supposed it must be the town's colors, for it matched the color of the flag flying high over the gate, a greenish teal with a curled symbol for wind.

The man stared at him with some suspicion. Sylus did not blame him. He doubted people came down from the mountains very often. He could not help but wonder about his appearance; his simple traveling clothes were filthy, and he could feel the dust that clung to his skin and hair like a second skin.

Sylus smiled at the man as he approached, unsure of what to do next, and the soldier waved him forward.

"Name?" he asked, pulling out a piece of paper and a quill from a pouch at his waist.

"S-" Sylus managed, before his voice cracked and broke. He coughed and cleared his throat. It'd been days since he'd spoken to anyone. "Sylus," he finished.

The man raised an eyebrow.

"Sylus Edelhart," Sylus corrected.

The man nodded and scribbled Sylus's name on the list.

"Where are you from?" he asked.

"Hearthhallow, up the mountains," Sylus said, throwing a thumb over his shoulder.

The man's gaze flicked up to the mountains with a dubious look, and Sylus didn't see recognition in his eyes.

"Right," he said, making another scribble on his list, "Purpose in Windmoor, Sylus?"

"I'm looking for a ship captain, actually, Captain Bracken. Do you know where I might find him?"

"I don't know, kid, the docks?" the man said, sounding annoyed, "Do you have any idea how many ships dock here?"

"I'm twenty-three, and no," Sylus said truthfully.

The man looked at him like he was an idiot, then sighed, "Ask around at the docks."

"I intend to," Sylus said, taking a step forward.

The soldier held out a hand to stop him.

"Hold on there, lad. New arrivals must be screened before entering Windmoor. If you're carrying any Thaumatech devices, you must, by law, declare such items now. You must also declare your infection status. If you get to inspection and are found to have lied about either, you will be imprisoned for no less than three days."

"Thaumatech? No," Sylus said.

He'd heard of inspection, but he'd never been through one himself.

"Any infection? Even the smallest cut must be reported."

"I'm not infected," Sylus said indignantly.

The guard gave him a disapproving look.

"Listen, kid, this is important. Someone gets in and turns Reclaimed in the middle of Windmoor, and a lot of people could die. You understand that, right?"

Sylus regulated his tone, "Yes, sir, I understand that."

The man stared at him with narrowed eyes, finally nodding and making a mark on the list.

"Inspection is to the left. Do not attempt to enter Windmoor without going through inspection. You will be watched."

The man stepped aside and swung his head toward a building on the other side of the gate, just to the left inside the wall.

Sylus nervously shifted his pack and patted the letter in his pocket before walking through the gate, keenly aware that the soldier was watching him until he pushed open the door of the inspection station and went inside.

Another soldier sat at a desk across from the door, looking up in surprise as Sylus approached.

"Where are you from? No one ever comes in this way."

"Hearthhallow," Sylus said.

"Never heard of it," the man said.

"It's in the mountains," Sylus said, wondering suddenly how often he was going to repeat that.

The man grunted.

"Nothing to declare then?"

"No."

"Alright, let's go. Room one."

Sylus looked down the hallway, where a series of doors were marked with wooden signs. The man stood from the desk and gestured down the hallway. Sylus obediently went to room one and pulled open the door, blinking against the sudden brightness.

Inside was a plain room with a bench, some shelves, and a small table. The only interesting thing was a single Thaumatech glow bulb hanging from the ceiling, which cast an unnaturally bright light throughout the room.

"Is that a glow bulb?" Sylus asked excitedly.

The man's eyes flicked to the light and back to Sylus with a pained expression.

"They don't have glow bulbs in the mountain, kid?"

"No, and I'm twenty-three," Sylus repeated, annoyed.

"Sure you are. Let's get this over with. Bag on the table, get your clothes off, and place them on the shelves."

"My clothes off?" Sylus said in a strangled voice.

"Don't think I need to repeat myself. There's an easy way and a hard way, and my shift is almost over. Don't make it the hard way, kid, I don't have all day."

Sylus stared at the man with wide eyes, and the man stared back impatiently.

Sighing, Sylus dumped his bag on the table and began stripping off his clothes. He turned his back on the man as he did so, placing his clothes on the shelves. He could hear the soldier rummaging through his bag as he did so.

There was nothing to find, of course. Sylus owned very little, just a few changes of clothes, a few coins, and the letter from his mother, though it wasn't in the bag.

Once he was down to his undergarments, he began to turn back around, but the soldier said, "All of it now, nothing to be shy about."

Coloring fiercely, Sylus took off his last article of clothing and turned back to the soldier, covering his manhood with his hands.

"Is this really necessary?" he asked.

"You think I want to look at your bits? It's for everyone's safety," the man said.

He patted down Sylus's clothes that he'd left on the shelves. Once he was satisfied that Sylus was as poor as he appeared, the man turned back to him.

"C'mon, drop the hands, you know I gotta check."

Sylus let his hands drop to his sides, trying to ignore the man circling him, studying him from every angle.

"Alright, kid, you're good. Welcome to Windmoor. Grab your stuff and get dressed. You can leave when you're ready," the soldier said.

He opened the door with absolutely no respect for Sylus's nudity and stepped out without waiting, closing the door behind him.

Sylus dressed faster than he'd ever dressed in his life, not even getting his feet into his boots properly before opening the door. He avoided looking at the man at the desk, who gave him a curt nod as he fled from the inspection station.

Sylus trudged down the street, trying to forget everything that happened. He knew why it was necessary, of course. Hearthhallow wasn't so far removed from the world that Sylus didn't understand the dangers of Thaumatech, but still, for some reason, he didn't expect the inspection to be quite so… intimate.

Putting it out of his mind, Sylus turned his attention to Windmoor, wanting to absorb everything he could about his first taste of life outside the village. The street he was on ended shortly ahead of him in an intersection that stretched left and right, most likely because there was nothing on this side of the city but mountains. He could see people wandering across the opening and hurried to turn the corner to get his first look.

As Sylus turned the corner, he couldn't help but stare. The port opened up before him in a cross-work of wooden structures, narrow stone streets, and more people than he'd ever seen in one place.

Merchants called to passersby from the windows of storefronts or from colorful wooden stalls that lined the streets. Men hauled carts loaded with goods down the center fairway, waving to people they knew and yelling at those who got in their way. Musicians performed on open patios to cheers and song requests. Everywhere he looked, Sylus saw something he'd only heard about from Galleon or read about in books, and while he stared in open fascination, a parade of scents filled the air, reminding him that he had not eaten yet today.

Sylus wandered down the street, lost in his exploration, crossing stalls selling exotic tea leaves, medicinal plants, fruits, vegetables, and everything in between. No one seemed to pay him much mind except for the vendors, who called out to him the same as anyone else. Sylus thought that was unusual, for he felt like he stuck out like a sore thumb.

No one was dressed as poorly as Sylus. He picked at his dirty, simple traveling clothes, fully aware that everyone else was dressed in sharp leathers and clean linens. Not a single person seemed to have dirt covering them from head to toe, and he wondered if the town had Thaumatech that kept everyone so clean.

There certainly was enough Thaumatech in the city to suggest it. Many shops had glow bulbs outside their doors, though they were turned off in the midday sun. Sylus even stopped at a stall where a merry vendor roasted strange meats on a Thaumatech grill.

The man offered him the legs of some large insect, which a small sign described as a Glimmerbeetle. Of course, Sylus had never heard of it. The other meat was a large rodent called a Blademouse, about the size of his chest, roasting whole on a spit. They were clearly creatures of the Verdant Sea, and Sylus was filled with a strange desire to buy one of each, so much so that it almost overpowered his desire to see the Sea itself.

Sylus hesitated at the stall for a long time. Not just because he was fascinated by the grill, which, like all Thaumatech, functioned without any visible power source or fuel, but because the delicious smells held him captive as he debated using his few coins to purchase something to eat.

In the end, he pulled himself away. The money he possessed was needed for emergencies. There was no guarantee Sylus would find Bracken quickly, and he might need to stay in Windmoor for some time. If that were the case, he would likely be camping outside the city walls. Sylus was a decent hunter, at least when it came to setting snares, and if the creatures wandered close to the shore, he might be able to catch one on his own. He tried to fill his belly with the thought of his well-reasoned decision as he passed several other stalls selling foods he'd never heard of.

Sylus needed to focus. It wasn't hard to discover which way it was to the docks. Windmoor's streets seemed to roll down toward the shore, and after a few turns, he could see the docks stretching out before him, reaching into the Verdant Sea toward the horizon, lined on either side with the colorful sails of the airships docked to either side.

As if drawn by a magnet, the rest of the town seemed to fade away as Sylus walked quickly down the street. He forgot about his hunger and disheveled appearance, and barely noticed the people he almost bumped into. His eyes were locked to the place where green became blue, and his feet carried him out of the cobbled streets and onto the wooden dock boards in moments.

If anything, the docks of Windmoor were even busier than its streets. Sailors moved everywhere, either loading or unloading ships, cleaning the hulls, or simply standing around talking in loud, raucous voices.

The airships themselves held Sylus's attention almost as much as the sea. They floated along the dock, hovering a few feet above the blades, held aloft by air tanks filled with gases lighter than air. Their hulls were plated in shining metal to protect the ships from the blades and anything that lived within them, and there were as many designs as there were people.

Some featured side- or bottom-mounted air tanks, while others preferred the more traditional vertical masts with large sails. Others, however, opted for the newer style of suspending the ship beneath the air tanks, with a large variety of sails lining the sides of the vessels. Many also sported wide engines mounted to the rear of the ships, powerful pieces of Thaumatech to be used in case of an emergency. To Sylus, no two ships were the same, and he felt as if his head was on a swivel as he took his first steps onto the dock. He could not understand how everyone was ignoring the majestic sights before them.

As the dock extended over the green, Sylus moved to the side and peered over. Soft grass swayed under the pier, the blades so thick and numerous that you could not see the ground. This was new growth, barely a few inches tall. He leaned over and reached to touch the blades, stretching his fingertips out until they grazed the swaying tops.

They were warm from the sun and softer than Sylus imagined. He knew that fully grown blades were sharp and dangerous, but these caressed his fingertips as they swayed in the gentle breeze, and he smiled.

Pushing himself up, he began to run down the dock, ignoring the shouts of surprise and anger that followed him as he weaved in and out of the sailors. He ran, laughing, until he reached the end of the dock and stopped, panting.

The Verdant Sea stretched before him. He was only fifty feet from the shore, but Sylus knew the blades here were much deeper. Even though the Whispering Reach was considered a part of the shallows of the Verdant Sea, here off the dock, the blades could grow as tall as ten or twenty feet.

Sylus looked at the swirling grass, drinking in the colors as the wind played through the Green. He closed his eyes, trying to block out the sounds of the ships and sailors, the talking and smells, and listened to the sound of the wind moving through the grass. He could hear it, if he concentrated, beneath everything else. A gentle, whispering rustle. A continuous shushing and swishing in a gentle harmony. Sylus breathed in deep through his nose, filling his lungs with the rich, earthy smells of the Green. He opened his eyes and smiled, feeling like he'd finally come home after a lifetime away.

Sylus looked over the edge again, wanting to feel how the larger blades differed from those near the shore. Were they already sharp enough to cut? He lowered himself back down to the edge of the dock, stretching his hand toward the Green.

"I wouldn't do that if I were you," someone said.

Sylus paused, turning to see a man sitting nearby whom he must have missed as he ran to the edge of the dock. That man sat on a nearby dock post, staring out at the horizon. He wore a bandanna wrapped low around his head and a long, leather trench coat that looked as if the man might sleep in it. His leather boots were worn and unstrapped, and his hands were stuffed into his jacket pockets.

A soldier stood a little behind him, watching the man with a wary eye. Sylus recognized the armor and shoulder tassel of the city guard.

"Blades get sharper as they grow. Much sharper. Sharp enough to cut," the man said, without looking at him.

Sylus looked uneasily back at the blades, only inches from his hand.

"I know that," he said.

Galleon told him once of a man who fell overboard into the blades.

They may be long, but they're not strong enough to hold you. You go over, and you're falling to the depths. Not that you'll have to worry much about that. You'd be cut to ribbons long before you ever hit the bottom.

Sylus pulled his hand back with a shiver, pushing himself to a sitting position.

"Thanks, though," he said to the man, "Curiosity got the better of me."

"First time?" the man asked.

"Is it that obvious?"

"Nothing quite like it, is there?"

"No," Sylus agreed, staring at the swaying grass.

"Hard to believe something so beautiful is slowly swallowing the world, isn't it?" the man said.

Sylus shifted uncomfortably. His mother told him that the Verdant Sea was advancing and would one day cover the world entirely, but he'd always dismissed this as one of her irrational fears.

He was about to ask more when a shiny insect peeked out of the blades for a moment. It jumped into the air before disappearing into the Green once more.

The man chuckled, "Only the creatures of the Green know the secrets she keeps."

He seemed to be quoting something, and Sylus saw the soldier roll his eyes.

"Are you a sailor?" Sylus asked.

The man looked at him for the first time, "I was."

"Was?" Sylus asked.

The man took his hand out of his pocket and pulled down the shoulder of his trench coat. He wasn't wearing a shirt underneath, but where there should have been skin, metal machinery glittered in the sun.

Sylus drew in a breath despite himself, "You're a Thaumatechne?"

The man nodded again, pulling his trench coat back up to hide the infected skin.

"Do you know any Wonders?" Sylus asked.

"Leave him alone, kid," the soldier said.

"It's fine, Marcus. He's a kid, he doesn't know any better," the man said, waving a hand as if to ward the man off.

"I'm twenty-three," Sylus said to no one in particular.

The man turned back to Sylus.

"Let me guess, you came to seek your fortune in the blades?"

"So what if I did?"

"Nothing, kid, just wondering if you truly understand the risks."

He raised his other hand, and Sylus noted that it was no longer flesh and blood; instead, it was like the opposite shoulder, metal and machine. He tapped his shoulder, producing a metallic clinking sound.

"I know enough," Sylus said.

The man sighed, "So did I."

He quieted, then after a few more moments, he spoke again.

"Let's go, Marcus."

The soldier nodded and helped the man to his feet. Marcus turned to leave, then paused and turned back to Sylus.

"Hey, kid, you got any money?"

"You can go to the Church," Marcus said before Sylus could respond, but the man shook his head.

"And listen to their crap the entire time? I'm not above begging."

Sylus looked up at the man. Now that he was standing, Sylus could see the infection was almost complete. It stretched across his chest to his shoulder and was inching up his neck.

"How long do you have?" Sylus asked.

It must be a rude question, for the soldier behind Marcus shot him an angry, scandalized look, but Marcus merely grinned.

"A bit longer if you give me some money to eat," he said.

Sylus sighed, then fished out one of his five coins. He held them out to the man, who held out his metal hand for Sylus to drop them into. Sylus held the money over the man's hand, but didn't drop it.

"Do you know a Captain Bracken?" he asked.

"Bracken?" the man said, his smile shifting to a look of confusion. "Can't say I do. What's his ship?"

"I don't know," Sylus admitted, then dropped the coins into the man's hand.

"Thanks," the man said, closing his metal hand around the coins. He peered at Sylus for a moment. "You could try asking at the Bladed Mare."

"Bladed Mare?"

"It's a pub, just at the entrance to the docks. All the sailors go there. I used to, but they don't let me in now."

"You're free to go wherever you like," Marcus said, "If you want to go to the pub-"

"Yeah, yeah. You know what I mean," the man said, turning away from Sylus and walking back toward the shore.

"See you later, kid," he said, throwing a hand over his shoulder.

Sylus watched the man go, listening to the two talking as they walked away.

"You know, I dunno why you're such a grump all the time, Marcus, it's me who's dying..."

Sylus watched the man go. He'd only ever met one other Thaumatechne in his life, and they were very different than the man he'd just met. Of course, the first one was a Technepriest, a servant of the Church, not some random sailor.

He appeared in the village one day, claiming he was traveling through the mountains on a mission to bring Wonders to the poor and to heal the sick. Sylus's mother warned him to stay inside, saying the man was only trying to convert them to the Church. Sylus snuck out and followed the man anyway, despite the risk.

From a distance, Sylus watched as the man healed a broken bone in about two minutes. That moment sparked his fascination with Thaumatech. Not that Sylus would ever want to become a Thaumatechne, of course. The price wasn't worth the ability to perform Wonders, no matter how amazing they were. Thaumatech devices could perform Wonders without taking over your body, if you could afford it. Barring that, your only option was to head out into the Verdant Sea and find them yourself.

If Sylus had a machine that could heal like the priest, his mother would still be alive. At least, she would be if he could have convinced her to use it, but she had never accepted that Thaumatech was safe if used properly.

Sylus shook his head. There was no point following that line of thought. His mother was dead, and there was no bringing her back. He felt a sort of profound sadness at the pointless nature of her death, but he pushed the thought away and took another look at the Verdant Sea.

No matter what, he would not die some pointless death in the mountains. Somewhere out there, his future was waiting for him. It was time to find it.

3

The Captain

Sylus could not help but wonder if any of the ships he passed could be the one he sought. Windmoor was not a large port. It possessed only a single dock, and the ships that docked here ranged from small to medium-sized. It was nothing like the massive ports Galleon had told him about, with ships so big they needed crews of hundreds, and docks that held hundreds of airships. Those were the cities Sylus longed to see most.

It didn't take long to find the Bladed Mare; in fact, Sylus was surprised he hadn't seen it on his way past. The raucous bar was in full swing, with music that could be heard from the dock. Sylus stood outside for a moment, watching sailors drinking through the windows, despite it barely being half past noon. Sylus supposed that sailors didn't keep a regular schedule.

Taking a deep breath, he headed inside the open door, nodding to a large man who sat on a stool by the entrance. The man gave him a cursory glance and turned his gaze elsewhere. Sylus didn't blame him. He considered himself fit, but he was sure most people in the bar could pick him up and tie him in a knot with barely any trouble.

Sliding his way past massive shoulders and muscular arms, he made his way up to the bar, where a man working the counter served drinks to a crowd of thirsty men and women. Sylus recognized the spirits being poured as grasswine, a cheap spirit made from the young grasses of the Verdant Sea. There was no mistaking that pale green liquid and the sickly sweet scent. It was a favorite of Galleon's, who often traveled to Windmoor to buy it, but Sylus knew from the one time he tried it that it gave you a splitting headache the next day.

He waved to get the bartender's attention and waited until the man shuffled over.

"What will it be?" he said curtly.

"I'm looking for someone," Sylus said.

"This is a bar kid, not the lost and found. Buy something or beat it."

"If I buy something, will you answer my question?" Sylus asked.

"No."

The man shuffled away toward paying, less bothersome customers, leaving Sylus to sit there staring after him. He realized he was now out of ideas, a realization that struck him with a horrible sort of panic that he had no business being here. He felt a wild feeling come over him, and he reached over the counter to grab two empty metal mugs that lay abandoned. No one seemed to notice. At least, until Sylus stood up on his stool and started banging them together. The room quieted as the music stilled and all heads turned to him.

Angry heads, Sylus noticed. The words he was going to say seemed to be drying up in his throat, but he forced them out anyway.

"I-I'm looking for a Captain-"

"Shuddup!" someone shouted across him, and the follow round of laughter drowned out the rest of Sylus's words.

"If I could just-"

He never got to tell them just anything, for at that moment a cup full of ale sailed through the air and slammed into the side of his head. The force of the impact threw him off the chair, soaking him with sweet green sticky liquid and leaving him in a crumpled heap on the floor, surrounded by gales of laughter.

Dazed, Sylus barely registered when someone grabbed him by the collar and pants and hefted him bodily from the ground.

"You're outta here, kid," someone said.

He was still sputtering and trying to gather his wits when he felt himself fly briefly through the air before crashing back into the pavement once more.

Sylus could hear cheers and whistles from inside the bar as the music started up again. It took him a few moments to push himself to his feet. His shirt was plastered to his skin, and his hair was soaked. The grasswine was already drying, leaving him sticky to the touch.

He looked to the door, where the big man was now standing, watching him.

"Real stupid kid, interrupting the music," he said.

Sylus looked through the window stubbornly. Someone in there would know Bracken, he was sure of it.

"You're not going back in," the man said, as if reading his mind.

He folded his admittedly gigantic arms across his chest.

"Fine," he said, trying to shake some of the liquid off his shirt, "Would you at least tell me if you've ever heard of a Captain Bracken?"

The man leaned against the door frame, then rubbed his chin as if considering.

"Maybe I have," he said, "What's it worth to you?"

"Everything," Sylus sighed.

He found his bag and fished out his last three coins, offering them up to the man.

"This is all you got?" The man said, eyeing the coins, and then Sylus, with what might be pity.

"Yup. Everything I got. I was planning to eat with it, but hey!"

The man pocketed the coins before Sylus was finished talking.

"I know Bracken, he just left an hour ago. Hey, there he goes."

Sylus's head whipped around to follow the bouncer's outstretched finger. He expected it was a cruel prank, but was surprised to find that the man was actually pointing to someone. A broad-shouldered man with a black bushy beard was passing that bar on his way to the dock. Of course, the bouncer could just be pointing at any random man to get rid of him, but Sylus had nothing to lose.

"Thanks!" Sylus said.

The man was setting an impressive pace; he was already on the docks and moving quickly. Sylus dashed to catch up.

"Excuse me!" he said, but needed to repeat himself and practically step in front of the man before he got the Captain's attention.

The captain was a rough-looking man with an overlarge nose and busy black eyebrows to match his beard. Flecks of grey were visible in the man's beard. He did not much look like Sylus's mother, but Sylus didn't let that stop him.

"What do you want, kid?" the man said gruffly, looking over Sylus's shoulder impatiently. "I be busy."

He had an odd, tilted way of talking and an accent Sylus had never heard before, not that it narrowed it down at all. Sylus had never heard an accent before. His mother had never spoken with an accent.

"Are you Captain Bracken?"

"Aye, and what if I am?"

"Please, Captain, I have a letter from your sister. Linnora?"

Bracken's eyebrows drew up his forehead in surprise and clear recognition. Sylus smiled; he'd found his man.

"Linnora, you say?" grumbled Bracken in a deep voice, "And who do you be?"

"I'm her son. Your nephew," Sylus said.

Bracken considered him deeply for a minute, grumbling.

"I suppose you do have the look of her," Bracken said, giving Sylus a disapproving glance. "Well? Fork over the letter, I don't have all day."

"Well, it's about me," Sylus said, fumbling in his coat pocket for the letter.

He managed to pull it out and hand it over to Bracken, whose eyebrows were drawing back down.

"Twenty years and not a word, and now she be sending - Why's it wet?" Bracken asked, shaking the damp letter at him. "You been drinking, boy?" the man leaned in and sniffed him.

Sylus shook his head, "Someone threw a drink at me. I was looking for - it's not important. What's important is that I found you. I want to join your crew."

Bracken looked at him with a flat, expressionless stare.

"I think not, boy."

"Please, read the letter," Sylus said desperately.

Bracken looked down at the letter in his hands, then back up at Sylus suspiciously. Then he opened the envelope and unfolded the letter, holding it in calloused hands, his dark eyes darting across the page.

Sylus watched Bracken's expression as he read, and began to feel his hope start to slide away. The more the man read, the further down his eyebrows drew. Eventually, his eyes slid off the letter and up to meet Sylus's gaze.

"Linnora wrote this, did she?"

Sylus did not hesitate, "Yes."

Bracken blew out his mustache in a soft harrumph.

"Linnora, a woman who be so scared of Thaumatech she could barely stand to be near it, did write this letter asking for her only son to join my crew aboard a Thaumatech ship, to sail the Verdant Sea in search of the same?"

"She... changed her mind. About Thaumatech," Sylus lied.

"I be doubting that very much. As I recall, the last thing she did say to me was that she'd rather walk through the blades than get on a Thaumatech ship."

"It's true."

"Oh, and how's that then? What be changing her mind?"

"She was... dying," Sylus said, the lie twisting his gut.

For a fraction of a second, Bracken's expression seemed to slip from disbelief to what might be construed as concern. Sylus latched onto the lie. He wasn't sure why he said it, but he could feel his only chance at his dreams slipping away by the second.

"Was?" Bracken said in a flat voice.

"A Technepriest came to the village by luck. He used his Wonders to save her life. After that, she realized Thaumatech wasn't so bad. As long as you're careful with it."

"Is that so?" Bracken said, stroking his beard with his thumb and forefinger, as he stared at Sylus with his piercingly dark eyes.

Sylus held his breath.

For a moment, Bracken almost seemed to soften, but then he shook his head.

"Even so, I think not. Sylus, was it? The Green be no place for a boy."

He thrust the letter back into Sylus's shocked hands and stepped around him, continuing down the dock. It took Sylus a moment to recover from the rejection before he turned around and followed Bracken down the pier.

"I'm not a boy, I'm twenty-three."

"I no care if you be thirty-three or fifty-three. Your mother be wrong. Thaumatech is plenty dangerous. Especially for a dirt scrubber like yourself."

Dirt scrubber? Sylus shook off the unfamiliar term, refusing to accept no for an answer, "I'm well aware of how dangerous it is. And I'm not a… dirt scrubber. I know how to sail, I've studied ships, I know how they work, and I know how to work them. I can make myself useful."

"Studying is no the same as doing, boy. Tell me, have you ever been on a Thaumatech ship?" Bracken asked, turning a sharp eye on Sylus as he walked down the dock.

For some reason, Sylus knew the man would be able to tell if he lied about this.

"Not exactly," he admitted.

"You ever even leave whatever flyspeck village your mother went to hide in?"

"No," Sylus admitted.

"Then what business do you be having on a ship? A ship needs to rely on its crew, and its crew needs to handle the ship. The Green takes what it's owed, boy."

Sylus didn't understand a word of what the man was saying now; all he knew was that the answer was starting to sound like a definitive no.

"Please, Captain. This is all I have ever wanted."

The sad, desperate words slipped from his lips before Sylus could stop them. Bracken gave him a sidelong glance, then sighed and came to a stop, turning to face him.

"Trust me, lad. I be doing you a favor. There's no place for you in the Green. Stay here, find yourself a girl, and stay away from the blades. You're better off..."

"Is that your ship?" Sylus said sullenly.

He had his answer; he did not want to hear any more. They'd come to a stop in front of a medium-sized vessel.

Bracken glanced behind him, taken aback, but seeming to understand.

"That it is. This be the *Bladedancer*," Bracken could not keep the pride out of his voice as he named his ship.

Sylus could not blame him as his eyes scanned the ship, taking in everything, letting it distract him from the crushing weight of disappointment.

The ship was of the newer style, with the main hull hanging beneath the air tanks, which were attached to the vessel by a large metal frame. Orange sails fanned out from either side of the ship.

"She's newer," Sylus noted, his voice sounded hollow and empty, "Top-mounted air tanks with side sails. You've reinforced the hull, it looks like, and added several sets of ancillary sails for tighter turning. That would make her heavier, so the engines will be modified. Probably a quad burst thruster. That also explains the extra weight on the nose. If you needed to do a full emergency burst, you'd need the extra weight to avoid flipping over. Of course, that means you need to double the air tanks as well. You've got maybe two, four spare air tanks at the most?"

"That's right," Bracken said.

Sylus nodded, "Not quite enough air tanks, but I suppose the extra power is sometimes worth the risk. What's the crew size?"

"You know an awful amount about ships for someone who never set foot on one," Bracken said, ignoring his question. He was stroking his beard again.

Sylus looked at him. What did he have to lose?

"There was a retired sailor in the village. Old Galleon, we called him. He had countless books about ships, and I read them all. He taught me to sail, too. On an old ship. It didn't run anymore, of course, just sat on the ground, but..."

Bracken was staring at him with that flat expression again.

"A ship in the mountains?" he said.

Sylus felt himself coloring.

"It's the truth."

"How he be getting a ship up the mountain, boy?"

"I don't know! They can technically fly, can't they? It's been there as long as I can remember."

Of course, Bracken didn't believe him. Why would he? Everything Sylus had said was stupid and completely unbelievable. Why had he ever thought this would work? He stuffed his hands in his pockets and took one last look at Bracken, who was watching him now.

"Well, thanks anyway," he sighed.

He took another look at the *Bladedancer*. It really was a remarkable ship. Then he turned to go, walking down the dock, away from his plans, away from his dreams.

"I'll take you through the Reach," Bracken said.

Sylus nearly felt his heart explode as he turned around.

"What?"

"Green take me, I must be crazy. We're going to Boughhaven to restock before our next expedition. I'll take you with us."

"Boughhaven, the treeport?"

"Just as a trial, mind you. If you actually know how to sail, which I be doubting very much, and make yourself useful, I'll consider putting you in the crew."

"Are you serious?"

"At the lowest possible share," Bracken said sternly, "One eighth what the rest of 'em get, and you'll be getting the worst shifts and the hardest work on the ship. You understand?"

"Yes! I understand, and gladly accept. Thank you! I can't tell you what this means to me. I could hug you."

"Don't, or the whole deal be off. Maybe I be your uncle, maybe I don't, but on that ship, it's Captain Bracken. Off the ship, too, mind. And if I find you lying, I'll put you off at Boughhaven and leave you there, nephew or no."

"You won't have any trouble from me, uh… Captain Bracken."

"Go get your stuff, we leave as soon as you get back."

"Uhm, this is it," Sylus said sheepishly, suddenly aware of his dirty clothes and disheveled appearance.

Bracken slid Sylus a disapproving glance over his scant possessions.

"Do you have a shirt that doesn't be smelling like cheap wine at least? Wouldn't do to be meeting the crew smelling like that."

"Of course," Sylus said, hurriedly taking off his coat and pulling his shirt over his head, right there on the dock.

He dug out one of his two other shirts and pulled it over his head. It was barely any cleaner, but at least it wasn't wet and sticky.

"It'll have to do," Bracken said, turning back to the *Bladedancer*, "Hurry up now, you've delayed me enough already."

With that, he turned back to the ship, where it seemed their conversation had not gone unnoticed. Faces peered at them from over the ship's rails, but Sylus hardly noticed.

He was part of the crew! Or at least, he was closer than he ever dreamed. All he needed to do was prove himself.

4

The Crew

Captain Bracken led the way up the gangplank, with Sylus following close behind, his eyes wide as he took in the sails hanging overhead, so much so that he almost didn't notice when Bracken started talking to someone who met them on the deck.

"Any luck, Captain?" a man was asking.

"Of a kind, Holven, of a kind," Bracken said, turning his eyes back to Sylus.

"Who is this?" The man asked, turning his stern gaze to Sylus.

Holven was tall and broad-shouldered, standing in such a way that made him seem sturdy and commanding. His hair was dark and cut short, but messy, and his deep-set blue-grey eyes focused on Sylus. Sylus could not help but notice a prominent scar running diagonally across his jaw. He was dressed smartly, with a dark, heavy leather coat reinforced at the shoulders.

"Your new deckhand," Bracken said.

If Holven was surprised, he gave no sign.

"Is that so?"

"Sylus, this be Holven, my second in command. What he says, you consider it as if I said it myself. He be running the day-to-day around here on the ship."

"Pleasure to meet you," Sylus said, holding out his hand.

Holven's eyes ran over Sylus's dirty clothes for a moment before he reached out and took Sylus's hand in a firm grasp. His hands were rough, scarred, and strong. Sylus felt like the man's firm shake nearly lifted him off the deck.

"We shall see if it is a pleasure or not shortly, Sylus," Holven said, "See that it doesn't become the latter."

"Of course, uh, sir," Sylus said, getting the distinct impression that Holven would brook no nonsense from anyone.

"Holven is fine," he said, letting go of his hand.

"Listen to Holven," Captain Bracken said, "He'll get you acquainted with the crew and the ship, but be quick about it. We sail in an hour."

With that, he walked away, leaving Sylus in the care of the stern first mate.

"Well, Sylus, since it seems the rest of the crew has nothing better to do, you might as well meet some of them now," Holven said, turning.

For the first time, Sylus noticed that a small crowd was gathered around the dock, and they were all, for the most part, staring at him. A slender, willowy woman stepped forward from the crowd, her dark brown hair streaked with auburn highlights, bouncing lightly on her shoulders and framing an olive-toned face with piercing green eyes flecked with gold. She was wearing tight brown pants wrapped with a belt covered in pouches, and a billowing white blouse that was more open at the front than any Sylus had ever seen. A small glass vial on a chain around her neck bounced as she took Sylus's hand and shook it.

Sylus felt his face color and made sure to keep his eyes firmly on the woman's face.

"Cally, our navigator," Holven said.

"Aren't you a sight?" the woman said, smiling brightly at him, "Where did he find this one, Holven?"

"I'm from Hearthhallow," Sylus said, the woman was still shaking his hand absentmindedly.

"Never heard of it, it's here on Altaris?"

"Yup, I'm not surprised. No one has," Sylus said.

"I'll have to update the map," Cally said, still shaking his hand. She tapped a finger on her chin, then smiled at him again, “How old are you?”

“I’m twenty-three,” Sylus said, exasperated.

“Are you?” Cally said, beaming. “I’m only twenty-five, myself.”

“I think you can give the boy his hand back, Cally. Shouldn’t you be plotting our route?” Holven said sternly.

Cally looked down and let go of Sylus’s hand, laughing in a tinkling way.

“I could sail to Boughhaven with my eyes closed, Holven, you know that,” she said, then leaned in closer to Sylus, “Don’t mind him, he’s a bit stern but quite a bit of fun sometimes.”

Holven cleared his throat, and Cally winked at him, then followed the way the Captain went, humming to herself. Sylus found it hard not to watch her go. She had a rather bouncy way of walking that drew the eye.

“Careful with that one,” a man’s voice said, and Sylus felt someone clap him on the shoulder.

He turned back to find a stocky, muscular man shaking his hand. He had sandy-blonde hair, short and messy, and a faint beard that was equally uneven. He had oil smudges on his face and clothes, which were simple linens, covered with a leather apron. Minor burns and cuts adorned his arms, and a small notch was missing from one of his ears. A belt around his waist carried various tools, some of which Sylus recognized and many he did not. The man’s eyes seemed to be having trouble staying on Sylus; they kept flicking around to different parts of the ship.

“With Cally?” Sylus asked.

“Cally? Oh yes, Cally. Beautiful, but a bit, well…”

“Sylus, this is Virel, as I’m sure he’s getting around to telling you. He’s an excellent engineer when he’s not chasing women,” Holven said, clearly wanting to speed things along.

“Only thing I can’t seem to fix,” Virel chirped, “Heard you admiring the ship, I’d love to hear more about this Galleon character, you know, there was once a famous sailor…”

“Another time, Virel,” Holven cut in impatiently.

“Alright, alright,” Virel said.

His darting eyes finally caught something of interest, for he wandered off without another word.

There were still quite a few people milling about, though some were indeed working to get the ship ready for launch; many were still staring at Sylus as if he were an exotic animal that crawled out of the blades.

"You can meet the rest of your crew-mates later," Holven said, placing a firm hand on his shoulder and steering him around toward the stern of the ship.

"How many are there?" Sylus asked as he watched men and women hustling across the deck as they got ready to leave.

"With you, that makes thirty-seven," Holven said as he opened a door and led Sylus inside. As much as Sylus wanted to watch the ship prepare for his first voyage, he knew there would be time enough for that later, once he was put to work.

Holven didn't say anything else as they strolled along the corridors of the ship's interior, and Sylus didn't ask any more questions. Holven didn't seem like a very chatty man, and Sylus was too captivated by the interior of the ship anyway.

The only ship interior Sylus knew was the rusted-out old hull of Galleon's mountain ship, and that was nothing compared to this. By all measures, it seemed that the *Bladedancer* was an extremely profitable treasure ship. The corridors were floored with lush red carpets that seemed remarkably clean except for where Sylus's feet left dirt and dust in a trail behind him. The hallways were paneled with sleekly polished dark wood boards that came up to his waist, where they met with the metal hull of the ship, which too was polished to a glossy shine. On the left, they passed countless doors and hallways with pictures of all sorts hanging neatly. Some depicted strange creatures or ships sailing on the blades. On the opposite wall, clear circular windows showed the docks of Windmoor.

They passed a map of the ship hanging at an intersection for those who might lose their way aboard the ship. Sylus barely got a glance. Holven, who obviously did not need a map, led them to a stop in front of a larger door, with a sign that said "Infirmary" above it.

Without explaining what they were doing here, Holven pushed open the door and held it for Sylus, who walked through to find a clean metal room full of beds. A petite woman with silver-blond hair tied in a loose braid was unpacking what appeared to be medical tools atop a large table that adorned the center of the room.

The woman looked up as Sylus came to stand before her, revealing a sharp, angular face with soft, gray eyes that seemed to hint at blue. Her steady gaze seemed to take in everything about him in an instant. She was wearing a simple white dress with the sleeves rolled up, revealing an intricate pattern of scars along her left forearm. Her only other adornment was a copper bracelet and a scarf, which her braid was tucked into for some reason. She remained slightly stooped, as if she were used to leaning over something as opposed to standing up.

"Holven," she said, as the man entered the room behind Sylus, "Who do we have here? He's filthy."

"Valera, how are you today? This is Sylus, our newest deckhand. Sylus, this is the *Bladedancer's* resident doctor, Valera. She'll be performing a quick inspection."

Sylus felt his face begin to color, "I uh… The towns guard inspected me before I entered the town."

Valera snorted.

"The town's guard," she said with an air of disdain, "is not qualified to perform those exams properly. If you want to sail on this ship, Sylus, I will have to inspect you."

Sylus sighed. He considered asking if Holven would do it instead, but a quick look at the man's perfectly neutral face told him that wouldn't be an option. He set down his bag upon the counter.

"I'll wait outside," Holven said politely, and left the room quietly, closing the door behind himself.

Valera was studying him with a careful eye. After a moment, she pointed toward a curtained-off area.

"You can change in there. I will be there in a moment. Please, try not to get dirt everywhere, if you could."

Sylus nodded, eyeing the pristine medical bay, and removed what he could. He set down his bag, jacket, and boots before heading behind the curtain and pulling it shut around him.

Trying not to think about how this was the first time a woman would see him naked, he dutifully stripped down all the way.

"Are you ready?" Valera said.

"As ready as I'll get," Sylus said, covering himself as she pulled back the curtain and joined him in the small space. She was carrying a leather-bound book, which she flipped open and began scribbling in as if he weren't completely naked. Her eyes snapped from him to the book as she scribbled.

"Where are you from, Sylus?" she asked.

"A village in the mountains," he said awkwardly.

He could feel himself beginning to color as her eyes examined him.

"I see," she said. She stepped closer, "Raise your arms, please."

He did as he was told, aware that his face was turning beet red, but Valera did not even glance down. Instead, she began to measure him with a small tape measure that she pulled from her belt.

Sylus thought he might die of embarrassment when the woman leaned down to measure his legs, but in a moment she was standing again. She circled him, occasionally poking or prodding as she scribbled in her notebook.

Finally, she examined his eyes, mouth, and hair.

"Well, you seem healthy enough. You're probably underweight, but it doesn't seem to have slowed you down."

"And no signs of infection," Sylus said, covering himself again with his hands.

How many times was he going to have to do this?

Valera raised her eyebrow sternly, "Infection is not all we have to worry about out here, and it's only one of many ways you could die on this ship. You would do well to remember that."

She turned her attention back to her notebook, "All in all, I see no reason to deny you a place on the crew. Ruse will have you up to weight soon enough; he's the ship's cook, and a damn good one, too. As for your complexion, however..."

Sylus stiffened and caught the woman's eye. She was smiling slightly.

"I suggest you get used to exams, Sylus, we'll be doing them quite often. Any time you leave this ship and return, an inspection will be the first order of business. It's for everyone's safety and your health. Stay here a moment."

Sylus stood there awkwardly as she stepped out of the curtain for a few moments. He could hear her rummaging around, then a strange grinding sound. After a few minutes, she returned, bearing a cup of thick green liquid. She handed it to Sylus, who awkwardly shifted his other hand to keep himself covered.

"Drink this," she ordered.

Sylus sniffed at the cup; he could smell grasses mixed with earthy and floral scents.

"What is it?" he asked.

"Nutrients you desperately need. A mixture of a few unique plants I cultivate here on the ship. It'll give you some extra energy, which I suspect you'll be needing."

Sylus shrugged and took a sip, then nearly choked. The mixture was unpleasantly thick and bitter. He looked at Valera, who merely folded her arms across her chest and raised an eyebrow at him.

Sylus suddenly remembered he was still naked and hurriedly choked back the rest of the concoction. He handed the cup back to Valera, who took it with a sly smile.

Sylus wiped his mouth with his hand.

"Did I really need to be naked for that?"

"No," she said, turning to leave, "but I find it helps people take their medicine. You can get dressed now."

Sylus hurriedly stuffed himself into his clothes, realizing now that Valera was quite amused with herself. He supposed it was funny. He wasn't so sure about her herbal cocktail, but at least he didn't feel quite so hungry anymore.

When he emerged to grab the rest of his belongings, he found Valera back to work quietly unpacking her boxes.

She smiled at him as he headed to the door, "I'll be seeing even more of you soon, Sylus. Good luck!"

His face reddening again, he pushed open the door to find Holven patiently waiting for him.

"All good," he said, trying to force the red out of his face through sheer willpower. He didn't need Holven thinking he couldn't handle a simple inspection.

"Well, I should hope so, since you were already inspected in Windmoor," Holven said, leading the way down the hallway once more.

Sylus felt himself feeling conspiratorial as he stared after the man in shock. Were they messing with him?

He hurried to catch up with Holven, who turned into a tightly wound stairwell that curved down to a lower level. This level was identical, except it featured slightly smaller windows and more narrowly spaced doors. Holven led him halfway down the hall, then stopped in front of the door marked 'Thirty-three'.

"This is you," Holven said, handing him a metal key. "Your room is free to do with as you wish, but must be kept clean. There will be monthly inspections. The lavatory is at the end of the hall on your right. I suggest you coordinate bathing times with your crew-mates at a later time. Drop off your belongings. Quickly now, the ship should be just about ready to depart."

Sylus opened the door to his cabin and took a quick look inside. It was about what he suspected, a small room with just enough space for a narrow bed and a small wooden writing desk. He threw his belongings on the bed, ditching his heavy jacket, and rejoined Holven in the hall, anxious to get back on the deck.

"I hope you are ready to work, Sylus. Because now we find out if you were telling the truth," Holven said, as he began retracing his steps to the stairs.

Sylus followed, but he did not feel nervous. He felt pretty good. He was full of energy, and the life he had always dreamed of was finally about to start.

5

Setting Sail

Once they were up on the deck, Sylus could see that the ship was nearly ready to sail. Men and women moved across the deck, getting into position to unfurl and ready the countless sails that would propel and steer the ship. The air tanks would be filling by now, unless he missed his guess. Even docked, they were never fully emptied, but kept at a level that allowed the ships to rest on the top of the blades until it was time to sail.

Several men moved past Sylus, equipping harnesses. The harnesses would prevent them from falling from the air tanks above in the case of sudden ship movements.

"So, Sylus," Holven said, turning to face him, "The Captain has instructed me to test you. I must remind you that if you are lying about your capabilities, you will be removed from this ship the second we make port. Is that clear?"

"Yes, sir," Sylus said.

Sylus suspected that he should feel nervous, and he did, but it was the quiet, restless nervousness of excitement. Sure, he'd never worked on a ship this large, but the concepts were the same. The only thing that changed was the scale.

"You shall be joining the tank team today," Holven said, smiling politely.

He reached out and grabbed one of the passing men, asking for his harness. Confused, the man handed it over to Holven, who in turn presented it to Sylus. Sylus smirked. He supposed Holven was trying to unnerve him.

Maintaining the air tanks was a perilous, important job. For the tanks to maintain altitude, they needed evenly balanced pressure at all times. Any sudden pressure drops could cause the ship to tilt or even descend into the blades. Mainly, air pressure was controlled at the helm, where the helmsman, namely, the Captain, could raise and lower the pressure across all tanks via a Thaumatech control panel. The problem was that the Verdant Sea was unpredictable.

The blades were not of uniform length throughout the sea, nor did the heights stay static. The grasses were ever shifting, and though it was unlikely here in the Shallows, sudden waves could catch the ship, requiring quick pressure changes. A leak was also never impossible. In these situations, pressure needed to be maintained or shifted faster than the ship's systems could allow. That's where the tank crew came in.

Sylus took the harness from Holven without hesitation. With quick, practiced movements, he stepped into the harness and secured it around his shoulders and under the legs, adjusting the straps to fit his height and size. Finally, he checked the leather tool belt that hung from the harness to ensure everything was in order.

He pulled out and inspected each of the ten repair kits that were inside, and unscrewed the metal container containing the kit's sealing resin. He poked it with a finger in several places to ensure it wasn't hardening, satisfied with the way it clung to his finger each time. He nodded and moved on to the pressure gauge, a small device with a thin needle that could be stuck into the air tanks to read pressure in an emergency. He pulled off the cap and stuck his finger with the needle, wincing as he became very sure of its sharpness. He flicked the pressure gauge to ensure its needle wasn't stuck, then moved on to the final item on his belt.

This was the only item he handled nervously, for it was Thaumatech, and as valuable as it was important. It was a small, strange circular device. One side was slightly domed and perfectly smooth aside from four intake valves, while the other was flat and featured five small claws. When pierced into an air tank, it would immediately activate, drawing energy from the Source to rapidly convert oxygen into helium, refilling an air tank in seconds. It was intended for use in extreme emergencies only.

Like most Thaumatech, that singular Wonder was its only purpose, and once used, it could not be used again until it was cut from the tank, which would require a full replacement.

Sylus handled it with care, though there was not much to inspect. Primarily, he took it out and examined it for any visible signs of use or damage. He'd never heard of a Thaumatech device failing at its purpose, but with something this important, it paid to be careful. Seeing no visible cause for concern, he carefully tucked it back into his belt and looked back to Holven.

"It seems to all be in order, sir," Sylus said, careful to keep his expression neutral.

He wanted to impress Holven, and being cocky wouldn't win him any extra points. The best thing he could do was prove his knowledge and usefulness by working as hard as he could.

Holven merely stared at him for a moment. If he was impressed or annoyed, there was no way to tell.

"Good," he said, turning back to the man whose harness he had taken. "Introduce him to Jorran, get him in position."

The man nodded, giving Sylus a doubtful look, "Come with me, lad."

Sylus followed the man without hesitation, giving Holven a determined nod as he passed. He could feel Holven's eyes on his back as he marched away and made sure not to look back.

The man led Sylus to the side of the ship, where the base of the air tank bracing met the hull. A metal rung ladder was attached to the inside of the bracing, leading up to the tanks. Similar ladders were affixed to the rest of the bracing, which people were beginning to climb. A stout-looking, muscular man in a harness was shouting orders at the rest of the tank crew when he noticed Sylus.

"Absolutely not!" he hollered, marching over to Sylus, "No mud slapping flat-foot is climbing my tanks. Not under any circumstances!"

The man was older, with a rugged, seasoned appearance, and his lined face sported a head of short-cropped hair that was more grey than brown. His penetrating gaze as he ran his eyes over Sylus was the first time he'd felt nervous since approaching the Captain.

His eyes shifted to the man who'd led Sylus over, "Whose idea was this? Huh?"

"Holven's idea, sir," Sylus said. The man turned thunderous eyes back to Sylus, so he hastily added, "Given to him by the Captain. Sir. He says I'm to be tested."

The man was frozen with his mouth half open; clearly, he was about to yell in Sylus's face, but at the mention of the Captain, he seemed to be having second thoughts. His eyes flicked upwards toward the helm for a fraction of a second. Then he shoved a finger into the other man's chest.

"Next time you come to me first, it's my final say, no matter what Holven or-"

A shrill whistle sounded throughout the ship, and Jorran cursed loudly. He turned away from Sylus to bellow at the people who were watching the interaction with interest.

"What are you waiting for? Climb! Climb!" he shouted, and everyone was suddenly clambering for ladders.

Sylus did not move as Jorran continued to yell creative insults at his crew. When he turned back to Sylus, he seemed surprised to see him there.

"And? What are you waiting for?"

"Permission, sir. It's your final say," Sylus said.

The man's eyebrows drew down as if he was not sure if Sylus was mocking him or trying to flatter him, but Sylus could tell it was working. The man's frown softened a tad as he gave Sylus a renewed glance.

"I suppose you have the build for it," he muttered, then shrugged. "Fine. You want to kill yourself, be my guest, not like you can kill the rest of us out here in the Reach anyway."

Sylus nodded and turned to the ladder. Not only to prove he knew what he was doing, but because he did not want to miss the moment the ship left the docks, and atop the air tanks would be the best seat in the house.

Hanging near the ladder was a series of lifelines, strong cables that were anchored to the ship and the harness in case the tank crew fell. He attached one end to a pole that ran alongside the length of the ladder, and the other end he attached to the anchor point of his harness. Then he was scurrying up the ladder as fast as he could move.

He looked down to see Jorran watching him, surprise clear on his face. Sylus let himself smile and kept going. Halfway up the bracing, the ladder switched to the outside of the support. Hooking his arm around the rung of the ladder, Sylus switched his lifeline and then swung himself to the ladder on the opposite side before beginning to climb once more.

He didn't allow himself to slow down until he started passing the air tanks themselves. Cradled within the reinforced braces, the tanks were made of an ultra-light metal, salvaged primarily from structures and remnants of the old world found out in the Verdant Sea. They were strong, but not invincible, and it was now his job to ensure their safety. They would be slowly filling with helium, and any moment now the ship would begin to rise off the blades.

Now that Sylus was high enough, he could see that various other stations around the bracing, as well as the crow's nest, where Cally's auburn hair could be seen through the window.

Sylus climbed to the top of the tanks and took a quick scan. He was disappointed, but not surprised, to find all the stations on the tops of the tanks were already filled. Galleon had told him that people often coveted their favorite spots, either for superstition or the view. These would have the best view and are also the safest. He took another glance around and located an empty station to his right, near the tops of the tanks. It was a side mount, but that didn't bother him at all.

Careful to keep his lifeline moving with him, he made his way to the side mount and positioned his feet to rest in the grooves provided. This was the most challenging part, but would also be the most thrilling. Taking a deep breath, he let his body weight relax, and the lifeline snapped taut, supporting his body weight as he hung off the side of the tank, taking the pressure off his arms and legs, and freeing his hands for his work.

Not daring to look down yet, Sylus turned his attention to the bracing, where a series of gauges monitored the pressure of the closest tank. He checked the needles on each indicator, watching them steadily rise for a moment. Then, once he was satisfied that all was in order, he double- and triple-checked his lifeline.

Then, and only then, did he allow himself to look out from the ship. It wasn't that he was scared of heights, quite the opposite, he'd just been waiting for this moment since he put on the harness.

Windmoor's docks spread out beneath him. The *Bladedancer* wasn't quite so large a ship that he could see the entire town, but it was easily the biggest ship in the port, and he got an unparalleled view of all the ships and land around Windmoor. In the distance behind the town, the mountains were just visible, their tops hidden by the clouds. Somewhere in those mountains was Hearthhallow.

He stared up at the mountains for a moment, overtaken by a sudden feeling of melancholy. If he got his way, this might be the last time he ever saw them. No. Even if he didn't make the crew - and he would make the crew - he knew he would never return here. There was nothing for him here now.

"Goodbye, mother," he whispered at the mountains.

The ship suddenly lurched, and Sylus felt his stomach drop out for just a moment as the airship lifted from the dock. He spared a glance at the tanks, estimating them to be at seventy-five percent. That was good; it meant the ship still possessed quite a bit of leeway for sudden changes in the blades.

He looked down and could see the ship rising above the docks. Going up and over was, of course, the easiest way to get out of the docks, but you had to be careful not to rise too high. While the ships were technically capable of flight, they could not maintain it for very long.

Multiple angled sails unfurled all around the ship in a series of fluttering followed by taunt snaps as they caught the wind. The sails, unlike the tanks, were mainly controlled by the crew, except for the two main sails, which were controlled from the helm. The main sails could guide the ship in a broad sense, but tighter control would require the use of the many smaller sails. Maneuvering out of the docks, for instance, would need all the sails working together.

Sylus watched as the *Bladedancer* began to drift toward the Verdant Sea. Smaller ships passed beneath them as they rose up and over the docks, the nose of the vessel turning out toward the sea. There wasn't much for Sylus to do at this point. Despite being perilous, if the air tanks were functioning correctly, then there was nothing to do but monitor the pressure and enjoy the view. At least, that was the case according to Old Galleon and his books.

Of course, the Whispering Reach, as this section of the Verdant Seas was known, was also part of what was colloquially referred to as the Shallows. The Verdant Sea was shallowest near the continents, and the shallower areas were calmer and much safer, often used for shipping and trading. The deeper regions of the Verdant Sea were another story entirely.

Finally, the ship completed its turn, and Sylus moved his eyes to the horizon, locking onto that magical place where green hit the sky. The pressure in the tanks began to drop as the ship settled into a cruising altitude, a good couple of feet away from the blades. More sails were deployed, snapping taut as they caught the gentle winds, and the *Bladedancer* began to glide over the blades, away from Windmoor.

Sylus did not look back.

6

The Bladedancer

It wasn't long before Windmoor began to fade from view, but Sylus barely noticed. He was trying to keep an eye on his pressure gauge, but those first few moments made it hard to pay attention. The ship was picking up speed, and the emerald hues of the Whispering Reach began to slide beneath them.

Sylus leaned out from the ship as far as the lifeline would allow. He breathed in the clean, crisp air that whipped his hair back, enjoying watching other ships pass them by on their way to Windmoor. He kept an eye on the horizon, hungry for a peek at anything that wasn't Altaris.

There was quite a bit to see as they pulled further away from the shore. Birds of all shapes and sizes flew high and low over the Green, including some he'd never seen before, and some that seemed impossibly large.

It wasn't just the sky that was full of life, either. Though humans were not equipped to traverse the sharp grasses of the Verdant Sea, a variety of life made its home within the blades. Multiple times, he saw flashes of unknown wildlife poking up from the Green. He spotted what could only be the shiny carapaces of giant insects a few times, and once something thin and long that was gone in an instant. Everything he saw filled Sylus with a burning curiosity. He knew very little of what lived in the blades, as his mother's aversion to everything to do with the Sea meant she did not answer any of the questions he asked about it growing up. In general, he knew his education about the world beyond his village was severely lacking. If it weren't for Old Galleon and his books, Sylus suspected he'd know nothing at all.

A flicker on the gauge caught his eye, and he tore his eyes from the Green to investigate. His tank was losing pressure. Frowning, he tapped the gauge a few times to make sure it wasn't loose. No, there was no doubt about it; the tank was losing pressure very slowly. It was not a catastrophic issue. A ship this size possessed several extra air tanks for just such an occasion. The loss of one wouldn't affect the safety of the vessel, but he did need to investigate, and that meant inspecting the tank.

Before doing anything, he turned back to the station. Affixed near his lifeline was a medium-sized bell, secured against the wind. He quickly unsecured it and rang it once, then three times. That signaled to the others on the tank team who were close enough to hear that he'd detected a minor issue with the tank, and he was investigating.

He re-secured the bell and readied himself. This was where the danger of managing the tanks came in. Unhooking his lifeline from the station and affixing it to the ladder, he began to climb, carefully inspecting every inch of his section, looking for any sign of a leak. He did not see any, but even a small puncture would cause slow pressure loss; it might even cause tank failure if left unattended.

Pressing his ear to the tank, Sylus plugged the opposite side with his finger and tried to block out everything else. It was a trick Galleon had taught him. It wasn't easy; there was a lot of noise on an airship, but the air tanks filled with gas amplified sound easily, and if you were anywhere close to the leak....

Yes! Sylus could hear it. It was at the top of the tank. Too far to reach from here.

Blanking his mind against what he had to do, Sylus extended his lifeline as far as it would go. Double-checking it was secure, he took a deep breath and stepped off the ladder onto the air tank. Fabric handholds were attached across the tank for traversal, and the material was more than strong enough to support his weight. Moving carefully, he pressed his ear against the tank every couple of feet, moving diagonally until he was sure he was in the vicinity of the leak. Making sure his feet and opposite hand kept a tight grip on the holds, he began running his hand across the tank, ensuring consistency in his search, leaving no square inch unchecked.

After a few moments, he felt it, a cool stream of air against his fingers. Smiling, he heaved himself, inspecting the area. To call it a hole would be generous. A barely visible dot was allowing a small amount of gas to escape. Frowning as he inspected it, Sylus wondered what could have made such a tiny, precise puncture, but there was time for that later. Sylus fumbled at his belt for the repair kit, looping his elbow through the hold so he could use both hands. He shielded the kit from the wind with his body and selected a patch of the appropriate size from the kit. Opening the resin, he spread the sticky sap across the outside edge of the patch and around the puncture, then pressed them together.

The resin was collected from the great trees of the Verdant Sea, and like everything in the Sea, it was powerful. He held it in place as the resin quickly bonded. Once exposed to air for more than a few moments, it dried into a perfect seal.

Once the patch was complete, he checked it against his palm to make sure the seal was tight. Nodding to himself, he put away his tools and slowly, carefully, made his way back to the ladder. Climbing back down to his station, he removed the bell once more and gave three loud, clear rings - the all clear. The tank would need to be properly repaired at some point, but for such a small puncture, the patch could hold for months, maybe even years.

Settling back into a comfortable position, he sighed, relieved, as he watched the pressure gauges begin to normalize. Then he noticed someone was climbing up the ladder toward him. Sylus waited patiently until the man reached him.

"Shift change," he said, "Go get some lunch."

"Lunch?" Sylus said, "Already?"

How long had he been up here? It felt like it was barely an hour, but a quick check of the sun's position told him it was well after midday. Sylus shrugged and swapped positions with the man on the ladder. It was a bit of a dance, but before long, he was climbing down and stepping onto the deck, where someone was waiting for him.

"Everything alright?" Holven said. "I heard there was a problem?"

"Nothing major," Sylus said, "A small puncture in the tank, I will have to inform the engineers."

"I see. I will make sure they get the message. I thought I would show you to the mess hall. You have an hour for lunch, then it's back to work."

"Great, I'm starving," Sylus said honestly.

"Hand off your harness," Holven said.

Another man was waiting impatiently for Sylus to hand over his harness. He quickly unstrapped himself and handed it over to the man, who took it with a nod and hurried off to his station.

"Follow me," Holven said, leading Sylus back to the same door they'd entered before.

After a few twists and turns, they ended up at a large double door, somewhere in the middle of the ship. Holven pushed through the doors to reveal a large room with several long tables and benches. Across the back wall, a serving station, crewed by people in cooks' aprons, was serving a long line of waiting men and women, in front of a window that opened onto a barely visible kitchen.

"You'll have to meet our head chef another time. I'll meet you back on the deck in an hour," Holven said.

"Aren't you going to eat?" Sylus asked.

"I ate already, thank you."

"Do I have to eat in here? I'd like to go up the deck, if I could," Sylus asked, before Holven could turn to leave.

Holven eyed him warily, "If you want to, but do not be surprised if you lose your lunch in the wind. The plate will come out of your shares."

"I won't lose my plate!" Sylus said, frowning. Was it not clear he knew his way around a ship yet?

Holven did not respond, which Sylus suspected was his default response. He turned to leave without another word. Sighing, Sylus got in line with the others, anxious to see what was being served.

The line moved quickly, and though people chatted with their friends and colleagues around him, nobody seemed inclined to talk to Sylus. He did not mind; in fact, he understood. He would not be surprised if the entire crew knew about him by now and was aware that he was also here on a trial basis. Why bother getting to know someone who might not be here tomorrow?

He patiently waited until he got to the front of the line. Once it was his turn, he was offered a choice between two options: a steaming bird the cook referred to as a 'Whisperhawk' and a familiar-looking platter of insect legs that turned out to be the Glimmerbeetles he'd seen roasting in town. He chose the legs and a side of vegetables, and took his plate back toward the doors.

He could feel people's eyes on him, but he didn't care. He snuck a glance at some people enjoying the legs to see how to eat them. He snacked on one of the legs as he made his way back to the deck. They were crispy and crunchy, yet strangely hollow, as if whatever was inside them had been drained out before cooking. They were excellent, and he'd eaten more than half of them by the time he got to the deck.

He moved to the railing and looked out across the grass as he finished his meal, careful not to let the plate get away from him. He allowed himself to enjoy the moment. Once he was done with his meal, he carefully tucked his plate under his arm and stared out at the Green for a moment, watching for any sign of something on the horizon.

After a moment, something did catch his eye. He turned his head and felt his mouth fall open. Far, far in the distance, something, or rather, several somethings, shone in the sun.

There was no mistaking the metallic gleams for anything other than the metals of the old work, poking out from the tops of the grass, catching the sun, and drawing the eye.

"It's one of the ruins of the old world," a gruff voice said behind him.

Sylus turned to find his uncle standing behind him, following his gaze out toward the shining points.

"Or at least, the tops of one."

"Ruins?" Sylus said in wonder.

"That be a city, one of the few we know the location of."

"Ruins are where you hunt for Thaumatech, aren't they?"

"That they be," Bracken said, coming to rest on the railing beside Sylus.

"Have you searched there?" Sylus asked, unable to keep the excitement out of his voice.

Bracken chuckled low in his throat.

"Blades, no. Everything in the Shallows has been picked clean for decades now, boy. Anything worth finding be deeper in the Green."

"Ah, I see," Sylus said, disappointed.

He tore his gaze away from the shining city to scan the horizon for more sights.

"You know your way around the tanks, I hear," Captain Bracken said casually, without looking at him.

"I told you, I trained my whole life to work on ships," Sylus said.

"Hmph," Bracken said, "There be much more to sailing the Green than minding the tanks."

"Nothing I can't handle," Sylus said confidently.

Bracken chuckled again, "We shall see, boy, we shall see."

"Ah, Captain," said Holven's voice from behind them, "I was just coming to collect young Sylus here."

"I'm twenty-three," Sylus said to both of them sternly.

No one paid him any attention.

"It is time you got back to the tanks," Holven said, holding out a harness.

"No, I be thinking not," Bracken said, "The boy be wanting to sail the Green, so he goes on the sails."

"While we dock?" Holven said, once again showing absolutely no emotion one way or another.

"Especially when we're docking. You say you can handle it, boy?"

"Of course," Sylus said.

The Captain chuckled again as he pushed off from the railing and walked away.

"At least he has the attitude for it, eh Holven?"

Holven, unsurprisingly, did not respond. Instead, he motioned for Sylus to follow him and led him to take the place of a man who was manning one of the starboard triangle sails near the front of the ship.

Sylus knew that this particular sail was partly responsible for sharper turns. Like many things on the airships, the sail was part of a series of similar sails, so that if something happened to one, it was not catastrophic for the rest of the ship.

Sylus was beginning to see a pattern. He gave Holven a dry look, which Holven returned with merely a raised eyebrow.

"Something the matter?" he asked.

"Not at all," Sylus responded.

He turned to his task and began diligently checking all the ropes and ties that held his sail in place. How long Holven stayed to watch, Sylus didn't know. They were traveling straight, but the wind did not often stay the same on the Verdant Sea. As such, it was more important right now that his sail remain furled so as not to upset the course of the ship. Once they got closer to port, however, directions would be called out for the desired position of the sails. It would be his duty not only to follow those commands but also to monitor the sail and make any split-second decisions necessary. Once his ties and leads were all correctly positioned and tight, he took the liberty of turning his eyes back to the sea, which is when he saw it.

On the horizon, something green rose higher than the blades.

Boughhaven, one of the famous treeports.

Sylus could not help but watch in wonder as the great tree grew closer, as a treeport was something he'd been waiting his entire life to see.

For reasons unknown, the grass dominated all other plant life that might grow in the Verdant Sea, with few exceptions. Of those, a few exceptions were colossal trees that had absorbed the grass's ability to grow to monumental size.

The trunks could grow as large as mountains, with bark so gnarled and textured it resembled a fortress wall. Their sprawling canopies could stretch for miles, with branches as wide as city streets and sturdy enough to support bustling markets, homes, and ship docks.

As Boughhaven drew into view over the next couple of hours, Sylus could see more details emerge as the *Bladedancer* prepared to dock.

Across some of the lower branches, docks were built out from the thicker branches in enormous platforms, with the capacity for hundreds of ships of all sizes, which were coming from all directions. The branches the docks were attached to were covered with a sprawling array of wooden buildings, with walkways and bridges extending between branches, while cranes moved goods up and down from higher levels of the city.

Sylus watched in amazement as they sailed under the canopy, entering a deeply shaded area shielded from the sun by leaves larger than the airships and houses they sheltered. As the canopy opened up underneath the branches, Sylus could see some of the higher sections of the city, with residential boughs, markets, and even larger buildings all nestled among the interconnected branches. At the same time, a grand spiral staircase circled lazily around the great trunk, providing access for pedestrians and carts to reach the many branches at a gentle slope that tapered out of sight around the side of the tree.

The absolute scale of the city was hard to comprehend, and as they drew toward the dock, the number of people moving among the docks and city streets surpassed anything Sylus ever imagined. He was so busy gawking that he almost didn't hear the instructions being yelled by the sail masters.

"Set the sails!"

Sylus jumped, snapping his eyes back to his task at hand. He quickly loosened the ropes that held the sail in place, and it snapped open with a sharp crack as it caught the wind.

"Ready about!"

Sylus positioned himself to tack. He searched for the open dock position that the *Bladedancer* was headed toward, eyeing the angle the ship would need to turn into the wind to make a smooth landing.

As if on cue, the Bladedancer began to rise slightly to glide over the other ships. As it grew, Sylus kept a tight grip on his lines, waiting for orders.

"Take in the starboard sails!"

This would allow the ship to turn into the wind, as all the wind pressure would be directed against the opposite side, causing the vessel to turn lightly.

Sylus began to pull in the correct lead line to position his sail closer to the ship.

A wild crack filled the air as the rope he was pulling on snapped in two.

Sylus stumbled backwards as the tension broke, almost falling to the deck.

"Loose sheet!" he called desperately.

People began shouting, but Sylus didn't listen; he had a job to do. His sail was fluttering in the wind, interfering with the turn maneuver. The part of the rope that was still attached flailed wildly through the air, only a few feet beyond the railing.

Sylus did not hesitate. He ran to the railing and hooked his foot between the tines, throwing the top half of his body over the side, and grabbing desperately for the rope. He snatched wildly, straining to get enough distance to reach the rope. It flew by his hand, and he managed to grab hold of it.

With him holding the rope, the sail snapped full, catching the wind. Sylus yelled out as the sail tried to pull his arm free of its socket. If it were a larger sail, he might have been pitched over the side.

He gritted his teeth and got his other hand on the rope, pulling it with all his might to try to close the sail. Using all of his strength, he managed to get the rope back to the railing, his entire torso burning from the effort of not going over the edge. Using slow, careful movements, he dipped the rope under the railing and around it, using it as an anchor to release the tension from his body. Once it was secured, he let go and repositioned his hands to pull in the sail the rest of the way.

"Secure!" he called, once the sail was in its proper position.

He finally let himself fall back on the deck, gasping for air. The loose end of the rope he'd just secured swayed in front of him, secured to the railing.

Admittedly, the ship was never really in any danger. He realized now that what he just did was stupidly dangerous and unnecessary. The vessel drifted lazily into its docking position, coming to a safe rest, but Sylus was examining the rope.

He reached up to grab it, examining the loose end. It had snapped almost perfectly in two. One half of the diameter was frayed, with loose fibers unraveling in every direction, but the other half was a clean cut.

That was impossible.

"You trying to get yourself pulled overboard?" the sail master said, coming over to shout at him.

Sylus dropped the rope, and suddenly Holven was there, kneeling over Sylus, his face serious but expressionless. He placed his hands on Sylus's shoulder.

"Are you hurt, Sylus?" he asked, waving the sail master away.

"No," Sylus said, and pushed himself up to a sitting position.

He rotated his shoulder.

"Just tired myself out there for a second. That was... a stupid thing to do; he was right to admonish me. The safer thing to do would have been to cut the sail free."

Holven merely nodded, rising from his knee to offer Sylus a hand.

"It was an unorthodox solution," he said, "but if you aren't hurt..." he trailed off.

"No need for another inspection quite yet, sir," Sylus joked, taking the offered hand to rise to his feet.

Sylus swore he saw Holven's mouth twitch.

All around them, men and women scurried across the deck, securing the ship to the dock with a series of ropes.

"Well... I should get back to it," Sylus said.

"Not quite," Holven said, "The Captain wishes to speak with you. Follow me."

Sylus could not tell anything from Holven's expression, but he felt his stomach drop out as the man walked away. There was nothing to do but follow. He glanced back at the rope once and decided not to say anything.

7

Boughhaven

Holven led Sylus to the Captain, who was waiting impatiently near the edge of the ship. A gangplank was being lowered to the dock below, and the Captain's black beard swayed ominously as he tapped his foot with impatience.

"As requested, Captain," Holven said.

Without even a glance back at Sylus, he continued onward, disappearing into the interior of the ship, leaving Sylus under the scrutiny of the Captain.

"Captain," Sylus said respectfully, but Bracken only grunted and shook his head, turning his attention back to the gangplank.

So Sylus stood there, increasingly nervous, as they waited for it to be lowered to the dock. As soon as it touched the platform, the Captain waved for Sylus to follow him and trudged down the ramp into Boughhaven, leaving Sylus to scurry along behind him.

Men and women moved about the ships all around them. Snippets of conversation, shouting, and the noises of a shipyard surrounded them, offering a hundred places to look at once. Sylus ignored them all. Why wasn't the Captain saying anything?

Bracken set a brisk pace through the docks, and soon they'd left the *Bladedancer* behind.

"So, you know your way around a ship," Bracken said, and Sylus hurried his pace to walk beside the Captain so that he could hear, "Though I hear there be some trouble."

"Yes. Nothing I couldn't handle, but..." Sylus said, pausing, wondering if he should continue.

The Captain was looking at him out of the corner of his eye, and Sylus decided to take a chance, letting his words out in a rush.

"The strange thing about both incidents is that they were problems, yes, but not issues that would have endangered the ship. In each case, if I were, say, lying about knowing how to sail, they could be easily handled by a nearby crew member without compromising the ship or the safety of the crew.

A hole the size of a pin in the air tank. A rope, cut just enough to snap under pressure. Those weren't accidents. They were tests."

Bracken's face didn't change a hair, yet by the time Sylus finished, he was confidant he was right.

"Hmph," the Captain grunted, "Maybe you be my blood, maybe you do not, but you know how to sail, that much is plain."

"So does that mean you're taking me on?" Sylus said, unable to keep the excitement out of his voice.

"I suppose..." the Captain began, but Sylus was already shaking the man's hand.

"Thank you, Captain. You won't regret it. I promise you," he said.

"At the lowest share, mind you!" The Captain said roughly, pulling his hand out of Sylus's grip and giving him a frown.

"At the lowest share," Sylus agreed, beaming up at the man.

After a moment, the Captain's lips quirked upwards, and he shook his head, "Blades take me, I must be crazy. Your mother be owing me till the end of her days, family or no."

"I can't wait to write to her," Sylus lied quickly, trying to hide his guilt by finally letting himself look around the port.

"Won't be many chances fer letters, boy," Bracken said gruffly, "Now come on. We've got lots to do. I can't be taking on crew members who don't know the business."

"What do you mean?" Sylus said, falling to step beside the larger man.

"Sailing for Thaumatech be some of the most dangerous work on the Green," the Captain said, picking through the crowds.

"I know that."

"Do you? Tell me then, what do you know about it?"

"Well, crews like yours. I mean, crews like ours scour the Green for ruins of the old world and bring back what we can to sell for profit."

"That easy, is it?"

"Well, of course not. There are all sorts of monsters in the Green. Strange creatures, and the Reclaimed, of course..." Sylus said, suddenly realizing that he had no idea what was out there in the Green.

He didn't even know how crews went about finding places to plunder, or how they gained access to the ruins they discovered. Were there traps? Specialized equipment? Sylus looked up at the Captain, who was watching him again with that steely gaze.

"I'll uh... be sure to pay very close attention to everything you teach me, sir," he said.

Bracken chuckled and shook his head again, "You be eager, boy, that can be a good thing. But don't be letting it get to your head. There's no place for ego on a crew like ours. It's likely to get you killed or worse, get others killed."

The Captain picked his way through the crowd easily, or rather, his size and gruff looks meant that people got out of his way more often than not. He led Sylus up a flight of stairs and onto the first branch, which seemed to be a shopping street, before turning left toward the trunk and the grand staircase that circled it.

For Sylus's part, he had a lot more trouble getting through the crowd, partially because next to his uncle, he was a scrawny nobody who no one gave a second glance to, and also because his head was swiveling in every direction as fast as he could move it, trying to take in all the sights at once.

The streets were made of stone, laid directly into the branch, and that gave all of the buildings on the branch a flat surface to build from, though some had extensions that leaned out from the branch over open air. Sylus saw restaurants, shops full of weapons and trinkets, and more than one

Thaumatech store, watched over by steely-eyed men brandishing cudgels by the front door. Sylus wanted to ask about the things he saw, but there was little time for gawking and even less for idle questions. The Captain set a brisk pace.

"Where are we going?" Sylus asked, struggling to keep up with the larger man's stride.

"The Church," Bracken said, pointing above them.

Sylus followed his finger to a large stone building on a branch above them and to the right. He gaped. It was the largest building he'd ever seen, taking up the majority of the branch it sat upon, and it was visible easily from where they walked, behind and below it.

It was a majestic stone construction, the only fully stone building he could see, covered in steeples, towers, and stained glass windows the size of houses.

"Why the Church?"

"Blades, they be teaching you anything in that village?" Bracken asked.

"I know some things. A Technepriest came to our village once," Sylus said defensively.

"Hmph. Likely then he preached at your village for hours, so you know about the Binary Gods and all that, at least."

"I do," Sylus said carefully.

Sylus had listened to the man speak, but it was primarily out of hope that he'd perform another Wonder, rather than interest in what he'd been saying. But some people in the village took the man's words to heart, and Sylus knew how touchy some people could get about their beliefs.

"Now you be sounding like your mother at least," Bracken said, shaking his head, "It don't matter to me one whit if you believe or not, boy. It's not important anyhow. What's important is that the Government demands that any ship seeking Thaumatech take a Technepriest aboard. It's the law."

"Why does the government want us to take a priest with us?" Sylus asked, genuinely confused.

It never mattered too much up in the mountains what the Government did or didn't do; it never got up to Hearthhallow.

"The Church *is* the government boy, or near enough that it doesn't matter. The government doesn't take a piss without asking the Church if it be okay. Even if it weren't the law, you'd want to take one anyway."

They'd reached the grand curving staircase that circled the trunk of the great tree. Each step was well-worn wood, cut from logs of impossible size. The stairs were narrow where they curved near the trunk, and wide at the edge, where a wooden railing prevented people from getting too close to the edge. These wider sections were wide enough for enterprising merchants and street performers to set up small stalls and stages, trying to entice the heavy traffic that flowed in both directions along the stairway. Sylus wondered how far around the great tree actually was, for it appeared they needed to do a full circle upwards to reach the Church. They started upwards along the outer side of the stairs, close to the crowd that gathered near the railings.

"Why is that?" Sylus said, careful to stay close to the Captain in the moving throngs.

He never got his answer, though, for someone grabbed his leg as he took a step up to the next stair, almost causing him to go tumbling forward.

"Hey!" he shouted in surprise.

He twisted back to see a man slouching on the stairs, out of the way of the crowds, but close enough that he could apparently reach out and harass passersby.

His shout caught the attention of the Captain and a few others. Bracken turned quickly, his hand going to his sword, as Sylus tried to pull his leg out of the man's steel grasp.

"Change, sir? Please," the man said, his dirty face looking up at Sylus pleadingly—a beggar.

"I don't have any," he started to say, but was surprised as the Captain reached down and offered the man a few coins.

The man let go of Sylus's leg and smiled up at the Captain, "Thank you, sir! May Verdalis bless you!"

Once the man's hand released him, Sylus could see why he was not able to pull his leg free. The man was a Thaumatechne, and his hand was metal and machine. In fact, his unshorn feet were also made of metal, and Sylus could see the machinery upon the man's neck as well. He stumbled out of reach quickly, toward the Captain.

How much longer did that man have left? Weeks? Days? As he stumbled backwards, he could see a man in armor hovering nearby, watching the entire interaction with concern.

Bracken laid a hand on his shoulder and steered him back around, toward the stairs, and in moments the man was gone from sight.

"That's why we bring a priest, boy."

"Because of the Reclaimed?" Sylus guessed, "The infection?"

"It's not just the Reclaimed that can spread the infection, lad, any piece of Thaumatech we find out in the Green be carrying it. Any cut, any injury, even if you're carrying something as innocuous as a glow bulb, and it nicks your hand, you're as good as dead."

"Anything," Sylus repeated nervously. He knew that, of course, but now he understood why they needed the priest. "Anything not deactivated by a priest, you mean."

"Exactly. They know the Wonders that make Thaumatech safe to handle. The Technepriests come into the ruins with us, they do their Wonders, if it's safe, and we haul it out."

"What if it's not safe?" Sylus ventured.

"Then we haul it out - careful as can be, and they do their business on the *Bladedancer*."

Sylus could feel his leg itching where the man had grabbed him, but resisted the urge to stop and pull his pant leg up to check for infection. For some reason, Thaumatechne could not infect others, not until the infection reached their brain at least, and they became Reclaimed. Everyone knew this, but it didn't make his leg stop itching. He shuddered and almost missed what the captain said next.

"Of course, they be useful in other ways, too. Some of them can use Wonders to heal, and of course, they're always handy to have if you run into the Reclaimed."

"Do you believe?" Sylus asked, the question springing to his lips before he could stop it. The Captain looked at him again out of the corner of his eye. It was too late to stop now, so Sylus continued, "About the Binary Gods, the Reclaimed, The Source, all of that?"

The Captain did not answer for a long moment, and Sylus began to grow nervous.

"I'm sorry, Captain, I did not mean to pry," he said, dropping his gaze.

They walked in silence for a few more minutes, with Sylus regretting ever opening his mouth.

"I no be religious, if that's what you mean," The Captain said in a gruff voice, "But in our line of work, it's a good idea to keep a healthy eye towards the gods, you understand?"

"Yes, sir," Sylus said.

"We're here, anyway. Let's go fetch our priest," Bracken said, and for the first time, Sylus noticed that they'd circled the entire tree and were stepping off the stairs onto another branch.

8

The Church of the Binary Gods

Once again, Sylus could not help but gape at the scene that stretched out before him. Where the branches below were narrow stone streets and wooden buildings, this branch held a full stone plaza. An open square sat before them, lined with low stone buildings that were dominated in height by the rising steeples and shining glass of the church that rose on its far end.

A wooden sign with foot-high golden lettering near the stairs informed everyone that this was the Boughhaven Church of the Binary Gods, just in case it was not obvious. Sylus had never seen a church before. He supposed there was one in Windmoor, but if there was, it was nothing compared to this.

Open-air sermons were being delivered in the courtyard, along with what seemed to be tours, while important-looking men and women in robes of various colors passed through the courtyard on their way from one building to another. Sometimes small groups of younger people in plain gray robes followed these more important-looking people, and Sylus assumed they were apostles or priests-in-training.

Sylus was not sure what he'd expected, but it certainly was not the busy atmosphere that lay before him. He felt his neck begin to ache as his head once again whipped around on a swivel. He searched for any traces of a Technepriest, or even better, perhaps demonstrations of Wonders. He was disappointed as he followed behind the Captain, who strode through the courtyard as if it were no more interesting than the stones beneath his feet.

Sylus felt foolish. Wonders were not for demonstrations, not at the cost it took to perform them. Still, as if he looked around, he realized he was searching for Thaumatechne, but there were none to be found.

The Captain seemed to sense his unspoken questions.

"Not what you expected?" he asked.

"I guess I thought there would be more Thaumatechne, but most of these priests look like regular people," he said honestly.

The Captain laughed a low laugh.

"Thaumatechne no live long enough to run the Church. No, there aren't so many as you might think. The Church tries to recruit as many as possible to train them. Or as they like to put it, save them and give them purpose."

"Do they train them here?" Sylus asked, excitedly.

"Blades, no. Boughhaven be about as close to nowhere as you can get outside the Uncharted Green. Plus, the Church does no like people learning their secrets. Only ones here be fully trained, stationed here for hire by crews like us."

Sylus very much wanted to know what those other things might be, but they'd crossed the courtyard and were approaching a smaller building on the left-hand side, close to the main cathedral. Here, an opening in the building, not unlike a shopkeeper's window, revealed an older man in magenta robes who sat behind a thin desk beside stacks of ledgers, one of which he was writing in a small, neat hand. He did not look up from his work until Captain Bracken cleared his throat.

"Good day," he said politely.

The man's eyes flicked up at them, switching between the Captain and Sylus quickly before he finished what he was writing, then carefully placed his quill down before turning his full attention to them.

"Good day, Captain," the man said, with an air of familiarity. "For what reason has Verdalis guided you to me today? Let me guess, you are here at last for your contract."

"Indeed, I am, and I'll thank you to leave the sarcasm out of it," Bracken said gruffly.

"Let me see here," the man said, pulling one of the ledgers toward him and opening it, quickly finding a page with a practiced hand, and running one finger quickly down the list, "Here we are, the ship *Bladedancer,* Captain by the name of Bracken, humbly requests the services of one Technepriest and one Tek-Exalt for purposes of salvaging the Verdant sea, and so on. This all seems to be in order."

Sylus looked up at the Captain, burning to ask what a Tek-Exalt might be, but the Captain waved him off, so Sylus held his tongue.

The man closed the book with a sharp snap, looking over his glasses at Captain Bracken with a slight smile.

"Who do you be saddling me with this time? I no like the way you're looking at me," Bracken said, but with a joking air of professional acquaintance.

"Liana," the man said, settling his chin into a hand as he leaned on the book with an elbow, and the Captain visibly brightened.

"Really? Well then, where is she?"

"You know Liana. Never one to sit still and wait for her assigned appointments. I suspect you'll find her wandering the lower branches, tending to those who cannot tend themselves."

Captain Bracken muttered in an annoyed way.

"That girl, it could take me hours to find her. I be running on a schedule," he said.

"Well, that's what happens when you are late, Captain," the man said, still smiling softly.

He had a twinkle in his eye that even Sylus thought looked suspicious, so he was not surprised at all when the Captain's eyes narrowed.

"Who be the other?"

"Asphen," the man said.

"Oh blades!" Bracken said, this time sounding truly annoyed. "Do there be no one else?"

"Not for a fortnight. Do you have some complaint you'd like to register with the Church against Asphen, Captain?"

Bracken shook his head, "You know I do. The man drinks too much and leers at all the women besides. Where is he, if I be so bold to ask?"

"I think you know his favorite haunt quite well, Captain," the man said, returning to the ledger to his pile.

The Captain closed his eyes and pinched the bridge of his nose with calloused fingers,

"At least we only need to go to one place," he said to himself with a sigh.

"Through Verdalis' small blessings we endure," the priest said cheerily.

"Stick to your books, you prune," Bracken said without any heat.

Sylus, who could not believe anyone would talk to a priest like that, looked after him stricken. The priest had a slight smile on his lips.

"There are, of course, some forms for you to fill out," the man said.

"Aye, Aye," the Captain acknowledged with a sigh.

The priest was pulling out a stack of papers that looked much too large for simply hiring two people. The Captain took the quill the priest proffered to him and leaned over the stack of paperwork, muttering to himself, leaving Sylus to stand there awkwardly to wait.

He took a look around the courtyard, itching to explore, and was surprised to find the priests' eyes on him when his gaze returned to the counter.

"And you are?" he asked politely.

"Uh, Sylus," Sylus said awkwardly.

"Tell me, Sylus, are you a believer?"

"Er, not really. I don't know much about the Church."

"Oh, leave the boy alone," the Captain said, irritated.

The priest continued as if he had not spoken.

"You seem like you have an inquisitive mind, Sylus. Since you have a minute, would you mind if we spoke of the Binary Gods?" the priest asked.

Sylus was not really interested, if he was being honest with himself, but he also didn't want to be rude or embarrass the Captain. He glanced at his uncle, but he was busy swearing at the documents in front of him.

"Uh," Sylus said.

"You see, I'm sure you know two gods watch over our world," the priest said, "Verdalis, the protector, and Therithar, the destroyer."

Sylus tried to recall everything the priest had told his village all those years ago.

"Therithar is the one who created the Reclaimed, right? And the Verdant Sea?"

The priest smiled weakly.

"Almost, but not quite. It was Verdalis who created the Verdant Sea to save us from the mistakes of the Old World, which threatened to destroy our world and everything on it. But Therithar, who thought our mistakes deserved no second chances, corrupted it, causing it to spread uncontrollably. The only reason it does not cover the whole world, even now, is that Verdalis once again rose to protect us, slowing its growth, giving us time to rebuild."

"And that's when Therithar created the Reclaimed?"

"Indeed. It was the abuse of Thaumatech that doomed our world in the first place, and so, stymied in his attempt to destroy us through the Verdant Sea, Therithar corrupted Thaumatech with the curse of the Reclaimed. For a brief time, all who handled it were corrupted and made to serve Therithar."

"But we still use Thaumatech every day, and the Church itself promotes its use," Sylus said, pointing out the obvious problem with the story.

"Ah, that is because Verdalis rose once more to our defense. She slowed the rate at which Thaumatech infects the body, and in turn, created the Thaumatechne. Through her guidance, the Thaumatechne were able to learn to purify Thaumatech, making it safe to use if handled properly."

"So what did Therithar do next?" Sylus asked, despite himself.

"Ah, well, at this point, the conflict between the gods came to a head. They clashed, but in the end, Verdalis locked Therithar away, at significant personal cost. The battle took its toll on Verdalis, and to this day, she is recovering her strength for the day she returns to us. It is for that reason that the Verdant Sea still expands, and the Reclaimed still walk the world.

It is up to us to endure until she returns to guide us into the future."

"Right," Sylus said awkwardly, thinking it was all rather convenient.

"You know, if you are interested in learning more," the priest said.

"No time for learning," Bracken broke in, shoving the pile of forms across the desk. "We be leaving. Unless you'd like to stay, Sylus?"

"Uh, no. Thank you," Sylus said gratefully.

"I see," the priest said, smiling politely. "Well, in that case, the arms of Verdalis are always open to you, Sylus, as they are to you, Captain. May Verdalis guide you safely home."

The Captain hesitated, then nodded.

"May Verdalis shelter you," he said gruffly. "Come on, Sylus."

He walked away at a brisk pace, leaving Sylus to follow, his head buzzing with a thousand unanswered questions.

9

The Priest and the Exalt

As soon as they were halfway across the courtyard, Sylus remembered his earlier question.

"What is..."

"Listen, I'm not the person to be answering all sorts of questions about the gods," Bracken said, cutting him off. "If you like, you can ask Liana once we set sail, or Asphen if you're feeling brave."

"Oh, I was actually going to ask what a Tek-Exalt is?" Sylus said.

"Ah, that," grumbled Bracken, who was setting a faster pace than before. "Forgot how little you know. Technepriests aren't the only job in the Church that needs a Thaumatechne. Not everyone wants to be a priest, see, and there be another, uh, path to go down, and that path leads to becoming an Exalt. Where the priests are more about recruiting, healing, that sort of thing, the Exalts have one purpose, and one purpose only. They fight to eradicate the Reclaimed."

Sylus felt his eyes go wide.

"They fight the Reclaimed? With Wonders?"

"Look, don't go pestering me with a million questions. I don't know the answers to most, and I no think I want to. You can ask him yourself if you can stomach him for more than a few minutes," Bracken said as they reached the stairs, this time joining the throngs heading in the opposite direction, down the trunk.

"Is he really that bad?" Sylus asked.

"The Exalts are a rough batch. Nihilists, all of them. Think they're already dead, so they spend what little time they have left risking their fool necks."

"And the Church requires you to take them?"

"Blades, no. Most crews don't bother. They do drink their weight in booze and take a share of what we find to boot."

"Then why do you?"

"Because they're damn good at what they do, and if the choice be my crew dying or getting infected fighting off the Reclaimed, or losing some loot, I be losing the loot every time. Now, enough with your questions, and stay close. The lower branches can be rough, and we've got a schedule to keep. You get lost, and I'm leaving you here."

Sylus doubted that was true. For all his bluster, it was clear that the Captain cared for his crew and was a decent enough man. But still, it was better not to push his luck, so Sylus kept close and held his tongue as they made their way back down the stairs, passing the docks they arrived at, which sat at the lowest possible level. The stairs became a flat platform as they continued around the trunk to a series of branches that sat at the back side of the tree, on a similar level with the docks, just above the blades.

It was immediately apparent that these branches were not the ones people chose to live on if they had any other choice. The wooden buildings were ramshackle and crammed together, as if whoever built them was trying to see just how many dwellings they could fit onto a single branch, while still leaving space to walk between them.

There were no open streets filled with shops, only narrow, zig-zagging alleyways. Disheveled-looking people moved through them with their heads down and their gaze straight ahead. Others lay in the alleys and let others step around them in the narrow confines, not even bothering to beg.

The Captain paused for a moment at the entrance to one of these alleys, muttering to himself about how they would never find the priest in this. He tapped his foot impatiently for a moment, then, without a word, set off down an alley. Sylus could see from here that the streets were a maze, turning this way and that, and he was careful to stick to the Captain as close as he could.

Sylus, not wanting to be grabbed once again, was exceptionally watchful whenever they needed to step around or over someone slumped against a wall or sprawled out along the street. Twice, they passed a nervous-looking guard standing over a Thaumatechne, who eyed them and everyone else who passed with a twitchy eye and a tight grip on their sword. Sylus did not understand. Thaumatechne needed to be guarded, of course, for the day they were eventually Reclaimed, but he could not fathom why anyone who could perform Wonders was out on the street. A business might not want to take on a person who could turn Reclaimed, but the Church seemed perfectly happy to offer them gainful employment, which meant the government probably would as well. He wanted to ask the Captain as much, but the man was peering down every alley and muttering to himself in an increasingly frustrated way, and Sylus felt it best to leave him alone for now.

He was not sure how long they wandered the alleys, a half hour or so, before the Captain peered down a passing alley and came to a sudden stop, causing Sylus to crash into him.

"Liana!" Bracken called, waving to someone down the alley.

Sylus peered around the Captain to catch a glance at their missing Technepriest. Further down the alley, a woman was leaning over someone on the ground. Her clothing was a short, simple robe of some off-white cream color, remarkable only for its cleanliness. It stood out like a beacon among the dirt and grime of the cramped surroundings.

She did not look up at the Captain's call, and with a soft grumble, the Captain began making his way towards her with Sylus following eagerly behind. The Captain came to a stop some few feet away, and Sylus could see why. The woman was leaning over a filthy man, talking to him softly, her short blonde hair blocking her face. But the man was not the reason they stopped.

The woman was grasping the man's shoulder for support as she held her forearm over the man's chest. Her *metal* forearm. Though both of her hands were skin and bone, the forearm of her right arm was metal, leading up into her sleeve. The complex machinery was emitting a soft green light over the man's chest, and Sylus recognized a Wonder. He leaned forward around the Captain eagerly, straining for a better look, until a firm hand on his shoulder from the Captain stopped him from getting any closer. There was no danger to them, of course. Wonders could not transfer the infection, but that did not stop people from being uneasy around such a direct application.

The man was watching the green light with apprehension plain on his face. From this far away, Sylus could hear that the man's breath was ragged, a gasping rattle in the lungs that did not sound like it allowed much for air. As they watched, the man's breathing began to ease. The rattle died down to a soft gurgling, then ceased altogether.

The green glow faded, and the woman lowered her arm as the man took deep, calm breaths.

"How do you feel?" the woman asked in a light voice.

"I-I don't believe it," the man said, rubbing his chest. He looked up at the Technepriest, and Sylus thought he could see genuine tears in the dirty corners of the man's eyes. "I thought… I thought that it was the end. How can I repay you?"

"There is no need," the woman said, standing up. She tucked her blonde hair behind her ear as she did so, revealing a pale face crossed by a smattering of freckles and a breathtaking smile of genuine happiness. "I merely do as Verdalis asks of me."

Sylus suddenly felt his stomach flip over.

"Verdalis…" the man mumbled, still rubbing his chest.

"You will need to eat. Can you walk? If you can make it to the Church, tell them Liana sent you. They will get you something to eat."

"Walk?" the man said, pushing himself up the wall in a surprising show of strength, "I feel like I could run, for the first time in years!"

"Well, promise me you will not," Liana said, her soft voice was stern without being unkind, "I did not heal your lungs just for you to burst them running when you can barely walk. You need rest and time to heal fully. Promise me now."

Sylus silently agreed with her, considering what she'd just sacrificed to give the man a new lease on life. How much of her own life did she spend to heal a random stranger off the street? What kind of person would do something like that?

"I promise. Lady... Liana was it? I won't forget this. I won't. Thank you," the man said, clasping the woman's hand in his own. She laughed, a musical tinkling to Sylus's ears, and the man turned and stared at the sight of them, as if noticing they were there.

"Excuse me," he mumbled, and they moved out of his way so he could pass them in the narrow alley.

Once he was gone, they found Liana staring at them. Now that she was standing, Sylus could see she was about the same height and age as he was. Her short, light blond hair was falling across her face again, and she tucked it behind her ear once more. Sylus's stomach flipped again as the woman turned bright blue eyes on them, that dazzling smile seeming to light up the shadowed alleyway.

"Captain Bracken," she said, "I was supposed to wait at the Church, wasn't I? I'm sorry."

"Oh, I can no fault you for being yourself, Liana," the Captain said, with surprising warmth. His annoyance seemed to have evaporated on the spot. "How have you been?"

"Through Verdalis I endure," she intoned, shrugging. "And who is this?"

She turned her attention to Sylus, who felt himself go red and his throat constrict painfully under her attention.

"Sy-" was all he managed before his voice cracked and refused to work.

He felt himself go redder and ground his teeth as the Captain stepped in to save him.

"He be Sylus, a feral mountain boy I picked up in Windmoor. I thought his backwards antics might be entertaining for the crew, so I brought him on as a fool."

"Oh? Is that so?" she said, a smile broadening her lips as she peered askance at Sylus.

Sylus's head whipped around to stare daggers at the Captain. This was ridiculous. Why couldn't he speak? Twice today, a stranger had seen his naked body, but one pretty girl turned his throat to dust?

He cleared his throat loudly and forcefully.

"He's joking. I'm twenty-three. Twenty-three!" Sylus said.

"He be rather insistent about that," the Captain said.

Liana looked amused.

"I'll be sure to remember that, Sylus," she said with mock importance.

Sylus just felt miserable and sick, and fell silent, embarrassment driving all further words from his head.

"I suppose you have hired an Exalt?" Liana asked, turning her attention back to the Captain.

"Asphen," the Captain said, "He be down here somewhere too."

"I have not worked with him before," Liana said, frowning in thought. "But I've heard the stories. Are we leaving tonight?"

"I no be sure anymore. To be safe, I think we'll sail tomorrow first thing. Will you stay on the ship tonight?"

"I thank you for the offer, but I still have some small preparations to make. I shall meet you on the ship before first light."

"And not a mome-"

"And not a moment after," Liana said, her eyes were twinkling. "I have not forgotten your fondness for schedules, Captain. I will be there!"

The Captain grumbled incoherently, but in a good-natured sort of way.

"Nice to meet you, Sylus," Liana said with a smile, and they moved out of the way so she could pass them in the alley.

Sylus watched her go, his smile widening as he watched her make her way up the alley.

"Don't think about it," the Captain said.

Sylus turned back to him sheepishly, "Think about what?"

"You do know what. She's joining the crew to do a job, and an important one at that. So are you, for that matter. Don't be filling your head with any ideas otherwise. She's a woman of the Church, and she wouldn't be interested in you anyway."

"I wasn't-" Sylus tried to say, but the Captain waved him down.

"Don't be lying when the truth is so plain on your face, boy. Even if she wasn't a priest, she be a Thaumatechne. Their lives are short, no matter how beautiful they may be. Now come on, we have two more stops and I do mean to get back to the ship before dark."

Sylus didn't see much point in trying to defend his dignity any further; he'd left it all at Liana's feet anyways. He glanced at what he could see of the sky through the building-sized leaves of the massive canopy. It was hard to tell in the shade of the great tree, but it must be getting late.

The Captain was already striding away down an alley, and Sylus hurried to catch up.

"You know where to find the Exalt?" Sylus asked.

"I know of the place. It's not far, but it's a rough place. Keep your mouth shut and we be fine."

Sylus was too interested in meeting a Tek-Exalt to respond, so he followed the Captain in silence and contemplated what kind of person would spend their already shortened life putting themselves in harm's way, especially when the cost of any injury was so high.

It did not take long to reach what Sylus assumed was a bar. There was no sign. It was clear that the lower branches could not afford things like glow bulbs. Instead, they came upon an open door with several men standing outside, their hands clutching filthy glasses swilling with some brown liquid.

They eyed the Captain and Sylus as they trudged past and into the establishment, and Sylus could not blame them. Even his filthy, dirt-stained clothes were cleaner than anything he'd seen so far.

The bar was cramped and dark. With no windows to speak of, the only light came from the open door, and a few old oil lamps hung from the ceiling. There were only a few people inside: a rough-looking bartender standing behind the counter bearing a sword on his hip, a large, surprisingly muscular woman drinking alone at the bar, and another man who sat in a corner with a woman on his lap. The man was slamming his hand on the counter to call to the bartender for another drink while he told a loud story that the woman on his lap laughed along to outrageously.

Somehow, these two alone were making enough noise that Sylus was surprised they could even understand what the man was saying, because Sylus certainly could not. When the bartender did not move quickly enough, the man's hand became a fist that pounded the table even louder.

Sylus heard the Captain let out a deep sigh before he approached the table. The man did not notice them, for he now had his head in the woman's neck, and she was giggling capriciously. The bartender was dropping off more drinks with a sour look at the two. For a moment, he seemed about to say something, before thinking better of it and leaving without a word.

The Captain cleared his throat loudly, "Asphen."

Asphen looked around, pulling his head out of the woman's mess of curly hair, and the woman threw her arms around Asphen's neck as he spun around to face them. The Exalt had a stern face with shockingly handsome features. Short black hair covered his head, and his beard was a neat five o'clock shadow. He was not wearing a shirt, and as dark, intelligent eyes flicked between the two of them, Asphen leaned back, exposing a broad, muscular chest covered in a variety of gold chains. Metal worked its way up the man's right side. The woman started stroking his chest with a finger, though Sylus noticed her hand never strayed too close to the metal.

For her part, she was a sallow-looking girl in a corset and shirt that seemed much too small for her, pushing what was there up and forward in a manner that almost made Sylus's eyes pop out of his head. She smiled lazily at him as she noticed him looking, while Asphen, with his free hand, also covered in gold rings, took a sip from his drink.

"Bracken," Asphen said in a voice like smooth velvet. His intense gaze shifted to Sylus, and Sylus felt himself stiffen under the scrutiny. "And a boy. "Is it that time already?"

For once, Sylus felt no need to correct the man.

"It was," Bracken said.

Asphen's eyes shifted to the doorway for a moment, "It's too late to sail now. First light, I assume?"

"A fact I see you are well prepared for," Bracken said, nodding to the woman.

"I do have some business to take care of," Asphen said in a near growl.

His free, still human hand slipped around the woman and curved around her backside, causing her to giggle and hide her face.

"Asphen!" she whispered in mock embarrassment, though it was clear she did not mind at all.

"Consider the contract confirmed, Captain. I'll see you tomorrow."

"First light," the Captain reminded him.

Asphen was no longer paying attention; he had nuzzled back into the woman's neck, and she was giggling with glee as the sounds of kissing lips floated out from beneath her hair. Sylus felt his face go hot as the Captain turned to leave, and Sylus followed quickly.

Once out in the street, the Captain did not stop, but walked quickly into the alleys, in a beeline to the stairs.

"See what I mean?" he said to Sylus, "What kind of man behaves so in public? He be no better on the ship either."

"Couldn't you just ask for someone else?" Sylus asked.

"Then we'd have to wait, and I do have a crew to feed and pay, do I not? Besides, the damned fool is one of the best."

"He did seem to be doing well for himself," said Sylus, thinking of the amount of gold that adorned the man and the woman on his lap.

He was muscular and handsome, clearly wealthy, and considered one of the best. The man had made a name for himself on the Verdant Sea, exactly as Sylus wanted to do, if not precisely through the same path.

"The man spends coin as soon as he gets it, on whatever he wants in the moment. He lives life fast and hard, though I suppose, under the circumstances, I cannot say I do blame him."

Sylus shivered, thinking of the metal that was stretching up Asphen's torso. As always, he could not help wondering how much time the man had left. Yes, Sylus wanted fame and fortune, and he could see how fighting the Reclaimed would earn you that, but he could not imagine paying the price that Asphen did. No, Sylus would earn his fortune his way, through hard work and perseverance.

"It's strange, how people handle getting infected," Sylus said, "Most give up, it looks like, but some people. Like Liana and Asphen, they at least found purpose in their situation."

"There be no purpose in it," Bracken said roughly, "No rhyme, and no reason. You can turn to the gods or wallow in the streets in despair, but the result be the same: a short life and a meaningless death. Now come on, one last stop and we're back to the ship," Bracken said.

From his tone, it was clear that it was all the Captain was going to say on the subject. Sylus could not help but notice how much his uncle sounded like his mother.

Sylus fell silent and passed the long walk through the alleys and up the stairs, embroiled in a fantasy where Liana giggled on his lap, impressed by his calm demeanor and impressive exploits, and there was not a trace of metal, or clothing for that matter, on either of them.

10

Rumors

Eventually, they reached the docks once more, and the Captain steered them toward a building not far from the place where they began. From outside, the place looked like another bar, though a much cleaner one. Sailors sat huddled around clean tables, drinking and conversing at a normal volume as the sun set on Boughhaven, the leaves casting deep shadows over the city. Along the street, some businesses were turning on their Thaumatech lights early, filling the streets with splashes of bright color.

As they approached, the Captain spoke for the first time in at least a half-hour, "Now, there be one last thing you need to know about hunting Thaumatech, and that's how to find it."

"I was wondering about that," Sylus said, "After all this time, wouldn't most of the ruins be cleaned out by now?"

"Perhaps they would be, if we knew where they all were, or if they stayed in one place," Bracken said, pulling him aside out front of the bar, "But they don't. The blades be ever shifting. Sometimes they be taller than the last time you sailed them, sometimes they be shorter. They bring things to the surface or expose something from underneath the Green. You understand?"

"That makes sense," Sylus said slowly. A vast ocean of water once covered most of the world; perhaps it still did, underneath the Verdant Sea. Sylus once read of something called 'tides' which caused the water level to rise and fall. Why wouldn't the grass ocean do the same?

"So, how do we find them?" he asked.

"We don't. It be too dangerous to sail randomly around the Green searching without a purpose. Too much out there to kill us. So we rely on Rumors."

"Rumors?" Sylus said blankly.

"Not that sort. When a ship or a sailor spots something out in the blades, they report it to the guild," Bracken said, gesturing to the bar. Sylus looked askance at the bar, which for all purposes seemed just a lively drinking hole.

"The guild?"

"The Rumor Guild. They report what they saw, and approximately where it was, and the guild confirms it. They got special ships, fast ones. Anyways, if it be there, the one who reported it gets paid, and the guild then sells that information to crews like ours, for a price."

"This system seems... not great," Sylus noted, "You just said the Green is always shifting, what if by the time they confirm it, get back here, and sell the information, the temple is gone?"

"That's the rub of it. The Guild has ways to determine how long something might be there, if they think it will move, and how long it will be visible. Don't ask me how they get it, cause I don't know," Bracken said, holding up a hand to hold off Sylus's questions. "But you're right, sometimes we buy a Rumor, get there, and it be gone."

"Let me guess, you don't get a refund?" Sylus said.

Bracken smirked, "Of course not."

"Okay, so why can't I come in?" Sylus asked.

"Because the guild is full of suspicious types, and they don't like anyone else to be in the negotiations. Each Rumor is a closely guarded secret, you understand? They don't hand out the same Rumor to multiple crews, and they're rightly suspicious of folks trying to steal them, seeing as how valuable Thaumatech can be. So you wait here. Don't talk to anyone. I won't be long."

Bracken turned then and left him there, and of course, as soon as he was gone, Sylus thought of a hundred more questions he wanted to ask. What exactly was the Captain negotiating? The price? The validity of the Rumor? Something else?

There was nothing for it but to lean on a nearby table and wait for the Captain to return. Or at least, he would have leaned on a table, but a bartender came out and shooed him off for loitering. Instead, he stood awkwardly across the street, watching the sun slowly sink beneath the horizon, a line of green just barely visible underneath the gigantic foliage of the great tree.

Though his legs were sore and his stomach rumbled, Sylus realized with regret that he'd barely seen any of the great tree-port. There were dozens of branches above him with buildings visible, not to mention the terrifying bridges that stretched between them. What was the view like up there on the highest branches? Who lived there? How did this place get any food? Did the great trees perhaps grow great fruits?

There was so much he did not know about the world, and his appetite to learn everything he could was only growing, as was his impatience to set sail and see what else the Verdant Sea had to offer him.

The Captain came out after a half-hour or so, some sheets and a parcel tucked under his arm, and two wraps clenched in his hands.

"Thanks," said Sylus eagerly, taking the food. It was a dark meat with vegetables and sauce, wrapped up in a tortilla. Grease dripped from the bottom, and it smelled amazing.

"Thank yourself, it's coming out of your first share," Bracken said.

"Of course. So all good? How many Rumors did you get?"

"Three," the Captain replied, "One only a few days from here, the others a bit farther out, ready to head back?"

"More than ready."

They ate as they walked back to the *Bladedancer*, talking little as they ate, until at last they were back at the gangplank to the ship, where Holven was standing on the deck, waiting for them.

"Just a minute, kid," Bracken said, then thrust the package under his arm into Sylus's hands.

"What's this?" Sylus asked.

"Clothes. Can't have you dressed like some mountain lout on my ship, I got a reputation to uphold," Bracken said.

Sylus couldn't blame him, but was touched nonetheless.

"Thank you," he said.

"It's standard for all new crew members, so don't be thinking you're getting any special treatment, you hear?"

"Of course not, Captain."

"Good. Well then, get some rest. We leave at first light. Oh, after we report for inspection, of course."

With that, the Captain went up the gangplank towards Holven, who at once began telling the Captain how the ship was being stocked, what repairs were completed, and what sounded like a million other things.

For his part, Sylus followed after, no one paying him any mind, and made his way down to the Medical Room to undress himself for Valera. One that was done, and having been given nothing else to do, he made his way to his bunk. The rest of the hallway was empty, likely because most of the crew was still at work.

Sylus was glad for the solitude. He lay in his bed and stared out the small porthole into the night beyond, imagining what life had in store for him now. He'd done it after all. He'd fled the clutches of Hearthhallow, made his way onto a ship, and escaped the sad fate of his mother, who died after an empty life with nothing to her name.

Guilt shot through him at his harsh thoughts, and he hastily clawed them back. His mother did the best she could with what she had. It wasn't her fault that she was terrified of the Verdant Sea. It'd taken her husband, and most of her family, and she'd never forgiven it. He realized with a start that it was Bracken's family as well. He spent some time marveling once more at the different life paths the same events could create.

Sylus could see a single star out over the darkness, and for a moment, he decided it was his mother, looking down on him. Disapprovingly, no doubt. Still, he felt his heart ache, so he promised her he would be careful and drifted off to sleep.

11

A New Life on the Blades

Sylus awoke to the sharp ring of a bell in the hallway outside his room and sat straight up, peering out of the porthole. It was still dark outside, and he relaxed. That meant he didn't oversleep. Blinking what remained of the night out of his eyes, he got dressed in the new clothes the Captain gave him. They were nothing fancy, just a few simple sets of sturdy brown pants and a few pairs of clean linen shirts; there were even a few pairs of socks and undershorts.

He knew he needed to shower, but there would be time enough for that after a day of work. Instead, he went to the shared washroom and joined a short queue for the toilets, nodding to his new shipmates, who nodded politely back but otherwise ignored him. Sylus did not mind. When it was his turn, he freshened himself up and found his way up to the deck. Countless men and women were hurrying to their posts, and lines were already being loosened by the earliest risers in preparation to set sail.

Holven and the Captain stood on the deck above him, watching the sailors make ready to leave and shouting the occasional order.

Sylus realized he did not know where to go and had never been given assigned duties or a schedule. Not wanting to waste time or appear lazy, he marched up the stairs to Holven.

"Holven, sir," he began politely, but Holven only spared him a glance.

"Ah, Sylus. Just a minute, I am waiting for… Ah, here they are, Captain," he said, gesturing to the gangplank.

Sylus looked over the railing to see Liana walking onto the ship, carrying a small case, with Asphen following behind her, a cloth sack thrown casually over his shoulder.

"About time," grumbled the Captain, though there was not a trace of the sun in the sky yet.

He waved the two over, and they climbed the stairs to meet him. Not knowing what else to do, Sylus stood to the side and stayed quiet. Grateful, at least, that he was in clean clothes this time.

"Good morning, Captain, good morning, Holven," Liana said brightly, before catching sight of Sylus, "Good morning, Sylus, first day?"

Sylus felt his throat begin to close as she turned that smile on him, but managed to mumble, "Good morning."

"Bracken," Asphen said with a nod toward the Captain.

He leaned casually against the railing, still not wearing a shirt, and Sylus could see that his muscles were not limited to his chest, but ran down his stomach in hard lines before disappearing into his pants.

Asphen was facing the Captain, but his eyes flicked toward Liana with open interest.

For no logical reason whatsoever, Sylus felt his chest get hot as he watched Asphen roam Liana's form appreciatively with his eyes. Liana, for her part, either did not notice or did not care, for she paid him no attention. The Captain was right, the man was a dog.

"Good morning will be seen when we hit the Green," the Captain said gruffly, "Get yourself down to Valera, she'll do your inspection. Holven will show you the way if you've forgotten, then show you to your rooms."

"Oh, how I have missed Valera," Asphen said with a sly smile, before sauntering off without waiting for Holven.

"I'm looking forward to sailing with you all," Liana said politely, "May Verdalis guide this ship safely back to port."

"If you'll follow me," Holven said, "Captain, can you see to young Sylus for me?"

"Sure," Bracken grunted, who'd already turned his attention back to his checklist.

Liana gave him a little wave as she passed, and Sylus did not remember to move his hand to return the wave until she'd already turned back around.

"Schedule is posted in the mess hall, memorize it," the Captain said, without looking up.

Sylus twisted uncomfortably, and when he didn't move, the Captain looked up at him.

"Well? Get moving."

"The Priest, Liana I mean, and Asphen, have to do the inspection too? Why?"

"Why? Why?" Bracken repeated, distracted.

He tore his eyes away from his list to glare at Sylus, "Because they're Thaumatechne, that's why. You want them to turn to Reclaimed while on this ship? We have to keep an eye on their progress. Track its spread. Now quit wasting my time, and get to work, or I be leaving you here. You're on sails. Go!"

Without another word, he stomped off, leaving Sylus to find whoever was leading the sail teams this morning on his own.

As the first tinges of color streaked across the sky, Sylus was at his assigned position on the sails for their departure. With no more tests to worry about, he felt a bit more relaxed. Now that he was officially part of the crew, the others began to open up a bit towards him. Sylus had trouble keeping all of their names in his head, but he suspected it would all come in time.

By the time the sun peaked over the emerald green horizon, casting the Verdant Sea into an array of color and life, the *Bladedancer* was soaring over the blades at a decent clip, with Boughhaven slowly getting smaller behind them. Sylus watched it retreat in silent awe, still amazed that a tree could grow to be large enough to hold a city.

He was dismissed for breakfast then, and made his way to the mess hall, where they were serving simple eggs and toast, and got his first look at the schedule. It was posted on a large cork board and detailed nearly everyone's duties in a neat and orderly fashion. Sylus suspected the steady hand of Holven in the masterpiece of organization.

He noted without surprise that he was scheduled to work sails for the majority of the week, with night shifts on cleaning and ship maintenance. Most days were twelve hours or more. He did not mind. It was simply another test to see if he was a slacker and to test his commitment to the crew.

Maintenance was dirty work, and cleaning was dull. He stood staring at the schedule for a time, munching on his toast, preferring not to sit to avoid having to choose a seat. Not that he was shy or intimidated. He didn't know people very well yet and didn't enjoy awkward silences or small talk.

Liana and Asphen were not on the schedule, which also did not surprise him. He could not imagine Liana hauling sails or scampering over the air tanks. Asphen, he supposed, would make a fine enough sailor with all that muscle.

"Oh, they're putting you through it, aren't they?" came Liana's voice from beside him.

Sylus jumped and turned to find her standing beside him, observing the schedule and nibbling on a piece of toast as he was. She wasn't wearing white robes today, perhaps she only dressed like that while on duty as a priest, but instead was wearing a simple grey dress that left her shoulders exposed, and flared at one side to the knee. It was held in place with a sturdy leather belt and finished with simple black leggings leading into high-topped leather boots. It was a practical outfit for sailing, somewhere between casual and functional. Sylus could see that her light freckles continued down her pale shoulders, then realized that a remarkable amount of time was passing without him saying anything.

Liana was staring at him politely, her head tilted to one side in amusement.

He cleared his throat.

"It's uh, nothing I can't handle," he said, regretting it immediately. He sounded like he was bragging.

"Oh? And where does one learn to sail bladeships in the mountains of

Altaris?" she asked.

"How did you know-?"

"I asked," she said, "Your eggs are about to fall on the floor by the way."

He hastily straightened his plate, feeling himself turn red.

"Thanks," he said, and she giggled.

"Did they not have girls in your village?" she asked, and Sylus almost choked on his toast.

"What? Of course we did!" he sputtered.

"So they just didn't have Thaumatechne girls," she said, smiling.

"No, it's not... It's not that. I'm just distracted. You caught me off guard. I'm not... the Captain was joking. I'm not some mountain boy, or whatever he called me. I've met Thaumatechne before."

"Relax, Sylus," she said with a laugh, "I know you're not, I'm just teasing you. But you are a little obvious about staring."

"Sorry," he said sheepishly.

"It's fine," she said, waving away his apology politely, "I am used to it."

She tapped her metal arm as she said so, a faint pinging sound coming through the sleeve. Sylus realized that he was not being chastised for ogling her. She assumed he was staring because she was a Thaumatechne. He was not sure which was more rude.

"I don't want you to be awkward around me is all," she said, when he did not say anything, "I'd like us to be friends and colleagues, because I do truly want to hear the story of how you learned to sail the Verdant Sea up in the mountains, in exchange, I'd be happy to tell you anything you'd like to know about Thaumatechne. I can tell you have questions."

What was he supposed to say? That he wasn't interested in learning about Thaumatechne, which wasn't true, or that he was checking her out, which made him no better than Asphen?

"I'd like that," he said truthfully.

"Friends then," she said, reaching across to shake his free hand with her still-human one.

"Friends," he agreed sheepishly.

"I want to know about this Thaumatechne you met, too," she added.

"He was a Technepriest."

"Really? Do you know-"

But Sylus did not hear the question, because he caught sight of his shift captain leaving the mess hall out of the corner of his eye, waving for him to hurry up.

"I have to get back to work," he said, "Sorry."

"Of course. I'll see you around, Sylus."

With that, she turned on her heel, the skirt of the dress flaring out behind her, and he watched her go with some interest before he suddenly remembered he still had eggs to eat, and shoveled them into his mouth as he hurried to the door, dumping his plate with the piles of other dishes as he left.

He did not see Liana again at lunch, though he lingered in the mess hall, hoping she might appear again as he ate something called a Greensnake steak. There was no way to eat it standing, so he sat with people from his shift for the first time. They told him the meal was a scaled slice of some great serpent. It took up the whole plate and was pretty good, though you needed to cut around the scaly skin.

There was not much to see in the Green during the day. As Boughhaven faded away completely, they reached an expanse of the Verdant Sea where nothing could be seen in any direction except the shifting colors and patterns of the grasses they passed over.

Sometime after lunch, perhaps around two in the afternoon, Asphen wandered onto the deck, blinking and shielding his eyes against the sun. He passed by Sylus, who judged that having just woken up was the most likely case, since you could smell booze on the man from about five feet away.

Asphen got quite a few disapproving glares. The Captain's opinion was clearly shared by many of the crew, but Asphen ignored them all and took up a position in the middle of the upper deck, out of the way, but in plain sight to all. Then he began to exercise. Sylus had a pretty good view from his position. He watched as the man went through some stretches, then drew out two swords he kept in sheaths at his hip, and began to practice.

Sylus had never seen anyone use a sword before, and he found it fascinating. Asphen moved from one movement to another with a fluid grace that resembled dancing more than fighting. Each swing of the sword flowed into the next as smoothly as water. The man's muscled body quickly began to shine with sweat as he went through his routine, and Sylus could not help but notice that he was not the only person watching. Some of the crew, mostly women, were watching with appreciative looks on their faces.

Sylus spotted Cally, though she had no real reason to come down to the deck, leaning on a railing and watching Asphen practice with a moony look on her face. She caught Sylus's eye and winked at him, and he quickly turned his attention back to his work, though he did allow himself the small satisfaction that Liana was not among the man's admirers.

Around mid-afternoon, long after Asphen and his crowd of admirers dispersed back to their own business, Sylus's shift at the sails was over. He was free until after dinner when his late shift began. Not wanting to let himself wait around for Liana, he decided to explore the ship some more and familiarize himself with all the different rooms. After all, he'd barely been on the boat two days.

He found a particularly well-furnished leisure space, adorned with plush velvet couches and a few game tables where people played games he did not recognize with cards and a variety of metal pieces. Adjoining this was a small library with three bookcases full of texts which he perused with interest, selecting one on airships for later reading. He dropped the book off in his room and proceeded to wander, discovering a variety of storage rooms, and of all things, a small empty chapel. Eventually, he found himself near a door marked "Engine Room". There was no sign saying he could not go in, so he pushed open the door and gasped as the room opened up before him.

The room was massive, perhaps taking up the entire rear of the ship. A great machine dominated the center of the room, where Virel and several others were huddled together, covered in grease and oil stains.

Their heads whirled around at the sound of the heavy door slamming shut behind Sylus, who winced as all eyes turned to him. Virel, removing a set of incredibly dirty goggles, blinked at him, then left the group to stand in front of him.

"Syler, was it?" Virel said.

"Sylus," Sylus corrected him.

"Sylus, that's right, that's right. Well, what's the problem? We're swamped, you know!"

"There's no problem," Sylus said, his eyes wandering over the machine.

"What? No problem? Then why are you here?"

"I was just exploring the ship," Sylus said.

"My boy, this is no place for you, it's for engineers only, and besides which-"

"This is the emergency thruster," Sylus said, mesmerized, "Thaumatech. But, you've modified it, haven't you? What's the range?"

"Oho? Do you know much about engines?" Virel said, his attention focusing as quickly as his annoyance evaporated.

"Not too much, the ship I trained on had an engine, but it didn't work. My mentor explained how they work, though, well, as much as you can explain Thaumatech. I'm no engineer, but I have a memory for how things work."

"Is that so? Well, you have a good eye. Yes, this is indeed the Thaumatech engine. As for your questions, yes, I have modified it. That's not easy to do, modify Thaumatech, you know. The common thought is that each piece of Thaumatech was created for one purpose and one purpose only. For the most part, they're correct. But! Only recently, a few years in fact, have we started to discover how to modify Thaumatech. We can't change the function, oh no. But we can alter it. Enhance it."

Virel grabbed him by the arm, pulling him alongside the engine, his voice picking up speed as he began explaining the modifications with pride.

"You know then, that engines like these are two pieces of Thaumatech, yes? One generates fuel, you see these tanks here?"

Glass tanks filled with an odd black liquid perforated the machine at odd angles. They were cylindrical and filled to the brim. The thick black liquid inside sloshed with the motion of the ship. The bizarre thing was that no two of the cylinders were the same size.

"The fuel never overflows. The generator always makes the exact right amount, you see? So we theorized, correctly, that bigger containers would make more fuel. We keep any that we find, and it's not easy to find these, of course. Or buy them, for that matter. They're very valuable. Of course, we have to shut down the engines to replace even a single container. The fuel is highly volatile. Reacts with air, you see. Safer to burn it away and make more than to store it anywhere."

"And it's true that Thaumatech just makes the fuel from nothing?"

"Well, not nothing of course. Nothing comes from nothing. But we don't know how. It uses energy from the Source to convert materials in the air into fuel, I suspect. I suppose that's why they call them Wonders. Anyways, with more fuel, more range, as you so rightly noticed. We could get two days' travel from this, at a full burn."

"But with more fuel, wouldn't the engine overheat, since it was designed for less?" Sylus said.

"Perhaps at a full burn, but you'd never do a full burn."

Virel led him to the back of the room, where the wall of the ship was built around the output.

"Here are the thrusters, of course," Virel said, stooping suddenly to examine something and muttering to himself.

To Sylus, they just seemed a mess of metal pipes and chambers, all leading outside to the true thrusters, which he'd seen on the outside of the ship.

Virel popped up beside him suddenly, "Five chambers, five thrusters, for added stability at speed. We've modified this, too; we drilled holes to inject air into the engines, here, here, and here. You see? More air, a hotter burn."

"Why would you want that?" Sylus said, amused.

"Why? Why?" Virel said, seemingly confused. "To go faster, of course, not that we would, of course. I daresay a full burst from this engine might well shake the ship apart, if it did not simply explode."

"Then why modify it to go faster?" Sylus said, confused.

"Well, because I could. It's the spirit of engineering, after all."

Sylus was not so sure. He did not think he would want to fool around with Thaumatech and Wonders himself, but he could appreciate the man's enthusiasm.

Something of his feelings must have shown on his face, though, for Virel took him by the arm and led him back toward the door.

"Don't tell me, lad, that you're one of those people who think Thaumatech is magic?"

"I know it's not magic," Sylus said.

But Virel was no longer listening.

"Lots to do now, Sylus, lots to do. Thanks for stopping by!"

Without much choice in the matter, Sylus let himself be herded out of the engine room and found ways to occupy himself for the rest of the day.

12

Night Shift

Sylus did not see either Asphen or Liana again until long after dinner. He learned from his crew-mates during dinner that they'd been given private suites, two of four that existed on the ship for the express purpose of housing Thaumatechne away from the rest of the crew. Rightfully so, as many seemed to think. Sylus did not understand the fear and apprehension that people harbored for them.

It was one thing to fear a Thaumatechne living on the street, and quite another in Sylus's mind to fear those in the employ of the Church. As far as he could tell, it wouldn't benefit the Church to have its agents turning into Reclaimed while they were out working. Anyone infected who was determined to be close to the end was watched, even if they lived on the street. Sylus had seen that himself. The Church surely would not send out anyone close to being Reclaimed, or perhaps they followed a strict code of some kind.

Sylus was dying to know. Thaumatechne fascinated him, and he spent a lot of time after dinner wondering if Liana would tell him more about the condition if he asked. She wanted to be friends. Surely friends asked about their friends' fatal conditions, didn't they? He shook his head ruefully at his prepositions as he readied himself for the night shift, pulling on a pair of overalls.

On a ship, the work did not end when the sun went down, and rarely did a ship even stop moving through the Green, unless there was a good reason not to. Because of that, the list of nighttime duties was extensive and hated by everyone in the crew due to the long hours of solitary, tedious work.

There were two primary night shifts on a bladeship. One shift handled the sails and tanks as part of the midnight crew, who were a skeleton crew tasked with keeping the ship running throughout the night. It was a long, boring duty with little actual work to do and only the endless night to entertain you. This was preferred over the other shift, which was maintenance, to which Sylus and a few others were assigned.

The exhaustive list of his duties, as explained to him by the shift leader and reinforced by a checklist handed to him, included washing the decks, maintaining the lanterns, cleaning the lavatories, checking the gear, performing inventory on the ship's supplies, and about a thousand other little tasks divided up among a few unlucky individuals. This shift was hated not only because it was boring, but also because it was a lot of work.

Sylus did not mind, however. He expected to be placed on the worst shifts when he joined the crew. It was a sort of initiation, or perhaps a test, of all new crew members, to see if they would stick through the mundane and sordid tasks required of a life on the blades, or if they would complain and seek their fortunes in a new line of work. There was no room on a bladeship for lazy sailors.

Which is why Sylus took to his checklist with a smile on his face and a whistle on his lips. It was interesting for the first few hours to wander the empty ship, as most of the crew had taken to their beds for the night. The eerie silence inside the vessel was broken only by the creaking of the hull and Sylus's mopping and cleaning sounds. His first list of chores was the cleaning of a few hallways in a part of the ship he'd never been to before, but that he recognized as containing the guest quarters and the captain's quarters as well.

Aware that this was also a test of his work ethic, Sylus made sure the floors were shining. He was concentrating so hard that it took him some time to realize he could hear voices. He paused, mop in hand, as the sound of a conversation reached him from around the corner: a woman and a man, talking in low tones.

"No, thank you," a woman was saying in a soft, polite voice. He immediately recognized Liana. "I appreciate the compliment, but no."

"Are you sure? Not many options for people like us. Don't you want to let go once in a while?" The man said in a familiar, rough, low voice.

Sylus carefully set down his mop and crept closer to the corner, pressing his body against the wall to peer around the corner.

As he suspected, Asphen leaned with one arm against the wall next to the open door to what must be Liana's room, as she was standing in the door frame as they spoke. Asphen swayed in a way that seemed to have little in common with the motion of the ship, and he was blinking as if having trouble concentrating on Liana, who looked relatively steady.

"Verdalis did not put me on this ship to socialize," Liana said, folding her arms beneath her chest.

"Verdalis," Asphen said, waving the name away with his other hand, which was clutching a bottle, "Would want us to have some fun, don't you think?"

"I don't begin to suppose what Verdalis wants; I merely watch for her signs and interpret them as best I can."

"And right now..." Asphen said slowly.

"I'm interpreting the signs as a no," Liana said, with a tone of finality.

Asphen blinked, and a look passed across his face. It wasn't anger, and it certainly wasn't hurt. It was merely considering.

Sylus went tense. What didn't he understand? No meant no.

There was an awkward moment as Asphen and Liana stared at each other, and Sylus readied himself to intervene, though he was not sure what he would be able to do against the larger, much more muscular man.

"Well," Asphen said, pushing away from the wall, "Who am I to argue with a God?" He shrugged then, and murmured, "G'night."

"Goodnight, Asphen, try not to have too much fun," Liana said, closing the door firmly.

Asphen did not look back at the door, and Sylus felt himself relax once he heard the lock engage with a firm click. Asphen was already stumbling down the hallway, right toward Sylus, who realized this too late as the man approached the corridor.

He hastily dove for his mop and began swabbing at the floor in an attempt to look as if he'd just arrived and was not eavesdropping. Asphen did not seem to mind getting rejected much, and Sylus barely knew the man, but some men did not like others to see their business, especially their failings.

Asphen came around the corner and spotted him, and stumbled for a moment. Sylus realized he should not have worried. Asphen was so drunk that it was a miracle he could stand, let alone walk. Asphen stared at him for a moment, blinking again as if to focus.

Not knowing what else to do, Sylus said, "Good evening, Asphen. Everything okay?"

Asphen blinked at him, then took another drink from his bottle and took a step closer.

"Mountain boy," he said, "How old are you?"

"It's Sylus," Sylus said slowly, "And I'm twenty-three."

"You know, you're not bad looking, for a mountain boy," Asphen said, wrapping an arm around Sylus's shoulders.

"Uh, what?" Sylus said, trying to shrug the man off, to no avail.

Asphen swayed dangerously, and it took a lot of effort to remain standing with the man's muscular arm around his shoulders.

"What do you say to skipping off work for an hour or two? My room is right.... Over there," he said, nodding in another direction.

He was staring into Sylus's eyes in an unfocused, yet intense sort of way.

"Oh. Oh!" Sylus said, and felt his face getting hot, "I don't, I mean, I never..."

"Doesn't matter to me," Asphen said, "I could show you."

"I um, I'm uh, flattered. But I'll have to decline. I'm new, and I uh, I can't skip work. It's my first day."

Sylus knew he was babbling, but Asphen did not seem to notice. As soon as Sylus said he wasn't interested, Asphen withdrew his arm and shrugged again.

"Your loss," he said, and without another word, he stumbled down the hall and around the corner, perhaps in search of better prospects.

Sylus watched him go, shaking his head in amazement at the man's brazenness. It was only a shame that there was no one he could tell the story to. It was only then that Sylus noticed Asphen had spilled wine in a trail down the hallway, and was tracking dirt on his boots in a path across the floor Sylus had just cleaned.

With a groan, he set to cleaning up the mess and completing the rest of his tasks, careful to be extra quiet near Liana's room, from which soft music could be heard playing through the door.

After a long night, he stood at the railing of a freshly cleaned deck, waiting for the night winds to dry the deck before he walked over it once more. It was nearing the end of his shift, a few hours after midnight. He was watching the light from the ships' lanterns briefly illuminate the blades beneath, a deep green in the dead of night, before they disappeared into the darkness.

It was a clear night, but neither of the two moons was out, and so the roiling grasses of the Verdant sea in the distance were only distinguishable from the sky by their lack of stars. Sylus was staring at the line where the Verdant Sea hit the sky, and the heavens opened up above.

He'd always loved the stars, and living in an isolated mountain village afforded him plenty of chances to see them. It was one of the few things he did that his mother approved of. She'd taught him the constellations, and they would spend hours together pointing them out to each other. He was so lost in his memories that he almost jumped out of his skin when someone came up the railing beside him.

"Beautiful, isn't it?" Liana said. Sylus slipped on the railing and nearly pitched forward off the side before he caught himself.

"Whoa, careful there," Liana said, "I thought you said you weren't scared of me?"

"You keep sneaking up on me!" Sylus said, exasperated and red in the face again, "What are you doing up here?"

"Probably the same thing you are," she said with a smile, tucking her hair behind her ear.

She leaned forward and rested both her arms on the railing, the right forearm clinking against the wood and drawing his eye. He looked away quickly, embarrassed, but Liana did not seem to notice.

"They should be out any minute," she said, staring out into the night.

Sylus, of course, had no idea what she was talking about, and he did not want to reveal his ignorance. After a long moment, though, his curiosity got the better of him.

"What should be?" he said, peering eagerly out into the darkness.

Liana glanced at him, "Wait, you actually don't know?"

"I lived in the mountains, remember?"

"I know that, but I figured you might have seen them last night. They love the giant leaves, but wow. Okay, follow me. You can't see them for the first time here. Hurry!"

Liana hurried from the railing and turned toward the back of the ship.

"This way!" she said.

"I'm supposed to be..." Sylus said, staring over his shoulder at his mop and bucket.

He clamped his mouth shut as her hand grabbed his and started pulling him along. Her hand was warm and clasped around his in a surprisingly firm grip. He was not sure he could free his hand if he tried, so instead he forgot about work and merely followed her, perplexed. She led him up the stairs to the highest deck, then toward the back of the ship.

The decks were abandoned, even by other maintenance crew members, who had moved on to their final tasks for the night.

"Why the back of the ship?" he asked, as she pulled him toward the back railing.

"Less lanterns, see? It's much darker back here," she said, "Plus, they like to follow the ship."

"What likes to follow the ships?" Sylus said, coming up beside her.

"Shush, just watch," Liana said. She released his hand, much to his regret, and stared out into the darkness expectantly, her hair having fallen across her face once more.

She obviously had no intention of telling him what she was talking about, so he merely looked out into the night with her. Then, he saw it. In the shadowy darkness of the blades, something, or rather, many somethings, were crawling up out of the blades.

The creatures were about the size of his chest, whatever they were, and would have been invisible in the grasses if not for the fact that they seemed to be sparkling.

Sylus leaned forward as more and more of the sparkling creatures rose from the grass, shining in the darkness, and began to leap in tall arcs through the air, before landing back in the grass. Some did indeed appear to leap after the ship, jumping multiple times to follow in the ship's wake. More and more rose, until it seemed that the grasses were a reflection of the starry skies above.

Sylus gasped in amazement.

"What are they? There are so many!"

"Glimmerbeetles," Liana said, her eyes sparkling as she smiled at insects who filled the darkness in front of them.

"You mean, the kind we eat?"

"The very same," Liana said, laughing, "This is when people catch them. Hunting ships, I mean. The poor things follow the ships, and they scoop them right up. Their shells are a shiny, shiny black, so reflective that they catch even the light of the stars at night. They hide deep in the blades during the day to avoid predators, and us, I suppose. But on clear nights, they climb to the surface."

"Wow," Sylus said, genuinely amazed, "To do what?"

"I don't know," Liana said softly. "Just to play, it seems to me. One of Verdalis' great mysteries."

Sylus was not religious, and he felt a little awkward whenever Liana mentioned her god, if only because he didn't know what he was supposed to say, and didn't want to offend Liana.

Instead, he said, "It almost seems a shame to eat them."

"Doesn't it?" Liana said. "Except..."

"Except?" Sylus said, looking at her. She turned and looked into his eyes, smiling.

"Except they're really fucking good," she said, giggling.

Sylus burst out laughing; he could not help it.

"They are, they really are!" he said between fits of laughter.

When their mirth subsided, they both leaned on the railing and watched the insects play. Sylus knew he needed to get back to work, but he did not want to leave Liana.

"I can't believe you didn't know about this," she said after a few moments, shaking her head. "What were you doing at the railing, staring out into the darkness? Just taking a break?"

Sylus shifted uncomfortably, debating what to say, before deciding to be honest.

"I was thinking of my mother," he said.

"Ah," Liana said, "Are you two close? It must be hard leaving her behind, but you can always visit."

Sylus only nodded, not wanting to lie to Liana.

"Do you have any family?" Sylus asked. Her smile slipped, and she looked away.

"Not really," Liana said, and Sylus regretted asking.

"I'm sorry."

"It's okay," Liana said, but she pushed away from the railing. "I should get to bed."

"Okay," Sylus said, feeling awkward. "I should get back to work anyway."

They walked together in silence, toward his bucket and the entrance to the interior. Liana's smile returned, but he could tell she was distracted, and he made a mental note not to ask about her family again unless she brought it up. He didn't want their conversation to end like this,

"Thank you for showing me that," he said when they reached the door. "There's so much I haven't seen. And I want to see it all."

"Oh?" she asked, amusement returning to her eyes. "Is that the real reason you joined the crew?"

"That's right. I want to explore the world. See its hidden places, and find its forgotten secrets."

"And sell them to get rich?" Liana asked, raising a knowing eyebrow. "There are lots of ships that see the world, and most of them are less dangerous."

"Is that so bad?" Sylus asked, a little embarrassed, "People need Thaumatech. It makes their lives easier. We struggled in the mountains. If we'd had more money…" he trailed off, realizing he was getting too close to the truth again. "Well, our lives would have been much easier at least. I'm tired of struggling."

"Verdalis sends us hardship to give our lives meaning and form," Liana said. He noticed she was holding her metal forearm with her human hand. "It teaches us to endure."

"Well, then I hope Verdalis is shaping me for something great," Sylus said, feeling awkward and regretting it immediately. He did not mean to boast, nor did he want to mock Liana's beliefs.

Liana did not seem offended, because she smiled lightly.

"Maybe she is. Goodnight, Sylus."

"Goodnight, Liana," he said.

He worked the rest of his shift with a smile on his face, feeling for once like he might not have embarrassed himself too badly.

13

The First Rumor

Working from sunrise to after midnight was exhausting, but Sylus persevered through the next morning, determined not to let Holven's schedule best him. He felt sluggish as he stood in line for breakfast the next day, as the cook's assistants served a peculiar type of red spicy soup that smelled of grasses, with eggs floating in it.

He did not spot Liana in the mess hall, which embarrassed him, as he found himself watching for her everywhere he went. Nor did he spot Asphen, for which he was grateful. He hoped the man would not remember propositioning Sylus. There was someone else interesting in the mess hall, and they'd drawn a crowd of their own.

Cally, the ship's navigator, had taken over an entire table with her books and charts, while her breakfast sat on the seat beside her, looking thoroughly forgotten. She was standing over the charts, frequently leaning over the table to check this or that. Sylus supposed this was at least partially why she was drawing a crowd, as she was wearing a rather loose shirt that displayed a generous sight to anyone who happened to be across from her.

Telling himself that there must be another reason people were gathering around her, Sylus approached the table as well. He stood at an angle that wasn't so obvious, and peered around the men and women who gathered to watch Cally work. He couldn't make heads or tails of what was so interesting besides the obvious. Eventually, his curiosity overpowered him, and he nudged one of the men standing beside him, getting his attention to lean in.

"What's going on?" Sylus asked.

"Cally's tracking down the location of the Rumor, and making a bit of a show of it, as usual," the man said, a grin visible though he did not turn to look at Sylus, "You know, I wouldn't mind if..."

But at that point, the man noticed he was speaking to a stranger and cleared his throat before continuing, "...if I had another bowl of that soup."

He walked off without a word, leaving little doubt that soup was the last thing on his mind. Sylus shook his head ruefully and turned his attention back to Cally. With the man out of the way, he got closer to the maps to try to figure out what was so interesting. Cally was attractive, though. The way her auburn hair bounced as she flitted from map to map, the unique olive tone to her skin, and that peculiar vial of seeds that bounced right above her...

"Getting a good look, Sylus?" Cally said, and Sylus's eyes shot to hers so quickly that there was surely no possible way that she could have noticed where his gaze was straying to a moment before.

"I'm not sure what I'm looking at," Sylus said weakly, and Cally got a dangerously pleased look in her eye.

"Oh, I think you do, in fact, from what I hear, I think you know more than you let on," Cally said.

She had not straightened even an inch, and now she rested an elbow on the table and put her head in her hand, peering up at Sylus. He felt his willpower hanging by a thread, but managed to speak in a weak voice and keep his eyes on hers.

"You do? From who?"

"Well, the Captain, of course."

"The Captain?" Sylus asked, feeling so confused and overwhelmed that he thought he might pass out.

"Well, you learned all about ships somewhere in those mountains, don't tell me you didn't learn something about charts and maps," she said, tapping the pages.

"Maps," Sylus said thickly, then, so grateful for an escape, he began rambling. "Charts. Yes, I know about maps and navigation. Probably not as much as you, of course, but the basics. Yup, maps and charts."

Cally's smile only deepened as he rambled, and Sylus could not help but feel like the woman knew exactly what she was doing. Was every woman on the ship going to make him feel like a fool?

"Well then, sit down," Cally said, pulling out the chair beside her and patting the seat.

"I should probably get to work," he said, glancing around.

The crowd that was watching Cally only moments before seemed to have dissolved, but no one was making haste to the doors.

"Nonsense, breakfast only just started," Cally said, patting the seat again.

Not seeing any real reason to refuse, he sat, determined not to make a fool of himself anymore. He settled his gaze firmly on the charts in front of him and was careful not to flinch when he felt her draw closer, her hair falling across his shoulder as she leaned in.

"Tell me, what do you see?" she asked.

Sylus concentrated.

"You're using your own shorthand," he said, noting the careful writing in stylized code. He quickly analyzed a few passages, comparing them to the map spread out in the center of the table.

"Here's Boughhaven," he said, pointing to a mark on the map, "And here's how far we've traveled." He traced a line across the chart, counting the lines, estimating the distance.

"Not bad," Cally said, "but where are we going?"

He pulled her notebook closer to himself, finding himself excited, as if he was being let in on the secret. But when it came close enough to read, he saw a cipher so hopelessly complex that it lost all meaning.

"I have no idea what this is," he admitted, looking down at what could only be described as the notebook of someone suffering a severe mental breakdown.

"I'd have a heart attack if you could," Cally said, slipping the book out of his hand and snapping it shut. "It took me eleven years to create my cipher, and for good reason. Can't trust anyone when it comes to Rumors. Only I know the details, and this book, of course, but even if you were to steal it, it would be useless to you."

Sylus turned to look at her and found her still peering at him slyly.

"I'm not going to steal it," Sylus said, offended.

"How should I know if you won't?" Cally said with a smile, "A boy from the mountains who knows about sailing? You could easily be a plant from a rival crew, after our Rumors. You have to admit your story is patently unbelievable."

Sylus bristled. He did not like being called a liar.

"It's true. I'm not a thief," Sylus said.

"Perhaps you were sent here to seduce me and steal away my book," Cally said with a mock sigh. She bit the tip of one of her fingers as she looked at him and added, "It wouldn't work, I'm afraid, though it might be fun if you tried, don't you think?"

Sylus felt his face turning crimson.

"Oh, leave the boy alone before he bursts into flames, Cal," said a new voice, rough from shouting.

Sylus had heard it before, if only in passing. He looked up to find the cook, Ruse, standing over them.

"Sylus, is it?" Ruse said, "You have to watch yourself with this one, she's a horrible flirt, but she's harmless enough once you get to know her."

"You never let me have any fun," Cally said, sticking her bottom lip out in an exaggerated pout. Ruse smacked her on the nose with a spoon.

"Ow!" Cally said, grabbing at her nose. Ruse put down the bowl of soup he was holding in front of her, ignoring the look she shot him as she rubbed her nose.

"You let your breakfast get cold again," he said, "You think I'm made of ingredients?"

With a hugely sarcastic sigh, Cally dipped a spoon into the soup and took a bite. Ruse nodded and turned back to Sylus. Behind him, Cally stuck out a tongue at him, but continued eating the soup.

"At least this one eats everything I give him," he said.

"You're an excellent cook, sir," Sylus said, grateful to be rescued from Cally's teasing. "Best food I've ever had, honest."

"I know that," Ruse said, smiling, "No need to butter me up."

Cally finished her soup quickly since it was clear that Ruse had no intention of leaving until she did. Once she was done, he nodded, collected their bowls, and walked off without another word.

"He's the one you should ignore, the old badger," Cally said.

Sylus was still mad about being called a thief and glared at her.

"Oh, come on, I was just having a little fun. I know you're not going to steal anything. You're way too cute and innocent. Here, I'll make it up to you."

She took his hand in hers and slid her fingers in between his, then walked his hand across the chart, letting go when they'd gone a few paces.

"That's where the Rumor is?" Sylus said, calculating. "We could be there today!"

"That's where the Rumor was," Cally corrected.

She opened her book and flipped to a page, the teasing, flirty look falling away from her face as she concentrated. It was like watching a mask of sugar melt under hot water, revealing a fiercely intelligent concentration. Somehow, it made her more attractive.

"We're heading to where it was last spotted, that isn't to say it hasn't moved. This section of the Green experiences violent windstorms, causing the grasses to shift endlessly. Not to mention that the grasses around here are yellow, which changes things."

"The color matters?" Sylus said.

Cally blinked at him, "What? Of course, they matter. Did you think the Verdant Sea was all the same type of grass? No, there are hundreds of varieties, and their density and growth patterns change the way things move through them. Yellow varieties are thicker and stronger. That means the Rumor might not have moved much if it's thoroughly tangled, but it also means it could be pulled under at any moment."

"How can you tell?"

Cally peered at him and smiled again, the flirty mask reappearing on her face so quickly it was as if it never dropped. She snapped her book shut and wagged a finger in his face coyly.

"Now now, Sylus, I can't be just handing out all my secrets on the first date. You have to woo me if you want me to give up a navigator's secrets. I like flowers by the way, but only certain pink ones, it's up to you to figure out which ones."

Sylus could not help but laugh. This woman was definitely a little crazy.

"What's so funny?" Cally said, her smile widening, "Is it the fact that you're almost late for your shift?"

Sylus jumped up, just noticing now that the mess hall was half as full as it was when he sat down.

"Goodbye, Sylus! I look forward to our second date!" Cally called after him as he raced for the door, forgetting entirely to say goodbye as he ran to his station to begin the day's work.

He was back on the sails today, which, in light of what Cally shared with him, was a disappointment. On the sails, he did not have as good a view as he did on tanks, and he was anxious now to see what they were looking for firsthand.

The day passed quickly as he let his mind wander to what the Rumor could be. The Verdant Sea held the majority of the Old World within it, and he knew from Galleon that the things they left behind could be nearly anything. Sometimes they were buildings, freed from their ancient moorings and adrift within the green grasses, bobbing and waving through the sea until they occasionally broke the surface. The grand prize, of course, was a city, untouched. That was rare, however, for unless the town was built somewhere relatively high to begin with, most had already been swallowed whole by the Green.

The most common find, according to Old Galleon, was the vehicles of the Old World. Sometimes small things with wheels, occasionally massive water ships, and rarely, colossal airships. The airships of the ancients were miles apart from bladeships like the *Bladedancer.* Galleon said they were sleek metal monstrosities, all hard angles and triangles, with no need for air tanks at all, but no matter what, everything that the Verdant Sea tossed up for scavenging was filled with Thaumatech.

Before Sylus knew it, with only a break for lunch, it was afternoon, and he was broken out of his daydreaming by the sharp tones of a bell ringing out from the Captain's Perch. Sylus's eyes snapped to the horizon, scanning the empty line where blue met green for any break in the pattern, for the bell could only mean one thing. They'd sighted something in the blades. Activity on the ship around him picked up immediately. Sylus could hear people rushing past, while crew leaders barked orders. Sylus knew better than to leave his post on the sails, plus it gave him time to scan the horizon until he eventually saw what caused the alarm.

Far off in the distance, barely visible on the horizon, a lone silver peak rose from the flowing shades of green and caught the sun. To be visible from such a distance, Sylus knew it must be massive, and as he stared, he felt his excitement grow to a desperate hunger.

They had found the Rumor, and he would get his first taste of hunting for Thaumatech.

14

Silver Spire

It did not take long to reach their quarry. Sylus helped guide the ship toward the gleaming obelisk from his post on the sails, hungrily watching as it drew ever closer over the next few hours. Sylus guessed that they would arrive before dinner.

Though from a distance it was easy to mistake it as the top of a building, as the *Bladedancer* neared, it became evident that what broke the surface of the Green was far too angular and sleek to be part of any building.

The familiar lines of aerodynamic construction struck Sylus as the details came into focus, revealing the nose of a metallic triangle that expanded down into the blades in sections. Sleek lines of panels formed straight lines, broken here and there by unidentifiable sections of machinery that jutted out from the triangle in various shapes. Sylus could see multiple large rectangular sections with narrow tubes built into them, and many rounded turrets that ended in long cannons.

When the *Bladedancer* finally pulled up alongside the thing, close enough that you could reach out and touch it, the height of it dwarfed even the crow's nest, and Sylus could not help but wonder how much still lay beneath the surface. It was an airship of impressive size, though not quite as large as those Galleon described. Even if they had two more ships with them, Sylus doubted they could carry off a fraction of the Thaumatech that must lay inside.

As he finished tucking the sails, he joined the growing crowd that gathered on the deck, where a palpable excitement was growing louder as the crew gathered to stare at the spectacle. Sylus found an unoccupied barrel and took a seat, so that his head was above the crowd and he had a better view.

"Never seen anything like it," someone said.

"...look at the size of it!" said another.

Chatter surrounded Sylus, and the mood was ecstatic as the Captain strode onto the deck with Holven and Cally to address the crew. Sylus scanned the deck and found Liana, dressed in her white robes, watching the Captain with a serious look on her face. Not far from her, Asphen lounged against a wall, waiting. His arms crossed under his chest as he stared up at their prize with a frown.

Sylus spotted nearly everyone he knew from the crew in the crowd. Virel the Engineer was lugging a complicated-looking piece of Thaumatech across the deck, while Ruse laughed and clapped an annoyed-looking Valera on the back.

Sylus breathed in deeply and just let himself enjoy this moment. Setting sail had been the start of his new life, but finding lost ruins, delving into the Green in search of Thaumatech and riches, this was what he had lived for.

Cally was at the railing, doing several odd things, her face locked into serious concentration. She appeared to be throwing something connected to a fishing line into the grass repeatedly and pulling it back up. When she was done with that, she pulled a tiny glass vial from one of her pockets and opened it, pouring out the contents, which appeared to be fluffy seeds that floated away on the wind immediately. She scribbled something into her notebook, then she reached out and attached something to the metal ship that Sylus could not see. Whatever it was, she leaned in and watched it intently, resting one hand on the ruined airship and one on the *Bladedancer*.

Eventually, she gathered her various implements and returned to the Captain, then they both spoke quietly with Holven. Sylus wanted to wait, sure that everything would be explained in time. But once again, his curiosity overpowered him, and he jumped down from his barrel and sought out Ruse, who nodded to him as he came to stand beside the man.

"What are we waiting for?" Sylus asked.

"A hundred things, lad. Did you think we just walked right into the thing? Cally's checking if it's safe."

"What do you mean?"

"I mean, the whole thing could drop beneath the Green at any moment, and anyone on board the damn thing with it."

Valera peered around Ruse to see who he was talking to and nodded to Sylus.

"She's checking if it's stable," she added more politely, "She makes the calculations, but the Captain gets the final call."

"And if it's too dangerous, we just what? Leave it here?" Sylus said, scandalized.

"Would you rather die inside?" Valera asked.

"Well, no," Sylus admitted, "but to just abandon it..."

"You people are all crazy," Ruse said, shaking his head. "Verdalis herself could offer to show me her green tits and I wouldn't take a single step on-"

"Watch your language, Ruse," Valera chided with the tone of someone who'd said the same thing about a thousand times.

"You don't want to go on the ship?" Sylus asked.

"Blades, no. The quickest way to die is to get off this ship and into one of those things. I'm a cook, and I mean to keep it that way."

Sylus then realized he'd been waiting to ask one question, and one question only.

"Who does get to go on?" he asked, a bit more urgently than he meant to.

"The Captain decides who goes and who stays," Valera said, then eyed him carefully. "It's your first time on the ship, Sylus. I wouldn't get your hopes up. You don't know how dangerous it can be. If it were up to me, you certainly wouldn't be going."

Sylus felt his heart drop. Was the Captain seriously going to leave him behind?

"Excuse me," he said, and began to push his way to the front of the crowd.

He felt the sudden urge to get in front of the Captain and be seen. As he made his way to the front of the crowd, the Captain finished his conference with Cally and Holven and turned to face the rest of the crew. The chattering died down just as Sylus pushed his way to the front.

"Alright," Bracken said, in a voice loud enough to carry across the deck. "She's sinking, but she be sinking slow. Cally says it could be a few hours or all night. Let's get to work. Where be Liana and Asphen?"

Liana and Asphen made their way to the front and came to stand beside the Captain. They put their heads together for a few moments as Sylus watched on with interest, until they seemed to agree, for Asphen nodded and stepped up to the ship.

He stared at it for a moment before doing something odd. He removed his boot and placed his leg up on the banister, so that his metal foot was touching the airship. Sylus leaned in, trying to understand what the man was up to.

Asphen said something, but Sylus was too far to hear what it was. In a moment, light began to build up in Asphen's leg. He was casting a Wonder!

Vents opened along the machinery of his leg, revealing lines of strange lights and venting channels. Once again, there was that slight sense of something being pulled in. A tug in the air that seemed to pull toward Asphen, nearly imperceptible. Sylus could hear a few people take an involuntary step backward as the sensation passed through the crowd.

The light built to a crescendo and erupted from his foot. A wave of light seemed to pass through the metal of the ship, traveling almost too fast to see. In seconds, it traveled the length of what was visible and continued beneath the Green, but Asphen did not move. In another moment, the wave of light seemed to return, passing back the way it came, retreating into Asphen.

Sylus goggled as Asphen lowered his leg, which appeared to be venting heat in a cloud of steam, and held it away from his body as he returned to the Captain. By the time he'd stepped back up to the Captain's side and nodded, the channels in his leg had closed once more, leaving it looking as if nothing had happened before he slid it into his boot.

The Captain grimaced, then turned back to the crew.

"There be Reclaimed on board, so I'll only be taking volunteers. Who will join me on the ship?"

Sylus shot his hand into the air and was easily the first to do so.

The Captain eyed him, but said nothing, waiting until more hands rose into the air. Then he began pointing and calling the names of those who would be going. Sylus was not among the chosen. He felt his heart drop out of his chest.

"Alright, then, let's get to work. Virel, cut it open. The rest of you know what to do, so get to it," The Captain finished.

The crowd began to scatter with purpose, men and women moving in every direction. Those who were chosen to accompany the Captain stepped forward and gathered in a group. They began attaching a gangplank to the side of the *Bladedancer* that led to the silver airship.

Sylus could only watch, crestfallen. Unlike the rest of the crew, he did not know what to do. No one had given him a task, and no one said he could not stand there and watch. He was too hollowed out to do anything else. His first ruin, his first chance to prove himself, and he wouldn't be going?

Holven saw him standing there and frowned, but was pulled aside by the Captain before he could move toward Sylus.

Virel lugged the Thaumatech device he'd been hauling up the stairs across the gangplank. Sylus could see now that Virel was wearing a strange protective bodysuit and had strapped a pair of heavy goggles to his face. As he powered on the device, it emitted a thin stream of white-hot flame. As he pressed the tool to the side of the downed ship, a shower of sparks and light too bright to look at directly burst forth, making the day seem dark and dim.

Sylus's throat was dry, and he felt like he couldn't breathe. Holven had disappeared, and the Captain was now staring up at the top of the silver spire in concentration. Sylus would never get a better chance than now. He willed his legs to move and got within three steps of the Captain before Holven seemed to materialize out of thin air.

"Sylus," he said, laying a hand on Sylus's shoulder in an attempt to steer him away. "The Captain has made his decision."

"But I..."

"But nothing. You have no experience dealing with the Reclaimed. You do not understand the danger you seem so willing to volunteer for."

"I understand the risks," Sylus protested.

"Do you? One slip, one fall, one single cut inside that ship, and you're as good as dead. Worse, some might say. The Captain is protecting you."

"I do not need protecting," Sylus said, but let himself be steered away, for he did not see any other choice. "It is my life to gamble with, and I volunteered. We have limited time, and you need all the help you can get. I noticed there weren't many volunteers."

"There is a lack of volunteers because our crew is wiser and more experienced than you, and they know that to enter a ship crawling with the Reclaimed is to risk the only true thing of value in this world, their life.

This is not a discussion. You claim to be a man, so act like one," Holven said.

Sylus flinched, stung by the words, but he found no malice in Holven's face; it was the same expressionless mask he always wore. He stared at Sylus, waiting to see if he would argue further.

Sylus considered it, but decided it was pointless. He let his gaze drop, and Holven nodded.

"Good choice. A good sailor knows how to take orders. You will get your chance, lad," Holven said, giving him a pat on the shoulder. "Now go find something to do. We need more hands on the unloading crew."

Sylus nodded and took one last look back at the ship.

The Captain was watching him with hard eyes and an expressionless face. Behind him, Asphen and Liana watched him too. Asphen looked bored, while Liana gave him a small smile. With a sigh, he went off in search of something to do.

He soon found himself roped into hauling up the equipment that the boarding team would use from the storage rooms of the ship. It took three trips, and each time Sylus was on the deck, the hole that Virel was cutting grew larger, until, when Sylus placed the last box down upon the deck, the hole was complete.

Virel moved out of the way, and to Sylus's surprise, Asphen walked up and kicked the cut panel open.

With a sound of twisting metal, the entrance fell inward and crashed into something inside with a resounding slam. Sylus goggled, unable to believe his eyes. The piece that fell had to be two feet thick of solid metal, and Asphen kicked it aside as if it were a toy. Just how strong was he?

Asphen drew his sword, holding it at the ready towards the new entrance. With a start, Sylus realized that half the crew on the deck had obtained weapons from somewhere, with the majority holding blades or spears, including the Captain, and they all stared at the entrance without blinking.

Sylus held his breath, not sure what he should be doing, but after a few moments, Asphen seemed to relax. He sheathed his sword and grabbed up an oil lantern, lighting it. He pulled on a pair of thick leather gloves and leaned into the dark hole of the ship, peering inside with the lantern.

"It's clear," he called, hopping down from the gangplank. Only then did the rest of the crew relax.

The Captain began barking orders, and Sylus was once again set to work. The crew seemed to be moving three times their regular speed, and he was expected to do the same. The boarding crew gathered and began outfitting themselves in leather armor and protective gear, including thick boots and gloves.

Lead lines were affixed to the ship and lowered into the hole so that the boarding team could find their way out. In only half an hour since the hole was cut, the boarding team was ready to embark.

Asphen was the first to enter, using the rope to lower himself into the ship and dropping out of sight. He was followed by the Captain, Liana, and the rest of the boarding team. Holven watched them depart, and once they'd all entered the ship, he turned back to the rest of the crew.

"Be ready for anything," he said, and ordered several men to watch the entrance for any signs of trouble.

The rest of them were put to work clearing the deck and hauling up empty boxes for the recovered Thaumatech. Sylus worked diligently, but with a heavy heart. How was he supposed to prove he was capable of risking his life against the Reclaimed without actually risking his life against the Reclaimed? He found himself wondering if it was because he did not know how to fight or wield a weapon. He realized that the fact that he had never learned how to do so was a serious miscalculation on his part. How had he expected himself to fend off the Reclaimed? It's not as if he did not know he would be facing them out in the Green.

Why had Galleon never taught him? Well, that was easy at least. Galleon never really expected Sylus to leave the mountains. The man had taught him sailing and about the business because he was old, bored, and wanted to talk about the good old days. He never actually expected Sylus to try to make a life for himself out of it.

Sylus resolved then and there that he would learn the sword. He would ask Asphen, who, according to the Captain, was one of the best, and if he would not teach Sylus, then Sylus would find someone who would. Holven would know, or perhaps one of the crew members. He was not going to rest until he proved himself.

Holven paced the deck restlessly, though the boarding team could not yet have been gone for ten minutes. No one told Sylus to leave or do anything else, so he sat back atop his barrel and stared into the darkened hole.

Which is why he was the first to cry out when a metallic hand grabbed the edge of the hole and pulled itself up onto the gangplank.

15

The Reclaimed

The Reclaimed hauled itself out of the hole as Sylus's yell split the afternoon.

Those who became Reclaimed generally retained a human-like form, long after anything resembling humanity was stripped away. Its face, if it could be called that, turned toward him as it rose to stand in the light of day. With no need for things like mouths, ears, noses, or eyes, these were often converted to make room for whatever it was that the Reclaimed used to navigate the world around them.

What was left was an object that resembled a human head, but was a mess of metal plates, shifting machinery, and blinking sensors. No two Reclaimed were the same, and the longer they were allowed to roam, the further they got from human form, developing extra limbs, odd attachments, or changing into something else entirely. This one must be old, for though it stood on two mechanical legs, it had developed three arms, with the third jutting from its back and reaching over the shoulder at odd angles.

Sylus did not notice much what it looked like; only that it turned its eyeless gaze on him. There was something about being looked at by something that possessed no human features that sent a shiver of fear cascading down his spine, paralyzing him from taking any action at all.

The Reclaimed's joints hummed and whirred as it took a step forward. Its movements were slow and halting, as if it could not remember the fluidity of human movement. It raised one arm toward Sylus, an arm that ended not with a simulacrum of a hand, but with a strange mechanical blade.

That was as far as it got. As it moved to take a second step, Holven thrust forward with a long spear. He did not seem paralyzed with fear at all, not even when the spear glanced off the thing's chest in a spurt of sparks and the sound of metal sliding on metal. Its attention refocused to Holven as the man whirled the spear back around for another attack, careful to stay well out of the machine's reach.

"Keep it from getting on the ship!" Holven called, and Sylus realized that he was the only one who was frozen.

The crew surrounded the Reclaimed as it took a halting step forward and lunged in a jerky movement toward Holven. Its blade-arm sliced through the air menacingly, but was well out of reach of hitting him. More spears made their way to the front and stabbed forward at the machine, but they had little to no effect.

A glancing blow caught the creature in the middle of one of its halting steps and threw it off balance. For one moment, the thing whirled, off balance, and seemed to be about to careen off the side of the ship, before its entire body seemed to lock, freezing its fall in place. Balanced almost comically on one leg, the machine whirred as it set its foot back down and took another advancing step forward, seemingly unconcerned by the fact that it was outnumbered ten to one.

Men and women were shouting, trying to dart in to strike the creature with their weapons without getting in range of its slicing blade, but it paid them nearly no heed. It took one step off the gangplank and landed with a resounding thump on the deck of the *Bladedancer,* as if it were far heavier than a human being.

Its head spun around, stopping for a second on each surrounding human, as if assessing. Then its body began to fill with light. For one brief second, there was that sensation of something being pulled toward the creature, an intake of energy.

Sylus's eyes went wide, and he snapped out of his stupor.

"Get down!" he cried, too late.

Caught up in the combat of the moment, some of the crew closest to the Reclaimed did not realize what the buildup meant, and had no time to get clear before the energy in the creature built to a crescendo with a high-pitched whine.

A wave of blue energy blasted forth from the Reclaimed in all directions, throwing back men, women, and objects alike. The wave hit Sylus with concussive force and sent him rolling backward across the deck, where he slammed into a wall, gasping for the air that was knocked out of his lungs.

Stars popped in front of his eyes as he realized he was one of the lucky ones. Nearby, a man yelled in agony, his leg bent at an unnatural angle. One woman screamed as she hung from the side of the ship from a rope, the blast having sent her over the railing.

Sylus did not think; he moved. He pushed himself up, fighting for air and pushing through bruised muscles, and tottered toward the railing, sparing only a glance toward the machine that had caused all this chaos.

Its lights were dark, its head bowed as it vented heat in all directions, seemingly exhausted after using a Wonder. Men and women picked themselves up across the deck, but Holven was nowhere to be seen.

Sylus made it to the railing, locked his foot around a post, and leaned over the edge to grab at the woman as she tried desperately to clamber back onto the ship.

"Help me!" she cried.

Sylus scrambled to get hold of her arms.

Together, with him pulling and her scrabbling up the side of the ship, they managed to get her back on deck, where she sank with shaking legs, gasping for breath.

"How do we stop it?" Sylus gasped.

The woman could only shake her head as she caught her breath, terror and exhaustion rendering her unable to speak. The Reclaimed was beginning to stir once more, its head spinning and locking onto a nearby man who lay still on the deck. He appeared to be unconscious. The machine took a slow, halting step toward the man.

Sylus cast around for something, anything. A weapon, or something heavy to throw. His eyes landed instead on something that lay forgotten nearby, tossed perhaps by the Reclaimed's Wonder. Virel's cutting machine, the one he'd used to cut into the ship.

Desperately, Sylus dove for the machine. The Reclaimed took another halting step toward the unconscious man, as Sylus tried to figure out how to turn the machine on. There were levers, buttons, and gauges, none of which made any sense to him. He cast around for Virel, but the man was nowhere to be seen.

A hand fell on his shoulder and lightly pushed him aside.

"Good idea, lad," came Holven's voice.

The man's face was bruised, but impossibly, still completely expressionless, as if they were not all in mortal danger. He picked up the cutter and, with a steady hand, turned it on, the white-hot flame bursting to life.

Sylus fell back as Holven rushed the Reclaimed from behind. The Reclaimed's head spun completely around as Holven approached, as if it had eyes on the back of its head, but its body was much slower to react. It turned, slicing with its blade, but Holven deftly side-stepped the attack, bearing the cutting tool down on the area where the thing's head connected to its body.

Within the shower of sparks that erupted where the flame touched, the creature began to jerk violently, until at last, the creature's head fell free from its body.

It thumped to the deck, rolling across and coming to rest against the railing, sparking. Holven backed away as the body still whirled dangerously, though now without guidance. It swung its arms violently in random directions, taking halting, even more jerky steps, sparking dangerously. The crew moved to stay well out of its reach. They took up their spears once more and began stabbing at the thing, trying to find purchase, until one spear managed to slide in between two plates of armor and got caught.

A cheer went up as several men assisted the attacker by grabbing the spear, using their combined strength to steer the Reclaimed toward the edge of the ship. With one final push, they heaved the thing over the edge, where it fell into the green grasses below with barely a sound.

Sylus dashed to the railing, but the thing was already gone, lost beneath the Green. He breathed a sigh of relief and let himself drape across the railing, breathing deeply, trying to steady himself.

Nearby, someone donned a pair of thick leather gloves and picked up the remaining head, tossing it overboard to be reunited with its body at the bottom of the Verdant Sea.

"That was quick thinking," Holven said, appearing beside him.

"I thought Asphen said it was clear?" Sylus said.

"It could have wandered over after they left, or come from another part of the ship. Or, something could have happened to them, but it's unlikely. Asphen is supposed to take care of things like this."

Holven looked away, thoughtful, but all Sylus heard was 'something could have happened to them'.

"Liana," he breathed, and without thinking, he pushed himself up from the railing and dashed toward the opening in the ship.

"Sylus! Stop!" Holven cried, but Sylus was already leaping onto the gangplank.

He grabbed an oil lantern and plunged into the darkness of the silver ship, ignorant of whatever danger lurked beyond.

16

Mysteries of the Old World

Sylus stepped into the darkness, not bothering to grab hold of the rope, which turned out to be a mistake. As soon as he stepped onto the ship, he fell, but not straight down, as one might expect. Foolishly, he'd stepped into the vessel expecting there to be a floor, though the thing was pitched upwards at a steep angle.

There was a strange sensation of vertigo as he unexpectedly pitched forward instead of down. He flailed, and his foot caught the floor. Confused, he stumbled forward haltingly a few steps, then looked back at the entrance.

The hole to the outside of the ship was now on the floor, and Holven was shouting for him to come back from outside. Bewildered, Sylus could not spare a thought for the sudden change in orientation. Holven could be on him in moments. He held his lantern high and found the rope, lying on the floor, trailing off through an open passageway. He could not allow himself to think. If he thought about what he was doing, which was disobeying a direct order under the guise of worry for a girl he'd had three conversations with, he would certainly turn back.

He almost did, because his feet refused for a moment to move any further into the ship. There was a soft artificial light coming from the passageway that the rope led down. Not the light of oil lanterns, but the solid glow of Thaumatech. Curiosity overpowered his better judgment in an instant, and he followed the rope through the door, leaving the hole behind, and traveling, as he knew now, down into the ship, under the Green.

The passageway he entered was not much different than the passageways of the *Bladedancer*. Sylus could not imagine how many empty hallways must fill a ship of this size, but to him it was a rather plain metal hallway, though one filled with many oddities he'd never seen before. The light was a solid strip of softly flashing yellow that ran the length of the hallway, lighting his way every few seconds or so. There were odd channels cut into the walls everywhere, and tubes lined the ceiling.

Every thirty feet or so, a strange flat black surface flickered fitfully with white and black flecks. These he could not help but stare at. He'd read about them: a kind of Thaumatech window that sometimes displayed information. Not even the top experts were able to make them work outside of the ruins, and they were generally considered useless curiosities. Still, he ran his hand along one as he followed the rope.

As he moved down the hallway, he crossed other corridors and was grateful for the foresight of the rope. He quickly lost count of the many doors (which he noticed did not have handles), or hallways that bisected his at an angle, or hallways which seemed to lead nowhere at all. How did the Captain decide which way was worth exploring, and which wasn't? It might take a crew weeks to search a ship this size, or even longer.

His confidence in his decision waned quickly as he walked. He was going to be in deep trouble; there was no doubt about that. The question was to what degree, and how could he mitigate it? The only hope was to convince the Captain, who was sure to be furious, that he'd panicked in the wake of the Reclaimed attack and run into the ship due to worry about the rest of the crew. He hoped that newcomer stupidity might spare him dismissal, but he wasn't sure. Had he thrown away his new life before it even began?

He was worried. Just one of the Reclaimed nearly took out the entire crew, and it was barely able to shamble. Were they all like that? Or had they gotten lucky with a weak one? For that matter, if one just found the entrance to the *Bladedancer* by chance, how many more could be wandering the halls? Alone, Sylus wouldn't stand a chance.

Suddenly aware of every sound the ancient ship made, Sylus's footsteps seemed to echo down every hallway with the steady clank of his boots, and he picked up his pace.

He was not sure how long he had followed the rope, perhaps ten minutes, when he began to hear voices.

"-should have brought the cutter," came Asphen's voice, low and rough.

"There be no time, I'm telling you she won't open. They never do," came the Captain's voice.

"Quiet!" Asphen hissed, "Something's coming. Behind me, all of you."

Sylus took a deep breath. He did not have any good options, and he did not want to end up on the wrong end of Asphen's sword.

"It's Sylus!" he called, "I'm coming out!"

He walked around the corner to find the rest of the crew staring at him with a mix of expressions. Asphen was looking at him with suspicion, but it quickly changed to annoyance when he saw it was indeed Sylus.

Liana's face, surprisingly, showed concern, but it was the Captain's that commanded Sylus's attention, for it was turning red with fury.

"Sylus? What in Therithar's deep green are you doing here, boy!?" he roared.

Asphen hissed, "Keep your voice down."

The Captain took in a deep breath, and Sylus jumped into the gap.

"The ship was attacked," he said breathlessly, "A Reclaimed made its way onto the deck!"

"The ship?" Bracken said, some of the fury slipping from his voice as urgency took over, "What happened?"

"I-I'm not sure," Sylus said, allowing some real shakiness to enter his voice, as the events of the past hour came crashing down on him.

"It cast a Wonder. An energy wave that threw everyone everywhere, almost overboard. Holven barely got it down, and we managed to get it over the edge of the ship."

"Who died?" Bracken said in a low voice.

"Died?" Sylus said, "No one, I think."

"Then what the blades are you doing here?" he said, anger entering his voice once more.

"I-I panicked, Captain. Holven said something might have happened to…" his eyes almost flicked to Liana, but he managed to keep them still, "to the boarding crew. I jumped into the ship to-to-"

"To what? Rescue us single-handed? Are you that big of an idiot? Do you not be thinking we have things in place for that? Do you not be trusting the commands of Holven and me?"

"No!" Sylus said, dread setting in. "That's not it at all, Captain, I only wanted to,"

"I don't give two shits what you wanted. On my ship, we follow orders, and if you can't follow them, you won't be on it. Get back to the ship, I'll deal with you when-"

"Enough," Asphen said, drawing everyone's eyes toward him.

He was staring at Sylus again, though not with annoyance anymore. If anything, his eyes were analyzing Sylus with interest.

"The boy is here now. As stupid as it was to come in here, the kid has guts. Punish him later if you must, but keep your voice down now. If a Reclaimed found its way to the ship, then they know we're here. It's a miracle he made it down here alone; sending him back now would be sending him to die."

"Captain," Liana said, "It is not my place to get involved with the affairs of your ship, but in light of what Sylus has said, might it not be better if we all leave? If the Reclaimed know we're here, then the *Bladedancer* is in danger. Sylus's actions were misguided, but he was right to try to warn us."

Sylus flinched, her polite words doing little to hide how she felt about his coming in here.

The Captain was silent for a long moment, his face red from contained anger.

"The crew can handle themselves," he said finally, "Boy, you stick close to the rest of the crew. Touch nothing, and say nothing. When we get back to the ship, you are going to learn the meaning of discipline. I won't be leaving here with nothing. We press on."

Sylus could do nothing but nod and try to appear as remorseful as possible, which he was. As the boarding party turned to continue down the hall, Sylus fell in with the rest of the crew, who were either giving him dirty looks or ignoring him entirely. He could not begin to fathom the damage he'd done to his reputation with the Captain and the crew, and for what? A girl?

Even as he thought it, he knew it wasn't true. He did not come in here for Liana, or at least, she was not the only reason. He knew, deep down, that the only reason he'd entered the ship was because he wanted to. He wanted to explore, find Thaumatech, and prove himself. Concern for Liana and the crew was merely an excuse he used to justify his actions. He wasn't thinking clearly, or he'd have seen the giant hole in this logic. What was wrong with him?

The crew moved forward down another hallway. The Captain stopped briefly at a plaque on the wall, murmuring to himself.

"We're close. This way," he said.

Sylus peered at the sign as he passed it, but aside from some marks that were arrows, the rest was gibberish to him, written in the language of the Old World. He bit back the two hundred questions this raised, sensing that speaking would be a fatal mistake.

The Captain then led them around two corners and then through an open doorway. Beyond, they walked into a massive room. To Sylus's eyes, he supposed it was a storeroom of some kind. Gigantic metal crates were stacked in racks from the floor to the ceiling, some small, others twice as tall as he was. He goggled at the size of the room, which could have easily fit the entirety of the *Bladedancer* within it with room to spare. The Captain, however, did not seem entirely interested in the crates. He moved immediately to the left, to a closed door. It did not have a handle, and above the doorway, a small red light was blinking.

"Damn it all," the Captain said, walking up to the door.

As he approached, something above the floor flickered to life, a blue light. The blue light traced a line on the floor, which passed over the Captain several times. Sylus started, but the Captain did not seem concerned. He merely walked through the odd blue line on his way to the door. Once the light finished its circuit, a sound chirped from the door, a harsh tone that sounded negative.

"I was hoping it was open," the Captain grumbled.

He slammed his hand on the smooth surface of the doorway. The doorway, in response, emitted the same negative tone. Bracken sighed and turned back to the crew.

"Should have brought the damn cutter..." he muttered, "Well? Get to work! Spread out and start searching those crates. We might not have-"

The entire ship lurched. The crew stumbled, then froze.

"What was that?" Sylus said, unable to help himself, but the Captain did not seem to notice.

"She's starting to shift," he said, looking around the room. Some of the crates had slid off their shelves. He was eyeing the larger ones with a concerned look.

He turned back to the crew.

"We don't have much time. Find what you can, go!"

The crew began to spread out, and Sylus moved eagerly toward a smaller crate, but froze as the Captain jabbed a finger at him.

"Not you, boy! Stand right where you are and don't move."

Sylus nodded and leaned sullenly against the wall as the rest of the crew spread out and began trying to open some of the crates. Asphen, for his part, clearly did not see himself as part of the crew, for the man found a nearby crate to lean against. He rested one hand on his sword, his eyes scanning the darker sections of the storage room slowly. Sylus supposed it made sense. The two Thaumatechne were not part of the crew after all. It was dumb to assume they would help with manual labor. They had their jobs to do.

Sylus could not see much from where he'd been told to stand, so he found himself staring at the door the Captain was hoping would be open. There was a sign next to it, but of course, he couldn't read it.

"You really shouldn't have come in here, Sylus," Liana said, and he turned to find her standing beside him.

He peered around nervously for the Captain. Sylus could not see him anywhere nearby, but he was sure the man was watching, so he kept his voice low.

"I know," Sylus agreed.

For some reason, he did not want to look at her, fearing what her expression might reveal.

"So why did you?"

"I was worried about the crew," he lied.

"Is that all?" Liana asked.

He slowly turned to look at her, ready for her scorn, but to his surprise, her face still held that same polite concern it had before.

"I suppose you're going to tell me Verdalis frowns on greed," he said morosely.

"I'm not that kind of priest," Liana said, crossing her arms under her chest. "You don't strike me as a believer, and I didn't come on this ship to convert people."

"Why did you?" he asked, wanting to change the subject off of him.

"To help people," she said, "to protect them, if I can. That includes finding out why you would risk your life by coming on this ship, despite your attempts to distract me. Is it greed, then? You want to be rich so badly that you'd die for it? I did not think you were that shallow."

"It's not that," he said quickly.

"Then tell me, what is it? What do you believe in?"

"I can't explain it," he said. "Not without sounding dumb."

"Try me, I promise to tell you if it's dumb."

"I just… I want to be somebody."

"That is dumb," Liana said immediately, "You already are somebody."

Sylus gave her a rueful look.

"You know what I mean. Someone people remember, someone who means something. Someone people talk about and write about. Like Asphen."

"Please tell me you do not want to be like Asphen," Liana said, looking over at the man.

Despite the danger that exposed skin presented in a place like this, he still wasn't wearing a shirt.

"Of course not," he said. "But even the Captain says he's one of the best. People know him, they respect him. They look at him differently. See him."

"They see what he wants them to see, I think," Liana said, "But I get your point. You want people to see you."

Sylus did not know what else to say, and Liana seemed to be waiting for him to speak, so they stood in silence for a bit, staring at the door that wouldn't open.

"You don't approve," he said, not putting it as a question.

"I wouldn't say that," she said, "Ambition can be healthy, or unhealthy. There is nothing wrong with striving to distinguish yourself, if that is what you want."

Sylus felt his spirits lift a little.

"But it can be a double-edged sword," she continued. "What if you never become someone?"

"What do you mean?"

"I mean, what if you fail? What if who you are now is all you'll ever be? Will you be happy with that? Will life still be worth living? I guess what I'm asking is, what's wrong with who you are now?"

Sylus could not help but think of his mother, who had lived her whole life and had nothing to show for it but a small tombstone in some mountains that no one would ever see. He clenched his fists, fighting back the existential dread that swept over him.

"Is life worth living if no one remembers you?"

"Life is always worth living," Liana said, and her human hand drifted to her metal forearm.

She saw him looking and tucked both her arms behind her back casually. Sylus felt like the world's biggest asshole. Here he was complaining about wanting more out of life to someone who would never get to live a full one. He felt so uncomfortable that he desperately needed to change the subject.

"What did the Captain want in there?"

"Hmm," she said, and moved to stand in front of the door.

Like with the Captain, the blue light sparked to life once more and roved over her from head to foot, before disappearing and emitting the harsh tone. Liana ignored it and peered at the sign beside the door.

"It says Armory."

"Really?" Sylus said, pushing away from the wall and coming to stand beside Liana.

He was careful to avoid the path she took, so that the blue light wouldn't wash over him.

"Like Thaumatech weapons?"

"That's the grand prize, isn't it?" Liana said.

"I've heard that Thaumatech weapons can cut through the Reclaimed like butter. They're priceless," Sylus said, peering at the sign. It was still gibberish to him. "You can read this?"

"Of course, the Church trains us to read all the Old Languages."

"Why won't it open?"

"It's some kind of lock," Liana said, "Doesn't the light remind you of the Wonder Asphen performed earlier?"

"Yeah, actually," Sylus said.

"That wonder searches for the presence of the Reclaimed. So…." Liana said, leading him to the obvious conclusion.

"So the door is searching for a key," Sylus said.

"A key nobody seems to have. It's probably different for every ruin. You're not going to try it?"

"Uh…"

"Oh come on, it doesn't hurt," Liana said, putting her hands on his shoulders and steering him in front of the door. "It tickles kind of, look."

The blue light blinked into life and flashed over Sylus's face, blinding him for a moment. It moved over his entire body to his feet, and then back up over his face. It was warm and tickled slightly.

The lock finished its search. The light above the door flashed red and emitted its harsh tone. Liana giggled.

"I guess you don't have the key either," she said with a mock sigh, "It's a shame, can you imagine the Captain's face if it opened? All would be forgiven, I'm sure."

"If only it were that easy," Sylus chuckled.

It felt good to laugh; it lifted some of the weight of his bad decisions.

"Do you feel that?" Liana asked.

The floor began to vibrate, a deep hum, as if it were coming from somewhere deep in the ship. There was a loud whirring noise, and suddenly, the glow lights around the storage room began to flicker, then they turned on fully.

Cries from the crew filled the chamber as the storage room was suddenly flooded with bright white light. The metal walls, covered in dead panels and dull lights only moments ago, lit up as the ship suddenly came to life.

Above the door, the light suddenly flickered. It flickered feebly once, a deep red, then turned a bright, vibrant green. A pleasant chime sounded, and the door opened with a smooth click as the shaking and vibrating of the ship came to a stop.

The crew stood in shock. Sylus stared into the armory at racks and racks of weapons. Liana stared, open-mouthed beside him, but she recovered faster.

"Captain!" she called, but that was as far as she got.

The ship gave a sudden, violent lurch, and Liana grabbed onto him as she tumbled forward; at the same time, he was pitched off his feet. Together, they fell through the open doorway.

17

The Armory

They hit the metal floor in a tangled thud, with Liana landing on top of him and knocking the wind out of him. Even still, he could not help but notice the way their bodies pressed together. The ship tilted dangerously once more and then grew still. Liana was first to rise, pushing herself off of him and looking at him with a frantic look in her eye.

"Are you hurt? Are you cut?" she asked.

Sylus pushed himself up to a sitting position and gingerly felt at his exposed arms, then the back of his head. He winced.

"What is it?" Liana said, grabbing his head and turning it to the side so she could see.

"Uhm, ow!" Sylus said, "That's my neck you're wrenching on."

"Don't be a baby," Liana said.

Her hands roved through his hair, feeling the back of his head.

"I think it's just a bump," she said.

"I guess I got lucky," he said as she lowered her hands and rose to her feet.

She offered him a hand. His skin was tingling where she touched him.

"You did. One cut, one serious injury in this place and you'd be…"

She clenched her metal arm with her human hand, something she did not seem to know she was doing so often. A pounding sound spared them from the awkward silence. They turned. The door had shut itself behind them and was shaking slightly under what seemed to be a series of blows. Muffled voices could be vaguely heard from the other side.

Liana ran to the door and banged back.

"We're here! We're okay!" she called.

There was a pause in the banging, then a muffled response.

"I don't think they can hear me," she said, but Sylus was not listening.

He'd momentarily forgotten because Liana was sprawled on top of him, and then because she was running her hands through his hair, but now his eyes had found the contents of the room.

Row upon row of weapons lined the rooms. On one side of the room, strange metal spears lined the walls inside glass cases lit from within. In similar metal cases with glass tops, various other weapons lay displayed. Sylus walked forward as if in a trance, passing a pair of knives, then an axe, all comprised of complex-looking machinery.

Liana was calling him, but he was drawn to the other wall of the room, where even stranger weapons lined the cases of the wall. Some were long and cylindrical, some were short and oddly shaped, but none were bladed. They all shared an opening of some kind, on one end or the other.

"Sylus, we need to get the door open," Liana said, coming up beside him.

"Do you know what these are?" Sylus asked.

She glanced at the weapons for a moment.

"Some kind of projectile weapon from the old world?"

"Yup, they're completely worthless. Not a single one has ever been found that works." Sylus said, "Neat though. Can you believe this room? We're all going to be rich! How do you think we open the cases?"

The ship rumbled and tilted dangerously once more, almost knocking them both off their feet again.

"Sylus, the ship is sinking into the blades. I need you to open the door, come on!" Liana said, grabbing his hand and pulling him away.

He let himself be led, his head on a swivel, trying to see in all of the weapon cases at once.

Liana led him back to the door and pushed him in front of it. The blue light flashed to life and swept over him once more, but this time, the light again flashed red, and the door emitted a harsh tone.

"What?" Liana said.

"Maybe it's broken," Sylus said. He tried stepping away and then back into the light. It swept him again, but did not open. The ship trembled.

"I don't understand," Liana said, her voice growing nervous. "It opened before."

"The others will open it; they can get the cutter," Sylus said, trying to be reassuring.

"There might not be time for that. If the ship goes down, we all die. They'll leave us."

"The Captain wouldn't...." Sylus started to say, and Liana looked at him blankly.

"Yes, he would," she said, "We need to get this door open."

The pounding from the other side of the door started up again; it was louder this time, with a more metallic sound. Someone was beating on the door. Liana bit her lip and stared at the door.

Sylus felt fear begin to set in. He couldn't die down here, not when he was so close to such a prize, and on his first voyage! If he could get that door open, he was sure the Captain would forgive his disobedience. Sylus started wandering around the room, looking for something, anything, that might control the door.

"What are you doing?" Liana said.

"Looking around, keep trying the door!" he called back to her.

Sylus wandered between the cases. Thaumatech usually had a button, a lever, or a switch. He scanned the cases carefully, but saw nothing. Well, not nothing. Despite the danger of the situation, one case kept drawing his eye. It was the only case with only a single item in it. A sword. A sword unlike any he'd seen.

Channels ran down the length of the cutting blade, which appeared to be made of interlocking plates, and just underneath the hand guard was a trigger. He placed his hands on the glass to lean down and get a better look.

There was a clicking noise, and he jumped back quickly. A panel in the floor had slid open, and from the chamber within rose a pedestal. It was a simple metal rectangle with a single opening. Atop the rectangle, something was written, and within the opening was a red handle.

"Liana?" he called, and motioned her over when she turned to look.

She came quickly, and he pointed at the words on the top of the pedestal.

"Can you read this? What does it say?"

"Uhm, it says 'Release'," she said.

"Release? Like maybe a door release? Or for the cases?"

"I don't know," she said, shaking her head, "and you're not trying it."

"But look, this sword. It has a trigger. Maybe it could cut through the door?"

"If you touch that thing, you're as good as dead. You know that. Come back and try the door again," she insisted.

"I thought you could cleanse it? Make it safe to handle?"

"It's not that simple. It's connected to the ship. If I tried to cleanse it, my Wonder would attempt to cleanse the entire ship. The effort would kill me."

"Could you pull it safely?"

She shook her head, "You don't know how dangerous Thaumatech can be. It never reacts the way you expect it to. I know that from experience."

Sylus hesitated, looking at the lever.

"Sylus. Don't. It's not worth it, trust me."

Sylus turned; she was looking at him, eyes wide. Despite himself, despite his effort, his eyes flicked to her metal forearm. She flinched, but then he took a deep breath, nodded, and stepped away.

"What are we going to do then?" he asked.

"I might be able to get the door open with a Wonder," she said, biting her lip.

"You know a Wonder that strong?"

"I… maybe, but you might need to carry me out. Will you do that?"

"What? Of course, but what kind of a Wonder are we talking about here?"

"A big one," she said, turning towards the door.

Sylus caught her arm before she could get too far.

"Wait. What will... what is this going to cost you?" he asked, phrasing the question as delicately as he could. She did not turn to look at him, merely shrugging.

"A lot."

"And you don't even know if it will work?"

"It's the only chance we have," she said.

"No, it's not," Sylus said.

He let her go and put his hand into the obelisk, wrapping it around the lever.

"Sylus! No!" Liana said, but it was too late. He pulled the lever.

There was a sickening, wet sound. The case with the sword in it hissed and then opened, releasing a cloud of strange-smelling, white mist. The lid slid back behind the case and disappeared, while the sword rose on its stand, presenting itself to be taken.

"There, see? I..." Sylus said, turning to grin at Liana. But she wasn't looking at him; she was looking at his hand. Sylus pulled his arm out.

His hand didn't come with it.

The world rocked. The opening in the obelisk was dripping blood, a lot of blood. Inside, something wet and dark was wrapped around the handle. Slowly, in shock, Sylus looked at his hand, or what was left of it. It had been cleanly severed at the wrist. Sylus couldn't breathe. Why wasn't there blood bursting from his arm? Where was all of his blood? There was a loud whistling whine in his ears.

His head swam. Someone was shouting, but he couldn't look away from his hand. Something was forming at the edges of the cut, something metal. His eyes rolled up into his head, and he could feel himself falling backwards. Liana was trying to catch him, shouting something he could no longer hear. He hit the floor hard, and the edges of his vision began to fade.

Then his mother was there. She was leaning over him, her face blurry, barely visible through the encroaching darkness. He could barely tell it was her, but he could feel her presence, warm and comforting, envelop him. He tried to tell her he was sorry, but he couldn't speak.

She smiled at him and whispered, “I’ve been waiting for you.” Then everything went dark.

II

Thaumatechne

18

Infected

Sylus sat bolt upright, gasping for air, only for a pair of gentle but firm hands to push him right back down again.

"What? No! Where am I?" he said, confused.

"We're back on the *Bladedancer*," Liana said, replacing a cool cloth on his forehead.

"And you're lucky to be alive, if you can call it that," said a new voice.

Valera came into view, leaning over him. Sylus squeezed his eyes shut.

"Did you cut it off in time?" he asked.

"Sylus…" said Liana softly, "It was too late for that. The Thaumatech was already in your blood by the time we made it to the ship. It's… well, it was too late."

"No, no, no, no," Sylus said.

He tried to sit up again, but Liana held him down.

So instead, he opened his eyes and brought his hand up in front of his face. Except his hand was gone. In its place, Thaumatech was building him a new one. How long had it been since the airship? Hours? Days? The infection was already rebuilding his palm, and the beginnings of fingers were visible. He wiggled them. They moved.

"I think I'm going to be sick," he said, feeling the room sway.

"What exactly did you expect?" Valera said, "Sticking your hand into an unknown Thaumatech device?"

She sounded disgusted, and Sylus couldn't blame her.

He heaved, and Liana handed him a bucket just in time for him to lean over the side of the bed and empty his stomach.

"Doctor," Liana said, "Perhaps you could give us a minute before you get the Captain? I need to speak to Sylus."

"Fine," Valera said coldly, "There's nothing more I can do anyway. He's in perfect health, as all Thaumatechne are."

She walked to the door of whatever room they were in. Sylus didn't recognize it. Valera paused, one hand on the doorknob, and looked back.

"What was worth so much, Sylus? You're only twenty-three. Twenty-three," she said, her voice strained. "What was worth throwing your life away for?"

"Valera, please," Liana said.

Valera opened the door and left without another word. Sylus covered his eyes with his hand, his human hand, and lay back on the bed, trying to pretend this was a horrible nightmare.

"Don't mind her," Liana said soothingly, "Valera cares deeply for this crew; she sees it as her responsibility to keep them safe. And..."

"Did it open the door?" Sylus asked, without looking at her. He was afraid of the answer.

Liana did not answer for a few moments.

"No. The door opened on its own after you passed out. The crew rushed in, and the ship lurched again. The Captain wanted to cut your arm off to stop the infection, but it was already too late. If you don't sever the limb in less than a minute after infection, it's in your blood."

Sylus felt tears trickling down his face.

"And the weapons? Did they get anything?"

"Sylus, are you serious?" Liana said, her voice growing stern. "Do you not understand what's happening right now?"

"Did. We. Get. Anything?" Sylus asked again.

"I don't know. The Captain threw you over his shoulder, and we all made our way back to the ship. Maybe some of the crew grabbed things."

"So it was all for nothing then," Sylus said, only half listening. The tears were flowing freely now, and he hid his face under his arm, so Liana would not see.

"Sylus..." she said softly.

"How long?" he asked.

"We can talk about that later, after you've had time to-"

"How long, Liana?" he insisted.

She sighed, then answered him, "Well, it's started in your hand. Not as good as, say, the leg or the foot, but there are worse places. I'd say... Maybe five to seven years. A decade if you never injure yourself again or use Wonders."

Seven years. Sylus stifled a gasping breath as panic set in. Seven years if he was lucky. Seven years to be somebody. Seven years to live. The door had opened seconds later. What was wrong with him?

A million thoughts ran through his head as the tears fell. He could feel Liana sitting next to him, murmuring comforting words, but he barely heard them. He cried for a long time. When his tears finally dried out, he was left with a hollow, empty feeling.

The door banged open, and in walked the Captain, his face a mask of deadly seriousness.

"Captain, can't this wait?" Liana said, standing.

"Out," he said gruffly.

"Sylus is going through-"

"The consequences of his own decisions. Out."

Liana stared furiously at the Captain, but she had no real authority on the ship. She walked out of the room stiffly and closed the door behind her.

Sylus did not look at the Captain. He kept his arm over his face, so at least he did not have to see his uncle's disappointment. He heard the Captain drag over a chair and sit down in it with a heavy sigh.

"Why?" he said.

"Does it matter?" Sylus mumbled.

"It does. It matters because, based on the answer, I be deciding whether to have you thrown into the blades. I told you to stand there and touch nothing. I gave you a direct order, boy. And now... Why?"

"The door wouldn't open. The ship was sinking," Sylus said, "We found a lever that said release. I thought it would open the door. Liana wouldn't pull it, and I didn't want to die. What do you want me to say?"

"Liana could have opened the door, she said so herself," Bracken said.

"She also said the effort would have killed her," Sylus said.

"So?" Bracken said, and for the first time, Sylus looked at him.

He was not furious, as Sylus expected. Oh, he was indeed angry, but mostly he just looked frustrated.

"That be her decision, and her job, boy. She's already dead, you damn fool. Did you no listen to anything I tried to teach you? And now, because of your rash decisions, you're as good as dead too."

"Did you get the weapons?" Sylus said.

"The weapons? The weapons!? The Green take the damn weapons! You're a Thaumatechne now! Do you no understand what that means?"

Sylus just shut his eyes again, not knowing what else to say. He didn't want his sacrifice to be for nothing. He felt tears begin to well up once more in the corner of his eyes.

"No. We didn't get any of the damn weapons," Bracken said finally. "The greatest find I ever seen, sunk back to the bottom of the Green, and all I got to show for it is a dead boy."

He stood up then, the chair scraping backward. Sylus could hear him thudding toward the door.

Sylus knew the answer to his next question, but he asked anyway, "Am I still in the crew?"

The door swung open, but he heard the Captain pause.

"Even if you weren't a Thaumatechne, my crew's got no place in it for people who can't follow simple orders. As soon as we be back at port, any port, you're off this ship."

The door slammed behind him.

Sylus's last hope was that the Captain would be happy enough with the haul of Thaumatech that he would forgive Sylus and allow him to stay on the crew. Now he had nothing left. He had thrown away everything. His chance at a future, his chance on this crew, his chance to be someone. He threw it all away for nothing.

He was suddenly filled with an anguish so profound that he leaped to his feet and grabbed the nearest thing to him, the chair the Captain had been sitting on. He lifted it over his head and smashed it on the floor, letting out a howl of rage and loss.

He grabbed for the next nearest thing, a vase on a nearby desk, and threw it against the wall, where it shattered into a million pieces in a spray of glass. Howling, he searched for something else to break, but the desk was empty, so he smashed it with his fist, and nearly fell over when the beginnings of his metal hand crashed through the desk as if it were made of rotting wood. An explosion of wood chips blasted outward, and the desk snapped in two, then crumpled into a ruined heap.

He stared at the remains of the desk, momentarily shocked out of his desperate rage. He heard the door open again behind him.

"Well, at least you won't have to pay the Captain back for the damages, considering he's throwing you off the crew," Liana said, closing the door quietly behind herself.

Sylus glared at her.

"Too soon?" she said, "Sorry. You should be careful, though. You need to get used to your new… situation."

"What's happening to me?" he asked.

"That's a really big question," she said. "Do you want to sit down?"

"Fine," he said, flopping down on the bed. Liana came and sat down gingerly beside him.

"How much do you know about Thaumatechne?"

Sylus could only grunt and stare at the ceiling.

"A Thaumatechne is a human being who has fused with Thaumatech. We don't know for sure, but Thaumatech slowly takes over the body, converting it into metal and machinery, until it reaches the brain. At which point…"

"You become Reclaimed," Sylus muttered.

"The Church says it's Therithar's punishment for the sins of the old world," Liana said, "A bio-technological disease, but you probably know all of that. What you might not know is that Verdalis' protection balances Therithar's curse. The infection optimizes the human body even as it converts it."

"What does that mean?"

"It means that you won't ever get sick from any other disease again. If you had a disease when you were infected, you won't anymore. It will make you stronger and faster than an ordinary human, especially in the areas closer to conversion. Like your hand and arm. And as you already know, if you get hurt, Thaumatech will fix you, replacing any injured tissue with machinery, though of course, any converted tissue is another place for the infection to spread from."

"So it keeps me alive, even while killing me. If it can fix any injury I take anywhere on my body, what prevents it from just converting my brain, turning me Reclaimed right now?" Sylus asked.

"Nothing but Verdalis' protection," Liana said softly.

"Glory be to Verdalis' preservation or whatever."

Liana's lips pursed slightly. She might not be a preacher, but she still believed in God. Sylus did not care if he was being rude at the moment, though.

"If you want a scientific answer, it is that we don't know. The infection is everywhere in your blood, but for some reason, it only converts your body near the injury site. I believe that Verdalis preserves us, Sylus. Your life is not over," Liana said gently, "It has merely changed. The Church teaches that everything happens for a reason, so…"

"I thought you weren't going to try and convert me?" Sylus said.

"I'm not trying to convert you. I'm trying to help you. I believe that Thaumatechne exist for a reason, and that reason is to help people with the time we have left. Your life may be different now, but it can still have purpose. This thing inside of us is horrible, but it can also be a gift. The things you can do with Wonders, the things the Church can teach you, are wonderful. We can help so many people, Sylus. It's not a bad life."

"But using Wonders speeds up conversion, doesn't it?"

"Well, yes. The toll they take to perform is one of the only things that weakens us, even if the energy comes from the Source. But some really don't use that much energy, healing, for example..."

"Forget it," Sylus said roughly, "No offense, Liana, but I want to live. I want to live as long as possible. I'm never going to cast Wonders, and I'm certainly not going to join the Church."

He expected her to look wounded or upset. If he was being honest with himself, he was trying to hurt her. He had just lost everything, and it felt like she was trying to convert him no matter what she said. Liana only nodded, as if she understood completely. It made him feel even worse.

"Forgive me, Sylus. I thought maybe my words would help you, but you've been through so much in so little time. You need time to adjust."

She patted his hand and stood up, moving toward the door. Suddenly, he did not want her to leave. She was probably the only person on the *Bladedancer* who might talk to him after this, but on another level, he wanted to be alone. Alone to rage and to cry. Alone to figure out what the hell he was going to do. So he said nothing.

She paused by the door.

"Just think about what I said, okay? And get some rest. If you want, maybe we can talk more soon."

He nodded, not wanting to commit to anything, and listened to the door closing behind her. The tears were coming once more, and he let them fall as he held up his metal hand, watching his new fingers slowly take shape.

19

Uncertain Future

Sylus spent the next few days in a haze of regret and misery. No one came to see him except Liana, who kindly delivered his meals and sat with him despite his terrible company. She did not speak of the Church again, perhaps sensing his mood, which was often dark and foul. He could not sleep most nights and whittled away the days staring out the window of his room.

Sylus was surprised to learn that the Captain placed him in one of the guest suites, which were much larger and featured a private washroom, until he remembered that Thaumatechne were always placed away from the crew, who did not want to be near them. He doubted the crew would like to be near him either way. He had endangered them all with his reckless behavior, and now they were trapped with an unstable, miserable Reclaimed-waiting-to-happen.

He learned this from Liana, who told him that the *Bladedancer* would continue onto the second and third rumors purchased by the Captain. He felt Sylus had already cost the crew enough, and would not deprive them of their bounty as well. So Sylus had some time left to enjoy the shattered remnants of his hopes and dreams before he was cast off the ship, to rot away on the street somewhere like those he'd seen in Boughhaven.

Liana, for her part, did her best to try and lift his spirits, talking herself in circles, trying to show him the silver linings of his death sentence without directly mentioning the church. He did not say much back, but to her credit, she was persistent, and her visits were the only highlight in his days of misery.

He could not understand why she kept coming back. He wouldn't. He knew he was often rude, morose, inattentive, and not like himself at all. He was a wretch, and if he weren't such a coward, he would throw himself off the edge of the ship and be done with it.

BANG!

The door to his cabin slammed open with enough force to rattle the door frame, and Sylus tried to scramble to his feet off his bed, grabbing one of the scraps of destroyed furniture to use as a weapon.

But it was not an attack; to his complete surprise, it was Asphen. The man strode into the room, shirtless, and took in the scene with a disgusted look on his face. He wrinkled his nose at the piles of dirty plates and probably Sylus himself, who had forgotten the point of showering or caring for himself.

"Oh, it's you," Sylus said, flopping back down on the bed, dropping the useless scrap of wood he'd been holding. "What do you want?"

"Get up," Asphen said roughly, kicking the bed.

He used his metal leg, and the corner post of the bed snapped like dry driftwood, depositing Sylus onto the floor.

"Hey!" Sylus said, clattering through the dirty dishes and debris to rise once more to his feet. "What the blades did you do that for?"

"You've had enough time to mope and cry. This is your life now. Bitching about it won't change it, so you might as well make something of it."

"What do you care?" Sylus said.

"I don't," Asphen sneered, "But you do."

He tossed the long cylinder he'd been holding at Sylus. As soon as Sylus thought to catch the thing, his metal hand snatched it out of the air. He blinked in surprise at his arm, which he couldn't remember moving.

"You're moving well," Asphen said, nodding toward his hand.

Sylus did not answer; he was staring at the object Asphen tossed him. It was a sword in a sheath, with a metal handle and a strange trigger under the blade guard. With a shaking, human hand, he grabbed the handle and pulled the blade free of the sheath, exhaling heavily as the weight of the sword tried to drag his arm down.

It was, without a doubt, the same sword he'd seen in the armory.

"How did you get this?" he asked.

"That's what you wanted. That's why you ran onto the ship, that's why you went through that door when it opened, and that's why you stuck your hand in the box. I don't think you're an idiot, Sylus, no matter what the Captain says.

I think you saw a chance to get ahead, and you went for it, damn the consequences. Maybe you didn't think it all the way through, sure. But on some level, you wanted this."

Sylus eyed the man sideways. What was his game?

"You don't know anything about me," Sylus said, sliding the sword back into its sheath.

"Sure, I do. You're not that complex, kid. I could see ambition plain on your face from the moment you walked into that bar with Bracken, eyes as wide as the moons.

You want what I have—money, respect, women, and power. You wanted to be someone. You still can. But not if you piss the rest of your life away in the streets like the rest of the idiots, so afraid of dying that they can't see the opportunities being a Thaumatechne gives them."

"Like helping people?" Sylus said, "Liana's already been at me. You can give it a rest."

Asphen snorted derisively, "Blades no. I'm not surprised she tried to convert you, though. I may be part of the Church kid, but I don't give a single fuck about the Binary Gods or the Source or whatever else. It's all nonsense if you ask me.

You want to make something of yourself? Well, congratulations, it just got ten times easier. You're stronger, faster, and probably smarter too."

"So what? I should spend my last few years on a suicide mission fighting the Reclaimed for money like you? I saw what those things can do."

"You saw what they can do to humans. It's a bit different when the playing field is more even. Why don't you draw that sword with your other hand?"

Sylus looked down at the blade, then suspiciously back at Asphen.

"Go ahead, kid, I don't have all day."

Sylus wrapped his metal hand around the hilt and pulled the blade free. As soon as his hand hit the blade, it changed. Much like he'd seen when Asphen was casting a Wonder, his hand lit up with channels of light, and the blade responded in kind. He felt the sword tug at the air around him, drawing something in.

The strange red channel along the cutting edge began to vibrate, and in seconds, it was a blur; the air around the blade warped from the speed of the sword. Somehow, none of the vibration made it past the handle, leaving the sword steady in his grip.

Asphen knelt, grabbed a piece of wood from the floor, and threw it into the air. Sylus had never wielded a sword before, but unlike when he held it in his human hand, the blade did not feel heavy at all. It felt light as air and moved as smoothly as silk.

He swung, and there was a soft shearing sound as the blade passed through the wood. The two ends clattered to the ground, the cut perfect.

Sylus gawked at the pieces as they rolled around the floor. Swords were not made for hacking through wood, and a regular sword would never have produced such a clean cut.

"It's not quite as good against Reclaimed, but you get the idea," Asphen said.

Sylus flicked the trigger again, and the blade immediately quieted. He slid the blade back into its sheath.

"The Captain just let you take this?" Sylus said, "It's probably worth a fortune!"

Asphen shrugged.

"I bought it from him."

"And you're just giving it to me?" Sylus said suspiciously.

"I figured you paid a heavy enough price for it, you might as well keep it," Asphen said.

Sylus did not know what to say; he could only stare at the sword numbly.

Why would Asphen do that for him?

"Well, I said what I came here to say," Asphen said.

Sylus blinked at him, surprised.

"Stay in here and mope if you want. Drink your life away. Blades, throw yourself off the ship for all I care. Or, get off your ass and do something. Learn to fight. You could work for the Church or join a pirate crew. There are lots of lucrative opportunities for a Thaumatechne in this world."

"I don't know how to fight," Sylus mumbled, still not sure what to think.

"I practice most nights around midnight. We've got weeks left in this journey. Come by if you want."

With that, Asphen turned and headed for the door.

"Why are you doing this?" Sylus asked.

"You're already dead," Asphen said, without turning around. "Why not start living? Think about it."

Then he was gone, not even bothering to close the door behind him.

Asphen stood there for a long time, staring at the open door, then slowly slumped down to the ground. Was it that easy? Just walk outside, learn to fight, and become a mercenary. All in a couple of weeks. Was there a point? How much could he accomplish in under a decade? Would it be enough to be remembered? Would it be enough to be a life worth living? He wasn't brave, and maybe he wouldn't even be good at fighting, Thaumatechne or not. One wrong move in a fight and you're dead.

Except that he was already dead. He stared at his hand. Already, thin, barely perceptible lines of metal were streaking into his wrist. They were too small to be seen as more than glints of metal, but Sylus could feel them. Or he thought he could, anyway. They itched.

Of course, that could be the dirt. Casually, he lifted his arm and sniffed, then reeled back at the smell. Liana sat next to him while he smelled like this? He suddenly felt like death wasn't coming fast enough.

Then he blinked. Then he smiled. Then he laughed.

Something shifted inside him. Something loosened, just a little, and he pushed himself to his feet and walked to the washroom. He didn't know if he wanted to be a Tek-Exalt, a pirate, a Technepriest, or something else, but he did want to shower. It was a start.

20

One Day at a Time

It was already well past breakfast by the time Sylus worked up the nerve to make it out of his room, which suited him just fine. Most of the crew would be up on the deck, and he wasn't quite ready to face them yet. Liana had not appeared with his breakfast, as she did most mornings, so he assumed she was busy.

Sylus cautiously cracked the door of the mess hall and peered in. There were still a few people eating; those on the night shift, or those who had taken a day off. The cooks moved around in the kitchen, cleaning and prepping for lunch. He took a deep breath and walked in. At first, no one seemed to notice him. He grabbed a tray and some cutlery, and by the time he got to the counter, the cooks were staring at him. Well, glaring more like it, but there was a mix of looks across their face. He caught Ruse staring at him from the back and caught his eye hopefully, but the head chef merely shook his head and looked away.

The cooks serving him breakfast did not say a word, and they were usually a rather chatty bunch; instead, they served him his breakfast in complete silence.

Sheepishly, Sylus headed to a table and sat down alone to eat. He could feel the eyes of the other crew members on him, and he found himself subconsciously lowering his metal hand under the table, where it couldn't be seen, and wishing he had a glove. He ate his meal in silence, and slowly, whispers started to fill the room. Sylus assumed it was about him, but he tried not to care. After all, the Captain had not confined him to his room; he was still free to go about the ship, wasn't he?

Either way, his hand was irritating him. He did not understand how, but he could feel the things he touched with it. Wouldn't that imply that the hand was already connected to his brain? And if that was the case, why wasn't he a Reclaimed? Why weren't all Thaumatechne?

"Sylus?" came Liana's voice from behind him, breaking him from his train of thought.

"Hey," he said.

"You're looking better," Liana said cautiously, setting down her tray beside him.

"I showered."

"Yes, I can smell that."

"Very funny."

"What prompted this change?" she asked, beginning to eat.

Sylus did not know how to explain that Asphen, of all people, had shaken something loose in him, mainly because he was not sure yet what it was, beyond a desire to do more than nothing. So he just shrugged.

"Well, I'm happy to see you out of your room, whatever the reason, though I'm not sure what the Captain will say."

"He never said I had to stay in there."

"That's true," she said thoughtfully, "But he's still pretty angry. I was just in a meeting with him."

"Oh?"

"He doesn't talk about it or anything, doesn't mention you at all really, but he's rather short-tempered with everyone."

"Oh."

"I can see your conversational skills are still recovering."

Sylus looked at her. She was staring at him with that same concern she always seemed to have, and realized for the first time that her care was genuine. He'd thought she was helping him in an attempt to convert him to the Church, or in his more delirious moods, he'd even entertained a fantasy that she was interested in him romantically. The truth was that she was a kind and caring person who had dedicated her life to helping others. No woman would have sat with Sylus while he was horrible to them, wallowing in self-pity, and still be attracted to them. Besides, the Captain was right. There was no time in lives like theirs for things like romance, not if you wanted to get anything done.

"Liana, I'm sorry," he said, putting down his food. "I know that I haven't been myself lately. I've been rude to you, dismissive, and generally a bit of an ass. And you still brought my food every day and sat and talked with me, tried to help me.

You're a good person, and you barely even know me. I just wanted to say I appreciated it, even if I didn't exactly show it."

Liana listened closely as he spoke, her cheeks coloring slightly, and then waved awkwardly with her human hand as if to dismiss it all.

"Don't worry about it, honestly. I remember what it was like when…" she said, her hand moving to her forearm. She seemed about to say something else, but then she shook her head. "You don't have to apologize."

"Well, I wanted to anyway," Sylus said, "I hope we can still be friends."

Liana smiled at him.

"Of course."

"So what was the meeting about?" he asked.

"We're coming up on the next Rumor. Probably in the next few days."

"Do you think I should tag along?"

"Is that a joke? Are we making jokes again?" Liana asked incredulously.

"Don't worry. I have no intention of stepping off the ship again, even if the Captain would let me. I wouldn't be surprised if he locked me in my room, to be honest."

"Neither would I," she said.

The conversation seemed to die then, perhaps straying too close to everything that had happened.

"Well, I have to go," Liana said, as she finished her lunch. "What are you going to do?"

"I don't know," Sylus said honestly. "All I ever wanted to do was work on a ship, and now..."

"I meant today, but it's nice to hear you thinking things through."

"Oh, I don't know that either."

"You should go stare into the Green. It's a beautiful day out there. It might help."

"Maybe I will, yeah. Thanks."

"See you around, Sylus."

He watched her go, then pushed around the rest of his food for a bit, delaying the inevitable. It would be nice to go up the decks, but on the other hand, most of the crew would be up there, and he'd have to endure their whispers and looks. Maybe it would be easier if he just got it over with.

Sighing, he put away his dishes and made his way up the deck. He passed only a few people on the way, who stared, then patently ignored him. As he pushed his way through the door, he was met with shining sun, and he blinked in the sudden brightness of a clear day. He took a deep breath of clean, earthy air and looked out over the edge of the deck.

There wasn't a single cloud in the blue sky, but a breeze filled the sails and stirred the green grasses into thousands of swirling patterns. Above, one of the moons hung clearly in the blue sky.

He wished that it was all he could see. It was impossible to ignore the stares he got as he made his way to the railing. He could not help but feel the eyes of Holven, who stared at him from the upper deck with absolutely no emotion, yet somehow it still felt like disappointment. Sylus was not even sure Holven liked him before, and now he wasn't sure if the man disliked him either.

Luckily, the Captain was nowhere to be seen. Even though he did not explicitly tell Sylus he was not allowed to leave his room, he didn't want to push the Captain's anger any further, lest he follow through on his threat to have him heaved over the side into the Green.

He leaned over the railing and watched the swirling green for a time, awash with different shades and patterns. Strange birds of various sizes flew overhead, keeping pace with the ship. For once, the horizon was not a completely straight line; some unknown mountains were visible in the far distance, and Sylus could not help but wonder where they were, or if he'd ever get to see the cities and places that might live there.

Seven to ten years, and so much to see and do. Something inside him had decided not to give up, but that was as far as he'd gotten. What was the best way to make a name for himself and see the world in such a short time? It would have to be on a ship somehow; there wasn't enough land left to explore. Did he have time to join the Church and learn? How long did it take? What did they expect from you after? Was he willing to give up that time?

There were so many questions he needed to ask Liana and Asphen. Joining the Church would get him onto ships. No captain in their right mind would bring Thaumatechne into the crew permanently. It was too dangerous, though Sylus did not see the difference between bringing them on temporarily. Weren't the risks the same?

He stared down at his metal fingers and flexed his hand. For all he could tell, it was his hand. It felt no different than it had before, and worked the same, if not better. Yet it was not his. It belonged to the Reclaimed, and one day it would kill him.

He sighed and watched a nearby deckhand struggling with a loose sail line. The man was having a hard time pulling the line back in to tie it down. Suddenly, the fluttering sail caught a blast of wind and ripped free of the man's hands. This line was one of the bigger sails that controlled the ship's direction, and as it fluttered in the breeze, the boat began to drift slightly. Yells ran out across the deck for help, and men rushed over to try to grab the snapping lines when they got close to the ship.

The whipping ropes snapped back and forth in a frenzy, and no one seemed to be able to get a purchase on one, at least until one snapped right toward Sylus. He reached up and grabbed it without thinking, his hand faster, and more importantly, stronger than any other man's.

The rope tried to pull free of his grasp, but his grip was literally steel. The sail snapped straight as it caught the wind, and since his hand would not let go, it tried to pull all of Sylus over the edge. He instinctively locked his legs around the railing as the sail wrenched on him with tremendous force, threatening to rip him in half. Then the gale subsided, and the pressure on the sail fell. With a great pull, Sylus managed to secure the rope.

He turned to find the crew all staring at him. Holven stood nearby, observing. The sea of blank faces was nervous, as if his touching the ship at all was dangerous.

"Sorry," he muttered.

He walked away quickly, to the sound of whispers and muttering. He fled the deck, feeling vilified, and returned to his room, flopping down on his broken bed with a sigh.

He'd only been trying to help. With the wind, he was sure no man could have caught the rope without being ripped in half; they'd have to cut the sail free to get the ship under control and put up a new one when the wind died down. Their speed would slow, and it would cost the crew money. Sylus suddenly thought it was so stupid to be afraid of having Thaumatechne on a ship when they could do so much without even using Wonders. Sure, the risk of injury was high, but with protective gear, why couldn't he serve on a ship?

He sat straight up suddenly. Why couldn't he serve on *this* ship? If he learned to fight like Asphen, he'd be doubly beneficial. A crew-mate with exceptional strength and stamina when sailing, who could protect the ship when delving into the ruins. It was a win-win. Of course, the Captain would never go for it.

This did not stop Sylus from hatching a plan. He had a few weeks left on the ship before they returned to port. Would that be enough time to change people's minds? That was, of course, if Holven and the Captain let him prove himself at all.

The first thing he needed to do was reprove his dedication to this ship. He wasn't going to be let onto any of the critical jobs, so that was out of the question. There was a lot he could do to help the ship, and there were always jobs others did not want to do. That meant the night shift.

Sylus smiled, though he knew his plan was unlikely to succeed. It was at least something to do to pass the time and keep his mind off death. If he allowed himself to think about his impending fate too hard, he knew his resolve might crumble. He could feel fear gnawing at the edges of his mind whenever he thought about how much time he had left, and he could not afford to waste any more time paralyzed by regret and fear.

With that in mind, he began trying to repair the bed that Asphen had broken for no apparent reason.

21

Tek-Exalts

Sylus put his plan into action that very night. He waited until it was time for the night shift. He'd stolen a peek at the job board in the mess hall and found, unsurprisingly, that Holven had reworked the schedule to remove Sylus's shifts and assign the work to others. But Sylus remembered, vaguely, what he'd been supposed to do this week.

After everyone gathered their gear for the shift and left the supply room unguarded, Sylus slipped in and grabbed everything he would need, then hauled it up to the main deck. For this to work, he would need to endure some painful moments.

Which is why he slammed the door open a bit harder than necessary, drawing any eyes to him as he hauled his supplies out to the middle of the deck and began to clean. Another deck hand nearby goggled at him. Partly because this was probably his assigned deck to clean, but more likely because he was unsure how to proceed. His face flashed from confusion to anger, then to concern as he looked around for an authority figure.

Sylus ignored him, and eventually the man wandered off. Sylus focused on cleaning, and it took forty-five minutes for the man to return with Holven. Holven merely watched Sylus for a few minutes, his expression unreadable. Sylus ignored him too, but held his breath. This was the first and most likely place his plan would fail. If they would not let him work, there was almost no way he could try to change their minds about him.

He was not sure how long Holven watched, but as he did, Sylus made an impressive amount of progress. Liana was right. He no longer got tired as he once did. His muscles felt strong and full of energy, as if he were no longer powered by things such as food and rest, but drew energy directly from the Source itself. Which, he realized, might be the case. He would have to ask Asphen or Liana.

He was already halfway done with the deck when Holven disappeared for fifteen minutes and returned, much to Sylus's worry, with the Captain, who took one look at Sylus before his face became a thunderhead.

"Boy, what the blazes do you think you be doing?" Bracken yelled down at him from the deck.

Sylus paused, trying to find the best words.

"Working," he said, then added on a belated "Sir."

"You don't work for this crew anymore, did I no make myself clear?"

"You did, sir. I want to work anyway," Sylus said, continuing to do just that.

The Captain did not look like he was expecting this response, and stared down at Sylus with a furious expression, tapping his fingers on the railing.

"I no know what game you be playing, boy...." he warned.

"No game, sir. I want to help. I want to make amends," Sylus said, "This is the only way I know how that doesn't interfere."

"You little..." the Captain sputtered.

Holven touched his elbow, and with another furious look at Sylus, the Captain let himself be pulled into a conversation that Sylus could not hear, except that it seemed to be a quiet but heated argument.

Eventually, the Captain threw up his hands and came back to the railing to thunder down at Sylus.

"Bah! Work yourself to death for all I care! But you no be getting paid! Not a thing, you hear me!"

"I understand, sir," Sylus said, beaming up at him.

The Captain stared at him like he was about to throw him off the ship then and there, but then he shook his head, muttering to himself, and walked away. Holven stared down at Sylus, expressionless, then walked away as well, leaving Sylus to reel at his luck. He would have given anything to hear how that conversation went. Did Holven speak up for him? Or did the Captain decide to let him work on his own?

Either way, the first part of his plan was complete. As he continued to work throughout the night, various crew members stopped to stare at him suspiciously. They either expected he was up to something or didn't trust him; he could not tell which. For the rest of the night, he was never entirely alone.

Around midnight, having cleaned twice as many hallways and decks as he used to in half the time, he gathered up his supplies and returned to the supply room. Once it was clear he was no longer going to keep working, his unofficial chaperon, another deckhand who happened to be cleaning the same area as him for the last hour, wandered away.

Sylus took the opportunity to head directly to Asphen's room and knock on the door. He could hear voices through the door that suddenly cut off at his knock. After a few minutes of silence, Asphen opened the door and peered at him suspiciously. He was not wearing a shirt, as usual.

"What do you want?" the man asked, and Sylus could see that his eyes were slightly unfocused. The man was clearly in the early stages of getting drunk.

"You said to come by for sword training," Sylus said, uncertain if the man remembered. He held up the sword, hoping it would jog the man's memory.

Asphen stared at the sword for a moment, then said, "Oh. That. Come on in then, you might as well."

He opened the door wide, and Sylus stepped inside, only to see a furious-looking Cally standing there, her face red.

"Are you fucking serious, Asphen? We're not done talking," she said, then noticed that it was Sylus, and froze.

"I was," Asphen said lazily. "I never said I wouldn't mess around with anyone else, I never expected the same from you either."

Cally's eyes went wide, and Sylus could not blame her. His face went red, and he looked at the floor as he realized he was suddenly part of a very private conversation.

Cally took three steps forward and slapped Asphen so hard that the sound echoed down the hallway. His head was tossed to the side.

"How dare you?" she hissed.

Asphen slowly turned his head to look at her, one side of his face glowing red, then took a long, deliberate drink from the bottle in his hand, without breaking eye contact. He did not say anything; he did not even look mad. If anything, he seemed almost bored.

Cally took one venomous look at Sylus, her eyes red, and fled the room, slamming the door behind her.

Asphen sighed and put the drink down on a shelf, rubbing his face absentmindedly.

"Shame that, she was incredible, if you know what I mean?" Asphen said.

Sylus had an idea, but said nothing, wondering if he'd made a mistake in coming to this man. What had he just witnessed? At the same time, he realized it was none of his business.

"Help me move the furniture," Asphen said, beginning to shove his bed to the side.

Sylus obeyed, and together they cleared a space in the middle of the room. Then Asphen pulled two more bottles from somewhere and popped the cork off one of them. The scent of grasswine filled the room as Asphen drank, then offered the other to Sylus.

"No thanks," he said, "I don't know if I can concentrate if I drink."

"You'd be surprised," Asphen said, shrugging. "Whatever else this does to us? It makes getting good and drunk difficult."

Sylus did not know what to make of this; it meant either that Asphen frequently faked his level of intoxication or drank twice as much as Sylus previously assumed. Despite the man's drinking, however, his hands were steady as he drew his sword and settled into a practiced stance, guiding Sylus to do the same.

"The first thing you need to learn," he said, "Is how to hold a sword properly. It's all in the wrists."

He showed Sylus, and Sylus attempted to emulate him. Placing his human hand above his metal one on the blade. Asphen came over and lowered his arms, so he wasn't holding the sword so high, then corrected the angle of the blade.

"You might have an advantage here," he mumbled, "switch your hands."

Sylus did so and retook the stance as best as he could remember. Asphen corrected him again, but left his wrists alone.

"Angle the blade ten more degrees to the left," Asphen said casually.

"How am I supposed to do that?" Sylus asked, but realized he'd already done it, his machine hand tilting the blade the barest fraction.

"How did I…?" he said, staring.

"You may not know how to measure ten degrees, kid, but Thaumatech does, and it's a part of you now. That hand of yours is filled with more sensors and technology than anyone on this rock really understands, and people aren't exactly lining up to study it either. I bet you'll be able to hold that angle ten times out of ten."

And he was right. He had Sylus draw his blade ten times, and each time, he was able to hold it at precisely the right angle.

"I don't understand," he muttered, letting the blade fall.

"You know what angle you need to be at, because I told you this was correct. Your hand gets it even if you don't. If you thought another angle was correct, it would adjust. You learn, it learns better, you see?" Asphen said, opening the second bottle.

"No," Sylus said honestly.

"I suppose it doesn't matter," Asphen said, waving his hand lazily, "You'll learn faster, is the point, at least where your hand and wrist are involved. I'll have to show you certain things once, maybe twice. But the rest, footwork, stances, the forms, you'll have to learn that on your own, but holding the sword right is half the battle."

They practiced for several hours, Asphen showing him various ways to hold the sword in one hand or two, as well as a few defensive and offensive stances to practice. Sylus did not understand anything, but he kept quiet for the most part and paid attention.

Eventually, Asphen called it quits after his fourth or fifth bottle of wine.

"Enough for today," he said, his words slurring only slightly despite the amount he'd drunk.

Sylus let his arms fall. Even with his newfound strength, he was exhausted. He collapsed in a chair, and Asphen raised an eyebrow at him.

"Can I ask you some stuff? About being a Tek-Exalt?" Sylus said.

"Blades, kid," Asphen said, falling backwards onto his bed. "Do you know what time it is?"

"Not really."

Asphen sighed, then waved at him to go ahead.

"How long does it take for the Church to train you?" Sylus asked.

"A year, maybe. Depends on how good you are. Oi," he said, sitting up and peering at Sylus. "You actually considering it?"

"I don't know," Sylus said, "What do Tek-Exalts do?"

"A bunch of stuff, most of it to promote the Church's agenda, but our main job is exterminating the Reclaimed," he raised his glass in mock salute, "In Verdalis' name, of course. Fighting for money, kid, there's nothing quite like it."

Sylus did not doubt that for a second. His heart was racing just thinking about it. "But what is the Church's agenda?" Sylus asked, "What do they want you to do?"

"Same thing everyone wants, kid. Power, and power means Thaumatech. Who do you think buys most of the shit these crews pick up? How do you not know this?"

"I don't know much about the Church," Sylus admitted.

"Eh, forget about the Church. The Binary Gods are a fairy tale kid. You go there, they'll try to fill your head with that crap, but it's the Wonders, languages, and training you want. In my opinion, you can ignore the rest. The Church is no better or worse than the rest of us, if that's what you're worried about, but they are the only ones offering honest jobs to poor bastards like us."

"So you don't believe in the Binary Gods?" Sylus said, interested.

"What? About Therithar, Verdalis, and the Source? Blades no."

"But..."

"But nothing. There ain't no gods kid. The Reclaimed aren't some curse created by Therithar, Verdalis doesn't protect us from shit, and the Source isn't real."

"Well, now you have to believe in the Source at least, where do you think the power for Wonders and Thaumatech comes from?"

"Probably from some other piece of Thaumatech we just haven't found yet," Asphen said, sounding bored. "It's science, not magic. Listen, if you want to debate theocracy, talk with your girlfriend. She'd be happy to fill your head with garbage."

Sylus colored, but let it go. The man was doing him a favor; the last thing he wanted to do was aggravate him by pushing anything.

"Fair enough," he said, "but couldn't you just teach me the Wonders I need without me going to the Church?"

Asphen sat back up and stared at him, "You don't know how Wonders are learned, do you? Liana didn't tell you?"

"No," Sylus said.

"Well, first of all, no, I can't show you. Not only did the Church make me swear not to, but I wouldn't. Did you forget that using Wonders speeds the infection? I like you, kid, but not that much. Second of all, well, you gotta get hit by one."

"What?" Sylus said, his eyes widening.

"Yup," Asphen said, casting around for another bottle, "It ain't pretty if you don't do it right. It ain't fun either way."

"You actually mean," Sylus said slowly.

"You want to toss lightning around, or throw fireballs? You gotta take one first. It's the Law of Contagion," Asphen said, then added, "and don't ask me cause I don't feel like explaining it all. The Church will tell you."

"Okay," Sylus said, setting aside about a million questions, "Then how does the Church teach them?"

"Volunteers. People who don't want to live anymore, or are nearing the end. The Church is always open to Thaumatechne. Not that there are many other options. Now stop pestering me with questions. I may not be as tired as you look, but I do want some sleep tonight, since you chased away my company."

"Me?" Sylus said before he could stop himself.

Asphen chuckled, "I could have talked her back around if I felt like it. No one can teach you that. You gotta learn that one yourself."

He gave up his search for another bottle and lay back on his bed, closing his eyes.

Sylus rose, more shocked by the certainty in Asphen's voice than anything else the man had said. He had to shake his head to clear his disbelief.

He paused at the door.

"Hey, thanks, Asphen. For showing me all this stuff."

"Practice your forms," Asphen said sleepily.

Sylus could not tell if the man was actually passing out or merely faking it to get rid of him. He was snoring by the time Sylus closed the door behind him.

Sylus's mind was racing the entire way back to his room as he pondered what Asphen had told him. There was so much he didn't understand about the world. He was worried he no longer had the luxury of time to figure it all out. He needed to find a path forward. The Church certainly seemed like the quickest path to learning what he needed to know.

Could he take their training and then disappear? Would the Church come after him if he did? If he couldn't convince the Captain, could he, no, would he, steal a ship? Become a pirate?

Sylus wasn't sure he could be like Asphen. He wasn't sure he was brave enough to fight the Reclaimed after his first encounter. And then, if he wasn't strong enough to fight the Reclaimed, how could he turn his power and strength on humans as a pirate? He'd have to do things he wasn't sure he was capable of.

He sighed as he readied himself for a shower and bed. He did not ask nearly enough questions of Asphen, or of Liana, for that matter. There were too many paths to choose from, and not enough time to second-guess himself once he started down one.

By the time he reached his bed, Sylus began to wonder if he would have to give up his dream after all.

22

New Normal

The next few days passed quickly. Sylus spent his mornings enjoying the sights of the Verdant Sea and enduring the looks of the crew. Nearly everyone was ignoring him. If he caught their eye, they looked away; if he saw someone who was previously friendly in a hallway or on a deck, they would turn the other way.

Sylus realized his first morning that it wasn't entirely just because of what he'd done. Thinking back, he realized that the other two Thaumatechne had been ignored and avoided to a lesser degree by everyone but the Captain and a few others. Sylus was different now, part of a tolerated, but feared, class of useful, living weapons. That made him feel only a little better about the stares and looks. At least Liana and Asphen were still spoken to by other humans, while he had earned himself total isolation.

He forced himself to endure it, at least at meal times and in the mornings. If he was going to convince the crew to accept him again, he needed to be seen. He kept his eyes open for problems he could solve faster and better than another crew member, but the truth was that the Green was calm, and accidents on bladeships were far and few between.

Eventually, he would retire to his room and spend his time practicing swordplay. Then at night, he took up his supplies and began cleaning the ship. Holven appeared once again to watch him for a time, then disappeared and was replaced by a crew member.

He did not see either Liana or Asphen the first day, and when he arrived at Asphen's room to resume their training, his knock was met by Asphen's muffled voice telling him to 'go away!' followed by distinct giggling.

Sylus stared at the door for a few moments in shock. The man was relentless. He seemed to have a tongue of silver in addition to a metal leg. He considered knocking on Liana's door; he had a million questions that only another Thaumatechne could answer, but in the end, he went to sleep.

That became his schedule for the second day, with the only real difference being that he saw Liana on the deck in the morning. She caught his eye and waved, but she was walking with the Captain, who scowled at Sylus so fiercely that Sylus fled back to his room to practice early. That night, Asphen opened the door, grinning about the night before and making a crude joke. He informed Sylus that they had no time for a whole lesson tonight, because the *Bladedancer* might be arriving at the second rumor's location the next day, and he wanted to sleep. He allowed Sylus in for a half hour to check on his practice and offer suggestions and new stances to try.

It wasn't until the third day that things changed significantly. He was eating his lunch in the mess hall, alone as usual, when Liana set her tray down beside him and fell into a chair with a bright, "Hello!" Which, as usual, made him nearly jump out of his skin.

"Do you ever approach anyone from the front?" he mumbled, even though he could not help but smile as she laughed, tucking her hair behind her ear.

"Literally everyone but you."

It was normal for him to draw eyes, but with Liana there, crew members openly watched them disapprovingly. Sylus let his eyes scan around the room, trying to see if anyone would catch his eye yet.

They would not, either glaring him down and turning away, or avoiding his gaze altogether. He sighed and turned his attention back to Liana, who was watching him with interest as she spooned today's lunch into her mouth politely.

"I see you're just as popular as ever," she said, nodding to the others.

"Despite your best efforts."

Sylus blinked in surprise, "How could you possibly know..."

"....what you're up to? The whole ship is talking about it, though not openly."

"Huh," Sylus said, looking back around with interest.

"I wouldn't get your hopes up, Sylus. As happy as I am to see you out of your room, I don't think what you're doing is going to work," she said, swirling her soup with her spoon. She was smiling, but her eyes were cast downward into the soup. "We're not one of them anymore. I know it's hard to accept, but..."

"I know it probably won't work," Sylus said, looking down into his soup. "But it doesn't matter. It's the right thing to do anyway, even if they throw me over the side. I betrayed their trust after they took me in. The least thing I could do is do some shitty jobs nobody else wants to do."

The words were out of his mouth before he could register that he meant them. He was pleased to realize that his motivations weren't entirely self-serving. A crowd of crew members passed by their table, and he could hear them whispering, but he ignored them.

"Well, good," Liana said, sounding surprised.

"Hey, where have you been anyway?" Sylus said suddenly, "I'm new over here, and I need spiritual guidance, lest I stray onto a dark path."

"Oh? I can't really imagine you on a dark path."

"Well, you'd better start. Asphen said I should become a pirate," he joked.

Liana groaned and rolled her eyes, "Please don't tell me you've been going to that man for advice."

"He's not that bad," Sylus said, only a little defensively.

"He's a creep."

"Yeah, he's a gross human-Thaumatechne-whatever. But he's been helping me learn the sword, telling me about some of my options."

"Ugh," Liana groaned, pushing her bowl away, "Now I am sorry I've been so busy. It's the Captain. Well, it's the Captain, or sometimes it's Holven, or sometimes it's Cally. Suddenly, many people seem to want my opinion on a wide range of unrelated topics. Honestly, I'm pretty sure it's all the

Captain. I don't think he likes how much time I was spending with you."

"What?" Sylus asked, genuinely confused. "Why would he care?"

"Well, I was hired to do jobs on this ship, and I wasn't doing them," she said.

"Like what? This is what I mean, I don't know anything about being a Thaumatechne. I don't even really know what it is you do."

"I know. Just give it some time. He's angry at you. He'll let up in a bit."

"Is he talking about me?"

"He's not very happy about your stunts. I wouldn't push him any further any time soon. And actually, I have to go again."

She picked up her unfinished lunch and rose to leave, "Just promise me you won't listen to everything Asphen says, at least not until we can talk more.

I don't think he means you any harm, but Tek-Exalts usually have unique personalities. Their lives are shorter than even ours and full of violence. There are many different paths for a Thaumatechne, and it really only sounds like he's telling you about the ones he likes.

Plus, you would make a terrible pirate; you don't even have a beard."

"Hey! I could grow one!" Sylus said, rubbing his jaw.

"Prove it," Liana said, winking at him. "I know you must have a million questions, Sylus. We'll find some time to talk soon, okay?"

"Yeah, sure."

He watched her go with regret, realizing how much he'd missed speaking with her. He did not know how she managed to be so happy and cheerful all the time. She made it seem so easy to make jokes, so easy to forget that the clock was constantly ticking down, faster than everyone else around them.

He shook his head to clear it before he fell into a spiral. Pushing himself up as well, he gathered his dish and headed back to his room for his afternoon practice, making sure to place his dish in the bin for collection, where it sat under the disapproving eye of Ruse, who watched him with a frown.

23

The Second Rumor

It was nearly sunset when the warning bells rang out across the ship, and Sylus gratefully tossed down his sword, panting from his practice. It could only be the second Rumor, and he was anxious to see what it was. Quickly toweling himself off, he strapped the sword sheath to his waist with a bit of spare leather. It wasn't fancy, but if Reclaimed made their way onto the ship, he wanted to be prepared.

Sylus made his way to the deck, where the crew was already gathering to see what they'd found this time. For once, most people were too intent on seeing the ruins to pay him any attention, though a few gave him concerned and nastier glances than usual. He did not blame them. His decisions cost the crew the find of a lifetime, and there was no guarantee that anything they found here would make up for it.

One took note of his sword and nudged a compatriot, who turned to look, then pushed away through the crowd, most likely to inform Holven. Sylus grimaced, but ignored it. He had no intention of leaving the ship or disobeying a single order given to him. If the Captain demanded he remain in his room under lock and key, he would do it without complaint.

The sun was nearing the horizon as Sylus moved to the edge of the crowd, casting the sky into shades of orange and yellow, contrasting against the green of the blades as he tried to get a view of the approaching shape in the distance. The sun setting behind it cast the ruins into shadow, but his immediate impression was that this was no ship. He wasn't an expert by any means, but the shape seemed far too square to be aerodynamic, though it did seem to catch the sun in a metallic way, duller than the silver of the ship they encountered previously. Birds of various sizes could be seen circling the object, as if it had been there for some time. He vaguely wondered what part of the Verdant Sea they were in now, and longed for a look at Cally's maps, though he doubted she would allow him so much as a peek these days.

He scanned the deck for familiar faces and caught sight of Virel hauling the cutter onto the deck, while Valera, who was staring at him from among the crowd, had a frown creasing the smooth lines of her face. Something in her gaze made him uncomfortable, so he avoided her eye and swept the upper deck for signs of Liana.

Her blonde hair was easy to spot, and Sylus saw her marching behind the Captain with Asphen in tow. The Captain was speaking with Cally, their heads tucked together.

Holven suddenly materialized out of the crowd, and before Sylus could get up, the man leaned across the railing next to him, staring out into the Green, that implacable face neither acknowledging him nor giving anything away.

Sylus settled back into his own lean, not exactly sure what was about to happen.

"Where did you get that sword?" Holven asked.

"Asphen gave it to me, it's mine," Sylus said, perhaps a little more fiercely than he meant to. He adjusted his tone before continuing, "He said I paid for it with the rest of my life."

"I see," Holven said quietly, still not looking at him. "I hope that you are not planning any further theatrics?"

"No," Sylus said, sighing. "Nothing like that. I just wanted to see the ruins."

"And the sword?" Holven asked quietly.

Sylus colored but kept his head up, "To protect the ship, if necessary."

"It is not your job to protect this ship," Holven said, "Not anymore."

"This ship is my home, for now at least. There are people on board I care about. If you want to order me to my room, I'll go, but I'm a Thaumatechne now. I can protect the ship better than anyone else."

"A Thaumatechne less than a week old?" Holven said, "Do you even know any Wonders yet?"

Sylus felt hot, but he managed to hold his composure.

"I am stronger now, and I have much less to lose than any of you," Sylus said.

Holven did not answer for a moment.

"Well, I hope you are telling the truth. The Captain is not joking when he threatens to throw you over the side, even if you are his family. He has lost too much to risk more from you."

Sylus stared. He did not tell anyone of his relation to the Captain. Holven did not give him a chance to respond. The ship was nearing the ruins, and calls rang out across the deck, giving orders to pull the *Bladedancer* up alongside it. Holven pushed off the railing and sank back into the crowd, leaving Sylus to stare in shock at the place he'd been.

Holven was about as crafty as he appeared. He did not order Sylus back to his room at least, which was good, because as Sylus turned his gaze toward the approaching temple, he knew he would have regretted seeing this.

It was a building, or at least, it looked like the buildings Sylus saw in Old Galleon's journals. It rose from the blades at a slight angle, and whether it was still attached to the ground or floated freely in the Green, he could not tell.

His mind raced as he began to imagine it as the tallest building of some long-forgotten city. His eyes searched the swirling grasses for hints of ruins lying close to the surface. How impossibly tall was this building to reach above the blades so high? The old world's constructions must have rivaled the great trees for size and height.

The building itself was a dull grey metal, perhaps worn down by age and elements. It was dotted with many rectangular openings, which Sylus supposed must have been windows. The glass was long gone, leaving shattered edges here and there and empty cavernous mouths in other places. No light flickered within the building, as it had with the ship, but that was not to say it would not light up when the crew set foot inside. Virel took one look at the building and began hauling the cutter back inside, his grumbling loud enough to be heard over the quiet conversations of the crew.

Once the *Bladedancer* had moored itself beside the building, the Captain stepped up to the railing of the upper deck to address the crew. Sylus only half listened as he gave his directions, trying to avoid notice and catch Liana's eye at the same time. She eventually saw him and gave him a little nod, but her face was focused and serious. This was her job, and she was not to be distracted from it.

Sylus took the hint, and as Cally began her measurements of the building's stability, Asphen moved closer to the building to perform the strange Wonder that would scan for the presence of Reclaimed.

Sylus yearned to move closer to the two, both to see what Cally was doing and to see if he could learn Asphen's Wonder simply by being close enough. If what the man said was true, Sylus would have to be in the building for it to 'touch him'.

Eventually, Cally moved back from her machinations with a smile on her face, and Asphen finished his scan. They both relayed their information to the Captain, who announced to the crew that the building was not only free from Reclaimed but also stable, which, judging from his scowl, was not a good thing.

Sylus supposed that stable, danger-free temples had a pretty significant chance of being discovered and looted, which might mean there was not much to find and scavenge. Still, there were more volunteers than the first time to join the boarding crew, and Sylus stood and watched as they donned their protective gear (except for Asphen, who seemed allergic to anything that might cover his muscles).

As the rest of the crowd dispersed, Sylus caught the Captain looking at him. The man was scowling and seemed to be debating whether or not to come over and say something to him. Sylus sighed and pushed off the railing to walk toward the Captain. He could not avoid the man forever; he might as well get it over with.

The Captain crossed his arms and watched him approach with a face like a thundercloud.

"Captain," Sylus said stiffly, letting one hand rest awkwardly on his sword in what he hoped seemed casual and confidant, like he'd seen Asphen do. Liana, who was standing behind the Captain, gave him an exasperated look. He ignored her.

"I no know what you be up to, flaunting that fool sword around, but I promise you, boy, you set one foot off this ship and the rest of you will follow, you understand me?"

"Perfectly," Sylus said, "you have my word."

"I had it before, it's not worth much, is it?" Bracken said, turning away.

Sylus flinched, but it was a fair comment, given the circumstances. Liana gave him an empathetic look, and he retreated to his spot on the far railing to resume his watch. Asphen gave him a nod on the way back, and Sylus returned it, feeling oddly better after being praised by the impressive man.

Eventually, the boarding team was ready, and Sylus watched them march into the remains of the building with no small amount of trepidation. Even without the presence of the Reclaimed, the building was far from safe. He'd taken the safety of the old world's ruins for granted and paid the price. He wouldn't wish the same fate on anyone.

Time passed slowly, and after the first hour had passed, Sylus found himself worrying about Liana.

Asphen could take care of himself, and Sylus suspected the Captain could as well. The rest of the crew had volunteered, so they knew what they were getting into.

He chastised himself for the thought, because so had Liana. This was her job; she knew what she was doing. If she were confident that she could force a Thaumatech door to open by force, she would need to know offensive Wonders. It wouldn't make sense for the Church to send out its priests defenseless.

Yet still, his anxiety only increased as time went on. One scratch, somewhere on the neck or the upper torso, and her time would be cut in half. A scrape on the face, and she might never return from the building. He knew, without a doubt in fact, that she would not. She would choose to stay, or perhaps cast herself into the blades like so many chose when their time came, hoping that the fall would prevent them from joining the countless Reclaimed who wandered the Uncharted Green.

The idea that their shortened time might be cut even shorter terrified him. Realization sank into him slowly, like a chill settling into his bones on a cold night. It was no surprise that he was attracted to Liana, but he thought he'd given up any romantic aspirations. He was no longer sure that was true. Maybe two Thaumatechne *could* have a relationship, bonded by their mutual demise. He was sure it had happened before; why could it not happen here? With him?

Liana had rejected Asphen, though. You would have to be blind not to notice how attractive he was. The man was so handsome that even Sylus almost regretted rejecting him. If Liana wasn't interested in Asphen, then what would she possibly see in Sylus? Even if she did somehow see something in him, how much of his time would a relationship cost?

A barrage of complicated emotions and thoughts did not help Sylus get any closer to an answer on what he felt, and he found himself thinking in circles. By the time several hours had passed, he'd only gotten as far as admitting he was still interested in Liana in a romantic way, even though she'd made it clear she was not looking for anything beyond friendship. If that was her decision, then he needed to respect it, he told himself. But his feelings would not subside, and by the time the boarding crew returned, hauling boxes of Thaumatech, his relief at seeing Liana step back onto the ship, unharmed, had him halfway across the deck before he realized what he was doing. Liana noticed him approaching and smiled, and he felt himself suddenly get awkward.

He awkwardly changed directions and offered a random crew member help carrying his box, earning himself a glare and a foul sneer for his effort. Sylus didn't care. He was getting used to it, and Liana was safe.

Sylus did not even mind much when the Captain appeared and glanced around the deck, his eyes locking onto Sylus, who was now standing awkwardly in the middle of the deck among the boxes that were being unloaded, with nowhere to hide.

The Captain grunted, perhaps in surprise, or because he regretted not having a reason to toss Sylus into the blades.

Once the crew had gathered around once more, he launched into a short speech.

"Good work, everyone. We did find enough to make it worthwhile for everyone on the ship, and we still have one Rumor to check!"

He glanced at Sylus, then added, "Well, almost everyone on the ship."

Sylus could hear the snickers that surrounded him, and hunched his shoulders against the crew's scorn. He thought the remark was uncalled for, but what could he do?

"Let's get this stuff to the holding bay so that Liana can get to work. Over the next few days, we can have a closer look at the haul, get a better idea of what we got."

Sylus perked up with interest. He'd forgotten that it was Liana's job to make the Thaumatech they found safe for use, and he was suddenly much more interested in what it was she did on the ship. Before anyone could stop him, he took hold of the nearest box and started marching it toward the stairs. The crew stared, but no one moved to stop him, so he kept his eyes straight ahead and marched toward the door that led to the interior of the ship, barely noticing the weight of the box laden with strange machines.

He made his way downstairs and dropped the box in the holding room where Thaumatech was kept until it could be made safe. Afterwards, it would be marked and stored until it could be examined for anything the ship might need or want to keep. The rest would be sold for profit.

Other crew members shuffled in behind him, carrying their boxes, giving him suspicious looks.

For perhaps the first time since he'd been infected, one man angrily spoke to him.

"What do you think you're playing at? You aren't getting a single coin, you know that, right?"

There were angry mutters of agreement, and Sylus realized that they thought he was after their earnings. It was hard not to be afraid, with so many angry faces staring at him accusingly, but he did not want to back down either. If he backed down now, they would never forget it.

"I do," he replied, then louder, "I don't care that I'm not getting anything, I want to help anyway. It's the least I can do, after what I cost everybody."

It was a poor reason, and it sounded false and hollow, a blatant lie. But what could he do? It was the truth. Their faces did not change a bit, and no one answered him.

After a long, awkward pause, Sylus made for the door, muttering "excuse me" to the crew, who moved out of his way without issue, though whether it was because they believed him or their fear of Thaumatechne being contagious, he could not say.

Sylus was thankful to get away from them either way and hustled back to the deck to grab another box, so that he could be out of the holding room before any of the rest of the crew made it down with their second box.

24

Wonders

Once everything was stored away, Sylus took the chance for some dinner while everyone who left the ship underwent inspection. Since the Captain took issue with him and Liana spending time together, he made himself scarce by taking the food back to his room to eat so as not to betray his intentions of watching Liana disengage the Thaumatech the crew had recovered.

It was late by the time he figured it was safe enough to sneak out of his room, well past the time when he would typically be out doing his unsanctioned cleaning. He hoped his sudden absence would not trigger a search. After the day's events, the ship was quiet and empty, and he was able to get down to the storeroom without any trouble.

Cautiously, he tapped on the door, but when there was no response, he opened it to find Liana peering up at him from a table she'd acquired somewhere. She smiled and tucked her hair behind her ear, grinning at him.

"Now, why did I expect that you'd show up sooner or later?" she said.

"Is the coast clear?"

"Holven has checked in a few times. He insisted I go to sleep, but I said I wanted to get a start on cataloging."

"Cataloging?" Sylus said, joining her at the table. She had one of the crates open beside her on the floor and was in the process of pulling out objects to examine them on the table. In front of her sat an open notebook where she was taking notes.

"You really did just hop on a ship without knowing anything about the business, didn't you?" Liana said.

"I knew enough," Sylus said defensively. "I didn't join to run a business. I joined for..."

"...Fame and fortune, I know. Well, sit down. I don't know if Holven will be back, but if he finds you here, I can't promise he won't run you off."

Sylus sighed, "None of them trusts me anymore."

"Well," Liana said.

"Yeah, I know," Sylus said, pulling up a chair across from Liana. "It's just hard. The way people look at me, it's like they no longer even see me. Just this."

He waved his metal hand in the space between them. Liana's hand drifted to her metal forearm, and she looked away.

"You get used to it," she said unconvincingly, "I know what you mean, though, it's like in some ways they don't even see you as a person anymore. Most people are either afraid of you and want nothing to do with you, or want you to do something and then leave them alone. Like you're just another piece of Thaumatech."

Sylus blinked, surprised by Liana's openness. She sounded sad. For a moment, he didn't know what to say.

"That, uh, sounds lonely," he said honestly.

"It can be," Liana admitted, "But not everyone is like that."

She turned back to him and smiled.

"You weren't. When you saw me performing that Wonder, you didn't back away. You tried to get closer, but the Captain stopped you."

Sylus blushed, embarrassed that she'd noticed so much about him.

"Anyways, I'm dying to learn about the many exciting jobs of a Techne-priest," he said quickly.

"Oh? And here I thought you just wanted to hang out with me," Liana said.

"You convincing me that this is more interesting than becoming a pirate is pretty much the only thing holding me back, so...."

Liana snorted, "You're not going to become a pirate."

"I've started on the beard."

Liana ignored him, shaking her head, but the corners of her mouth were turned up mischievously.

"Pirates are rogues like Asphen, who only care about themselves. You're not like that."

They were only joking, but Sylus felt himself wondering. He stared at his metal hand, an inseparable reminder of his selfishness. Asphen's words came back to haunt him: *some part of you wanted this, some part of you wanted power.*

Sylus suddenly wanted to change the subject again.

"So what are we doing here?" he said, "Is this stuff safe to touch?"

"For us, yes. Technically, it's as safe as any other Thaumatech for humans, which is to say it's fine as long as it doesn't cut you. That's why they always wear the gloves, just in case."

She reached into the box and drew out a metal cylinder. It was about a foot in length, with cut channels on one end.

"Take this, for example," she said, "have you ever seen one before? They're pretty common."

Sylus shook his head to say he had not.

"It's a torch, sort of," she said, pressing her thumb into an indent around the middle of the rod. There was that odd, sort of pull toward the rod for a split second, then the channels lit up with bright white light, and Sylus, who had stupidly been staring directly at the thing, was forced to cover his eyes until Liana turned it off.

"No sharp edges, nothing that can hurt anyone," she explained, "But it's still worth disengaging, just in case."

"Disengaging," Sylus said, leaning forward excitedly, "That's what removes the infection, right?"

"It removes the potential for Thaumatech infection," Liana corrected. "If someone cuts themselves with this, or god forbid, bashes someone's head in, they won't become a Thaumatechne."

"I'm guessing that it doesn't stop an active infection?" Sylus asked.

"Sadly, no."

"Can anything?"

"That's part of what we're here to find out," Liana said.

"What do you mean?" Sylus asked.

"Do you think the Church just sends us out here for free?"

"I assumed they did it because it was the right thing to do."

"Ah, an optimist," Liana said, "As much as I wish that were true, it's not. We're searching for Thaumatech just as much as the crews are."

Sylus had to mull this over, not sure what she meant. To give himself time to think, he changed the subject.

"So Disengaging, it's a Wonder?" Sylus asked.

"A very minor one, but yes."

"And you have to cast it on every single piece of Thaumatech?" Sylus said, his eyes growing wide. "Is it... How much?"

He did not know how to ask how much of her life it would cost her. He could not imagine burning away his remaining time on this.

Liana shook her head.

"It's not like that. Some Wonders are complex, but some are simple. Complex creations, such as fire or lightning, require extra energy from the Source. Those are the Wonders that are dangerous to use. Others are so minor that they only require the energy you already have, the kind used by your Thaumatech. I can't disengage everything in here at once, but over the next few days? It's safe, if that's what you're worried about. Do you want to see it?"

"You're going to do it right here?" Sylus asked.

"It's not that exciting," Liana said, putting down the torch.

She pulled up her sleeve, revealing her metal forearm, and for the first time, Sylus got an idea of how far her infection had spread. Her arm was metal up into the sleeve as far as he could see, and down to the wrist, where it was beginning to take her hand, the opposite of his own.

She held her arm out over the object.

"Disengage," she said in a clear voice.

A blue light shone from her forearm, one quick flash that bathed the table, then disappeared. She made a note in her book and placed the torch into a box at her feet. Then she folded her hands politely and stared pleasantly at Sylus.

"Wait, that's it?" Sylus said.

"That's it," Liana said, "The crew can keep this one. They're pretty useful, so they fetch a good price."

"What do you mean they can keep it? Do they not get to keep all of it? They found it!"

"That's what I was saying before. Why do you think these crews are required to have a Technepriest on board?"

"So the Church is taking a cut?" Sylus asked.

"It's not like that," Liana said, shaking her head. "It works like this. The Church provides a priest to disengage Thaumatech. In exchange, I get paid, but the Church also gets first rights on anything the crew finds. It's not so we can sell it, either, so wipe that look off your face."

Sylus hastily composed himself, not wanting to offend Liana.

"If the crews come across anything new, anything we don't understand, or anything that seems potentially dangerous, it gets sent back to the Church for further study. If it's deemed safe, the crews get it back," Liana continued.

"Why is the Church so interested in undiscovered Thaumatech?" Sylus asked.

"A lot of reasons, but I think it's mostly to find a cure," Liana said.

"A cure?" Sylus said. "I thought you said it was impossible."

"As far as we know it is," Liana said, "but the old world created so many strange and powerful things. Who is to say it's not out there?"

"Is that why you became a Technepriest?" Sylus asked, "To try and find a cure?"

Liana looked up at him through her eyelashes for a moment, considering.

"The Church has been looking for a cure for a very long time, Sylus. I don't have any illusions, and neither should you."

Sylus could not help but notice that this was not an answer to his question.

He looked at the stacks of boxes Liana had lined up to go through, and she followed his gaze.

"I know it's probably not what you were expecting," she said, "But it's important work. You don't have to stay if you don't want to."

"It's not that," Sylus said quickly. "It actually is pretty interesting. I can see the appeal of finding Thaumatech that no one has ever seen before. That's exactly what I wanted to do when I came out here, but if the Church keeps it..."

"We only keep things that will help people," Liana cut in. "Water purifiers, well drills, that sort of thing."

Liana drew another piece of Thaumatech from the box. It was a large flat square, with black glass facing upwards.

"Hey! I've seen one of those before," Sylus said. "It's a cooker, right? It heats things. Someone in the village had one; it was like the only piece of Thaumatech we had."

"I think," Liana said, moving her hands around the edge of the box, "you may be right."

She found what she was looking for, and there was a barely audible click.

Again, there was that feeling of something being pulled toward the object. It pulled at Sylus, but this time, he noticed that it also seemed to pull him away at the same time. There was a sudden sense of great distance, but it was gone in a moment.

The top of the Thaumatech device began to emit heat immediately, and a strange, curled pattern glowed red underneath the glass.

"Do you feel that pull when you turn this stuff on?" Sylus asked. "I felt it before, but ever since this happened to me, it feels different."

Liana looked up at him as she adjusted her sleeve.

"Yes," she said, "The Church believes it's a sort of resonance between us and Thaumatech. We can feel it drawing energy from the Source."

"You believe in the Source, then?"

"Of course. How could you not?"

"Asphen says it's probably just another piece of Thaumatech somewhere."

"He would," Liana said, "but it doesn't feel like that when you cast a

Wonder, it feels... well, it's hard to describe."

Liana shut the cooker off and made a note in her book before holding her arm over it.

"Disengage," she said, and the blue light flashed. Liana put the cooker in the box with the Torch. "The Captain will be pleased, these are so valuable, and I think I saw a few more in there."

"Do you have to say the word?" Sylus asked, wondering how she could do this all night. "Asphen didn't speak when he did that scan thing."

"Not really. Technically, you only need to concentrate," Liana said, looking at him sideways. "You have a lot of questions for someone who never wants to cast a Wonder. Do you want to try it?"

"Try it?" Sylus said nervously.

"I promise, this one won't cost you anything. You should know how to do this stuff, if only so you know the process."

"I don't know. I thought you're not supposed to share the Wonders the Church teaches you?"

Liana shrugged, smiling mischievously.

"Just because I work for a Church doesn't mean I don't know how to break the rules."

Something in the way she said that made Sylus's face flush.

"I still don't know," Sylus said, "Asphen sort of explained how it works."

"Then you know that this one won't hurt you, because it won't work on you. But you'll learn it. Or rather, your Thaumatech will. Trust me!"

Liana looked so excited that he couldn't find a good reason to say no. If it wouldn't cost him anything, what reason could he have to refuse except that he didn't trust her, which wasn't true. There was something about Liana that was too honest not to trust.

"Uhm, okay, sure," he said nervously.

Liana beamed. She held her forearm out over his hand.

"Ready?"

"I guess so?"

"Disengage."

The blue light flashed across his hand and was gone. He waited for something to happen. Liana stared at him expectantly.

"Did it work?" he asked.

"Give it a minute," she said.

A whirring sound emanated from his hand, and it jerked softly. Sylus turned it over. In the palm of his hand, the metal plates were shifting. He leaned in, fascinated, as they rearranged themselves, changed shapes, and moved, until finally a small channel opened in the palm of his hand. Inside was a tiny glass-like bulb. Then the channel closed, and his hand lay still.

"There you go," Liana said happily.

"I don't understand," Sylus said.

"It's the Law of Contagion. The same way it spreads from Thaumatech to people is the same way it learns, from contact. Your hand just built itself whatever it needs to perform the Wonder."

"How could it possibly know how to do that?" Sylus asked.

"If we knew that, we wouldn't call them Wonders, dummy," Liana said with a laugh.

She pulled another object from the box; it was a screwdriver.

"That looks like a screwdriver," Sylus noted.

"It is, Virel will love this," she said, pushing a button. There was that sensation of being pulled in, so slight this time he could barely feel it, and the head of the screwdriver began to turn itself. "Looks like it works. Go on, give it a try."

She set the screwdriver down on the table, nodding to Sylus.

He felt oddly nervous for some reason as he held his hand out over the small piece of Thaumatech.

"So I just say the word?" he asked.

"If you want to," Liana said, "the Thaumatech inside you knows what to do; you just need to concentrate on what you want to change. Focus on making this Thaumatech safe to use. That's the important part."

Sylus nodded, staring at his hand. He thought about what he'd seen Liana do, picturing the flash of blue light, and focused on the intention of disengaging the infection.

"Disengage," he said shakily, holding his breath.

He expected to feel something, an intake of energy perhaps, but there was nothing as the chamber on his palm slid open, and a flash of blue light erupted over the screwdriver.

In seconds, it was over, and he turned his hand up to look at it. The channel with the small glass bulb had already closed.

"Huh," he said, "I thought it would feel different."

"Yup, not much to that one. Not much power needed, whatever is already in your body is usually enough, and the more Thaumatech you have…"

"…The more energy your body stores," Sylus finished, catching on.

Liana nodded and placed the screwdriver with the other disengaged items. Then she tucked her hair behind her ear and smiled secretively at him.

"Want to learn something a bit more exciting?"

"Uhm…"

"Well, if you're scared…"

"I'm not scared," he protested.

Liana ignored him.

"That's okay, but eventually, you're going to choose how you want to move forward, and no matter what that choice is, you may need to defend yourself."

"I just don't want to…" Sylus trailed off, squeezing his eyes shut against the dread that swelled up inside him.

He felt Liana's hand slide over his human hand. His metal hand was much closer to her, but she'd reached across the table to grip his real hand instead. There was something strangely intimate about the gesture. Her hands were soft, and his skin tingled where her skin touched his.

"I understand," she said quietly. "It's up to you, but I really think it's a good idea to have a Wonder in case of an emergency."

Sylus took a deep breath, then blew it out forcefully.

"Okay, okay," he said finally, "A small one, okay?"

Liana pushed up from her seat excitedly.

"Of course!" she said, drawing him out of his chair.

She led him to an open area free from boxes.

"How do we do this?" Sylus said, feeling very awkward.

"Well, you said Asphen told you. I have to, well, I have to use it on you. But don't worry!" she said quickly, seeing the look on his face. "It doesn't hurt that much. You would learn the Wonder if I hit you anywhere with it, but for obvious reasons, we don't want to give you an actual injury.

That's why I'm going to use it on your hand. Not only will it barely hurt that way, but it won't advance your infection by causing an injury that Thaumatech has to repair. You see? Relatively safe."

"Relatively?"

"Hold your hand out, please. And hold still, obviously."

"I think I'm going to be sick," Sylus said.

"Oh, come on! You said you trust me, right?"

"Right," Sylus said, and held out his hand. His arm was shaking, but the unnatural metal of his hand was still and quiet. "What are you going to do?"

"I think you'll like it. It's a little Wonder, it causes a sort of electric shock. It probably won't hurt a Reclaimed. I doubt it could even seriously hurt a person, but it's enough to stun either for a few moments."

"What's it feel like?" Sylus asked.

"You're about to find out," Liana said, holding her forearm close to his hand and furrowing her brow in concentration.

Two small metal spikes emerged from her arm. She flicked her gaze to his.

"Are you ready?"

"I don't-" Sylus said, but Liana spoke right over him.

"Spark!"

It happened quickly. There was a slight pull of energy toward Liana, and then blue sparks burst between the metal spikes and *jumped* to his hand in an arcing flash. The spark hit his hand, and all of his muscles suddenly seized.

A short, sharp pain laced through him from his hand to his feet, and he tried to spasm for a moment, mouth open, but his muscles completely locked, and no sound came out. In less than two seconds, it was over.

He swayed slightly as he stumbled forward, his muscles turning to jelly as they unlocked. He had the strangest sensation of his hair standing on end.

"What did you do that for!" he cried, rubbing his metal hand, though there was no lingering pain. "I didn't say I was ready!"

Liana gave him a knowing look, "Oh, please, it's more unpleasant than painful."

"Yeah, unpleasant would be one way to put it," Sylus said.

Liana's eyes flashed up to his head, and she suddenly giggled, raising a hand to her mouth.

"What?" Sylus said, "What is it?"

He had a sudden, intrusive vision of himself with his hair on fire, and clamped a hand to his head. But his hair was intact, and he relaxed, though Liana kept giggling. She stepped close to him.

"Your hair looks ridiculous," she said, reaching up a hand.

She ran her hand through his hair, trying to flatten it back against his head. She was standing very close to him, smiling as she concentrated on fixing his hair.

Her bangs fell across her face as she did so, and without thinking, he reached up and tucked her hair behind her ear, as she usually did herself. As he realized what he was doing, he froze, and so did she. They stood there for a moment, both of them touching the other's hair, looking into each other's eyes.

Sylus was suddenly overcome by a desire to kiss her, and the thought collapsed him into full-blown panic. He froze completely, the color draining from his face. Liana's eyes widened, and she stepped backward, pulling her hands away from his hair and moving away from him. Her eyes went down, her face colored, and she tucked her hair behind her ear herself.

"Sorry," Sylus said, embarrassed.

He was sure his intentions were as plain as day on his face in that moment; no wonder she stepped away. He scrambled to make it seem like he wasn't crazy.

"I shouldn't have touched your hair without asking," he said.

He would later wonder for hours why he had said this, out of all the things in the world he could have said in this moment, and would come up with no good answers.

"It's fine," she said, the awkwardness dropping away slightly as she smiled at him again. "I was touching yours after all."

She turned away and walked back toward the desk. Sylus didn't move for several moments. He desperately wanted to know how she could just let things go so quickly.

"I take it then," she said slowly, sitting back down, "from what you've said, that Asphen has tried to recruit you to become a Tek-Exalt?"

"Not in so many words," Sylus said, trying to emulate her by sitting back down and forcing the color from his face. "But basically, he says to use the Church for what they can teach me, but also..."

"...That the entire religion is a lie?" Liana guessed, pulling some more things from the box at her feet.

"Pretty much."

"He said pretty much the same thing to me," she said.

Their conversation seemed a little stilted now, and Sylus wasn't sure how to fix it.

"Anything to add?" Sylus asked.

She sighed, "Well, obviously, I'd add that he's an ass, but he's not wrong about what the Church can teach you. He's not telling you the whole truth, though."

"And what's the whole truth?"

"That most Tek-Exalts die within a year fighting the Reclaimed," Liana said, "That their lives are violent, full of death, and even shorter than ours. Don't get me wrong, what they do is necessary; it protects people. It just doesn't seem like a good use of the gifts Verdalis gave us."

"You see this as a gift?" Sylus said, shocked. "I thought the Church says it's a curse?"

Liana looked at him thoughtfully before answering.

"The histories say that before Verdalis intervened, anyone infected became Reclaimed in moments. Now we get years. Besides that, I can heal people from wounds that should kill them. I can drive sickness from the body. I can bring hope to people who have none. These are miracles, Sylus. Aren't those things worth the price? My sacrifice for countless others? Maybe it's a curse for us, but how we use it in the time we have left. I have to believe that it's a gift."

She looked down, suddenly seeming sad, and added, "I have to."

Sylus knew it was inappropriate to ask, but all he knew was that Liana had been infected at a young age, and he wanted to know more about her.

"Liana," he said carefully, "Do you mind if I ask how…?"

"How it happened?" she offered with a weak smile.

"You don't have to tell me if you don't want to."

"I don't really remember much, to tell you the truth. I was only fifteen. My father was a merchant, and he bought a bad shipment of Thaumatech. He didn't know it at the time, but it hadn't been properly disengaged.

Among the things he bought was a little music box. A beautiful little thing. He was so excited to show me what he'd bought that he hadn't checked it. I dropped it, and the edge cut my arm and the top of my leg, and that was that."

"That's horrific. Such a simple mistake…"

"It happens a lot more than you'd think."

"Is that why you joined the Church?"

"My parents didn't really want me around after. They were scared of me. I didn't want what happened to me to happen to anyone else, so I joined the Church. I didn't really have anywhere else to go."

Sylus felt horrible. He regretted asking. Liana was tracing little circles on the table. He didn't know what to say.

"I'm so sorry," he said.

Liana shrugged.

"It's not that bad. The Church took me in, and now I get to help people. So it all worked out in the end."

Sylus thought she was being incredibly generous with that assessment.

"What if it hadn't happened? What did you want to do with your life before you were infected?"

Liana didn't answer and didn't look at him. She busied herself for a moment, drawing things out of the boxes and placing them onto the table in front of them.

After the box was empty, she finally spoke.

"It doesn't matter, because that's not what happened. Verdalis placed me on this path, and I'm grateful for it. Look, Sylus, this has been fun, but I actually do have a ton of work to do."

"I could help," Sylus offered, not sure what he'd done wrong.

She looked up at him and smiled, though it seemed pained.

"I appreciate it, but there's no reason for both of us to be stuck here all night. You should get some sleep."

Sylus could not think of a reason to refuse, and he could not think of a reason to stay. All he could think of was that he'd done something wrong, and that a moment had passed that might not ever come again. His mind sought a solution, but eventually the silence that passed became too long to bear.

"Okay," he said, feeling like an idiot for not having the right words to fix whatever he'd broken. "Good night."

He stood up from the table.

"Good night, Sylus. See you tomorrow," Liana said, clearly trying to return her attention to the task at hand.

She kept her eyes on her book, scribbling small notes, and did not look up as he left the room.

25

Out of the Depths

Sylus closed the storage room door quietly behind himself and pressed his forehead against the cool wood of the door, trying to let the swaying of the airship soothe away his regrets. What was wrong with him?

How was he both so impulsive that he'd thrown his life away on a whim, yet so hesitant that he became paralyzed with fear whenever a pretty girl looked at him?

He let the scene play out again in his head: their hands in each other's hair as they stood less than a foot apart, Liana staring up at him, the light spattering of freckles across her nose, and then her pulling away, and the following awkwardness.

Was he supposed to have kissed her? Or was that urge entirely in his head? She'd been pretty clear about only wanting friendship. It seemed to him that she realized he was thinking about kissing her and pulled away. He was, probably, maybe, imagining things.

He sighed and pushed away from the door, heading back to his room. There was no one on the ship he could ask for advice, since so few people were speaking to him. Sylus fetched his sword, intending to see Asphen for further training.

As Sylus made his way there, he realized he could speak to Asphen. Asphen seemed to have a way with both women and men, but Sylus quickly discarded the idea. First, it was a terrible idea; secondly, Asphen would realize Sylus was interested in Liana, and he was not sure what the result of that would be, but he did not feel great about it. What if he told her? What if, worse, it renewed the man's interest in her?

Sylus stopped halfway down the hall to Asphen's room. He no longer felt like training. What he felt like doing was going to his room and banging his head on the floor until the world started making sense again, but he settled on going to the deck for fresh air instead.

The mid deck was abandoned, except for a solitary crew member who saw him and turned away. Sylus retreated to the upper deck instead, finding it blissfully empty and with a better view besides. He leaned on the railing and looked out into the clear night. The larger of the two moons was a half moon tonight, bright enough to bathe the dark grasses in pale shades of grey, allowing just enough light to watch the wind swirl patterns in the blades.

He breathed deeply, filling his lungs with the earthy smells of the Verdant Sea, and tried to settle his mind. Why was he suddenly so focused on Liana? Didn't he decide, just recently, to take the Captain's words to heart and forget about romance to focus his short time left toward achieving his dreams? Was he using Liana as a distraction from the stark fact that he'd made zero progress with the crew? He'd also made zero decisions regarding what to do once he was kicked off the ship. All the while, his precious time was ticking away.

Sylus held up his hand in the light. The metal was still working its way down his wrist. There had been no progress that he could see, but it was progressing as surely as the ship swayed in the wind. He needed to make up his mind. He should pick a path forward, stick to it, and ignore Liana. She was a distraction at worst, and at best, the only thing that seemed to lessen the existential fear that pervaded his every waking moment.

He wished he knew how she did it. How did she stay so positive and hopeful in the face of certain death? Not only that, but she used it as motivation for dedicating her life selflessly to helping people. He could do the same. Join the church, heal the sick, help the injured. He'd seen the look on the man's face when Liana healed him in the alley. It wouldn't be a bad life by any means, but would he be happy?

The grasses swelled in the distance, the blades seeming to rise and fall without rhyme or reason, with some of the swells passing harmlessly under the ship.

The sword weighed on his hip, and he was forced to consider what Liana said about the Tek-Exalts. He did not want to die any sooner than he had to, but if he worked to become as good as Asphen was, could he rise to fame and wealth quickly? He could train and train until he was sure he was ready, and only then go out on the ships. He could explore forgotten ruins, find new and amazing Thaumatech, and make a name for himself. The life he'd always wanted, if only he could survive its impossible dangers.

Another swell passed under the hull, and this time the tips of the blades brushed the bottom of the ship. A soft brushing sound filled the air, despite the sharp edges of the blades. The *Bladedancer* rocked slightly from the contact. A bell chimed, and Sylus watched as the ship rose higher, to avoid the grasses that seemed to be growing rougher despite the lack of wind and clear skies.

Glimmerbeetles rose from the grasses, perhaps disturbed by the rough swells, and perched on top of the blades, shook themselves, and took flight into the night sky. Sylus, who did not know they could fly, watched in amazement as a veritable swarm rose from the grasses around the ship, their sparkling shells glinting in the moonlight as they flew into the darkness and out of sight. He wished Liana had seen it.

He stared out into the night, watching the grasses swell, and just tried to quiet his brain into silence, hoping to match the empty night. Which is why when he saw something roiling within the swells, he thought for a moment it was another swarm of beetles, but the color was wrong. Something was roiling beneath the swells, something only slightly shiny, and not the jet-black reflective shells he was used to seeing.

Whatever this was, it was only slightly visible in the undulating grass as it rose and fell. He caught sight of it in one swell, and then another, and then once more, in a sudden wave of grass that rose high enough to touch the ship as it passed underneath. In that moment, Sylus, looking straight down, got a passing glance as something moved through the swell of grass. In glimpses, he spotted a creature of long, overlapping reddish plates. It was impossibly long and moving impressively fast. A faint, rhythmic clicking rustled through the grasses, nearly inaudible over the sound of the wind, but hard to ignore once you heard it.

Suddenly, Sylus began to see flashes of the same reddish carapace everywhere he looked. With rising horror, he stumbled back from the railing as he realized the creature was not riding the swells, but causing them. What appeared as random patterns of wind-blown grass snapped into clear focus. The waves weren't random at all, but instead moving inwards in a spiraling pattern as if circling the ship.

Sylus stumbled away from the railing, and his eyes darted around for an alarm bell. He felt like he should be screaming something, but his throat had closed up. He caught sight of one of the bells and ran for it. At the same time, something rose from the Green and rammed into the side of the ship, sending the *Bladedancer* tilting dangerously to the side.

Yells rang out into the night from above, as the night crews cried out in surprise and confusion. Sylus nearly lost his footing as the ship swayed, but managed to catch himself at the last second. He threw himself at the bell, ringing it as hard as he could, splitting the night with piercing tones in short bursts of three, the standard signal that the ship was under attack.

As if it knew it had been discovered, the faint clicking suddenly grew much louder, filling the air with a chitinous cascade, like stones tumbling down a mountain before a landslide. Sylus felt someone thunder up behind him.

He turned to see a very angry-looking crew member approaching him, but whatever the man was shouting was suddenly drowned out by a warbling, alien shriek, and a horrific, violent ripping sound as something burst from the blades in a spray of shredded green.

Sylus only had time to see the massive insect-like body, a plated carapace, and hundreds, if not thousands, of grasping yellow legs, as the creature arced its gigantic body into the air with the grating sound of carapace pieces sliding against each other. The monster slammed into the *Bladedancer*, its weight sending the ship into a dangerous tilt and throwing Sylus and the other crew member to the ground.

Some of the tank crew were not so lucky. Sylus could hear screams and the distinctive sound of snapping lines. He caught sight of one unfortunate person falling from the heights, the sound of their scream cut suddenly short as they slammed into the blades.

The ship veered, then began to right itself as the creature sank beneath the Green once more. Sylus forced himself back to his feet and back to the bell, ringing it again and again, until more bells split the night as the signal was taken up. Shouting rang out through the night. Sylus thought he could hear the Captain's deep baritone cut through the noise, and the ship began to rise, perhaps in an attempt to get out of the insect's range.

In another burst of grass on the opposite side of the ship, the monster reared out of the blades once more, rising to tower over the *Bladedancer* as the bladeship tried to rise into the sky. Sylus forgot about the bell as he got his first full view of the thing attacking them.

Rising high into the night was the most enormous creature Sylus had ever seen; an impossibly large centipede covered in ridged plates that ran down the length of its long body, along with countless hundreds of legs that ran from the creature's head down into the blades, each one tipped with a scything claw that produced the horrible clicking noise.

Its head surveyed the ship for the briefest moment, a triangular, angular thing tapering to a sharp point surrounded by four mandibles, and topped by two whip-like tendrils. They twitched and flicked around its body like a snake's tongue might taste the air, and beneath them sat two clusters of black glassy orbs, arranged in a crescent shape, seeming to glow faintly in the dark.

It clacked the four massive, interlocking mandibles, revealing for a moment a circular inner mouth lined with hooked teeth. The creature reared backwards and let out a true roar, a deep, resonant vibration that shook the ship.

Without warning, it fell forward, expertly snaking its way through the gap between the air tanks and the deck. Its many legs grabbed onto the ship and propelled it forward in a countless series of clacking legs, crossing over the deck and driving itself off the other side.

Sylus watched in horror from where he'd fallen as the creature's body kept coming, a never-ending series of legs and carapace. Once the head had disappeared over the side, it quickly reappeared at the front of the ship, wrapping up over the railing and encircling a mast before clattering over the opposite side once again, and still its body kept coming.

With a sudden dread, Sylus realized the creature was trying to encircle the ship to prevent it from fleeing, and they'd barely reacted yet.

The crew member who fell beside Sylus seemed just as stunned and lay watching in the same stupor.

"Leviapede..." he said, only audible because they'd fallen in a tangle as the creature encircled the ship.

Men and women were pouring onto the deck now. The ship lurched left and right as the creature worked its machinations to encircle its prey. One man thundered up the stairs, visible over the top of the rapidly moving Leviapede's body. He yelled and struck at the creature with a sword, only for the speed of the creature's movement to rip the blade out of his hand, tossing it into the night.

There was a sharp crack, and the man followed the sword into the air, screaming. A jagged cut streamed blood from his chest across the night. Had the creature had the capacity to strike out with one of its thousands of legs?

The creature's velocity seemed to slow, perhaps finally running out of body with which to encircle the ship, and the man beside him pushed himself to his feet as the creature's body began to undulate, scraping back and forth across the deck, cutting them off from the lower deck, where shouts could be heard.

"We can't stay here!" the man beside him cried, as the creature's thrashing brought its body closer to them.

"Wait!" Sylus called, but the man grabbed hold of a nearby ladder, making to climb up onto the tank network and go over the creature that way.

Another roar shook the ship, and Sylus saw the creature's head rise and strike the lower deck like a snake strikes its prey. Screams followed, and the creature's head reappeared, tossing a man caught in its mandibles into the air. It swallowed him whole as he fell back down screaming, right into the creature's waiting maw.

Sylus scrambled to his feet and tried to follow the man up the ladder, his mind racing. Desperately, he attached a lead rope to his belt, having no better alternative, and threw himself up the ladder two rungs at a time.

As he rose higher, he began to see the full extent of the monster that encircled their ship. It rose from the surface of the blades about fifteen feet, and underneath the airship, churning patterns of green suggested it still hid a good portion of its length. It was wrapped around the center section of the hull, once at the upper deck, and again at the lower deck, preventing the *Bladedancer* from rising any higher. Furthermore, it appeared to have encircled the hull, its legs clinging impossibly to the metal surface, giving it purchase to strike at the decks themselves.

Despite the creature's apparent intelligence, it had not yet made a move toward the air tanks, which were likely the only thing preventing the ship from being pulled into the Green. Sylus passed one of the tank stations on his way up and noted that the air pressure was at full capacity. Such an amount would generate an incredible amount of lift, and yet the *Bladedancer* rose no further.

The creature writhed, and the ship shuddered, metal creaking ominously as it tightened its grip. Sylus lost his hold on the rungs with his human hand and swung imperiously out into open air; only the unbreakable grip of his metal hand and the lead rope prevented him from falling to his death.

He needed to get to the main deck. Once he reached one of the horizontal rails, which allowed for travel, he switched his lead rope and moved toward the front of the ship. He passed over the length of the creature that barred his way and made his way down the next ladder as the sounds of yelling and battle filled the night air.

Sylus slid the final distance down to the deck and landed in a scene of chaos. Men and women hacked at the sections of the creature's body they could reach, though their weapons had no effect. Many were forced to retreat as the Leviapede's slashing legs would retaliate with sharp cracks whenever someone got too close.

Vaguely, Sylus clutched at the sword at his hip, drawing it, and staring at the trigger embedded in the handle. Could its vibrating blade pierce the creature's carapace? He found himself shaking as he considered joining the fray. A fire had somehow started on the deck, and men and women rushed to extinguish it. Sylus swallowed and looked around for the creature's head. He could not see it, but another of those eerie roars sounded toward the front of the ship, and the *Bladedancer* shook as something hit it hard, followed by the sounds of screams. Perhaps if it was distracted, he could...

Sylus took two steps toward the men and women trying to pierce the creature's body. He could see Virel, blood running down his face, trying to get close enough to heave the cutter against the creature's body, but the slicing legs were proving too challenging to get past with the heavy machine. As Sylus took his third step, he watched as a woman attempted to slice off one of the legs, only for it to whip forward with a sharp crack, as if the creature could sense danger to every part of its body. The woman went flying backward with a scream, a deep puncture wound in her shoulder.

She crumpled to the ground at his feet, and he could see inside her body through the hole in her shoulder. Her insides were red and raw, and blood poured in torrents from the wound as she screamed. All he could hear was the pounding of his own heart in his ears, and a horrible, high-pitched buzzing.

He felt the sword fall uselessly to the ground as his stomach churned and his mind reeled at the horrific sight in front of him. He felt like he was going to throw up, then someone shouldered him out of the way.

It was Liana. She fell to her knees in front of the woman, her short blond hair streaked with blood, and turned to look up at him, shouting something. The shock and relief of seeing her, alive, seemed to flood some awareness back into his senses.

Liana was shouting at him.

"Sylus! Snap out of it! I need you to put pressure on the wound!"

"What?" he said, shakily.

"Dammit, Sylus! She's dying!"

"Right!"

He fell to his knees beside her and placed both of his hands over the hole in the woman's shoulder. She'd stopped screaming because she'd lost consciousness at some point. Her eyelids flickered weakly. Sylus leaned into the wound, trying to ignore the feeling of hot blood seeping up between his fingers.

Liana held her forearm over the wound, her sleeve long since torn away.

"Heal! HEAL!" she cried.

There was that strange intake of energy, that pull toward something distant, and green light bathed out over his hands and the woman's shoulder. It was strangely warm. It cast the red blood into a deep shade of purple, and as he watched, fascinated, as the blood stopped seeping from between his hands. The woman's breathing became less shallow, and color slowly returned to her face.

The green light winked out, and Liana slumped. Without thinking, Sylus moved his hands to catch her, but she reached out and caught herself.

"I'm fine," she said, sounding pained. Sylus looked back at the woman's shoulder in amazement. The gaping hole was gone, and all that remained was blood-soaked skin.

"We need to get her below deck," Liana said, "Can you help me?"

Sylus looked to where his sword lay nearby, "I…"

Liana followed his gaze.

"There are people who need us, Sylus," she said. "You could help me. I tried to heal you when you lost your hand; you should already know the Wonder."

"That sword is Thaumatech; it might be able to hurt that thing," Sylus said.

"Are you sure about that?" Liana asked.

Sylus hesitated. Liana's eyes were red-rimmed, and she seemed exhausted. The question was not meant to be hurtful; she was asking an honest question.

"No," he said honestly.

Liana nodded, "Well, I am sure that you can save lives. Help me get her up."

A sudden crash drew their attention. Asphen appeared, apparently retreating from the creature as it reared up for another strike. The man held two swords out in front of him and stood alone on the deck as the creature retracted itself from where it had just punched a splintered crater in the deck, trying to grab him.

Asphen did not turn away from the creature, but his eyes flicked back toward them, taking them in. Virel and the crew members who were trying to attack the creature's body took one look at the Leviapede, which was undulating above the deck, and fled from the creature's sight.

"We need to move," Liana said, trying to pick the woman up.

The creature struck, slamming into the deck in another attempt to grab Asphen. He dodged deftly to the side, and the creature's mandibles cut deep gouges into the deck boards as it slammed into the ship hard enough to send the *Bladedancer* tilting. As he dodged to the side, Asphen struck, slicing not at the creature's armor, but at its rows of legs.

There was a spray of green blood, and Sylus saw several legs go sailing into the darkness. If the loss of a few legs bothered the creature, it showed no sign. Instead of rearing up again, it swept its entire body sideways, legs working furiously to scuttle sideways in a broad sweep toward Asphen, using its head as a mace.

Sylus heard a clattering and saw his sword sliding across the deck toward the railing. Struck with sudden inspiration, he dived for it, ignoring Liana's calls of surprise. He managed to grab hold of it before it could totter off the edge, scrabbling back to his feet.

"Asphen!" he called, "The sword!"

Asphen did not even look at him, and Sylus did not blame him. The creature was trying its best to crush Asphen, thrashing across the deck as he dodged in a series of dives and deft movements. In the flickering firelight, however, Sylus could see that the man was drenched in sweat. He couldn't keep this up forever, and for a brief moment, his eyes locked onto Sylus.

"Throw it to me!" Asphen called.

"Sylus!" Liana called, "Help me!"

She was still trying to drag the woman to safety.

All of this shouting seemed to draw the creature's attention. It had been crawling across the deck toward Asphen, but now it turned, one set of eyes focusing on Liana and Sylus. This turned out to be a mistake.

Asphen charged forward and struck, not with his swords, but with a kick. His Thaumatech-enhanced leg drove into the side of the creature's head. The Leviapede was thrown backwards with surprising force, its head slamming into the wall with a mighty crack.

"Throw it to me!" Asphen called, motioning to Sylus.

Sylus drew back his arm, and the creature, furious, crawled up the wall and launched itself at Asphen. Asphen dodged, but did not see the body section of the gigantic creature rising behind him, independent from the movement of the head.

"Look out!" Sylus called, too late. The creature slammed into Asphen from behind, tossing him like a toy. He sailed across the deck and slammed into the same wall he'd kicked the monster into with a sickening crunch, where he fell and lay still.

The creature writhed, mandibles clacking, and advanced on his unconscious form.

"Asphen!" Sylus called.

Without thinking, he drew his sword and engaged the trigger, the blade becoming a blur as it vibrated. Perhaps it could hear the vibration, for several of the glowing green orbs turned in his direction, and the creature changed direction, rearing up to loom over Sylus and Liana.

There was a strange sort of intelligence to the insect. It swung its head left to right, mandibles clacking, as it peered down at Sylus as if trying to assess this new threat.

Sylus began to sweat profusely as the creature hovered, and he let his gaze drift to Liana. She was huddled over the woman she'd been trying to save, apparently trying to stay relatively still. She was looking at Sylus with a desperate expression on her face.

Sylus licked his lips. He was no fighter, at least not yet. But with Asphen down, he knew there was no one left on the *Bladedancer* who stood a chance against the Leviapede. If he fought the creature, he would surely die, but if the creature took the ship down, he would die anyway. So would Liana, Asphen, and everyone else.

The creature seemed wary of the blade, but began to sink closer toward him. Its body writhed left and right, searching, watching him, probing the defenses of this new challenge to its supremacy.

Without warning, it struck, head lancing down toward him. Sylus got one look at the mandibles opening, revealing that inner mouth, and dove without thinking. He felt the creature pass over his legs, smashing through the railing with the sound of splintering wood.

Sylus scrabbled away, his Thaumatech sword leaving deep cuts in the deck. His mind was unable to form coherent thoughts. He crawled toward Liana, who pushed herself up and ran to him, helping him to his feet.

She looked into his eyes as the creature reared itself back up. It was fast, but it needed time to recover after striking.

"Together," she said, nodding. "I think I can stun it. Cover your eyes, okay?"

He nodded, and they turned to see the creature turning back toward them. It opened its mandibles, and the splintered remnants of the railing clattered to the deck. It reared back, ready to strike.

"Now!" Liana said, holding up her arm, "Flash!"

Sylus closed his eyes just in time. He felt pulled toward Liana, pulled toward something far away, and white light burned his eyes even through his eyelids. There was a screech of surprise and pain from the creature.

Sylus opened his eyes as the monster thrashed on the deck, its head smashing into the wall and the air tank supports as if it were blind. The filaments on its head flicked wildly in every direction, trying to find them.

Sylus moved. He ran forward, screaming, and the creature paused mid-trash, as if hearing him, but it was too late. He dodged under a whipping antenna and slashed the vibrating sword across the Leviapede's body, not bothering to aim. The sword cut easily, sending burning blood spraying across the deck, passing through a leg and sinking deeply into the creature's carapace.

The Leviapede convulsed, its entire body thrashing violently. Hot, green blood poured from where Sylus's blade was stuck. The creature's thrashing pulled Sylus into the air, threatening to rip his arm from the socket. In surprise, Sylus released his iron grip on the hilt and fell back onto the deck as the monster screeched.

There was nothing he and Liana could do except back away, dragging the woman's body with them, as the creature rampaged, bellowing in pain.

Slowly, it calmed, its head coiling down to where Sylus's blade was stuck in its body, no longer vibrating. It hissed at the wound, and then, horrifyingly, it moved its head forward and grabbed the blade with its mandibles, pulling it free with a horrible sucking sound. The irritating weapon removed, it dropped the sword on the deck, where it clattered uselessly onto the deck boards, coated in green blood. With the crack of one of its legs, the creature sent the sword clattering away. Its many eyes focused on where Sylus and Liana stood.

"Get behind me," Sylus said, putting himself between Liana and the Leviapede as it lowered its head slowly toward him. It swung its head one way and then another, as if shielding one eye at a time from any more tricks.

Sylus watched as the creature's head approached. It was cautious, intelligent, watching, knowing. Sylus knew then that he was going to die. He felt Liana's hand on his arm.

"I'm sorry," he said, eyes burning.

The creature lowered itself to their level, its eyes level with them. It was close enough for Sylus to notice that Asphen had cracked the carapace on the side of its head with his kick. The rolling green orbs assessed, then the creature opened its mandibles wide, reaching toward them.

Sylus did the only thing he could.

He raised his hand.

"Sp-Spark," he mumbled. Two small spikes slid out from his palm as the inner mouth approached, but this felt different; instead of feeling a pull toward something far away, he felt something flood into him. Energy suddenly built up in his metal hand and then released.

A pathetically small, blue, arcing light jumped from his extended hand, straight into the creature's mouth.

The creature convulsed, its many thousands of legs jerking violently in all directions. It reared backwards, spasming so violently, smashing so hard into the walls and air tank supports, that Sylus was certain the ship would come apart from the rampage. The entire creature's body shuddered, its eyes rolled and trained on Sylus and Liana, mandibles snapping a warning, and it emitted an ear-piercing screech, forcing them to cover their ears with their hands. Suddenly, the creature's legs started scuttling backwards, retracting the Leviapede's body away from them as it hissed warily.

Its speed increased as the many legs clinging worked overtime to untangle itself from the ship. Sylus did not dare to move, lest the creature change its mind. They stared as the head disappeared toward the front of the bladeship, only to reappear, still retreating, still watching them, over the deck once more, then under the deck and out of sight.

There was one last view of the creature's head, and then the stars began to move as the ship, free from its living anchor, began to rise into the night sky.

There was a stunned moment of silence, which was broken when Liana, her hand still clasped tightly on his arm, said, quite clearly and quite loudly.

"Blades below... Sylus, you did it."

She spun him around, her beaming face covered in red and green blood, and shook him so hard his teeth rattled.

"SYLUS, YOU FUCKING DID IT!"

Sylus felt his knees give way, and he slumped to the ground, nearly pulling Liana down with him. All of the fear and stress bubbled to the surface, and Sylus did the only thing you can do when you survive certain death by sheer dumb luck: he started laughing.

26

Voices of Praise

It took some time for the laughter to stop, and as Sylus wiped the tears from his eyes, he realized others were joining them on the deck. Cautious faces of crew members appeared around corners, and out of the doorways leading to the interior of the *Bladedancer.* After a moment, they ventured out, their faces a mixture of relief and disbelief.

"People are hurt," Liana said, wiping her eyes.

They'd slid down to the deck, holding each other as they'd sobbed and laughed, even though small fires burned on the deck. Now Liana let Sylus go, and he nodded regretfully as reality began to set back in. The laughter was a release, but the ship was still in danger.

"Asphen," Sylus said suddenly, his eyes falling on the unconscious man.

Liana was busy checking on the woman they'd worked so hard to save, so he stumbled over, his legs still shaking, and held a hand to the man's neck to feel for a pulse. It took a few seconds to find it, but he did. Asphen was alive, but for how long remained to be seen.

"How is he?" Liana's voice said, and she knelt beside him.

"Alive," Sylus said.

He was not a doctor. Liana had more experience, and she carefully checked his head and face for serious injuries, careful not to move his head from where it lay. Sylus realized with morbid horror that she was making sure the man was not going to become Reclaimed from his injuries.

Men and women were gathering around them now, staring, and Sylus saw Virel, Ruse, and Cally in the crowd.

"Uhm, Liana?" he said, feeling nervous, and she turned to see the crowd hovering near them, as if waiting for something. Her face grew serious.

"They are making sure we don't turn," she whispered. Then, more loudly, to the crowd, she said, "We're fine. No serious injuries. Sylus drove the creature off."

Sylus winced. He doubted he was the reason the monster retreated. To him, it looked like the Leviapede decided the *Bladedancer* was no longer worth the effort and moved on to easier prey.

The entire crowd started whispering, repeating Liana's words through the crowd. Suddenly, the crew gave way, and the Captain pushed his way through, yelling for people to move out of his way until he stepped into the wide circle that surrounded the three Thaumatechne.

He had his sword out, and his face was a thundercloud. He had a long gash and a deep bruise forming above his right eye, but the blood that seeped from his face into his beard looked to be drying.

On his heels were Holven and Valera. Holven seemed to have no injuries nor expression, and surveyed the scene calmly, taking in the three on the ground with a measuring gaze. Valera immediately shouldered past the Captain before he could even open his mouth to speak.

"I'll be the judge of your injuries, if you don't mind," she said in a sharp voice, but her face was painted with concern as she knelt beside Asphen and began performing a thorough inspection.

The Captain eyed them all with a dark look that lingered on Sylus before turning to Valera.

"How is he?" he asked.

"There's no immediate danger, but Liana should probably heal him."

"Liana can barely stand," Sylus said before he could stop himself, causing all eyes to swivel to him.

He wanted to wither under their combined glares, but he forced himself to remain defiant, meeting the Captain's eyes.

"I'm fine," Liana said, pushing to her feet, "Captain, there are people who need me."

"None of you is going anywhere. Not until we can be sure. Inspection, immediately. When you be cleared, come to my office. I want to know what happened, and I want to know it yesterday."

Inspection? Now? Sylus knew they were dangerous if injured, but this was ridiculous. He opened his mouth angrily, but Liana laid a hand on his shoulder, and he stopped, turning to meet her steady gaze. She nodded reassuringly.

"Of course, Captain," she said.

Sylus clamped his mouth shut and allowed himself to stew, focusing on the feeling of Liana's hand on his shoulder as he turned back to the Captain and nodded curtly.

The Captain watched this exchange with a strange look on his face. It was dark, but not angry. If anything, the Captain suddenly looked simply tired. Then he caught sight of one of the fires, and his face became stern yet again. He turned on his heel and began yelling at the crew and pushing through the crowd.

"What are you all staring at? Somebody get Asphen to the medical bay, and the rest of you, do you no see the fires? Get those flames under control! Virel! Where be Virel? Get me a damage report! And for the sake of Verdalis, will someone tell those mudstompers on the tank crew to get our height under control before we breach the blades-damned clouds!"

The Captain's further commands were drowned out as the crew sprang to action, hurrying off to get the ship under control. More than a few lingered, still whispering and staring at him and Liana. Holven, surprisingly, was one of these, watching them with that expressionless face.

Sylus sighed and moved out of the way as two men with a stretcher stepped forward to gather Asphen. Once he was gone, Valera turned her attention to Liana and Sylus.

"You two come with me," she said.

Sylus nodded to Liana and moved to follow, but was stopped by Holven. The man laid a hand on Sylus's shoulder to stop him as he passed, and what remained of the crowd grew quiet.

Sylus looked up at the older man defiantly, not sure what to expect.

"Is what Liana said true? Did you drive it off?"

A part of him wanted to accept Liana's words. He'd been looking for a chance to do what no other crew member could, and this was it. The seconds ticked by, and Sylus found that he could not. He shook his head.

"Liana did just as much as I did, but I have no idea why it left. We just got lucky," he said.

Holven considered for a moment, then nodded, and drew out something he'd been holding behind his back. It was Sylus's sword, though the sheath was missing. Sylus was certain both went over the edge, but the sword survived at least. The blade was covered in thick green blood. Holven held it out to him.

"This is yours, I believe."

Stunned, Sylus took the sword from Holven. Holven, in turn, nodded.

"Good work, Sylus," he said.

The crew looked on for a moment, then erupted in cheers. Sylus was stunned by the sudden noise as his shipmates whooped and hollered. Some men reached out to clap him on the back, while others merely gave him thankful nods. Sylus could only look on, frozen by the unexpected reaction.

Valera pushed her back through the cheering crew members and grabbed Sylus's hand, pulling him through the crowd as the crew shouted words of thanks.

Sylus had a hard time recovering from this outburst of emotion. He was sure that people hated him. He found himself still stunned a few minutes later, as Valera pushed him and Liana into separate showers in the medical bay.

Sylus washed himself in a daze, and when he was finished, did not even protest as Valera swept in and demanded he remove his towel so she could inspect him.

"You don't seem to be injured at all," Valera said, as she circled him, scribbling on her clipboard, "Nothing serious anyway. Superficial injuries and bruises."

She came to a rest in front of him, her face a mask of genuine concern,

"I am not a religious person, Sylus, but if this isn't a miracle, nothing is."

"We got lucky," Sylus repeated.

"Lucky? Lucky? Leviapedes are ship killers, Sylus, and they're smart. They leave the air tanks intact so they can eat the crew one by one. If the ship goes down, it loses its prey, you see. As it is..." Sylus watched the woman's face fall, and realized that what Liana said was true.

Valera was stern, but she genuinely cared about every single person on the ship.

"How many?" he asked solemnly.

Valera looked away for a moment.

"Too many," she said.

When she turned back, her clear eyes were red-rimmed.

"Six people. Three lost to the blades, and three to the Leviapede."

"I'm sorry," Sylus said, and reached up to awkwardly pat the doctor on the shoulder.

"It would have been more, if not for you and Liana," she said. She stared at the hand on her shoulder and raised an eyebrow. Sylus hurriedly removed it, feeling awkward. She continued as if nothing had happened.

"Did you use Wonders? Do you know any?"

"Yes," Sylus said reluctantly.

Valera stepped forward and took up his metal hand, examining it closely. Then she pulled a small metal device from her pocket. It resembled one of the tools Cally used to mark distance on a map. Valera put it down and drew out a notebook, then placed that back down and placed the tool on his wrist, on top of the metal.

"What are you doing?" he asked, as she adjusted the other arm of the device to the place where metal became skin.

"Measuring how much damage you've done to yourself," she said softly, shaking her head, "Every time you cast a Wonder, you weaken yourself."

"Liana says energy for Wonders comes from the Source," Sylus said, voicing a sudden thought, "Why does it allow the infection to spread?"

"The energy may come from the Source, but casting a wonder still puts strain on your body. The strain lets the infection spread."

She looked him in the eye.

"Using them will kill you faster, Sylus, but if you hadn't, I guess we'd all be dead."

She turned her attention back to her measurements. Sylus looked away. He did not want to know.

"Well, whatever you did, it did not seem to affect you much. There isn't much growth. Maybe a centimeter, maybe less," Valera said, sighing, and making a note in her book. "You are lucky."

"Does that mean I can get dressed?"

"Oh, yes, of course. You're clear to go. Don't forget, straight to the Captain."

"Do you know what he wants?" Sylus asked nervously.

Valera shrugged, "I long ago gave up trying to understand that man. You'd better hurry, though, Liana has already gone ahead."

Sylus hesitated, halfway to reaching for his clothes. He thought of the massive flash and the fireball Liana cast.

"How is she?" he asked carefully, trying to seem casual as he began to pull his undergarments on.

Valera raised an eyebrow at him, "You know I cannot tell you that. It is her business. If she wants to tell you, she will."

"Right," Sylus said.

Valera studied him, tapping a finger on her chin.

"I would not get overly attached, Sylus. You've already lost so much, I would not want to see you lose more."

With that, she swept from the stall, leaving him gaping at her back. Did that mean Liana did not have much time left? Or was it the same warning he'd received from the Captain?

Sylus did not know how much time Liana had left. It did not seem like the type of question you asked someone, and the only way to find out would be to see her naked. He colored at that, and tried to focus on putting on the rest of his clothes before hurrying to the Captain's office. He was suddenly aware that Liana had been naked only a few feet from him.

Sylus did not see anyone while making his way there, but he could hear people rushing around on the decks above. A quick look out of the window told him they'd lowered the ship's cruising altitude, though not back to the surface of the blades. Eventually, they would need to; the air tanks could not sustain that kind of lift indefinitely, even with Thaumatech providing a near-infinite supply of helium.

He knocked on the Captain's door, and it opened to reveal Liana on her way out. She was no longer covered in blood, but her hair was still wet. It glistened in the lights of the Captain's office. She smiled at him, tucking her hair behind her ear.

"Good luck," she whispered.

He let her pass, then moved inside and closed the door. The Captain was sitting at his desk, head in one of his hands as he held a sheet of paper with the other. An open bottle of purple grasswine sat on the desk, with an empty cup beside it.

Not knowing what else to do, Sylus took the chair in front of the Captain.

"Eleven sails," his uncle said suddenly, reading from the page, "Two dented support struts, twenty-four windows shattered, fire damage to all three decks, and more holes in the ship than I do care to count."

"And six dead," Sylus added grimly.

The Captain met his eyes. A fire burned in them, but it was not one of anger, or at least, not anger at Sylus.

"Aye, and six dead. May Verdalis shelter them in her eternal green grace."

He put down the page and let out a deep sigh, weariness melting the hard edges from his face. He ran a hand down his face and threw his beard, focusing on Sylus.

"That creature tore my ship to pieces, killed my people, and nearly pulled us down into the blades, and yet you walk away unharmed. How?"

"How, sir?"

"We were losing. Nothing could hurt it. It took down Asphen. So, tell me what happened. I want to know everything."

"I don't think I know," Sylus said, earning himself a raised eyebrow.

So Sylus started from the beginning, without embellishment, telling the Captain how he'd noticed the Leviapede while out on the deck and rang the alarm bell. How the creature rose from the Green and attacked the ship, and how he was too afraid to do anything for fear of being injured. He described how it defeated Asphen and how he and Liana together made one last desperate attempt to defend their own lives, which had not worked. He finished with his casting of the Wonder and the creature's seemingly meaningless retreat.

"I don't think it was any one thing I did, Captain. We hurt it, sure, and the Wonder certainly seemed to scare it, but it doubt it did any real damage. I honestly don't know why it left. If I'd given Asphen the sword the moment I saw him, instead of waiting, he could have killed it. He's a warrior, I'm not. I'm a coward."

He finished and thumped back onto his chair, the words he'd been silently thinking all night finally out in the open. That was why the crew's reaction bothered him. He didn't deserve it. Six people were dead because he was a coward. The sword was the only thing that hurt the thing, and he'd done nothing useful with it. If he had acted sooner, maybe some of them would still be alive.

The Captain leaned back in his chair, studying Sylus with a shrewd look.

"You be many things, lad, but I no think a coward be one of them."

He opened a drawer on his desk and pulled out another glass. He picked up the bottle of grasswine and poured out two glasses, offering one to Sylus.

Stunned, Sylus took it.

"But, if I had acted sooner, if I hadn't been so scared..."

"I do believe I told you when you asked to join the crew, that the Green had a thousand things that would kill you as soon as look at you?"

Sylus nodded.

"Well, a Leviapede is one of the bigger ones, and not even the meanest. Pray to Verdalis that we never run into a Hydrantis. The point is," he said, sipping his wine, "If being scared was all it took to make a coward, everyone would be one. Blades, I nearly soiled myself when I saw that thing crawling across the deck toward me.

You could have run and hidden below deck. You wouldn't have been the only one, and even if you had, I wouldn't call you a coward.

No, you may not have wanted to, you may not have done everything you could, but when that thing looked you in the face, you didn't run. You fought.

I don't know why the beast gave up; maybe you just scared the hell out of it. A shock down the gullet can't be enjoyable. But whatever be the reason, we might all have died if not for you. For that, and on behalf of the crew, I thank you."

He raised his glass toward Sylus and drank deeply.

Numbly, Sylus raised the glass to his lips, feeling a slow warmth blossom in his chest as the liquid filled his belly.

The Captain drained his wine and placed his glass down on the desk, smacking his lips appreciatively. Sylus didn't drain his. He felt like, maybe, just maybe, he had a chance to get back on the crew. He opened his mouth to speak.

"Don't go spoiling it now," the Captain said, and Sylus changed what he was going to say.

"Captain. Sir," he began.

"Ah, sir, again now is it?" The Captain said, bemused, but he gestured for Sylus to go on.

"I just wanted to say that I was truly sorry for what I did at the ruins. I disobeyed your direct order, and beyond that, I put the entire crew at risk. I honestly can't even tell you why. I just wanted to get those weapons for the crew so badly. I wanted to prove myself, but that's no excuse. It was stupid, and selfish, and it cost me everything. I just wanted to tell you that I was sorry."

It was not what Sylus was going to say, but it was true nonetheless. It wasn't the right time to ask to be on the crew again. He was beginning to suspect that Liana was right, and that his plan had no hope of ever succeeding, but his uncle still deserved an apology.

The Captain harrumphed, blowing out his mustache.

"You're a damn fool, Sylus. You be a brave fool, but a fool all the same," he said.

Sylus's spirits dropped, but then the Captain's face softened a moment, and he looked embarrassed.

"Still, I suppose… perhaps I've been too rough with you. You've paid a high price already; there be no need to punish you further."

"Does that mean…?" Sylus said hopefully.

"It means," the Captain said sternly, "That I no throw you over the side of the ship. I don't know what kind of life you might have, given your circumstances, but if you'd like, I can introduce you to the Church. You can stay on the ship until we reach a port where they train your kind, and I'll pay you a small wage for the work you do to help you get on your feet. Not a share of our finds, mind you, a wage.

I know it's not what you wanted, but you'll get to sail the Green, and you'll get to risk your fool neck as often as you please, something you seem determined to do anyways."

Sylus's heart dropped. Of course, the Captain would not know that both Liana and Asphen were already offering to introduce him to the Church, but Sylus could see that the man was offering an olive branch. So he swallowed his disappointment and forced a grateful smile onto his face.

"I'd appreciate that, sir. Thank you," he said.

"Right," the Captain said, suddenly picking up the papers. "I have a ship to run, Sylus."

"Of course, sir. I understand," he said.

Sylus quickly finished the rest of his glass. Purple grasswine wasn't something you wasted. Then he set it down and let himself out, heading back to his room.

As he fell onto his bed, Sylus thought he should feel exhausted, but for the first time in days, he just felt good. It didn't seem like he was going to change the Captain's mind about letting him stay on the ship, but at least his uncle didn't seem to hate him anymore. It was a start. Perhaps things would be easier with the rest of the crew as well.

Then there was Liana.

Sylus closed his eyes and remembered the moment Liana spun him around, shaking him in her excitement to be alive. Even splattered with blood and covered with green monster goo, she was gorgeous. Her eyes had sparkled with excitement, and perhaps, admiration?

A warmth filled his chest, and he was content to daydream for a while, floating in the warmth of the idea that maybe, just maybe, his short life wasn't entirely hopeless.

A sudden headache split across his temples, so strong he sat straight up, clutching at his forehead.

You did well.

Sylus, panicked, looked around the room for the source of a woman's voice. His head felt like it was about to split open. There was no one in the room, and Sylus didn't recognize the voice.

If I see you, she sees you. Seek me out. Seek the Source.

"Where are you? What is this?" Sylus asked the empty room, his panic spiking even as the pain began to fade from his skull.

There was no answer, except for the rising realization that the voice he'd just heard had originated inside his head.

27

The Binary Gods

Sylus awoke the next day disheveled, but not tired. That was surprising since he didn't sleep much. As he showered and readied himself for the day, he tried to tell himself he'd heard the voice due to stress. Nearly being eaten by a gigantic insect was surely a reason to start imagining things, yet he could not believe this to be the case. The voice was too vivid, too real.

Sylus felt haunted as he made his way to the mess hall, jumping at the once familiar noises of the *Bladedancer* as it sailed over the blades, but the voice did not return.

As he walked, he began to notice that the ship was in rough shape. He passed several hastily patched holes in the hull and one shattered window, which had been sealed with a metal cap forged just for such occasions.

With the air tanks intact and the damage to the ship mostly superficial in nature, Sylus found himself wondering if they would continue to the third Rumor. It would have come down to the number of spare sails the *Bladedancer* carried to replace the eleven it lost. Of course, it still possessed enough sails to continue its journey, but its speed would be affected, as would its ability to maneuver, should something else happen, and that might make it too much of a risk.

As Sylus entered the mess hall, he was not sure what to expect. What he received, thankfully, was both less than he feared and more than he expected. Many members of the crew nodded to him as he passed, and several thanked him for defending the ship as he waited in line for his breakfast.

When he got to the front of the line, the cook who was serving him gave a start and ran to fetch Ruse from the back, who appeared a moment later.

"Here he is, the hero of the hour," Ruse said.

Sylus colored and shook his head, "I just did what I had to."

"Had to? Had to? You had to get the hell out of there and try to avoid pissing your pants. That's what you had to do. Do you know we were readying the lifeboat when you drove that thing off? The Captain was about to give the order to abandon ship."

"I didn't," Sylus said, surprised.

Ruse nodded, "So not only did you save the ship, but also my paycheck. And for that, you get a special breakfast."

He snapped behind him at some cooks standing behind him, who handed him a bowl of something green and thick.

"You really didn't have to," Sylus said, feeling embarrassed, but Ruse spoke right over top of him.

"Least I could do. This is my spicy grass stew. It's not exactly a breakfast dish, but it is my specialty. The crew goes wild for this one, but it's a real mess to make. I stayed up all night. It takes about six hours."

"Wow," Sylus said, taking the bowl.

Inside was a thick green stew, filled to the brim with vegetables and floating chunks of meat. The aroma that wafted up to him was fragrant and spicy.

"Well? Go on," Ruse prompted.

Sylus, who'd eaten grass stew before and found it to be a rather plain and cheap dish, dipped a spoon into the steaming bowl and tried a bite. Instantly, his mouth was filled with a hearty spicy flavor that was more flavorful than hot. The vegetables were perfectly tender, and the meat was of the perfect consistency.

"Wow," Sylus said again, "What exactly is in this?"

"Ain't your grandma's grass stew, is it?" Ruse chuckled, clearly pleased. "Wish I could tell you, but I'd have to kill you."

"I need to go sit down and eat this," Sylus said honestly.

"Go on then, enjoy. It's only a shame you didn't kill that thing. We'd have eaten like kings!"

"You can eat those things?" Sylus said, gathering up his tray.

"My boy, you can eat anything if you put your mind to it!" Ruse called as he turned back to the kitchen. "And there's more where that came from!"

Sylus hurried to a table, not noticing that some of the crew were motioning for him to sit with them. Instead, he sat at an empty table and dug in, his troubles momentarily forgotten. But as his bowl began to empty, his mind began to fill.

If he was imagining the voice, why would he imagine a need for himself to find the Source? He knew next to nothing about it, except that it was the name given to the energy that fueled Thaumatech and the power of Wonders. Asphen seemed to believe that the Source must be a piece of powerful Thaumatech, and those who sailed the Verdant Sea had long fantasized about finding it. Like all legends, there were a thousand tales surrounding it and the powers it might hold, but they all agreed that it must be a limitless source of energy and immense power.

"Good morning," Liana said brightly, sliding into the seat beside him. "Wow, is that Ruse's spicy grass stew?"

"Yeah," Sylus said, distracted.

"Do you think I could get some?"

"Probably, you helped save the ship as much as I did."

"I'll be right back."

She left the table, and Sylus stirred the remainder of his stew absentmindedly, his thoughts trying to dredge up everything he knew about the Source. He'd never paid the legends much mind. The power for Thaumatech came from somewhere; that much was clear. Nothing came from nothing. But why would he be imagining a reason to seek it out?

Liana sat back down with a steaming bowl of stew a few minutes later, digging in hungrily, talking to Sylus between bites.

"Asphen is going to be okay. He had some broken bones and some bruises. He should be healed in a couple of days. I heard he's awake, though, if you wanted to see him."

"That's good," Sylus said, still distracted.

Liana eyed him sideways, "You seem quiet this morning, considering the entire crew seems to be talking like you're some hero. I thought you'd be on top of the world. Is everything alright?"

Sylus considered.

"What do you know about the Source?"

"The Source?" Liana said, "I don't know, as much as anyone from the Church, I guess. Why the sudden interest?"

Sylus hesitated. What was he supposed to say, that he heard a voice in his head? He did not like to lie, and he especially did not want to lie to Liana.

"I'm... thinking of joining the Church," he said.

It was partially true, at least, but it still made him feel guilty, especially when Liana beamed at him, tucking her hair back behind her ear as she leaned in.

"Really? Sylus, that's amazing. Trust me, you won't regret it. I knew you'd come around to seeing the good we can do. What changed your mind?"

"I don't know," Sylus said awkwardly, "I haven't really made a decision yet, but I guess I just want to learn more about the Church. I don't know much about the faith side of things, like the Binary Gods or the Source."

"Hmm. Well, I suppose you could come to one of my sermons in the chapel, but I warn you, they're pretty long."

"You give sermons in the chapel?" he asked.

Liana snorted.

"You make it too easy. I told you, I'm not that kind of priest. I do some of that, but only if people ask me to privately. If you're worried you'll have to stand around giving speeches, don't be. The Church uses human priests for that stuff. We Thaumatechne are far too valuable for such mundane tasks."

Sylus felt like they were getting off topic from what he wanted to talk about, "So, what does the Church say about the Source?"

Liana looked thoughtful as she ate her stew, having a few bites before answering.

"The Source, according to the Church, is where the energy for Thaumatech comes from. They say that when the old world was on the verge of destruction, they prayed for salvation. Verdalis and Therithar heard their prayers, and together they created the Verdant Sea as a means to save our world. Of course, it wasn't quite the Verdant Sea we know today..."

"Wait, they worked together?" Sylus said.

"At first," Liana replied. "Don't interrupt. With disaster averted, the Binary Gods shared the source of their own power with humanity, which is where it gets its name, of course.

The ancient world harnessed the power of the Source, allowing them to create a paradise of technology under the guidance of the Binary Gods, who worked in tandem to preserve the balance between preservation and destruction.

Naturally, humankind abused the power of the Source and warred over its control, throwing the world into ruin. Those who could see the end was coming prayed once again for salvation. It was here that the two gods split. Verdalis believed that, while flawed, humanity was worth saving, whereas Therithar, incensed at the abuse of the Source, decided that humanity itself was the problem and vowed to purge it from this world.

It was Therithar who struck first, corrupting the Verdant Sea, causing it to swallow entire cities, ever-expanding, and driving humanity to the brink of extinction. Verdalis, in turn, slowed the growth of the deadly grasses, giving us time to rebuild.

Unwilling to wait for the slower growth of the Verdant Sea to destroy us, Therithar corrupted the very technology we used to access the Source. He infected it with the Reclamation Virus, meant to return us to the gods by turning us into Reclaimed.

Verdalis shielded us from this new threat and slowed the infection, teaching the infected people how to channel the Source directly through their new bodies.

Verdalis realized the conflict would never end, and used the last of her divine strength to cast Therithar into exile and seal him away from the

Source so he could no longer use it against us. Afterwards, she herself retreated to the heavens to recover, though she still offers guidance and protection to those who will listen. Therithar, they say, whispers in the dark, waiting for the day he will break free and finish the work he started.

That's why they say that this is a time of trial, a test to see how humanity will survive, or if it deserves to. It is the Church's mission above all else to ensure that humanity endures, as Verdalis willed."

"I see," said Sylus, noting that this told him very little about what he wanted to know. "But is the Source a place? Or is it just everywhere? What is it?"

Liana gave him an odd look, as if he wasn't paying attention.

"Some people in the Church believe the Source is a place, or a thing, like Asphen does. Other people believe it's just a story. A story told by flawed people."

"I don't understand, how can people in the Church follow the teachings, but not believe in its mythology?"

"The Church has many Sects. There are even some in the Church who advocate for the total abandonment of Thaumatech. It's possible to believe in a higher power that watches over us and guides us, but not every single story someone tells you about it.

It's a creation myth, a valuable lesson about the dangers of abusing power, and the importance of enduring in the face of adversity. A way to make sense of a harsh world full of dangers we don't understand. That doesn't necessarily mean it's accurate or not true. You have to decide for yourself."

"So when we cast Wonders, and we feel that pull, or that push, from something far away, that's not the Source?"

"Many people believe it to be,"

"What do you believe?"

Liana laughed, "You may have noticed that I am trying very hard not to tell you what I believe. You should form your own opinions, Sylus. Faith isn't about adopting someone's beliefs, it's about finding your path."

"Okay, but I want to know what you believe. Your opinion is important to me."

Liana shot a smile at him and tucked her hair behind her ear.

"I believe that Verdalis watches over us and offers guidance to those who listen. And yes, I believe that the Source is what we feel when Thaumatech or Wonders are used. We are connected to it, and through it, to the Binary Gods."

"Has the Church ever, you know, tried to find it?"

"You are awfully interested in the Source all of a sudden," Liana noted. "What's actually going on here?"

He considered telling her, but she was smiling at him that way she did sometimes, when it seemed like he was the only person in the world, and he could not imagine telling her that he'd heard a voice once. So he shook his head.

"Nothing, it's just interesting, that's all. I've heard a lot of stories about people trying to find it, like it's some big treasure."

"Are these stories from the mysterious Old Galleon you keep mentioning?"

"Yes, actually. He tried to find it himself."

"Is that how his ship ended up on top of a mountain?" She asked, eyebrows raising.

"You know, he was never really clear about that," Sylus said honestly.

"You really must tell me more about this mysterious mountain man. Are you aware that there was a notorious pirate by the name of Galleon who went missing over thirty years ago?"

Sylus laughed, "Old Galleon? A pirate? Trust me, if you met the guy, you'd know how funny that is. Kindest old man you ever met, wouldn't hurt a soul."

"Oh, good. So you understand why the idea of you being a pirate is so funny to me."

He shoved her playfully as she laughed at him.

"You are the worst, you know that?" he said.

"You love me," she said, chuckling.

Sylus felt color rising to his face and hurriedly cleared his throat, casting around for something else to talk about.

"How was your inspection?" he asked in a hurry, realizing he'd never asked. "All good, obviously?"

"Oh, yeah. All good," she said, smiling as she looked down into her stew. "I should get going, though, I still have lots to catalog in storage."

"Oh. Okay," he said, wondering what he was going to do with his day. She stood up to go, then hesitated and looked back at him.

"Are you going to offer to help, or just let me do it all by myself, alone, in a dark room for hours, with no one to pester me with questions?"

"Oh! Would you like some help?"

"I thought you'd never ask," she said, smiling. And he rose to follow her, gathering up his bowl.

Seek the Source.

Sylus nearly dropped the bowl as the voice spoke to him, though it was not as clear as the night before. He wheeled around to see if anyone else had heard it, but no one was reacting. Liana stared at him questioningly.

"Are you coming?"

"Yeah. Sorry."

He tried to put the voice out of his mind.

What was happening to him?

28

Seeking Answers

The next few days might have been the most enjoyable Sylus experienced since joining the crew, were it not for the voice. After an afternoon cataloging Thaumatech with Liana, Sylus returned to his nighttime duties. Though it was becoming clear that the Captain was not going to change his mind about allowing a Thaumatechne to join the crew, Sylus felt awkward lounging around the ship without contributing. If he were going to start a second new life after they made port, he would need the pay that the Captain was offering.

And so Sylus suited up and cleaned the ship, which unfortunately gave him time to think as he scrubbed empty decks, hallways, and bathrooms. The voice did not speak again until late that first night, repeating the same command: *Seek the Source.* Sylus was asleep at the time and sat bolt upright in bed with the unsettling sensation of a disembodied voice speaking within the silence of his empty bedroom.

Afterwards, it would return at seemingly random intervals. Because of this, Sylus found himself increasingly obsessed with learning about the Source and why he was supposed to seek out something that may or may not exist. In his desperation, he even considered that the voice might belong to Verdalis. Liana seemed convinced that Verdalis could speak to people, but Sylus was not even sure he was spiritual, let alone religious. He could not fathom a reason why Verdalis, if she existed, would speak to him, but such was the state of his desperation.

Either way, Liana knew little more of the Source than what she'd told him before, and he did not want to ask too many questions of any one person. Luckily, the rest of the crew seemed to have accepted him again, if not as one of their own, then with the same sort of tolerance they showed Asphen and Liana. With lots of free time on his hands, he tried, without making it seem obvious, to question the people of the crew about what they knew about the Source.

Ruse, a great lover of stories, told him several amusing tales about people who had tried to find it. All of them seemed to end with the person going missing, being eaten, or dying in the attempt. The only thing that Sylus learned from that was that most people seemed to agree that if the Source did exist, it was somewhere in the Uncharted Green.

Virel seemed to share Asphen's opinion that the source was nothing more than an undiscovered Thaumatech device. He was adamant that any such technology would be gargantuan in size and thus easy to find. While interesting, the discussion provided very little of value.

One day, Sylus attempted to visit Asphen but was informed by Valera that he was not accepting visitors. Taking his opportunity to casually ask if she'd read any books about the Source in the ship's small library, Valera replied that she had no interest in such things and shooed him from the medical bay.

Sylus thought about asking Holven, but rejected the idea almost immediately. The man seemed to be exceptionally sharp, and Sylus did not want anyone to connect the dots about what he was doing.

The rest of the crew had little to offer, since most were only interested in the very tangible profitability of Thaumatech, and not theoretical questions about where it came from, or if what powered it even existed. To most of the crew, it was a foregone conclusion that it did exist, but in the mythical legend type of way, that was both frustratingly vague and completely useless.

Despite the voice's constant interruptions and the fact that Sylus was getting nowhere with his attempts to understand, it was hard to be concerned about it when he was so happy. He got to work on the ship, sail the Verdant Ocean in search of Thaumatech, and spend nearly all of his free time with Liana, who was beautiful, funny, and intelligent. He tried not to think about how it would all come to an end after they found the final Rumor.

One morning, a few days later, at breakfast, Cally stopped by his table, a bundle of maps under one arm, and her other arm planted on her hip. As usual, a couple of vials of herbs and sands dangled from her neck in small glass vials.

"Yo, hero," she said, "I never got a chance to thank you for saving all of our lives."

Sylus, who immediately remembered that the last time he saw her was in Asphen's bedroom, was not sure how he was supposed to act.

"Oh, hey, Cally. I didn't really, it was me and Liana," he said.

"Don't be modest now. I wanted to thank you, and I thought you might like to come up to the bridge and learn more about navigation."

"Wait, are you serious?" Sylus said, staring up at her. She smiled knowingly.

"Deadly serious."

"And the Captain is okay with it?"

"Well, he doesn't like anyone up there, but I convinced him you earned it."

"Okay, when?"

"Right now, let's go."

Sylus nearly fell out of his chair in his haste to get up, and Cally laughed as she swayed toward the doors. Sylus could not believe it. The perch sat beneath the air tanks, but above the decks. It was only reachable from a Thaumatech lift that ran up the central support pillar. It was where the Captain controlled the ship with a small crew of officers.

Cally led the way, but she kept looking back over her shoulder at Sylus, flipping her hair around.

"You know, I always thought you had something about you, Sylus. A certain, I don't know, daring? I get why you went onto that ship. Who doesn't want to be rich? And then facing down a Leviapede? Are you kidding me? That's impressive. I heard not even Asphen could kill that thing."

"Well, neither did I," Sylus pointed out.

"So modest," she said, chuckling to herself as they approached the lift.

Cally swung open the door with one hand, revealing a small metal cage held aloft in the shaft by a series of thick ropes and guided by metal wheels and rails.

"It's a little cramped, but I'm sure you don't mind?" she said, opening the cage and stepping in.

Sylus gave the lift a doubtful look. It was not designed for more than one person at a time. Cally knowingly smiled at him, tilting her head as if to question what was taking him so long. It was then that Sylus noticed she was wearing what could only be described as her most revealing outfit yet. Short pants bared long, perfect legs, and a sleeveless top that opened generously at the front, revealing enough to make any man's eyes pop.

Sylus's eyes nearly fell out of his head until he got control of himself.

He hesitated, sensing a trap of some kind.

"Hurry up now, Sylus, or I'll begin to think you don't want to," Cally said.

Sylus was only human. He squeezed in opposite Cally, who lounged casually against the small handrail that lined the box. They were forced to intermingle their legs, mostly because she was not standing up straight. She seemed amused as Sylus was forced to step over her to get inside the lift.

Cally closed the door and pressed a button affixed to the inside of the cage. He felt nothing from the button and had to assume the actual mechanism lay high above them. A moment later, the metal cage started to slide up the rails, pulled by the ropes overhead.

"Pretty neat, isn't it?" Cally said.

Her legs were pressed against his. Sylus tried not to notice.

"Yeah, I've never ridden in one before," he said, uncomfortable.

Luckily, the ride was short, and the lift came to a stop at the perch after only a few moments. Cally opened the door to reveal a room smaller than

Sylus had imagined.

There was a series of metal control panels across the front of the room, where the Captain and several others stood. Aside from the wall with the lift, the room was mostly made of windows, offering a complete view of the surroundings. Toward the back of the room were a few desks with slanted surfaces and a board attached to the wall, covered with maps and charts.

Various crew members, whom Sylus recognized as some of the ship's officers, monitored the many gauges and control panels, while the Captain stood at the helm. To Sylus's surprise, he was speaking to Liana, and they both turned toward the door as the lift opened. Cally waved to the Captain and headed toward the navigation desks, and Sylus shuffled sheepishly behind her.

The Captain merely nodded toward them, but Liana gave Sylus a questioning look, which he returned with a shrug as he followed Cally to the map table.

"Here we are, my navigational oasis," she said, spreading out some of the maps she'd brought with her on the largest desk, pinning the corners down with small pins she pulled out of a drawer.

Sylus stared at the various maps with fascination. Cally had shown him localized charts of the area they were in, but here, pinned to the walls and desks, were maps of regions larger than he could imagine, and one that he suspected might be the entire world. Much of it was covered in various shades of green. That was the Verdant Sea, and its known regions were labeled in small, neat text. A large share of the map was also blue, and Sylus, who'd never seen a water ocean, found himself reading the names, trying to imagine a body of water so large that you could not see the other side. He tried to find Altaris or Boughhaven, but couldn't spot them on the vast map.

Cally came up and stood beside him, "Impressive, no? Not much use in navigation, of course, but I like to have it up here. Reminds me how much there is to see in this world."

"What is this?" he said, pointing to the largest green patch in the Verdant

Sea, colored a green so dark it was nearly black. If he had to guess, it covered about a fourth of the map.

"You're kidding. That's the Uncharted Green."

"It's that big?" Sylus said, amazed, and Cally giggled.

"It's cute how little you know about the world," she said, resting a hand on his shoulder lightly, "Come over here, let me show you."

She led him over to the map table and pulled out a chart from a cubbyhole underneath, spreading it out across the table to reveal a map centered on the Verdant Sea, marked out in shades of green.

"We've really only charted about forty percent of the blades," Cally said, pinning the map down.

"I had no idea the Uncharted Green was so big," he said.

"Well, that name is a bit of a misnomer," Cally said.

"What do you mean?"

"Well, the Verdant Sea is constantly spreading outwards, growing taller all the while. Some of what we now call the Uncharted Green was once explored, but as the blades grew taller, the Sea grew deeper. Much of what we knew was lost under the Green.

We call it uncharted, and most of it, to be fair, isn't charted, but really it's just a name to signify the most dangerous parts of the blades."

"And no one is interested in charting it?"

Cally giggled again and sidled closer to him.

"Of course they are, but it's way too dangerous. You think the Leviapede was bad news? There are things in the Uncharted Green that make it look as harmless as a Glimmerbeetle. Not to mention all the Reclaimed."

"The Reclaimed?"

"Oh yeah, tons. You know how, when someone uhm…" her eyes flicked to his hand, and she visibly changed what she was going to say, "You know how some of the Reclaimed wander into the blades? Well, their metal skin helps them survive a walk along the bottom, with the added benefit of slicing them up for conversion. Some, not all, but some, must head toward the Uncharted Green."

"How could we possibly know that?" Sylus asked.

"Well, because there are so many there. It's the only thing that makes sense."

Cally lowered her voice,

"They're not just hanging out in ruins either. They have ships."

"What? Ships?" Sylus said, remembering the halting, shuddering monster that boarded the ship. He could not imagine a crew of the things manning a bladeship.

"It's true. They'd been known to sail out of the Uncharted green to capture ships that stray too close. They convert the crew, then commandeer the ships and sail them back into the Uncharted Green to add to their armada."

"Why would they need ships? Or an armada?"

"Well, to invade the rest of the world and convert us all, of course. People say they're smarter out there, faster."

Sylus felt a chill. Cally seemed to be enjoying herself.

"Look, here's Boughhaven, in the Whispering Shallows," she said, pointing. She traced her finger from there into a different part of the Sea, colored a different green. "Here was the first ruin, and here was the second. Here's where we are now," she said, her fingers tracing a path across the map that led closer and closer to the Uncharted green.

"The next rumor isn't that far off from the Uncharted Green," she said, "Maybe a few days' journey. We should be safe, but..."

Cally looked at him and bit her lip, a worried look on her face. Sylus suddenly realized just how close she was standing. She leaned over the map to whisper into his ear. Her chest hovered just inches above his hand as her lips drew close, and Sylus found himself suddenly paralyzed as he struggled to keep his eyes on the maps.

"I do get scared by the idea of a Reclaimed ship. Sometimes at night, when I'm all alone, I like to..."

"I believe I said you could bring Sylus up here to learn about navigating, not to be filling his head with nonsense and whispering sweet nothings to each other," said the Captain's deep voice from behind them.

Cally was suddenly standing two feet away. Sylus did not see her move.

Liana stood a few feet behind the Captain. She was smiling mischievously, her eyes flicking between Sylus and Cally.

Sylus's face turned beet red.

"Just having a bit of fun with him, Cap," Cally said sheepishly.

Sylus realized she'd been pulling a prank on him again.

"There are no Reclaimed ships?" he said, frowning.

The Captain shot Cally an annoyed look and rolled his eyes.

"Oh, there be sightings of such things in the Green," he admitted, "But they no be sailing out to capture any ships or building no armada. Most likely, they be nothing but ghost ships whose crews were lost to the Reclaimed, adrift on the Green. Anyone who says otherwise be spreading tall tales, and nothing more."

Cally shrugged coyly under the Captain's gaze, but winked at Sylus as soon as the Captain turned back to Sylus.

"What about the number of Reclaimed out there? Is that true?"

The Captain sighed.

"There be more Reclaimed out there because there be no people to drive them off. Now, no more questions about nonsense. And you," he jabbed a finger toward Cally. "I do regret letting you bring him up here in the first place. Don't be filling his head with any more nonsense. And, what did I tell you about the dress code on the bridge?"

"You don't like it?" Cally said, pouting.

The Captain raised a bushy eyebrow, but remarkably, merely shook his head in annoyance and walked back to the helm, grumbling. Liana smirked and wagged a finger at Cally.

"You'll go too far one of these days," she warned, but her eyes sparkled with amusement.

"Nothing is too far for me," Cally said, but she was looking at Sylus.

Sylus tried to ignore her. He caught Liana's eye and gave her a sheepish grin. She rolled her eyes.

"Don't be too rough with him, Cally," Liana said, turning on her heel to rejoin the Captain.

"They're no fun," Cally whispered, suddenly right beside him again. She laid a hand on his shoulder and leaned close to him, "But I can be."

Sylus suddenly regained the use of his free will. He took two big steps away from Cally, who giggled, her eyes sparkling. He could never tell if Cally was teasing him or being serious, and he suddenly found that he didn't care much either way. What he did care about was what Liana thought was going on. Why had she been smiling like that?

"Uhm, where's Altaris?" he asked awkwardly, trying to get Cally to focus on the maps.

She smiled knowingly, but began searching for an appropriate chart to show him. They spent the rest of their time looking over maps, with Sylus asking a lot of questions to keep Cally from flirting with him. He barely absorbed any of her answers.

Sylus's mind struggled with two warring lines of thought. One was the supposed presence of Reclaimed in high numbers in the Uncharted Green. Something about that was bothering him, but he could not figure it out, because the other half of his mind was worried about what Liana was thinking.

Eventually, the Captain called out that Cally had work to do, and Sylus made his way to the lift. Before he left, he snuck a look at Liana and caught her eye. She winked at him.

Sylus left the bridge feeling as if he would never understand women if he had a hundred years.

29

The Voice of God

Sylus spent the rest of the day with a nagging sense that he'd done something wrong, despite all evidence to the contrary. Cally liked to have her fun, but everyone on the ship thought she was harmless, and no one was spared her flirting. The only one immune to her teasing was Ruse. However, some of the things Cally said struck Sylus as forward enough to make his ears burn. It was impossible to deny that Cally was a beautiful woman, and Sylus knew for a fact that she was more than comfortable with Thaumatechne. There was nothing real going on between him and Liana, so why did he feel so bad about being flirted with?

Sylus talked himself in circles like this for a few hours, a little grateful to have something else to worry about besides a disembodied voice telling him to seek out a nebulous legend. So much so that when the voice flared in the afternoon, telling him once again to seek the source, he found it far easier to ignore.

Despite himself, Sylus kept wandering the halls near Liana's room, waiting for her to return, and feeling foolish for doing so. By dinner time, she had not appeared, so Sylus ate with some members of the crew who called him over. He half-listened to them discuss the battle with the Leviapede with enthusiasm, relating their own experiences across the ship. At the same time, Sylus pushed his food around with his fork and scanned the room for a flash of blonde hair that would announce Liana.

After dinner, Sylus convinced himself that Liana was avoiding him and was unable to think of anything else. Feeling a strange urge to explain himself, he made his way back to their shared hallway and hovered outside her door, trying to decide whether or not to knock.

"Sylus?" Liana said from behind him, causing him to jump.

He turned and found her standing there, arms crossed beneath her chest. She was not smiling, though she just snuck up on him again. It was not a good sign, in Sylus's opinion.

"Uh, hey," he said awkwardly, "Can we talk?"

"It's been kind of a long day," Liana said.

"It's important," he insisted.

Liana gave him a considering look, then shrugged.

"Okay, come on in."

She stepped past him and unlocked her door, gesturing for him to follow her inside. He did so, finding a suite very similar to his own, except, of course, the bed was not broken, and the furniture was not rearranged to provide space for training. Sylus, who had never been in her room before, was not surprised to find few belongings. The bed was neat, and the desk uncluttered, and there was not a single item of clothing on the floor. Sylus made a mental note to keep his room cleaner as he took the chair that Liana offered him, then waited as she flopped down on her bed with a sigh, staring at the ceiling.

"Okay, what's up?" she said, not looking at him.

"I wanted to talk to you about..." Sylus began, but found himself not knowing how to continue.

What was he supposed to say? How did he apologize for letting Cally flirt with him without revealing that he was interested in Liana? He was assuming that she cared at all, even though Liana specifically said she wanted to be friends. Though she'd just said that she'd like to be friends, not that she'd *only* like to be friends, which meant that...

"Sylus?" Liana said, pushing herself up on her elbows to look at him. "Talk about what?"

Sylus colored, "Talk about today."

"What about today?" she said.

"Just what happened, and what it meant," Sylus said, floundering.

"You are being so strange lately. I know Cally is gorgeous, but surely she doesn't scramble your wits that much?"

Sylus nearly choked.

"She's annoying," he blurted out.

"You didn't seem annoyed," Liana said casually.

She lay back down and stared at the ceiling.

"I don't think I've seen anyone annoyed by Cally's attention. Are you joking?" she continued.

"Not really," Sylus said honestly. "She's always saying things and making me feel like a fool."

"Well, that's a mistake. She's amazing. And super smart. Her ditsy thing is a bit of an act. I don't know why she does it, but you should give it a try, honestly. I think you two would get along if you got to know her."

Sylus felt himself gaping at her, "I… what?"

"She's clearly into you, Sylus," Liana said. "Did you really need my help to figure that out?"

She started playing with a piece of her hair, holding it up over her head so she could see it, then letting it fall back onto her face.

Sylus started ringing his hands and did not know what to say. Was this a test? If Liana were only interested in friendship, why would she test him? He resolved to find someone to ask about women.

"I think she's just like that," Sylus said carefully, "Besides, she's with Asphen. Or at least, she was."

"Seriously?" Liana said, sitting straight up and looking at him in shock. Sylus cringed; that was not his secret to tell, but it was too late. So he related to Liana what he'd seen in Asphen's room.

"Oh, Cally…" Liana said, leaning her face in her hand. "Poor girl. Still, though, it sounds like she's available now. You could ask her for a drink or maybe go to her room, honestly, she likes guys to be bold."

"I'm not interested in Cally," Sylus said firmly, his face coloring. Liana peered at him, her big blue eyes studying him oddly.

"Why not?" she asked. "Is it cause you're a Thaumatechne? Cally obviously doesn't care if she got with Asphen."

"I'm just not," he said moodily.

"Sylus, I know it can be hard to form meaningful relationships. I gave up on that sort of thing pretty early on, once I realized all the guys my age wouldn't even look at me, but that doesn't mean you shouldn't try."

"She's not my type," he protested again.

He was distracted by the idea that anyone could overlook Liana. Sylus felt overwhelmed and unhappy with the way the conversation was going. Why couldn't he say what he wanted to say?

"You are being so strange," Liana said, sitting up to look at him again.

Sylus was starting to get a little annoyed.

"Why do you keep saying that?"

"Because I spend practically every day with you, and I can tell when you're being strange."

"You're the one being strange," Sylus countered, "You barely even acknowledged me on the bridge today."

"I was busy."

"You're always busy, but you always make time for me anyway."

Sylus felt his face go red under Liana's scrutiny and realized how foolish and childish he sounded. He was floundering, drowning in his inability to talk to women, and there wasn't a life jacket in sight.

Liana's eyes narrowed as she studied him. Sylus felt himself begin to sweat.

"You're hiding something, aren't you?" she said.

"What?" Sylus said, genuinely confused.

Liana suddenly smiled.

"Aha! I don't know what it is, but you've been acting suspicious for the last couple of days. We're supposed to be friends, Sylus. Is it Cally? You already got with her, didn't you!"

She laughed. Sylus sputtered and went beet red. Liana snapped up to a sitting position, leaning forward eagerly.

"Oh my god, you did! Didn't you? She was all over you earlier! Maybe you could be a pirate, you sly dog! Still, I don't see why you felt you had to hide it from me, we're all adults here, Sylus, honestly."

Sylus couldn't handle it anymore. Liana looked far too proud of herself, and his face was so red he felt like he was going to explode.

"I'm not seeing Cally!" he said desperately.

"It's not a big deal, Sylus, you deserve to have some fun."

"I've been hearing voices!" he shouted.

Liana's mouth dropped open mid-sentence, and Sylus snapped his jaw shut. He had not meant to say that, but it just slipped out. It took Liana a few moments to answer.

"Hearing voices?" she said.

"Yes, okay? It started right after the fight with the Leviapede. I keep hearing a voice, clear as day, but it's inside my head."

"All the time?" Liana asked.

"No. Maybe once a day, sometimes more."

Strangely, Liana's expression was one of curiosity, instead of disbelief and judgment.

"What does it say?"

"It keeps telling me to find the Source. I don't know if I'm going crazy, or what, but it just keeps repeating that."

"Is that why you asked me all those sudden questions a few days ago?" Liana said thoughtfully.

"Yes, I've been asking everyone. I don't know what else to do. I don't even know if the Source is real, or if I believe in it. I don't know why I'd suddenly be suggesting to myself to find it. I thought if I knew more about it, the thoughts would stop, or go away, or something."

Sylus realized with a start that a heavy weight seemed to lift from him as he spoke. He had no idea how much stress he was under, and what a relief it was to tell someone. He finally looked up at Liana, who was not staring at him like he was crazy, but strangely smiled and tucked her hair behind her ear.

"Sylus, you're not going crazy," she said softly.

"What do you mean?" he asked, confused.

"It's not abnormal for some Thaumatechne to hear something similar," she said.

She seemed to be searching for words.

"Instructions?" he probed.

"Well, sometimes. It's not like every Thaumatechne hears a voice, but it's not uncommon. It's well documented by the Church, but, for obvious reasons, we don't talk about it."

"Liana, what's happening to me?"

"I suppose that depends on what you believe. Some people hear instructions to do something specific, while others hear vague things. Some people hear things that seem to serve no purpose at all, not all of them pleasant."

Sylus felt cold.

"What is it, though?"

"Is the voice you hear a woman, by any chance?" Liana asked.

"Yes!"

"Well, in that case, some people in the Church believe that what people are hearing is the guidance of Verdalis. Oftentimes, it tells people to do good things. Like go somewhere or do something where they can serve the best purpose in helping others."

"And if the voice was male?" Sylus said.

"Therithar," Liana said, "He gives different instructions. I wouldn't worry too much about that. It's rarely ever been recorded."

"What about those who aren't in the Church?" Sylus asked, starting to feel a strange numbness.

"Well, that depends on who you ask. Doctors assume it's a delusion, of course. Something to do with the way Thaumatech interferes with our brains in its attempts to take over."

"What happens if you don't listen?" Sylus asked.

"What? Nothing, of course. No matter what you believe, the voice is just a voice. I know what I believe, but you have to choose for yourself."

"Have you heard it?" Sylus asked, hopeful.

"No," Liana admitted, and she seemed genuinely disappointed. "I'd like to, though, one day."

Sylus fell silent, considering everything Liana had told him. He didn't like the idea of a god speaking to him directly. Liana pushed herself up from the bed and came over to him, placing her hand on top of his. She forced him to look at her by placing herself directly in front of him.

"Sylus, you're okay," she said softly, "It's very common. If I'm being honest, most people ignore it. It's just another part of being a Thaumatechne."

Despite everything, Sylus could not help but feel better looking into Liana's eyes. It felt as if a weight was lifting off his chest.

"So please stop being so weird," Liana said, her eyes twinkling.

He shoved her playfully, and she fell over laughing. He could not help but laugh alongside her until their laughter died out. She sat up, chuckling, tucking her hair behind her ear, and looked at him oddly, hugging her knees to her chest.

"What is it?"

"Do you think you could tell me what it sounds like? The voice, I mean."

"Oh," Sylus said, taken aback.

"You don't have to," Liana said, her eyes widening. "I know you're freaked out."

"No, I don't mind."

Sylus realized that hearing what she believed to be her god was probably a profoundly moving, possibly even spiritual experience to her. He searched for the right words. Most of the time, the voice sounded commanding. But the first time he'd heard it was different. Aside from the pain, the voice had been soft, gentle. Complementary, even. He remembered thinking, at first, that it might be the voice of his mother.

"She sounded like my mom at first," he said finally. "Gentle. She said I did well against the Leviapede. But since then, it's just been the command to find the Source."

Sylus could not tell how she felt about that. Liana seemed to be looking through him, lost in thought, but after a few moments, she nodded and refocused on him, her eyes sparkling mischievously.

"Are you seriously not interested in Cally? Are you blind?"

"Verdalis, give me strength," Sylus said, shutting his eyes tight in mock despair.

"You should think about it. You deserve to be happy."

Before Sylus could answer, a knock at the door drew both of their eyes. They looked at each other in confusion, then Sylus pulled Liana to her feet so she could answer the door.

To their surprise, Asphen stood outside, shirtless, leaning casually against the door frame.

"I thought you might be here, Sylus," he said.

His eyes flicked between the two of them, a slight smile playing at the corner of his lips.

"Did you forget about our lessons?"

"Right now?" Sylus asked, "Are you sure you're up to it?"

"I'm alive, thanks to you two," he said, nodding to each of them in turn. "And I've never felt better. Let's go."

Sylus looked at Liana. She shrugged.

"I should get some sleep. Go, have fun," she said.

Sylus hesitated. He couldn't shake the feeling that he'd just missed yet another moment to tell Liana how he felt. He'd had so many chances, what was he so afraid of?

Asphen was already walking down the hall. Sylus took one last look at Liana. She smiled at him, and she seemed to be waiting for something.

"Good night then," he said awkwardly.

"Good night."

He followed Asphen down the hall, hurrying to catch up to the man's long strides.

Sylus, preoccupied with his conversation with Liana, did not say anything as they walked down the Hall to Asphen's room, so he was surprised when Asphen spoke suddenly.

"You shouldn't listen to everything she tells you, kid," Asphen said. "I know she's pretty, but she's a deeper believer in all the Binary God stuff than she lets on."

"What?"

"The voice, it's not real."

"You heard?" Sylus said, mortified.

"You shouted it pretty loud. I was outside at the time, and I listened to the rest."

"You were eavesdropping, you mean?"

Asphen shrugged.

"I wanted to know if you guys were going to get it on."

"That's... not cool," Sylus said.

"Whatever. The point is, all that crap is just religious nonsense. We have a disease with the specific purpose of rewriting our flesh and our brain, yet it has to be a miracle when some of us hear voices. Good people hear voices telling them to do good things, and bad people hear voices telling them to do bad things. It's all very convenient. It's not that hard to figure out. We're dying. The brain is grasping at straws. The sooner you accept it, the happier you'll be."

"We?" Sylus said excitedly, "You've heard it too? What does it say to you?"

"It doesn't matter," Asphen said forcefully, "Because it's not real. The gods aren't real, the Source isn't real. There's nothing for you to go out and find. It's just a side effect of the infection, and no one ever died from ignoring it.

You're too smart and too talented to fall for this crap. You stood off with a Leviapede for fuck's sake."

Sylus realized that Asphen, who was unconscious at the time, did not see what happened, and his curiosity about Asphen's experience with the voice was momentarily overshadowed by guilt.

"About that. I don't think I even hurt the thing," he said, but Asphen waved him off.

"Doesn't matter. As soon as we dock somewhere civilized, and word gets out about that... Well, your dreams of being famous might start sooner than you think."

Sylus completely forgot what he was about to say.

"Do you really think so?"

"It's pretty likely, kid. Not too many Leviapedes in this part of the Green. That story is going to take flight. It'll carry you to the top, if you let it."

Sylus didn't know what to say; he considered the fantastic possibilities as Asphen opened his door and led Sylus inside to where they would train, the space in the middle of the room already clear.

"It will carry me too," Asphen added as he passed. "I'd appreciate it if you didn't mention the part about me being knocked unconscious. I have a reputation to uphold, you understand?"

"Of course," Sylus said quickly, "I wouldn't have survived without everything you taught me, Asphen. You did just as much as I did, if not more. I got lucky."

Asphen considered, then nodded.

"Feel free to tell people that part too. But your luck is going to run out one day if you don't know how to fight. That's why we're moving forward with your training. Tonight, we start sparring."

He strode to the side of the room and grabbed two wooden practice swords that were leaning against the wall. He tossed one to Sylus, who caught it out of the air easily.

"Sparring?"

"I can't teach you how to talk to girls, an area you desperately need help in, by the way, but I can teach you this. I'm alive because of you, and I value being alive beyond anything else. This is the least I can do."

Sylus found himself feeling grateful for the exertion; it was the first time he'd relaxed in days.

30

Untethered

Sylus returned to his room in a rare state of exhaustion, covered with bruises that were already in various stages of healing. It was odd, being a Thaumatechne. He worked out, got tired, and recovered within an hour as if he'd taken a whole night's sleep.

Increasingly, he got the impression that he needed less and less sleep every day. Liana and Asphen did not seem to sleep much either, and the idea was both frightening and exciting. He was unsure if he'd stop needing sleep entirely, but he wondered what more he could accomplish in his short life if he could use every day to its fullest.

As he showered, Sylus was happy to notice that his first few weeks of training were beginning to pay off. His arms were growing larger, and his torso was becoming toned. He was moving away from being wiry, with the beginnings of muscles starting to emerge. He was nowhere near Asphen, of course, but with more time? He amused himself with a fantasy of being a man who walked around with his shirt off, while women goggled. He abandoned the image when all the women became different versions of Liana.

Sighing, he left the shower and dried himself off.

Seek the Source.

The voice, absent for the day, sent his happiness spiraling away as he stared at himself in the mirror.

"No," he said to his reflection, "Do you hear me? Verdalis, Therithar, whoever, no!"

There was no reply.

Sylus banished the voice from his mind, resolving not to think about it as much as possible. He was not ready to believe, as Liana did, that the gods were speaking directly to anybody, let alone him. That raised too many theological questions he was not prepared to face. He could not even decide what to do once the *Bladedancer* made port, let alone figure out if gods were real.

Sylus dried his hair and flopped onto his bed, though he felt no desire to sleep. He stared at the ceiling and tried to clear his mind. After a few minutes, he opened his eyes, annoyed. The ship was too loud. The *Bladedancer* always hummed and creaked as it sailed over the Green, but this was different.

Sylus tried to block out other sounds as the hum grew even louder, transitioning into a growing whine. His teeth began to chatter as his bed started to vibrate, sliding slowly across the floor. Things rattled and fell off his desk. The entire ship was shaking! The whine grew louder, and suddenly, with a massive hollow boom, Sylus was thrown from the bed as the bladeship lurched forward with sudden speed.

Sylus tumbled from his bed and rolled across the floor as the ship accelerated, and a roar reverberated through the air. He tried to stand, but the increasing acceleration stopped him halfway, throwing him backwards and pinning him against the wall. The entire ship rattled dangerously, and his furniture followed him into the air, smashing against the wall, narrowly missing him. He felt like he was going to be crushed as he lay spread-eagle across the wall, unable to gather his voice to scream.

Sylus could only guess that the roar was the emergency engines, though what would necessitate such a sudden and violent burst of speed, he could barely imagine. It came to an end with a hollow boom from the back of the ship, followed by the horrible sound of twisting metal. The ship shuddered as the acceleration stopped abruptly, and the roar of the engines began to fade. He could feel the pressure on him decreasing until it finally released him, the roar trickling to a whine, and then to eerie silence as he fell to his knees on the floor of his bedroom, gasping for breath.

It took him a few minutes to gather his wits, and when he tried to stand, he could tell the ship was tilting dangerously to the left, causing him to slide toward the wall as he tried to get to the door. Shouting and the sounds of alarm could be heard from the decks above, but Sylus's thoughts immediately went to Liana. He pushed open his door and ran down the hall, stumbling and sliding across the tilting hallway. Others ran past him in other directions, but he paid them no mind. He threw himself at Liana's door and pulled it open.

"Liana?" he shouted.

The room was empty. Like his, the furniture had smashed against the wall, as if a giant wave had swept through the room, sweeping everything to one side.

Feeling a rising dread, and with no idea what was going on, he abandoned Liana's room. He ran down the hallways, joining the crew members who were heading for the upper decks as alarm bells began to ring along the ship.

"What happened?" he cried to a passing man as they ran for the stairs.

"Emergency engines!" he called, pulling ahead of Sylus and thundering up the stairs.

Why would the emergency engines engage in the middle of the night? Had something attacked the ship?

Sylus followed up the stairs and burst onto the deck. Immediately, he saw that three of the six support pillars for the air tanks were bent and twisted, warped under the stress of the sudden acceleration. The air tank frame was leaning at an odd angle, and Sylus could tell at a glance that at least three air tanks were punctured, the venting gas filling the night with a steady hiss.

The *Bladedancer* was rotating in a wide, aimless circle, and most of the sails were nowhere to be seen. Splintered masts stuck out at odd angles from the ship, and toward the rear, a large column of dark smoke was rising into the night sky, visible against the light of the moons.

The Captain's voice boomed from the upper deck, filling him with relief for his uncle's safety.

"Get those tanks under control before we sink into the Green, you blade-touched idiots! Somebody get Virel up here now! Cally! Put that down and figure out where the fuck we are!"

His commands continued to ring out as Sylus stumbled forward, drawn across the deck to where he spotted a green glow emanating from around a corner. He was forced to grab onto things to haul himself across the deck, fighting the slope of the ship until he forced himself around the corner to find Liana kneeling over a man who was bleeding from the head, the Thaumatech on her forearm bathing the man in a green light.

"Liana! Are you okay?" he called, using the wall to move more easily over to where she knelt.

"I'm fine," she said, focusing on her healing.

"What happened?"

"I don't know. I was in bed when it happened. I was thrown across the room."

"Me too. People are saying it was the emergency engines."

"Why would the emergency engines fire?" Liana said.

The green light faded, and she turned to look at him. She had a large, dark bruise above her right eye, but otherwise looked okay.

"I don't know," he said.

"Here, help me, we can't leave him here."

"He's probably safest against the wall; the ship is tilting."

Liana bit her lip, looked at the man as if trying to decide, then nodded.

"Did you see anyone else hurt?"

"No, but I'm sure there are more. Come on, I'll help."

He offered her his hand and helped pull her to her feet. She looked up at him with wide, red-rimmed eyes, fresh from sleep.

"What's happening, Sylus? It's like..."

But at that moment, Holven hauled himself around the same corner Sylus had, his eyes taking in the scene quickly.

"Good, you're both unharmed. Liana, Valera needs your help. Sylus, I'd understand if you're unwilling, but she may need your help too."

"I'll come. I-I can heal them too," Sylus said, only hesitating slightly.

Holven merely nodded.

"Follow me. I'll have someone bring him below deck. We're setting up a triage in the mess hall."

Holven led them back to the main deck area. While the ship was beginning to tilt dangerously toward the Green on the starboard side, it seemed the crew was working to right the ship. Sylus's eyes flicked upwards to note that air tanks on the higher side were being vented to level out the *Bladedancer* while tank teams worked to repair the leaks. Already, the deck was becoming easier to walk on.

Wounded men and women were being dragged by others toward the stairs that led into the ship. Liana looked aghast.

"Stop dragging them!" she cried.

She ran ahead to stop a man who was trying to pull a woman with a splintered railing jutting out of her side, leaving a wet blood trail. Asphen appeared, and his eyes locked onto Holven.

"Holven! Where are we? What happened?" he demanded, but was shoved out of the way by a cook carrying a man with severe burns visible on his face and arms.

"Help!" the man cried, laying the man down on the deck.

It was Ruse.

Sylus forgot all about Asphen and ran to kneel at the friendly cook's side. His skin was red, raw, and blistering, even tearing open in places.

"What happened?" Holven demanded.

"Found him in the kitchen. He must have been doing late-night cooking. He does that sometimes when he can't sleep. There was a soup pot nearby...
"

Sylus didn't need to be a doctor to see that Ruse was dying. He didn't think. He held out his hand.

"Heal!"

Sylus felt that eerie draw, stronger this time, and energy flowed into him. His hand rearranged, and green light bathed outwards from his palm.

Where the light touched, open wounds began to knit themselves back together.

"Cut his clothes away," Sylus called, and someone complied as he worked.

Sylus watched, wide-eyed, as the raised, fluid-filled blisters drained away, the extended skin becoming smooth as the fluid was absorbed. The red, angry skin cooled and faded to its standard color, and missing skin regrew before his eyes. The worst part was the eyeballs. A fluid Sylus did not want to think about was leaking from Ruse's closed eyes, but it soon retracted itself. Sylus was careful to make sure he checked everywhere for burns to heal.

The entire time, a strange sense of power flowed into him from somewhere distant and out through his palm, taking with it, he knew, minutes, possibly hours, off his lifespan. He didn't care. He understood Liana now. What were minutes or hours compared to the rest of Ruse's life? Sylus's life was already over; why should others share his fate when he had the power to prevent it?

Eventually, Ruse's breathing grew stronger, his eyelids flickered, then opened. Sylus could find nothing else to heal, and let the Wonder blink out, feeling as amazed as the people around him looked.

"Where am I?" Ruse mumbled, then he screamed, sitting up so suddenly that Sylus fell backward.

Ruse was feeling at his face and chest wildly, but when he did not find horrific burns, his eyes landed on Sylus.

"You… did you heal me, lad?" he said quietly, before his eyes rolled back into his head, and he collapsed once more, unconscious.

Sylus moved forward, but Holven pulled him back.

"He's fine, Sylus. Get him below with the others," Holven commanded the bystanders. He dragged Sylus to his feet. "There are others."

Sylus only nodded, determined.

Holven led him to another injured man. Then a woman. For an hour, he worked alongside Liana and Valera, who appeared on the deck, treating those who could be treated with medicine. Holven disappeared, and through it all, the Captain shouted commands, stabilizing the ship, getting those of the crew who could work to patch up the *Bladedancer* as best they could and assess the damage.

Finally, there was no one left to heal. Sylus slumped down as the man in front of him was lifted away, the gash in his thigh completely healed, leaving only blood-soaked pants. He nodded numbly as the man thanked him, feeling oddly tired, in a way he'd never experienced.

Sylus sat back against the nearest wall and rested until Liana appeared and sat next to him.

"Are you okay?" she said, slumping down next to him.

"Yeah," he said.

She was close enough that their legs were touching.

"You did a good thing here today, Sylus," she said. "A lot of people will live because of you."

"I know," he replied, and smiled.

Asphen was standing nearby, leaning on the railing, his face not visible as he stared out into the night. He had not helped heal people. Perhaps he didn't know how, but Sylus got the distinct impression that he didn't want to. The thought left him hollow and a little sick. Liana followed his eyes.

"Some people just don't get it," she whispered.

Sylus didn't answer because he did not know at that moment how he felt. He looked up to Asphen, but did not understand how the man could stand by while others might die around him.

Captain Bracken stomped down the stairs, Virel and Cally leading the way. Many of the crew were milling about on the deck, resting, or otherwise waiting now that the immediate crisis had passed. The Captain would explain. He always did.

Virel and Cally joined the crowd, many of whom stood as the Captain paused at the top of the stairs, and swept his eyes over the assembled crew, a dark look on his face. An eerie silence fell over the crew, with all eager to hear what had happened.

"I will no lie to you," he said, his voice quiet, but carrying easily across the deck, "It be bad. Virel tells me that the emergency engines ignited, burning through all our fuel, before burning themselves out. We be lucky they didn't tear the *Bladedancer* to pieces. The engines are damaged, but Virel thinks he can repair them with time. That be the good news."

Sylus shared a worried look with Liana. What could be worse than that?

"Cally says we're adrift in the Uncharted Green."

Dead silence met this announcement, the kind of silence that stretched until something broke it, and what broke it sent Sylus into a panic.

"What did you do, Sylus?" came Asphen's voice.

It was cold and quiet, but it carried across the deck as easily as the Captain's. Sylus couldn't see the man, as all he could see was Liana's wide-eyed look of utter bewilderment, and the turning heads of the crew.

"What?" Sylus sputtered.

"I said," said Asphen, emerging from the crowd and marching straight up to Sylus, "WHAT DID YOU DO?"

Asphen was on him before Sylus could react. He reached down and grabbed Sylus by the collar, hauling him to his feet and slamming him against the wall, knocking the air out of him. Shouts of alarm rang out from the crowd.

Liana reacted first, trying to grab Asphen, but Asphen shoved her aside without even looking, and she went sprawling to the floor.

"Nothing!" Sylus cried, trying to push the man off of him, until Asphen's sword appeared between them.

Asphen held Sylus off the deck, his feet dangling in the air, with one forearm, while his other hand was holding a sword point to Sylus's neck.

Sylus stopped struggling immediately. Sweat poured from him as he stared down the blade. He barely noticed the crowd frozen around them. The Captain was there, frozen with one hand toward Asphen, about to pull him off. Asphen eyed the crowd without letting Sylus leave his gaze; his eyes were wild and red-rimmed.

"Asphen," the Captain said, his voice low, "What be the meaning of this?"

"He did this," Asphen spat, refocusing on Sylus, "Admit it!"

"I didn't! I have no idea what you're talking about! He's lost his mind!"

"Shut up! All your nonsense about hearing voices, telling you to seek the Source. Thought you'd take us on a little trip? I'm not the one who's lost it."

Sylus felt the blood drain from his face as Asphen's words rang out. He saw glances pass between members of the crew and heard the murmurs that swept the deck. How many of them did he ask about the Source recently? He felt cold as a look of concern passed over the Captain's face.

"I didn't. I wouldn't! I don't know how!" Sylus spluttered.

"You've killed us all, you know that, don't you?" Asphen whispered, yet the sound seemed to sweep across the deck. His eyes were hard and cold.

"YOU'VE KILLED US ALL!"

He raised the blade, but hesitated and glanced to the side. Sylus felt it too, a great pull toward Liana. She was rising to her feet, lines of light shining from her Thaumatech, visible even through her clothing.

"PUSH!" screamed Liana, coming to her feet.

Asphen tried to turn, but was blasted backward by a solid wall of energy as it erupted from Liana. Sylus, already against the wall, felt himself crushed against it as the wave passed over him, but Asphen flew across the deck, landing in a sprawl, and many things happened at once.

Asphen tried to rise to his feet.

"Hold him down! Stop him!" cried the Captain, moving forward quicker than anyone else.

He caught Asphen by the wrists and twisted, trying to get him to drop the sword. Asphen snarled, his grip not even shifting, and threw off the Captain's hands. Asphen took two steps toward Sylus before the rest of the crew joined in. Men and women piled on Asphen, wrestling him to the ground as he tried to fight them off. Eventually, he was overpowered and forced to the ground.

Sylus could only watch from where he'd fallen, too confused and panicked to do anything else. Liana was at his side, helping him to his feet.

"Are you okay?" she asked, checking him for injuries.

Sylus could only nod numbly.

Eventually, heaving with exertion, Asphen stopped struggling.

"Alright!" he cried, "Alright!"

The crew did not let him up. Five men held him down, one holding each limb, with three for his Thaumatech leg, and another physically sitting on his back, all of them looking exhausted and nervous. The Captain collected Asphen's swords, breathing heavily.

"Everyone get a hold of yourselves!" he roared.

Silence fell once more across the deck, and he looked down with a deep frown at Asphen.

"Asphen, Sylus, what in the blades is this about?"

"He didn't do it, Captain," Liana began, but he cut her off.

"I no be asking you, Liana," he said, his voice making it clear she should not interfere.

She fell silent, looking angry, and held onto Sylus's arm, stubbornly glaring at Asphen.

Asphen glared at Sylus with pure hatred.

"He's lost it. I overheard him tonight talking with her," he spat, "Talking about hearing voices, telling him to seek the source. He's been asking all over the ship about it. I'd heard he was asking around about the Source, but I never thought he'd sink this low. He's crazy. Impulsive. We should get rid of him now."

Sylus was shaking his head as the Captain's eyes flickered over to him. He seemed to find his voice at last.

"I was just curious, you absolute psychopath!" he shouted at Asphen, "How the fuck would I sabotage the ship? I don't even fucking know how the engines work!"

"Sylus," the Captain said, turning to him, "Is what he's saying true? You be hearing voices?"

Sylus felt the fire die down as the question brought the ship to silence once again.

"Well, yes. But, so does he! He said as much to me when I told him about it. It's normal, it's…." he turned to Liana, who was looking uncomfortable.

She was not the only one. Many faces in the crowd were now looking at him with suspicion.

"Liana?" he pleaded.

The Captain turned to her.

"It's not something we talk about, but many Thaumatechne hear voices," she said quietly.

Murmurs ran through the crowd, and she raised her voice.

"Many in the Church believe that these voices are the will of Verdalis, guiding us toward greater purpose!"

Sylus winced, even as his heart swelled.

You could tell just from the tone of her voice that she genuinely believed in Verdalis and thought this would help his case. As much as Sylus admired her faith in this moment, he was certain that the crew did not want to hear that he thought he was hearing a god.

"I don't know much about that. I ignore the voice, as many others do! It's just a part of our condition."

Suddenly, Valera was pushing through the crowd.

"Captain, if I may…" she said, continuing when he nodded. "This isn't the first I've heard of this. It's been documented before. It's true, at least, that some Thaumatechne are similarly afflicted."

The Captain nodded, and Valera stepped back, but he still did not look convinced. He sighed, running a hand through his hair, then came to stand in front of Sylus, looking him in the eyes.

"Sylus," he said, in a voice so cold and still that it sent fear running up Sylus's spine.

"I be asking you this once. Did you sabotage my ship?"

"No! Captain, of course not! I would never do that. Why would I? I just risked my life for this ship! I healed people who were hurt! I would never put people in danger just for my…" he died off, for he knew that he had put people in danger for selfish reasons before, and everyone knew it. But still, he shook his head.

"No. Captain, I didn't do this. I was in my room when the engines fired. I probably have bruises all over my back from where I was slammed against the wall. You can check!"

"Oh, for blade's sake," came another voice.

Virel stepped out of the crowd.

"Captain, I talked to Syler once when he wandered into the engine room asking questions."

A suspicious murmuring spread through the crowd, and Sylus groaned. The man could never get his name right.

"Oh, shut up!" Virel called to the crowd. "Captain, this boy may be a good sailor, hell, from what I hear, he may be a great one, but he doesn't know shit about Thaumatech, and certainly he knows less about engines. You barely know how to work the damn thing without me, Captain. You think he figured it out?"

The Captain raised an eyebrow at him, and Virel shuffled his feet as if he had just remembered who he was talking to.

"That's just my thoughts about it, uh, sir," he said, then retreated into the crowd.

The Captain returned his attention to Sylus, his dark eyes switching back and forth between Sylus's as if trying to catch one of them in a lie. Eventually, after an eternal moment, he breathed out.

"I believe you, Sylus," he said, loud enough for everyone to hear.

"Then you're a fool!" Asphen spat, struggling again against those holding him down.

"Take Asphen to his room and lock him in there to cool down," the Captain said, glaring at Asphen. "And Asphen? If anything happens to Sylus, you be going into the blades the very minute I find out. That goes for all of you, you hear? We're going to get to the bottom of what happened, and whoever be responsible, if anyone, will be paying the price. Until then, no one takes action without my order. Do you all understand?"

There were murmurs of assent, but as Sylus surveyed the crowd, he found many pairs of eyes lingering on him; he could tell the crew was not entirely convinced.

"Now get out of my sight. I want damage reports finished by first light, and repairs being made as soon as we get them. If we be getting out of this mess, we're all going to have to work together. I want round-the-clock watches, and I want us hovering as high off the blades as we can safely get! Go! Get to work!"

Bracken stared down the crowd until they began to disperse. They took their time about it, staring around the Captain to shoot furtive glances at Sylus while Liana hovered near him protectively, one hand on his shoulder, glaring back at them all.

The five men holding Asphen eventually hauled him to his feet, and while he no longer struggled, he stared poison at Sylus until he was taken below deck and out of sight.

With a deep sigh, the Captain glanced back at Sylus and Liana.

"It's probably best if you go back to your room. I'll have a watch set on Asphen's room, but lock up just the same."

With that, he thumped off, barking orders at anyone he caught not actively doing something.

"Come on," Liana said, trying to pull Sylus to his feet.

Sylus felt numb. He did not understand why Asphen would suddenly attack him like that, or why anyone would think he would sabotage the ship and strand them in the most dangerous part of the Verdant Sea on purpose.

It took some effort on Liana's part to get him to his feet, but eventually she guided him back to his room.

31

Admission

Sylus followed the Captain's advice and locked the door as soon as Liana was gone, then tried a hot shower to clear his head. It didn't work. He didn't know what to think. Could the emergency engines have fired by accident? The possibility was never mentioned. If it were not an accident, who would sabotage the ship? Surely, no one in their right mind would send them into the Uncharted Green on purpose.

There were more reasons than just the Reclaimed not to come here. As the deepest part of the Verdant Sea, it was also home to its most enormous creatures. Beyond that, great storms were common, and the movement of the grasses was unpredictable. No one who wanted to live sailed into the Uncharted Green willingly, and to be adrift here was a death sentence.

The Captain had put the best spin on it he could, but Sylus felt hopelessness in the way Asphen reacted and the sluggish movements of the crew. Without sails to steer and move the ship, the *Bladedancer* was as good as doomed. Whoever did this had sentenced them all to death. The best they could hope for was to repair the emergency engines and pray the ship drifted out of the Uncharted green.

Sylus stayed in the shower a long time, trying to use the hot water to ward off the sense of dread and defeat that was slowly spreading through him. It was like the universe itself was conspiring to break him down. Every single time he felt like his shortened life wasn't hopeless or that there was some silver lining, disaster struck to remind him that he'd thrown everything away.

He had no idea what time it was when he finally got out of the shower, but it was likely very early in the morning, nearly three or four am, which is why he was surprised to hear a knock on his door as he finished dressing. All of his nerves stood on end, and he dashed for his sword, pulling it free and wheeling to face the door.

"Who is it?" he called, staying as far back from the door as he could manage.

Sylus didn't want to hurt anyone, but if they were going to toss him overboard for something he didn't do, he wasn't going to make it easy on them.

"Sylus?" came Liana's voice through the door.

Relieved, Sylus put down the sword and cracked open the door to find Liana standing there, looking worried. She was alone.

"Liana?" he said, confused.

"Hey. I couldn't sleep," she said.

Sylus nodded, "Me either."

"I don't feel great about you being alone here with everything going on. Could I come in and, I don't know, hang out?"

"Uh... Sure, I guess," Sylus said, feeling awkward.

His room was a disaster. He'd not had time to try and salvage any of the furniture except to push it into the corner and lay his mattress out on the floor with his sheets and blankets, but he appreciated the offer of company. Sylus opened the door all the way, and Liana strolled past him into the room. Sylus quickly closed the door and locked it again.

Liana wandered a bit around the room, seemingly aimlessly, then settled herself cross-legged on his bed.

"It's a mess in here," she noted.

"Yeah, sorry. Haven't really had much time to clean it up," he said, sitting down on the bed a few feet away. Liana played with his blanket, twisting it around her fingers.

"Are you okay?" she asked, not looking at him. "I know Asphen was sort of like a mentor to you."

"I don't know," he said honestly, "I just don't get why he would suddenly think it was me."

"People do strange things when they're scared."

"You think he's scared?" Sylus asked, surprised.

"Aren't you? We're lost in the Uncharted Green. No engines, no sails. It's about as bad as it gets."

"Yeah, but I didn't think anything could scare Asphen."

"I'm not trying to make excuses for him or anything, but the idea that someone would sabotage the ship..."

"It's crazy," Sylus said.

"Yeah."

Liana was still focused on the blanket, twisting it between her fingers absently, but shot a furtive glance his way. She shifted around on the bed, seeming anxious. Sylus suddenly felt cold. There was apprehension in the look she shot him, gone a moment later as she turned her gaze back downward. Sylus suddenly got the impression that maybe she wasn't as convinced as he thought.

Sylus shifted uncomfortably.

"I can't imagine who would do something like that. Like, what would be the point?" he asked, trying to make it clear it wasn't him.

Liana's fidgeting seemed to build, and she pushed herself off the bed in a rush.

"What pisses me off is how anyone suspects it was you," she said, "Why would you risk your life fighting off a Leviapede, then sabotage the ship. It just doesn't make any sense."

She glanced at him quickly, then continued pacing, her voice picking up speed.

"After sabotaging the ship, why would you go out onto the decks and heal people, sacrificing... well, everything! Which, by the way, I'm honestly so proud of you for doing. You sacrifice yourself for them, and they turn on you. Why would you do that?"

Sylus just felt numb. He could feel her leading him toward the inevitable question. She'd defended him on the deck when he was in danger because she was a good person, but she was just as hesitant to believe him as the rest of them. He let his gaze fall to the bed.

"I didn't do it," he muttered.

Liana stopped her pacing. He couldn't see her, but he heard it.

"What?" she asked.

"I didn't sabotage the ship. You don't have to beat around the bush. I understand if you don't believe me."

"Oh, Sylus," she said, then she was there, sitting back down beside him on the bed.

He felt her arm wrap around his waist, and her head lean onto his shoulder.

"I don't think you did it, you idiot," she said softly.

He looked down at her, and she tilted her head to look up at him.

"You don't?"

"Of course not!" she said, sitting up so they were level with each other. "It just pisses me off! I thought the crew was better than this. It's not like Asphen had any evidence it was you, but they were all happy to believe him because then they could blame a Thaumatechne. As if it's a crime to be curious!"

She threw her hands up in the air, and her hair came loose again. She did not seem to notice as she shook her head in disbelief.

"Maybe the engines just blew up. Or maybe it was someone else. No one even mentioned another option."

Sylus appreciated the support, but he knew it had little to do with him being a Thaumatechne.

"I get it. I mean, it doesn't look good for me," Sylus admitted.

"Sylus, you would never do something like this. You would never be so selfish!" she said, real heat entering her voice.

"You might be a little impulsive, and I know you don't really think much of yourself at times, but I've seen you risk your life for others multiple times with barely a second thought. You don't have it in you to hurt other people, Sylus. That's why you'd make such a terrible pirate."

She smiled at him, a dazzling, beautiful smile, encouraging him to join in on the joke. He wanted to listen to her encouragement. He wished he could accept the warmth and kindness she was offering, but there was still a creeping numbness threatening to re-swallow him at any moment.

"I've done a lot of things I regret," he said.

She smiled and took one of his hands in her own.

"We all have, dummy. But you've done a lot of wonderful things, too. Don't let your mistakes outshine the good you've done."

They stared at each other, and Sylus felt an unbearable heat building in his chest. He could feel his heartbeat thundering in his chest, his blood pumping in his ears, and he felt a sudden, overwhelming desire to kiss Liana. He, of course, froze completely instead.

Liana was smiling at him, and her hair was falling across her face. She seemed to be closer than she was a moment ago. She tucked her hair behind her ear absently, without breaking eye contact with him. Her face was only inches from his own.

"I truly think you're meant for great things in this world, Sylus," she whispered.

Then *she* was kissing *him*.

One moment they were apart, the next she reached out with both hands to pull his head down to hers. Their lips met, parted, and met again as she kissed him with a sudden passion, hungry and fiery. Her hands twisted in his hair, and all Sylus could do was try to keep up or be swept away. He had no idea what he was doing.

Sylus went to wrap his hands around her waist, wanting to pull her closer, and she let go, pulling away, looking both shocked and mortified. Her face was turning red, and her eyes widened with panic as she retreated across the bed. Sylus was left with his hands hanging awkwardly in the air, the heat in his chest roaring for more.

"Fuck. Sylus. I'm so sorry. I shouldn't have... that's just... so inappropriate of me. I'm so sorry."

"It's okay," Sylus stammered, more confused than he'd ever been in his life.

"No," she said, a little out of breath.

Her eyes flicked to his and away again as she became even redder than before.

"It's not okay, I shouldn't have done that. It's not a good idea. I just let my feelings get away from me for a minute. It was stupid... it was..."

Her feelings? Sylus didn't hear anything else she said, because the warmth in his chest erupted into an inferno, filling him with a sudden confidence. Words rose in his throat and escaped before he knew what he was doing.

"I like you, Liana. I have for a while now. I want this," he said, probably a little too loudly.

Liana seemed frozen, her brilliant blue eyes locked to his. For the barest moment, she smiled. Then the smile fell away, and she shook her head.

"No, you don't," she said.

"Yes, I do."

"Well, you shouldn't," she said, looking away. Her voice grew quiet. "You deserve someone with more to give you."

"I don't care. I don't want anyone else. I want to be with you," he said.

He moved right next to her and reached for her hand. He placed his hand over hers, and she turned back to look at him. Her eyes were red-rimmed, though she smiled softly.

"Sylus, I don't have that much time left. Hardly any at all. In a few months, maybe a bit more, I'll be..."

"I don't care," he repeated, then he leaned forward and kissed her.

Liana kissed him back, but pulled away once more, their lips only inches apart, to stare into his eyes. Her eyes, on the verge of tears, looked deeply into his own.

Then her arms wrapped around his neck, and Liana was kissing him so furiously and holding him so tightly that Sylus could barely breathe. She pulled him toward her, and they fell backwards onto the bed, with Sylus on top, their legs awkwardly tangled until the natural rhythm of their kissing entwined their bodies.

They took desperate deep gasps of air in the seconds their lips were apart, the blazing heat in his chest combining with the growing inferno that rose from Liana as they pressed together. An entirely new type of heat built, one that wiped away rational thought, fear, and nervousness in a wave of passion.

Liana rolled him over and straddled him, leaning forward to continue kissing him as her hands tore at his shirt, pulling it over his head in a flurry.

They rolled again, and Sylus was kissing her neck, Liana's breath hot and heavy in his ear as his hands roamed her body, undoing buttons and slipping between the folds of her clothing.

In moments, their clothing fell away, though Sylus could not say how. He drank in the sight of her with nothing between them. Liana's eyes met his own with a strange mixture of shyness and ferocity. Then she wrapped her arms around his neck once more and pulled him on top of her, their bodies melting together for the first time.

That was the last thing Sylus remembered before all rational thought fled him for some time.

32

Fate

Sometime much later, Sylus regained his senses. Liana lay asleep in his arms, her body snuggled close to his. One of his hands was clasped tightly within her own, although she breathed in and out with the soft rhythms of deep sleep.

Sylus was not asleep. He could not sleep, for he was so enraptured with Liana and the sudden fulfillment of his innermost desires that he would spend the rest of the night staring at her. He traced his fingers lightly across her body, fixating on the places where metal met skin. In her nakedness, he could see that the infection traveled from where he'd always known it on her forearm, claiming her entire arm to the shoulder, and traveling back down her side from under her arm, wrapping underneath her left breast and working its way down her side toward her thigh. This path of the infection did not concern him, for while it was extensive, in many ways it was much better than those above. He ran his fingers lightly across the nape of her neck, where thin lines of metal were beginning to reach upwards, like small metal fingers of death, on their relentless path toward her brain and the end of her life.

Liana's admission that she didn't have much time left was easier to accept than seeing it with his own eyes. He meant what he said about not caring and about spending whatever time they had left together, but now that rational thought had returned, he could not help but stare mournfully at those metal fingers.

Sylus hated how they seemed to be reaching up to steal something that was quite instantly more precious to him than any amount of fame or fortune. He realized, with sudden alacrity, that he'd found the one thing he wanted more than his dreams, and like his dreams, it too was doomed. Even if they could somehow escape the Uncharted Green alive, he and Liana were both fated to die, and nothing could change that.

Seek the Source.

The command, for once, was easy to ignore. Sylus was far too busy wondering how it was possible to feel so happy while being filled with despair at the same time. He clasped Liana's hand tightly, never wanting to let go.

III

The Source

33

A Ship Adrift

Sylus was nervous when Liana woke up, afraid that she might say that the night before was a mistake and reiterate that they shouldn't be together. Instead, Liana merely turned to him and smiled, blinking away sleep and whispering good morning before kissing him. That led to more kissing, just as deeply as the night before, with the same result, her need outmatching even his own.

Eventually, however, to stay in bed any longer during a life-or-death situation would arouse suspicion. They showered together, which took admittedly longer than showering separately, playing and giggling as if the ship weren't adrift in the most deadly part of the grass sea.

It was a surreal experience to bathe in momentary happiness among a disaster. Neither of them wanted it to end, knowing that eventually they would have to talk about things, but wishing to delay that moment as long as possible.

Liana was trying to find her clothes, wandering the room in nothing but a towel, shooting him furtive glances and small smiles.

"This is ridiculous," she muttered, finding her underwear, which somehow ended up behind the desk.

"Don't look at me," Sylus said, unabashedly watching her, "I'm not the one who threw them across the room."

She shot him a dirty look, which barely hid her smile as she tucked her hair behind her ear, then turned to stare at him.

"Well? Turn around!" she demanded.

"Are you being serious?" Sylus asked, amused.

He reached for her towel, but she darted out of his reach.

"Stop!" she teased, "Seriously, it's already late. I'm supposed to be on the bridge. Turn around!"

"I don't think regular schedules are being kept right now," Sylus said.

He held his hands up in mock surrender and turned around under her warning stare. He heard the towel drop and immediately peeked, enjoying the shape of her body as she pulled on her clothes.

"That's not the point! If we show up around the same time, people are going to realize."

"Is that so bad? I'm pretty sure everybody already knew I was into you," Sylus said.

"I didn't!" she protested.

"I don't see how," Sylus said.

"Hey! I don't have a ton of experience with this, and boys are confusing."

She checked her outfit in the mirror and turned to him, finding him only half dressed.

"Sylus, what are you doing? Come on, get dressed."

"What does it matter if people find out?" he asked, catching the pair of pants she threw at him.

His thoughts on the matter must have been obvious, because she paused, peering at him, then came over and took his face in her hands.

"Now's not the time, and it's also none of their business. And I want to keep you to myself."

"Liana..."

"No, we don't have time right now, just listen," she said, putting a finger over his lips. "This thing, us. I've never had anything like this before. I want to keep it all to myself. I'm sorry if that makes you feel bad, but I don't want to share you yet."

Sylus looked into her eyes and saw worry, maybe even fear. He could tell that their magical night was fading away, that reality was beginning to set in. Whatever Liana was afraid of, he didn't think it was people finding out, but he didn't see a real reason to push the point.

"You won't have to," he said, and stood up and kissed her.

She returned the kiss, pulling him into her, then pushed him away again, pointing an accusatory finger at him.

"None of that. I'm going to sneak out. You go out first and go to the mess hall. And stop smiling, we're in legitimate danger! I need to go to the bridge and see if there's anything I can do."

"Fine. No smiling," he said, smiling at her.

She smiled back, then opened the door, poking her head out first to see if the way was clear before slipping out and closing it behind her.

Sylus sighed, got dressed, and followed Liana's orders to wait five minutes before leaving the room.

Seek the Source.

He shook his head. The voice seemed louder today, but he'd already decided to ignore it, so that's what he did.

He passed no one in the hall, and the usual sounds of the ship seemed different. Boots thumped on the deck above him, and twice he saw people heading through the hallway, faces grim. There were no sounds of conversation floating down the halls, no distant laughter at a joke. The change from the normal sounds of life on a ship unnerved Sylus, and it was enough to wipe the smile off his face, especially when he entered the dining hall.

It was late for breakfast, and few people were eating. Many sat alone with their heads down. Anyone speaking did so in a whisper, adding to the quiet sounds of cutlery and the kitchen. All together, it made for a tense atmosphere, the air heavy enough to cut with a knife.

The magic feeling of the previous evening faded entirely as Sylus got his food and sat down, absorbing the bleak mood as an accurate representation of the situation. This was a ship on the edge, with a crew facing down nearly certain death that they could do nothing about. The reality of it, momentarily forgotten in the night, came crashing down into Sylus as he picked at his breakfast.

The door to the mess hall opened, and Asphen walked in. Sylus locked eyes with the man immediately. He shot to his feet, his chair scraping across the floor, drawing all eyes to him as his entire body tensed, not sure what to do. All noise in the mess hall ceased as everyone saw what was happening.

Asphen glared at him, frozen in the doorway. Sylus, for his part, did not glare back but watched apprehensively. The rest of the crew looked between the two, a few looking like they'd halfway stood up themselves, but whether to help Sylus or Asphen, Sylus was no longer sure.

After a moment that seemed to stretch forever, Asphen broke the stare and walked over to the counter to get his food. Everyone, including Sylus, let out a collective sigh, and Sylus took the opportunity to flee, leaving his meal half-eaten on the table. He was not sure what Asphen might do, but Sylus didn't want to find out. It was yet another problem he was not sure how to deal with.

Sylus made his way up to the deck, only to find a vastly different scene from the one he was used to. The entirety of the ship was still listing slightly to the side, but it was flat enough to walk without much difficulty. Instead of men and women seeing to the business of running the ship, they stood around the perimeter of the deck holding weapons. Each of them watched the Green nervously, their hands shifting anxiously on weapons they did not put down. More than one had a looking glass out to scan the empty green horizon for any sign of a threat. Sylus did not doubt that more were on the bridge and crow's nest, watching for signs of danger from beneath the blades as well as above.

Virel stood nearby, directing a crew of engineers who were studying the bent support posts and broken sail-masts, discussing how they might be repaired. Nearby, crew members appeared to be stitching together sails, likely all of the extras the ship could carry, to replace the main sails they lost.

Sylus thought this was a risky gamble.

The main sails were enormous; they needed to be to push the ship, but some smaller sails were necessary to steer it as well. A few main sails might be able to steer the *Bladedancer* in a general way, perhaps enough to get them out of the Uncharted Green if the winds were favorable, but if there was a storm or strong winds, the stitching wouldn't hold, and they would lose their last hope of controlling the ship at all.

Sylus felt the grim mood of the crew wash over him. Very few people spoke, and their faces were a mix of determination and nervousness, with tension heavier here than in the mess hall. Sylus suddenly felt very foolish and selfish for being happy at all. What were he and Liana thinking by pretending, even just for an evening, that the entire ship wasn't on the verge of panic?

Suddenly miserable, he caught sight of the Captain and Cally standing on the upper deck, Cally speaking in low tones, with the Captain nodding along, his expression dark.

Seek the Source.

Sylus shook his head forcefully, ignoring the voice. It seemed louder and more insistent today, but he couldn't let himself get pulled into that now. Sylus didn't see Holven anywhere, so he made his way to the upper deck, trying to ignore the way that some of the crew were staring at him. It was about an even split between open suspicion and nods of tense acknowledgment. Sylus supposed the crew was split on how to feel about him right now.

Sylus hunched his shoulders and went to join the Captain at the railing. Cally noticed him coming and stepped around the Captain to intercept him.

"You doing okay, Sylus?" she asked.

"What?" Sylus said.

"Are you doing okay? You know, mentally?" she said. "You look stressed."

"I didn't do it," Sylus said, shifting uncomfortably.

"Never said you did," she muttered distractedly.

Cally's eyes flicked down to the still-open notebook in her hand, a look of concentration on her face. She returned her gaze to him a minute later.

"I just heard what happened with Asphen. He's a dick. Well, you know that, obviously. Ignore him. No one thought you did it before he ran his fat mouth."

Sylus felt a sudden rush of affection for the woman.

"Thanks," he said.

"Have you seen Liana this morning?" she asked.

"No, not yet," he said quickly, his face coloring.

Cally looked at him oddly.

"Okay. Well, if you see her, tell her I'm looking for her," Cally said, turning back to her notebook.

Sylus did not think he'd seen her so serious. Gone was the open smile, flirty laughter, and casual stance. She stood with her shoulders hunched and a haunted look in her eyes.

"What about you? Are you holding up okay?" he asked her.

"It's not looking good, Sylus. If we can't find a way to move the ship…"

"Is there something you needed, Sylus?" Bracken broke in, giving Cally a dark look that snapped her mouth shut.

"Just looking for some way I can help, I guess."

"It's about time. Where have you been all morning?" he said suspiciously.

"Nowhere!" Sylus said quickly. "Just in my room."

Bracken merely grunted.

"You've been going through the Thaumatech with Liana, right?" he said.

"Y-Yes," Sylus muttered nervously, feeling ridiculous.

No one knew. Was he going to blush every time someone mentioned her name? He struggled to control himself.

"Get back down there then. Look for anything useful. I do remember seeing a few things that may help us. I'll send an engineer down to you in a few hours, and Liana, once she's done in the Chapel.

It's a good time as any for Verdalis to offer guidance, though I can't say I see her plan in this mess."

Sylus merely nodded.

"Get going. And Sylus?" the Captain said.

"Yes, sir?"

"Every second could count. There be things in this part of the Green that can tear this ship apart in moments, you understand? Anything you find, send for me or Holven immediately."

"Yes, sir."

Sylus made his way to the storage room, finding it abandoned, and got to work searching through the crates for anything that might be useful. There were several items he did not recognize, though none of them seemed helpful in their current situation.

He stopped for lunch, but took it back to the storeroom with him, rather than stay in the pallid atmosphere of the mess hall. He was not interrupted until Liana appeared in the doorway sometime in the afternoon, looking exhausted.

"Oh, hey!" he said, setting down the piece of Thaumatech he was investigating, which he thought was a device for heating water.

"Hey," Liana said, coming over and pulling up a chair beside him.

"What's up?" he asked, concerned.

"Have you been up there? It's bad," she said. "They're scared, and it's starting to get to them. There was a fight up on the deck just now."

"A fight?"

"They almost killed each other over nothing. They both needed healing, and then the Captain locked them in their rooms."

Sylus felt an odd flash of anger.

"They're fighting at a time like this, and you healed them?"

She looked at him, eyebrow raised, "Of course, why wouldn't I?"

"I..." Sylus said, searching for a reason, "I don't know."

"It was pretty bad," she said.

Sylus tried not to acknowledge that the only reason he would care was that he now knew how little time Liana had left, and that her giving it away to heal people who willingly injured each other was time she would no longer have with him.

"You should have come and gotten me," he said instead.

She raised another eyebrow at him.

"I could have helped," he said evasively.

"Sylus, I can't stop doing what I was put here to do. Not even for you," she said.

Something in the way she said it suggested that a small part of her wanted to.

"I wouldn't ask you to," Sylus said, "Even if I wanted to. It's selfish, I know. But you could let me help. I have..."

"...More time left?" she offered, then shook her head sadly. "This is what I was talking about. It's why I shouldn't have kissed you. Shouldn't have let myself get attached. Why we shouldn't be together."

"Don't say that," Sylus said, "Please."

She looked back at him, and her gaze softened. She sighed, then suddenly leaned her head onto his shoulder.

"I'm sorry," she said, looking up at him, "This is all new to me. I don't regret it. I just don't want to hurt you."

"You won't."

"I will. I can see it when you look at me. As soon as you woke up today, you were already counting the days until I go. That's why Thaumatechne don't usually form relationships."

Sylus wrapped his arms around her.

"The ship is adrift in the most dangerous part of the Green," he said, "At any moment we could be attacked by some horrific monster, or the Reclaimed. If that doesn't happen, we die a slow death of starvation, or a fast death when the crew loses their minds."

"Where are you going with this?" she asked, looking genuinely confused.

"Last night and today were the happiest days of my entire life. I never thought anything would happen with us. I never dreamed you would be interested. I never let myself think about it, and now you're all I can think about.

I know how it will end, Liana. I won't lie and say it doesn't terrify me, but at the same time, I don't care. I want to spend every single second I can with you. I know it's selfish, but I can't help how I feel."

He finished in a rush, and Liana stared at him for a very long time, her eyes looking up into his. Then she kissed him. When she pulled away, she was smiling. The kiss stirred to life something in his chest, washing away the fear and tension of the ship's situation.

She grinned at him. He kissed her again. Her arms reached up, her hands in his hair. When they broke apart again, both of their faces were flushed.

"We really shouldn't," she breathed.

"Definitely not," he agreed.

"It's a bad idea. Someone could walk in at any moment," she said, but her hands did not loosen their grip on his hair, and her breathing was fast and shallow.

"It's a terrible idea," he whispered.

Liana's eyes flicked to the door; their rooms were not that far from here.

Her eyes locked back onto his.

The rooms were too far.

34

Whispers in the Night

Over the next few days, the situation on the ship only grew more dire. There was no way to repair the supports that held the air tank in place, not without a shipyard. The Captain even asked the Thaumatechne if they possessed any Wonders that might help. Still, Liana and Asphen were adamant that the risks of damaging the ship further were too significant.

Eventually, Virel was forced to reinforce the twisted metal pillars in the hope that they would not twist further. The patchwork sails were installed and ready, consisting of two main sails and a single ancillary sail for steering. With so few sails, the ship could move, but it wouldn't be making any tight turns or course readjustments easily. The only reason they hadn't yet tried to escape their predicament was the complete and utter absence of favorable winds. According to Cally, they were drifting in the wrong direction, deeper into the Uncharted Green, and the Captain was unwilling to risk their makeshift sails for anything less than a sure chance.

Holven and the Captain held frequent meetings to provide what hope could be offered, which wasn't much. Discussions of using the ship's sole escape craft to send a small crew for help were raised, but fell apart when it was pointed out that no rescuers would be convinced to sail into the Uncharted Green. Any who left would be leaving the remainder to die, and there was no guarantee they would escape on the much smaller craft.

It was put to a vote, but as yet, very few were willing to sign the death warrants of the rest.

Cally spent her days in a constant vigil of the wind, sometimes staying up for fourteen hours straight, afraid to miss the winds that might see them home. Dark circles haunted her face every time Sylus saw her, but her suggestive jokes stopped completely, a worrying sign.

Virel spent nearly all day, every day, trying to repair the engine with the rest of the engineers. They surfaced only for meals, then returned below to continue working. The fuel was regenerating slowly, thanks to Thaumatech, yet the emergency engines still refused to fire.

Valera darted around the ship, fists full of herbs and tinctures to help with nerves, insomnia, and panic. Despite the toll it took on her and their supplies, she never denied a single request.

Ruse did his best to raise the ship's morale with quality meals. Luckily, food was not yet an issue. Even in the Uncharted Green, Glimmerbeetles were plentiful and easy to catch. The meals were often accompanied by a lively story of Ruse's invention, delivered to crew members who were barely listening, in an attempt at humor that was brushed aside.

Asphen, for the most part, stayed in his room and worked his way through the ship's alcohol, which was for the best, as every time he emerged, his mood was so dark and foul that he started arguments and fights everywhere he went. Eventually, he needed to be watched to ensure he did not cause any trouble.

The rest of the crew spent their time alternating between pointless busy work and standing guard, a duty that required multiple shifts to ensure twenty-four-hour coverage and full crew participation.

Liana spent most of her days in the ship's chapel preaching. She worried in private that it was not her vocation, and that she was not good at it, but her sermons seemed to draw a larger crowd every day. For support, Sylus attended often and learned about the hopeful message of Verdalis' protection. Liana's sermons focused on the spirit and merit of endurance in the face of hardship. He was not moved to become a full believer as Liana was, and she never pushed him for more, but she was grateful for his support.

Yet Sylus and Liana were still able to steal moments of happiness in isolation, not only at night, but in any spare moment they could find. Their relationship was filled with secret passionate rendezvous, perhaps spurred by the looming threat of death, and quiet, heartfelt moments of genuine connection, talking while lying in each other's arms at night.

It would be foolish for Sylus to deny that his feelings for Liana were wildly out of control, for he spent nearly every minute thinking about her or wanting to be near her, which was both a blessing and a curse. His heart felt like it would burst with joy at the sight of her, and yet he wanted to curse and scream at the unfairness of the ticking clock that hovered over their time together. He found he could not help but stare at the metal that crept up her neck as she slept, hating its slow crawl toward the inevitable.

Sylus knew he was falling wildly, madly, desperately in love with her, and he was reasonably sure she felt the same way, but as of yet neither of them had said the words. Sylus hesitated, uncertain and new to love, not wanting to hear that she didn't feel the same way, though he was just as sure at points that she was on the verge of saying it first, and held back herself for some unknown reason.

Very little changed in those grim first days in the Uncharted Green, and they were, without a doubt, the happiest in Sylus's entire life, at least until one night, after a week of being adrift. Liana lay sleeping, and Sylus lay awake, haunted by the increasing awareness that their time was doomed to be short. It floated like an unspoken promise between them, one that Liana seemed content to ignore, fully engrossed in enjoying the present in a way that only she seemed able to accomplish. Sylus loved her for it, but he could never stop wondering what would happen when the time came.

He didn't see Liana choosing to let her body walk into the blades, where it might be used to hurt or infect others. Would she turn herself into the Church? Or, and this was the worst scenario that taunted him, would she turn to him, whom she trusted, and ask him to perform the deed? It was unlikely, but the nightmare haunted him. Could he do it? End her suffering and prevent the virus from claiming her as its own? Sylus was sure she would prefer that to letting Therithar have her, as she believed. He unwillingly tried to imagine taking his sword and striking down Liana, and the thought made him physically sick.

Sylus felt so helpless and powerless that it was all he could do not to weep, his heart aching at the unfairness of it all. He was rapidly spiraling him down into a private despair that he could not share even with Liana. He was terrified that if she knew how much he dreaded their parting, she might end their relationship early, convinced that it was a bad idea in the first place, and he could stand that even less.

Seek the Source.

The voice cut through his thoughts like a knife, and he pressed his hands against his face, trying to push the voice out of his head. Most of the time, he could ignore it, despite its insistence growing stronger, but in times like these, when he was alone and fragile, it dominated his thoughts.

Sylus willed the voice to leave him alone, willed it away with all his might, screaming all of his frustrations and weakness silently into the void. For a moment, he was even sure it worked.

Seek the Source.

It repeated. This was its new tactic, to repeat itself, sometimes many times, driving him ever deeper into despair.

Seek the Source.

Sylus removed himself from the bed, careful not to wake Liana, before pacing the floor as silently as he could, trying to drown out the voice.

Seek the Source.

He shut himself in the washroom and closed the door, splashing cold water on his face from the basin. His own eyes, haunted by dark circles from lack of sleep, stared back at him from the mirror.

Seek the Source.

The voice was more insistent than usual today. Sylus could feel the tears forming before they began to flow, feeling overwhelmed as his eyes became red-rimmed.

Seek the Source.

"Why?" he whispered to his reflection, "Why, damn you! Why should I?"

There was no answer, of course. He waited anyway, letting the tears fall silently into the sink. And then, a splitting headache. Sylus let out a horrific gasp as the pain struck him like a bolt of lightning. The wash basin fell to the floor, knocked to the ground by his shuddering, and shattered across the floor. Only his sudden grip on the washstand kept Sylus from falling.

"Sylus?" came Liana's voice, heavy with sleep, from the other room. Then again, with more concern, "Sylus!?"

The Source could save her.

Sylus's shocked face stared back at him as his eyes snapped back to the mirror, the pain evaporating as quickly as it appeared.

Liana was knocking on the door.

"Sylus? Are you okay?" she asked, but he wasn't listening.

The voice never changed what it said. Never, not since the very first time it spoke to him. The memory returned to him in a rush, both the splitting headache and the words.

The knocking became a pounding. Sylus turned in a daze and opened the door to find Liana staring at him, concern written across her face.

"Sylus? What happened?"

Sylus looked desperately into Liana's eyes, wondering if he should tell her. Liana shook him slightly, trying to get him to answer, but he could not.

Had he imagined it? Was he so worried and obsessed with the idea of losing Liana that his psychosis was evolving a new line to torture him with? Or had the voice listened to him and responded?

His skin broke out into goosebumps as the voice returned.

Seek the Source.

It was barely a whisper.

35

A Ship in the Green

Though Sylus told Liana that it was just a nightmare, he could tell in the morning that she did not believe him. She sat with a thoughtful look on her face, her legs pulled up to her chest as she watched him get dressed.

"You're never up first," she noted.

"I couldn't sleep anymore," Sylus said honestly, sneaking a glance in her direction.

Her hair had fallen in front of her face again, but she seemed too suspicious to notice. Sylus debated telling her the truth. Liana may believe that her god was speaking to people, but so far, they hadn't discussed what the voice was telling Sylus to do. He wondered what she would say if he told her that her god said there was a cure for their condition. Would she believe him? Or would it seem a desperate lie, proving all the doubts she had about their relationship? Would she leave him to protect him? Worse, would it contradict her faith? Cause her to question? Abandon the Church?

Sylus didn't want that. He still wasn't sure what to believe, but he knew that Liana drew strength from her beliefs, and he could not, would not, take that from her. No, there were too many risks to tell her the truth.

Liana was still staring at him.

"What?" he asked.

"You haven't even noticed that I'm still in bed," she said.

When he didn't respond, she rolled her eyes.

"And I'm naked? When have you seen me sit around in bed naked unless there was a good reason?"

Sylus felt heat bloom in his chest at the suggestion, flutter, then suddenly die out. It left him feeling gutted and empty. He forced a smile to hide the sickening feeling in his stomach.

"Sorry, I think being stuck out here is just starting to get to me. I'm a little distracted."

"Which is why I thought maybe you'd like a different distraction?" she said, smiling coyly at him. "I can tell something is bothering you. So if you don't want to talk about it, you might as well come over here and..."

The sharp tones of a bell rang out from the deck above, drowning out Liana's words. It was followed quickly by more as others picked up the warning, echoing the signal throughout the ship.

Three long rings, two short. A ship.

Liana and Sylus looked at each other in shock, and Liana flung herself out of bed, getting dressed in a flurry as Sylus searched the room for his sword. In moments, they were ready, and Sylus flung open the door, Liana right behind him, only to find Valera standing there, her hand raised as if about to knock.

"Oh," she said in surprise, staring at Sylus. Then her eyes slid to Liana standing behind him. "Oh."

Sylus glanced back at Liana as his face colored. Liana's cheeks colored only slightly, and she met the other woman's eyes with a defiant look. An awkward silence passed in which the two women communicated telepathically.

After what seemed like a long time, Valera tore her eyes away from Liana and looked back at Sylus.

"Good, you're both here. The Captain sent me to find you. We're going to need you on deck."

"There's a ship, right?" Sylus said.

"Yes," Valera said, the urgency of the situation seeming to overpower the awkwardness of the moment. She motioned for them to follow and began walking down the hall toward Asphen's room.

"It's a bit too far to be sure, but there's no flag. No colors. No one visible on deck."

Sylus and Liana followed her down the hall, sharing a glance and a shrug; they could deal with being discovered later.

"What does that mean?" Sylus asked.

"No one sails the Uncharted Green unless they have no choice," Valera said, her words terse.

"Reclaimed," Liana whispered, turning Sylus's blood cold.

Valera pounded on Asphen's door. There was a muffled, angry response. Valera pounded on the door again.

"Asphen, get up. You're needed!" Valera shouted through the door, giving the other two an apologetic look.

Sylus shifted uncomfortably. Likely, the man was hungover, or worse, still drunk. Sylus did not fancy having Asphen open the door to discover him standing there, as they still hadn't spoken since that day on the deck.

There was a grunt, then the sound of something falling over and glass breaking, then muffled curses. Eventually, the door opened to reveal a very angry-looking Asphen, his eyes red-rimmed as he took them all in. His gaze lingered on Sylus suspiciously for a moment before focusing on Valera.

"What is it?" he said, his voice rough.

"A ship," Liana said, disapproval heavy in her voice. "Can't you hear the bells?"

"A ship?" Asphen asked, suddenly seeming much more alert. "Rescue?"

"We don't know," Valera said. "Could be trouble. Come up to the deck."

Asphen shook his head as if to clear it, then swore and held a hand to his head.

Valera sighed.

"Take this with water," she said, passing him a vial of herbs from her belt pouch.

"Fine," Asphen muttered, taking it from her. He shut the door in their faces.

Valera shook her head.

"We'd better go," she muttered and led them up to the deck.

They joined a crowd gathering at the railing of the lower deck in the early morning sun, many peering through eyeglasses at the horizon where blue met green. Sylus squinted and was just able to make out a ship in the distance. Sylus glanced around to the upper deck, where the Captain, Holven, and Cally stood at the railing as well. The two men spoke in low voices and looked through eyeglasses at the approaching ship. Cally alternated between squinting at a chart and glancing toward the sky.

Something about her expression worried Sylus.

"Come on," he said, grabbing Liana's hand and pulling her through the crowd to the stairway. Out of the corner of his eye, he spotted a bleary-eyed Asphen make his way up onto the deck, shielding his eyes against the light.

They made their way to the Captain, who was muttering under his breath.

"Captain?" Sylus asked.

Bracken pulled the eyeglass away from his face for a moment to see who it was.

"Stay close, you two. The ship be coming from the wrong direction. Cally?" he said, putting the eyeglass back on his face.

"I've checked and double-checked," Cally said, frowning and folding up the map.

"That ship's coming from deeper in the Uncharted Green, Captain."

"Therithar's thorny balls," Bracken muttered.

"Is it the Reclaimed?" Sylus asked. The ship was moving impressively fast. Already, it was visible without squinting. No one answered his question.

"Captain, there's no one on the deck," Holven said.

"Quiet!" Bracken said suddenly, "Do any of you hear that?"

"Hear what?" Sylus said.

"QUIET YOU LOT!" Bracken bellowed.

The crew below hushed. Sylus held his breath and strained his ears.

Just audible over the noise of the ship, a low but powerful hum filled the air, growing louder with each passing second.

"That's a Thaumatech engine," Sylus said.

"Captain, we have to accept the possibility…" Holven said cautiously.

"Can't be," Bracken muttered, "It's only rumors!"

But the captain was the only one who seemed unable to face the simple truth.

"Verdalis protect us," Liana said.

"Captain, we have to ready the crew," Holven insisted.

Bracken swore again, then pushed away from the railing, hurrying to the nearest alarm bell. He grabbed it and began ringing it in a constant pattern of five short rings, the sharp tones piercing the hush that had fallen over the ship.

"ENEMY SHIP!" he roared, "ENEMY SHIP!"

There was a minute of stunned silence, then the *Bladedancer* erupted into chaos.

36

Battle on the Blades

Men and women swarmed the deck in every direction. Some hauled in the remaining sails, while most hurried to gather weapons and defensive implements from the ship's armory. Metal spikes were affixed to railings, and nets were raised to impede attempts to board the deck. The damaged support pillars were barricaded with anything they could find to protect them during the attack.

The Captain roared orders left and right, with Holven hot on his heels. All the while, the encroaching ship sped toward them, the dull roar of its engines growing louder and louder.

Sylus grabbed up someone's dropped eyeglass as it rolled across the deck. The approaching vessel was close enough now to see that it had no sails. What use were sails on a ship crewed by those who did not grow hungry or sick? They could afford to wait for engines to recharge. Its deck was empty, and there was still no real sign of the Reclaimed, but no natural ship had empty decks at any time, let alone during daylight.

Liana hovered at his shoulder, her face a grim mask of determination as she stared out at the horizon. As Sylus lowered the eyeglass, she caught his eye and nodded tightly. He knew her well enough to know that this was reassurance. She wasn't worried for herself or the ship, but for him. He reached out and took her hand, giving it a tight squeeze.

Asphen pushed through the crowd suddenly, his eyebrows drawn down as he scanned the deck. As soon as his eyes saw them, he marched directly toward them. Sylus felt his already stretched nerves go into high alert, but to his surprise, Liana stepped in front of him protectively. Though his chest filled with warmth, he gently moved her aside. He could fight his own battles. She let him draw her back beside him, but refused to move behind him.

Asphen stopped in front of them and crossed his arms.

"All of this won't stop the Reclaimed for a minute," he said bluntly, gesturing to the efforts of the crew. "These defenses are meant for human beings. The Reclaimed will tear through them like paper, and the crew won't fare much better."

Sylus licked his lips, glancing around at the crew hurrying back and forth. He'd assumed as much, but hearing it out loud drove it home. They were in serious trouble, but Asphen didn't need to tell them that.

"You have a plan?" he asked.

"We three could take the escape ship. With all three of us, they won't be able to stop us."

"No," said Sylus.

"No!" said Liana, sounding disgusted.

Asphen shook his head.

"It's our best chance, Sylus. The best chance you're going to get to survive this mess." His eyes shifted to Liana. "And for her to survive this mess."

Sylus paled.

"What you're suggesting is mutiny. You would be sentencing the entire crew to death," Liana spat, "We'd rather die than do that."

Asphen ignored her, still only looking at Sylus. To his eternal shame, part of Sylus considered it. Liana would hate him, and more than that, she would never agree to come with them. Without her, there was nothing to think about.

"You heard her," he said firmly, but he could tell by Asphen's face that the man knew what he was thinking.

"Was worth a try," he said, shrugging. "We will very likely die here then."

"I'd rather die trying to save these people than live as a coward," Liana said, her voice dripping with venom.

"Is it cowardice to flee a hopeless battle?" Asphen said coldly, turning to her for the first time. "I call it prudence. But so be it. If we're going to stay, we're going to have to fight. All of us, together. We're the only chance this ship has."

He turned back to Sylus, "There will be no time for hesitation, no time for freezing up. We need to take these things down fast and hard. Can I count on you to have my back?"

"Have your back? You tried to kill me!" Sylus said, his voice rising.

Asphen stared at him for a long time before answering, "I was wrong."

He didn't elaborate.

"Is that all you're going to say? Are you fucking serious?" Liana said, taking a step forward.

"We don't have time for this," Asphen sneered, "If we don't work together, we are all dead. Are you with me or not?"

He was right. Even if they had a choice, Sylus would take any chance he could to keep Liana alive. He nodded and drew his sword.

"You should take this," he said, offering it to Asphen. "You're better with it than I am."

Asphen stared at it, but shook his head, "No. Even with my skill, it will work better for you." His eyes flicked toward Liana, "You might want to get a weapon. Meet me below."

With that, he turned on his heel and left, leaving Liana and Sylus to look at each other.

"Do you trust him?" she said.

"I do, actually. He's a lot of things, but his selfishness works in our favor here. He wants to live."

Liana nodded, but her eyes flashed fiercely, "I'll watch your back."

The confidence in her voice that she would be able to protect him from Asphen was so resolute that he nearly picked her up and kissed her right there. She was staring suspiciously after Asphen, but turned when she caught him staring at her, her hair falling across her face.

She tucked it behind her ear with a smile, "What?"

The urge to tell her how he felt threatened to burst out of him, but he couldn't decide if this was the right time, even if they might not ever get another.

"I want to kiss you so badly," he said instead.

"No time," she said, but her smile widened. "Help me find a spear, it's the only thing I know how to use."

They found one easily enough, a straightforward thing. Sylus doubted it would be any use against a Reclaimed.

"Maybe you should take the sword," he said to Liana as they approached Asphen.

"Don't be an idiot," Asphen said.

Liana shrugged.

Captain Bracken appeared on the deck. He was wearing metal armor and gripping a sword tightly in one hand. Holven strode behind, clutching a spear. He gave them a curt nod, his face completely blank.

"There you are," Bracken said, "This may go without saying, but we be relying on you. Sylus, I know you don't know much about fighting, but I must ask you-"

"I'm going to fight," Sylus said quickly.

Bracken looked a little surprised. He opened his mouth as if to say something more, but then closed it as if he thought better of it, and merely nodded, turning his attention to Liana and Asphen.

"You two, we survive this, I'll double your pay and your share of the loot, you understand?" he said.

"That's not necessary," Liana said politely.

Asphen merely grunted.

Sylus wondered what the Captain would say if he ever found out that Asphen tried to convince them to steal the only escape ship.

Bracken nodded.

"Then may Verdalis shelter us. If ever we be needing her strength, it be now."

He turned to go. Holven turned to follow, then paused and looked back at them.

"Good luck," he said, before following the Captain to stand nearby.

"They're coming," Asphen said.

The ship was bearing down on them, showing no signs of slowing.

"If they ram the ship, we're done for," Asphen growled.

"The *Bladedancer* no be defenseless," Bracken growled, then turned and called to the crew, "Raise the spikes!"

The call was repeated along the deck, and a few moments after the call ran out, a great cloud of steam released from somewhere under the ship, billowing up along the railing at set intervals. The sound of metal doors sliding open filled the air, and Sylus leaned over the edge to see what was happening.

Great metal spikes were emerging from hatches along the side of the ship. Steam hissed from the openings as they slowly extended outwards, a deterrent against ramming. The pikes were wicked, cruel-looking things, barbed with thick metal brambles to ensure they did maximum damage to an attacking ship.

"There they are," Asphen said, his eye still to the looking glass.

Sylus turned his attention to the incoming ship, where movement was now visible on the deck. He could see sunlight glinting off metal.

"It be true," Bracken muttered, sounding slightly disbelieving.

"Captain," Holven said.

"Not yet," Bracken said, his voice strained.

Sylus looked around at everyone. He felt like people should be screaming, but most just looked grim. Were they not going to do anything else but sit here and get rammed? His voice dried up in his throat. Everyone was positioning themselves close to something they could grab, and many were tying themselves to something with a length of rope. His heart was pounding out of his chest as the roar of the approaching engines filled the air.

The ship bore down on them.

"Captain?" Holven asked quietly. It seemed to be the only sound aside from the engines.

The Captain hesitated, then hollered, "NOW!"

Whatever plan was in place, no one told Sylus about it. The *Bladedancer* suddenly lurched as a loud hiss filled the air, and Sylus was nearly knocked to the ground as the ship swung. They were venting one of the air tanks!

Desperately, he grabbed onto the railing beside Liana.

"BRACE!" the Captain called, and the enemy ship was all Sylus could see.

The angle was barely enough. The *Bladedancer* completed its last-second spin, and the Reclaimed vessel crashed against the side of the ship.

Screams finally rang out as the two metal airships ground against each other at high speed. Sylus held wildly onto Liana as some of the metal spikes sheared away, while others tore through the hull of the Reclaimed ship with the horrendous noise of wrenching metal, cutting thick jagged lines into the enemy ship before catching. With a gut-ripping sensation, the two decks became hopelessly entangled, and the momentum of the attacking ship suddenly changed the direction the *Bladedancer* was spinning, throwing more people to the deck and sending both ships spiraling across the blades.

Sylus clamped his metal hand onto the railing as his feet left the ground, his other arm wrapped around Liana. The railing splintered under his iron grip, but held. Others weren't so lucky.

The sounds of snapping ropes and screams of panic could be heard as some crew members were flung free, sliding across the deck and slamming into walls. Sylus saw at least two people fall over the side, but there was no time for anyone to do anything about it.

Sylus struggled to his feet, fighting against the motion of the entangled ships as they spun, their momentum slowing to a lazy drift. The Reclaimed hardly reacted to the collision. By the time Sylus got to his feet, the first of the once-human monstrosities rose from the opposite deck.

With an effortless leap, the Reclaimed launched himself onto the deck of the *Bladedancer.* The net did little to stop it from landing with a heavy thud three feet from Sylus. With a yell, Sylus pulled Liana away from the railing, as two more Reclaimed made the jump, their blank, eyeless faces sweeping the deck.

Shouts filled the air as the crew rushed the monsters with spears. Sylus felt Liana pull free from his grasp and turned to see what happened, only to see her short blonde hair disappearing into a crowd as she rushed a Reclaimed that landed on their other side.

"Liana!" he called.

Sylus tried to follow, only to have another monster land right in front of him. He was lucky the Reclaimed moved so haltingly and reacted so slowly, for he froze as the creature turned its eerie gaze toward him. This one had a large, single red light in the center of its otherwise smooth face plate. Then it raised not one or two, but three arms toward him, and took a halting step toward him.

Sylus drew his sword, the Thaumatech blade humming to life in his hand. The creature seemed to hesitate, its head cocking to the side as it examined him and the weapon for a moment before it lurched forward once more.

There was no time to think. It reached for him, and Sylus slashed, bringing the sword up in a flashing arc. There was a spray of sparks, and the metal hand that was reaching for him clanked to the deck.

The Reclaimed did not react to its injury. It swiped at Sylus with hands that ended in too many bladed fingers. He was forced to duck wildly, then dodge backwards as the creature swiped at him again and again, creating space between them.

With horror, Sylus watched as the sparking stump of the machine's arm began to rebuild itself, the metal around the severed wrist shifting and flowing.

It was easy to get away from the thing, but battles raged on all sides of Sylus. As he retreated from the Reclaimed, he suddenly felt his back slam up against another person, and then a sharp pain in his ribs as the butt of a stabbing spear caught him in the ribs. He grunted, pain blossoming across his torso, but even as he fell, the creature in front of him took another halting step toward him.

Setting his feet as Asphen taught him, Sylus stopped retreating. There was nowhere to go. No one was coming to help him, and he had no idea where Liana was or if she was safe. It was that more than anything that drove him forward, a roar bubbling up in his throat and tearing free from his lips.

The creature's arms reached for him, and with two arcing slices, Sylus cut them both off at the elbows. The Reclaimed stopped its advance, and lights flashed across its body. Sylus felt that familiar feeling fill the air, energy being drawn in, and realized it was about to perform a Wonder. He dashed forward, blade outstretched, and his blade pierced the thing right through the eye sensor. The Reclaimed's body spasmed, lights flashing across its surface, then blinking out. The feeling dissipated, and the creature collapsed to the deck.

Sylus let out a ragged breath, then went flying as something collided with him and threw him to the ground. Stars popped in front of his eyes as he tried to roll the heavy object off him. He pushed it away from him, gasping, and realized it was a body. The man's eyes stared up at him, his face frozen in a scream, and a deep cut in his neck oozed dark blood into Sylus's lap.

Shuddering, Sylus rolled the man off of him and struggled to his feet, slipping in the blood. He looked around for Liana, took a step, then nearly tripped when something grabbed his ankle.

Horrified, Sylus looked down to find the dead man holding his leg. Metal blossomed from the wound in the dead man's neck, and his body jerked and twitched as it spread rapidly up the man's head, turning skin, muscle, and bone to metal before Sylus's eyes. It was a grotesque and gruesome transformation, and Sylus tried desperately to yank his leg free from the thing's grasp.

Suddenly, Asphen was there, sweeping down with his blade. His sword sheared through the man's arm, freeing Sylus's leg.

"You have a sword, fool!" he hissed.

He drove his other blade directly through the man's eye. The metal had enveloped the lower half of his face already, but at Asphen's final strike, the transformation stopped immediately.

"Don't let them turn!" Asphen said, then cut the man's head off and kicked it overboard, sending it sailing out into the night. Then he was gone, back into the chaos of battle, and Sylus was left staring at a bloody stump as blood pooled into a giant puddle on the deck.

Liana.

The thought of losing Liana was the only thing that kept his stomach from emptying itself. Sylus tore his eyes away from the corpse, kicking the hand free from his leg while trying not to remember if he'd known the man's name or not.

Nearby, several crew members kept one of the Reclaimed at bay with a coordinated effort of spears, though the Reclaimed wielded a weapon of its own. One of its arms was a long blade, which it was using to slash jerkily at the spears keeping it back. Sylus could understand why no one was trying to engage with it; a single slash from that blade meant infection, and it was already red with blood.

But he was already infected.

He pushed through the crowd at the creature's back, shouldering men and women out of his way. He raised his blade and plunged it through the thing's back, the vibrating blade sliding through metal like hot butter. The thing spasmed and stumbled, falling to one knee. Horrifically, its head turned all the way around to regard him, its metal face made of two plates with a vertical slit.

A resounding clang crushed the thing's head in as a massive hammer struck it from the other side. Sylus pulled his sword free as the thing teetered, then fell to the deck. A man struck again with the great hammer. Sylus thought he might be one of the engineers. A hulking man, he raised it and brought it down again and again, flattening the Reclaimed's metal skull in a furious rain of blows.

Sylus left him to it. There were more Reclaimed than Sylus ever hoped to see in one place. Three were visible on the deck, with one fighting the Captain and several other crew members, and another fighting Asphen. Two lay defeated on the deck, but the sounds of battle floated down from the upper deck. More must have boarded the ship since Sylus stopped paying attention.

A woman suddenly burst from the stairway that led below deck, her face covered in blood that she didn't seem to notice. Wild, panicked eyes locked onto Sylus.

"They're inside the ship. Oh gods, they're in the ship!" she said, stumbling over to Sylus.

Sylus felt his blood run colder. In the tight quarters of the hallways, fighting these things would be a nightmare. He glanced around wildly for Liana, or even a flash of her hair. Why did she run off?

"You have to help them. I barely got past... I barely..." the woman said, swaying.

Sylus reached out to steady her.

"You're bleeding," Sylus said, "Are you alright?"

The woman raised a shaking hand to her temple, where a shallow cut was bleeding freely. She wiped at it with her fingers, and as she wiped away the blood, Sylus saw the glint of new metal. Her face blanched as she felt it with her finger.

"Verdalis... no..." she whispered.

Absolute horror made its way into the woman's expression, and she began to shake violently. The wound was too close to her brain; the woman might have minutes at most.

"I can't..." she whispered, taking a step back.

"Hey, wait!" Sylus said, reaching for her.

"I CAN'T! I WON'T!" the woman suddenly screamed, clutching her face. "OH VERDALIS, NO!"

Sylus watched, stunned, as the woman turned and ran, directly to the edge of the ship. He realized too late what she was going to do.

"Stop!" he called, but what could he do?

The woman pitched herself screaming over the side of the ship and disappeared into the blades. Sylus was left standing with his hand outstretched, battles raging around him.

For the first time, Sylus prayed to Verdalis. He prayed desperately that Liana was alive and for Verdalis to grant her some protection.

Seek...

Sylus did not have time for the voice. He didn't have time to think about what he just saw. He rushed down the stairs and into the hallways of the ship, glancing down each hallway he passed, watching for threats as he skidded around corners. He raced down the hallway and into the mess hall, only to feel a familiar feeling as he entered the room.

Energy was being drawn in, but this was different. Too much. Overpowering.

"PUSH!"

Sylus flew through the air with stars popping in his eyes. The world spun, merely colors and pain. He hit the wall, feeling like he'd been slapped by a giant, and fell five feet to the ground. Something fell on top of him. Something heavy bit into his forearm.

He groaned, dazed.

"Sylus!?"

It was muffled, but it was Liana's voice.

"Sylus!? Are you okay?" she was panicking.

Why couldn't he move? His thoughts flowed through molasses. There was a rough scraping noise.

"Help me, get it off him! It's dead; you can touch it. Hurry!"

The weight was lifted from him, and light flooded his blurry vision. He blinked as a crowd of people pulled a Reclaimed off of him. As soon as it was clear, the men and women dropped it and stepped away, wiping their hands on their aprons.

Then Liana was there, hovering above him, concern plastered across her face, her hair in disarray. She took his head in his hands.

"Sylus? Sylus? Are you okay? Can you hear me?" she said.

"What happened?" he groaned.

Relief painted her features. She was so beautiful it hurt. Or maybe that was the pain. He felt it start to fade as his healing kicked in. His arm stung.

"I-I don't know. I used a wonder, but it was different. Stronger. Let me see you," she said, disappearing.

She was patting him down.

"I'm okay, really," he said.

His head already felt clearer. He pushed himself up to a seated position.

"No, you're not. Oh, Sylus, your arm."

He held up his forearm so he could see it. A long five-inch gash was visible, or rather, what had been a gash. It was a relatively minor injury, and his Thaumatech had already taken care of it. He was looking at a shining metal scar, a new vector for the disease.

"I'm sorry, I didn't see you," Liana said, observing him.

He honestly did not care. He was too grateful that Liana was okay.

He shrugged. "

It could be worse. Are you okay? Why did you run off?"

Liana threw her arms around him and kissed him.

A couple of the bystanders murmured in surprise. Sylus heard quiet laughter, and at least one person distinctly said, 'I told you so. '

"Uhm, Liana?" he said when she pulled away.

"Screw them," she said, smiling, "I'm just so happy I didn't kill you."

"Not as happy as I am that you're okay. You ran off, and I..."

"There are only three of Sylus," she replied firmly, lifting him to his feet. "We can protect the ship better if we split up."

"But..."

"But nothing. I'm not made of glass, and you're not going to treat me like I am. Do you understand?"

Sylus was taken aback, but could not help his eyes from flicking toward her neck. Veins of metal were peeking up out of her collar. She followed his gaze, then shook her head as if reading his mind. Sylus looked back into her eyes. Liana's gaze was firm, but then softened.

"Sylus, do you trust me?" she asked.

"Of course I do."

"Then trust that I can look after myself."

"Okay," Sylus said. She was right, and this wasn't the time to argue anyway. "What happened to my sword?"

Once he was standing and equipped again, he turned back to Liana.

"What are you going to do now?" he asked.

She smiled gratefully.

"I'm not much of a fighter. I came inside to see to the wounded, but then they got into the ship. I saw at least two more down here. I'm going to help the wounded. I can't help anyone who was cut, but there are plenty of injuries that didn't turn people."

"Just two?" Sylus said, taking in a deep breath.

Liana squeezed his hand.

"Be careful, Sylus, please."

"I will. You too. Please," he said, squeezing her hand back.

Their eyes met again, and again the words wanted to flood out of him. This was certainly not the right time. It might be his last.

The sounds of screams echoed in from the hallway.

"Go, they need you," Liana said.

Sylus nodded, trying to steel his nerves as he reentered the ship. He tried not to think about the absolute lunacy of what he was doing as he ran toward the sounds of people dying. He just kept telling himself that if the Reclaimed took the ship, they would all die. There was no choice but to fight.

He skidded around a corner near the engine room and came to a dead stop.

Two Reclaimed were trying to get into the engine room and were barely being held at bay by Virel and some engineers, who crowded the hallway in front of the door, leveling long pikes toward the machines, trying with little success to keep them from advancing. It wasn't going well.

Two men gurgled on the ground, metal growing from wounds in their chest to cover their torso as the virus tried to repair the damage and claim a new host at the same time.

The wounds were far enough from the men's heads that they might live for a while as Thaumatechne, but the wounds were large. If he could heal them before the virus did, they would live longer.

One engineer stabbed with his pike into the chest of one of the haltingly advancing machines, and to his apparent surprise, the pike pierced the creature's metal chest and got stuck. The creature grabbed the pike and pulled, and the man, too surprised to remember to let go, was pulled forward out of the crowd, landing in front of the Reclaimed.

The other Reclaimed lifted its leg and stepped on the man's head. He screamed as the creature pushed down.

"NO!" Sylus cried, diving forward, but it was already too late.

There was a wet popping sound, and Sylus's cries did little but turn one of the machines toward him. This one held a sword in a metal arm. It retained much of its human form, including two glowing red eyes in its face plate.

Sylus darted in, bringing his sword down, and the creature raised its own in a jerky attempt to block. It was just a regular sword, though, and it stood no chance against Thaumatech. The vibrating blade sheared right through the weapon, sinking deep into the Reclaimed's neck.

Sylus tried to pull the blade free, but the machine grabbed his arm in a crushing grip. Sylus cried out in pain as it started to squeeze. Desperately, he let go of his sword and grabbed at the hand. He screamed as he tried to pry the thing's fingers loose, squeezing with all of his might until at last there was a metal crunching sound, and the thing let go, its wrist a ruined mess.

Sylus stumbled backward and fell as something grabbed his leg.

He hit the ground hard and looked up in horror to see one of the men who'd been on the ground pinning his legs. There was a fresh wound through the center of his forehead, about the size and shape of a finger. The other one reared up on his other side and pinned his human arm to the ground. Behind them, the second Reclaimed stood. It had finished the men off while he was distracted, creating two more machines. He was outnumbered four to one.

"No!" he cried, struggling, as the creature with Sylus's sword stuck in its neck reached up and grabbed the hilt, yanking it free. The wound began to repair itself immediately. The thing lowered the sword toward Sylus and took a halting step forward.

Sylus looked around desperately as cold panic gripped him. The men at the end of the hallway couldn't help him, and he couldn't rely on anyone else coming by. He struggled desperately, but only his metal arm was free. He pummeled the machine that held him down. Its face was still mostly flesh, and though Sylus pulverized the former man's face with his metal fist, it didn't let go. Dark blood splashed over Sylus's face. The monster holding the sword took another halting step toward him.

In his panic, Liana's words floated back to him. Her Wonder was stronger; would his be as well? Desperately, Sylus placed his hand over the face plate of the creature holding him down and willed his Wonder to be as strong as possible.

"Spark!" he cried. It was all he knew.

He felt a strange sensation of drawing energy from a distant source. Except it no longer felt distant. The energy that flowed into him wasn't a trickle; it was a stream. His hand began to glow with light and vibrate dangerously before eventually releasing the pent-up energy.

A bolt of lightning erupted from his palm, not the tiny arcing jolt he'd produced before, but wicked, jagged, angry flashes. The Reclaimed's entire body convulsed as the energy passed through its head and arced into the wall behind it in brilliant purple flashes. The lights in the hall flickered as the bolts arced off the metal walls, and the creature's head exploded as Sylus's Wonder blasted a smoking hole through the thing's head.

Absolute silence fell across the hallway, and Sylus's hand began venting heat violently as the thing's limp hands fell from him. The other three machines seemed frozen, their heads clicking and whirring, tilting as if surprised.

Sylus's hand stopped venting heat faster than usual, much quicker than it usually would.

He didn't hesitate. Sylus wrestled the half-formed Reclaimed that was holding his legs off of him and scrabbled to his feet, raising his hand towards the most significant threat.

He braced his arm with his other hand and planted his feet.

"Spark!" he yelled, throwing all of his will and feeling into the Wonder. "Spark! Spark! Spark!"

Energy poured into him, and his hand vibrated so violently he thought it might shake him apart. He ground his teeth and tried to keep his gaze fixed on the Reclaimed. The lights in the hall seemed to dim, as if his Thaumatech was drawing in energy from everything around it. Even the Reclaimed shuddered as if the energy was being drained from them as well.

Purple bolts of lightning sprayed from his hand as he shouted the command, arcing across the hallway, jumping from the floor to the ceiling, leaving burning trails where the wild, uncontrollable arcs touched. He could smell the awful smell of burning human flesh as the half-formed Reclaimed closest to him was ravaged by electricity. The two creatures standing in the hallway seemed to draw the bolts as they arced through the hallway. They stumbled and convulsed until they finally fell, smoking and ruined.

Still, he kept shouting, and still, the lightning came. The lights in the hall grew so bright they burst, and Sylus's vision was a ruin of white lines. It was all he could do to keep his hand up until his throat was raw, and he stopped shouting the command. Finally, the energy dissipated, and he let his hand fall to his side, smoking and venting heat.

It took a few moments for Sylus's vision to clear. The hallway was filled with smoke, scorch marks, and the twisted metal corpses of four Reclaimed. Sunlight streamed in through the windows.

No humans were visible.

"Virel?" he said, coughing as acrid smoke filled his mouth. "Virel! You guys okay back there?"

The door opened, and for the first time, Sylus realized it was closed. The humans must have retreated inside the door and shut it while Sylus was frying the machines.

He let out a massive sigh of relief as Virel's head poked out of the door, taking a wide-eyed look around the hall, then focusing on Sylus standing in the middle of it.

"Therithar's great green dick, Sylus. What in the fuck was that!?" he called.

Sylus raised his hand in front of his face in wonderment. He pulled back his sleeve and nearly lost his footing at what he saw. He was afraid that casting so many Wonders that strong would cost him his entire arm. It would have been better than dying, but instead, he stared in wonderment at his metal hand. It had advanced, but only about an inch up his wrist.

He touched the still human skin of his forearm in amazement. "I have no idea."

37

Aftermath

It was a solemn scene on the deck as Sylus helped heave the last of the Reclaimed corpses over the side.

"Just eight of them," muttered one of the men across from him.

The man's face was grim as he stared out at the horizon, then he shook his head and wandered off, muttering to himself. Sylus understood the man's frustration.

The Reclaimed ship held only six of the creatures, but together they'd killed nearly fourteen people in less than a full hour. Sylus was certain there had been more of them, but when they got them all laid out on the deck and the ship was searched top to bottom with no more to be found, he was forced to admit the reality of the situation to himself.

He avoided looking at the row of bodies behind him, wrapped carefully in linen, lined up in a row. Nine members of the crew lay beneath the sheets, five dead, four turned and then killed. Five others were missing, presumably lost to the blades.

Sylus looked instead at the girl tending to them. Liana said words over the dead, a prayer, but he was too far to hear it. She was, blessedly, unharmed, though her face was the picture of sadness as she tended to her duties. She caught Sylus's eye for a moment, which they did every chance they got. It was an unspoken but sorrowful reassurance of the other's still being alive.

As happy as Sylus was at that, he felt sick at the thought of those who did not survive. These were people with lives, friends, family, and a whole world outside of this ship. Sylus turned away and leaned on the railing, looking out at the horizon. He kept playing every moment from the attack over in his mind, remembering every misstep, every hesitation, every decision he made in painstaking detail. Which ones cost people their lives? Which ones made the attack worse instead of better? How many could he have saved if he'd acted differently?

He knew it was a stupid thing to dwell on, but he couldn't help it. He was alive, and they were not. It didn't seem fair, and it wasn't right, and there was absolutely nothing he could do about it.

He found his gaze drifting back to his arm, as he was doing more and more often as the day continued. He ran his hand over the human skin that by all logic should be metal. He wanted more than anything to talk to Liana about it, but there hadn't been a chance. It was not the only thing he wanted to talk about. He'd been in a battle, used a Wonder that seemed far too powerful, and been tossed bodily across the room and into a wall, not to mention the other injuries he'd sustained. Shouldn't he be exhausted and covered in bruises, even with his enhanced healing abilities?

His inspection, which everyone went through the moment the ship was declared safe, had perplexed Valera. His injuries were healed entirely, and he wasn't tired at all. He felt amazing. His body was practically buzzing with energy. His every step bounced, and hauling the Reclaimed around seemed easy even though they weighed hundreds of pounds. He could not stop thinking about what it felt like to cast a Wonder out here. The energy he drew in felt so close. He itched to cast something again, to explore that feeling. At the same time, he was afraid that casting anything right now might endanger the ship.

What changed?

"Could have been worse," came a voice.

Sylus blinked in surprise, finding Asphen standing beside him. He had one foot up on the railing, staring out in the same direction that Sylus was, toward the horizon. He puffed on a small pipe that had smoke drifting from it lazily. Sylus had not seen the man in hours. He did not help with the bodies, but Sylus heard from others that the man was responsible for downing at least three of the Reclaimed, and did not have a scratch on him.

"What?" Sylus said.

"The attack. It could have been worse. A lot worse. I've seen fewer Reclaimed kill a lot more in an enclosed space. You did well. I told you, you got a future in this."

It took Sylus a moment to understand what the man was saying.

"Oh. Yeah, I guess," he said awkwardly.

Asphen glanced sideways at him.

"You still pissed? We're good now, as far as I'm concerned."

Sylus locked eyes with the man. Despite everything, something inside him wanted to trust Asphen. He was rough, callous, possibly unhinged, but he'd been something of a mentor to Sylus. Sylus would undoubtedly be dead right now if it were not for him.

"Yeah, we're good. I'm just tired," Sylus said.

Asphen only nodded.

"We might get out of this," the man continued, "If they find what they're looking for."

Sylus looked over his shoulder to the enemy ship, still tangled with the *Bladedancer*. A while ago, Holven and Virel led a team across to see if anything could be salvaged to repair the *Bladedancer* and get them out of the Uncharted Green.

"Hopefully," Sylus said.

"Imagine the stories we'll have once we get back to shore? Two Tek-Exalts - once you finish your training - that have faced down a Leviapede, survived the Uncharted Green, and repelled an attack by a Reclaimed *ship*? Do you have any idea the rates we'll be able to charge?"

Sylus turned back to the man and was taken aback by the stare Asphen was giving him. Ambition was plain in his lopsided grin and unfocused eyes. Sylus could smell liquor, and the mystery of where Asphen was for the last few hours was solved. Sylus couldn't keep his face from twisting with disdain. Asphen seemed to misinterpret the look.

"What? You can't seriously still be thinking of becoming a priest, can you? Come on. We could be legends, you and I!" he said, clapping Sylus on the shoulder.

Sylus didn't know what to say. He glanced toward Liana, and Asphen followed his gaze.

"Look, man, I get it. She's a really cool girl and all, but well, our lives are short, and frankly, I think hers might be shorter than most. We're not going to be on this ship forever. She's going to go back to the Church, and you? You could be great. Truly great. There will be more girls waiting on the other side, trust me."

A fiery anger leapt to life in Sylus's chest, and he pushed himself away from the railing before he said something he would regret.

"I'm gonna grab something to eat," he said, heading toward the stairs.

"Hey, we should celebrate after!" Asphen called after him, producing a bottle from somewhere.

Sylus put the man and his infuriating comments from his mind. It wasn't his fault. Asphen was a completely different person from Sylus. He had his way of looking at the world. If the man was happy to be alive and wanted to celebrate while fourteen other people were dead, well, that was his right, no matter how disgusted it made Sylus feel.

Sylus didn't head to the stairs; instead, he went straight toward Liana, not caring if Asphen noticed or not. Liana had finished her prayers, and the bodies were being lifted reverently by crew members. They would be stored in a special sealed room on the ship, kept on ice, for proper funerals once they returned to shore.

Liana turned to look at him as he approached, her eyes sad but focused.

"Hey," she said softly, and slipped her arms under his own, pulling him into an embrace.

Sylus was a little surprised, but wrapped his arms around her as she turned her head and leaned against his chest. Sylus could feel eyes on them, and concentrated on the feeling of Liana in his arms instead.

"Uhm…" he whispered, "Is this okay?"

"Oh, they all know at this point," Liana said, her voice low and muffled. "Cally even pulled me aside before the funeral to ask if we'd done it. Before the *funeral*."

"Did she?" Sylus said.

Liana pulled back to look at him, a knowing look on her face.

"Something on your mind?"

"Am I that obvious?"

"Yes," Liana said, smiling. "I can read you like a book."

Sylus felt his heart expand at that, even if he could not say the same about her. She remained as wonderful and mysterious to him as ever.

"Can we go to your room?" he asked. Her eyebrow raised.

"Really?" she asked.

"To talk," he added.

"Sure," she said with a doubtful smile.

Liana grabbed his hand and headed toward the stairs, but they were interrupted by the appearance of the Captain and the rest of the crew on the enemy ship's deck. Many of them were holding boxes full of scavenged parts. Those on the deck gathered around as the Captain stepped back onto the *Bladedancer*.

"We'd better stay and listen for a minute," Liana said.

The Captain didn't seem to want to make a speech, but he gave the gathering crowd a wary look and cleared his throat before speaking.

"I no be wanting to get anyone's hopes up," he began, "We did find no sails, the Reclaimed no seem to care for using them. But Virel says there's a chance, a chance, mind you! That we be able to repair the engines."

He got drowned out momentarily by whoops and cheers from the crew, who were unable to contain themselves. Liana turned and beamed at him. It took a few minutes for the crew to control themselves, but eventually the Captain waved them down to near silence.

"It be taking a few days, and we be in no small amount of danger until its complete. I want triple shifts around the clock. If so much as a Glimmerbeetle hops in the Green, I want to know about it. Holven! Gather up some men to see to whatever Virel needs, and the rest of you..."

"Come on," Liana said, tugging him toward the stairs, "Let's sneak away before he puts us to work."

"You want to sneak away from your duties?" he asked, shocked.

She merely took his hand and gave him a thin-lipped smile, with a look on her face that shut him up quickly as he followed her back to her room.

The door wasn't even completely closed before her mouth found his, her hands tugging at his shirt, trying to pull it off while continuing to kiss him.

Sylus struggled to get words out.

"I... actually... did... need to... talk to you!" he mumbled in the seconds their mouths were apart.

"Shush," she said, putting a finger over his mouth, and pushing him backwards, toward the bed, "We could have died, Sylus, but we didn't. I'm alive, and I want to feel alive. We can talk later."

She gave him a hard shove, and he fell backwards onto the bed. Liana pulled off her top and crawled on top of him, and he completely forgot the things he wanted to talk about.

38

Hope for a Future

Some time much later, Liana finally looked up from where she lay on his chest, a content smile on her face.

"So what did you want to talk about?" she asked.

Sylus, who was entertaining a fantasy about this moment lasting forever, took a minute to respond.

"I'm sure you heard what happened," he said slowly. Liana merely nodded.

"You mean your Wonder," she said.

"Not just mine. Yours too. I've seen you use push before, Liana. It was never that powerful. The Reclaimed are heavy, and you tossed it through the air like a doll."

"I know," she said.

"And when I cast Spark? Liana, it was like an entirely different Wonder. It *melted holes* through the Reclaimed."

"I saw them," Liana said.

"Well? Don't you think that's strange? What is going on?"

"I don't know," Liana said.

She pulled herself up into a sitting position in the bed, wrapping a blanket around herself so they could talk.

"It's like our Wonders were getting a huge power boost. When I cast Push, I could feel this huge amount of energy flow through me. I remember

I was worried my Thaumatech might explode."

"Me too!" Sylus said, sitting up, excited, "And did you notice? Look at my arm. My infection barely moved! Yours too, from the look of things."

Liana shifted uncomfortably and looked away for a moment, pulling the blanket up a little higher. Sylus knew she didn't like talking about her infection, and she didn't want him looking at it, even now.

"I know."

"Well? What could cause something like that?" Sylus pressed.

"I don't know," she said, turning back to him, "Frankly, I don't want to know."

"What? How can you not want to know?" he asked.

"Because it's a miracle," Liana said, meeting his eyes. "Six Reclaimed in an enclosed space? We should be dead. Again. But we're not, because of those Wonders."

Sylus put the pieces together, "You think it was Verdalis?"

"What else could it be?" she asked, a little defensively. "I know you don't believe as I do, but as soon as that ship appeared, I started praying to her. To save us. To save you. I think she was listening. I don't know if I want to question that."

Sylus nodded. He felt a little bad; he had not meant to question her beliefs.

"I hadn't thought of that," he said honestly, and she gave him a questioning look.

"Liana, I don't know what I believe anymore. Lately, I've found myself wishing I did believe as you do. That there's something out there, something watching over us. Watching over you. I suppose it could have been Verdalis, that's true."

Liana stared at him for a moment as if she couldn't believe what he was saying.

"I'm not just saying that, either. I honestly don't know what I believe, but I'm more on the fence about things than I was in the past."

She nodded, "You have your own theory, don't you?"

"I won't force it on you if you don't want to hear it, but I'd really like to tell you," he said. She nodded, so he continued, "What if the Wonders are more powerful because we're closer to the Source?"

Liana stared at him thoughtfully for a long moment. She sighed, but then nodded.

"I mean, everyone says the Source is in the Uncharted Green somewhere, if it exists at all. And if it's where Wonders get their energy from, then I suppose being close to it would make them more powerful."

"Yes! You get it!" Sylus said excitedly, "We've been adrift in the Uncharted Green for nearly a week. Maybe we've been drifting toward it this whole time. Think about it, Liana. We could find the Source."

"Slow down, Sylus," Liana said, shaking her head. "I didn't say I agreed, I just said it would make sense. Plus, why would you even assume that we'd be randomly drifting toward the Source?"

Sylus felt himself coloring. Her eyes narrowed.

"What aren't you telling me?"

"Nothing!"

"It's because of the Voice. Isn't it? That's why you're starting to believe. The Voice is telling you to find the Source, and now that you think we're close to it..."

"Well, why not?" Sylus said a little defensively. "You said yourself that some people in the Church believe the Voice could be Verdalis, guiding us. Well, what if it *is* Verdalis, and she wants me to find the Source? What if she did extend her protection to us today? What if this is where we're supposed to be?"

Liana, strangely, looked uncomfortable.

"I should never have told you that. It's not a widespread belief; it's more of a fringe belief, not the Church's official position."

"Oh," Sylus said, deflating a little, "What is the Church's official position?"

"Uh..." Liana said, looking down at the blanket, twisting a fold of it between her fingers. "It's that people who hear the voices are potentially suffering from an acute form of mental distress brought on by their condition?"

"What?"

"I'm sorry, Sylus. I just. I liked you, and you were so lost. It took you so long to come out of your room and act like yourself again. I didn't want you to spiral into a depression. Maybe it was the wrong thing to say, and if so, I'm sorry for it."

"Then why did you say it?"

Liana colored and looked away, pulling the blankets up around her chin.

"Because it's what *I* believe," she said quietly.

"Oh," Sylus said.

Sylus sat back and thought for a moment, while Liana glanced at him nervously.

Eventually, he shook his head.

"Don't be sorry. You were trying to help me. Maybe the Church is wrong, maybe it is Verdalis."

"Sylus..." Liana said.

"I want to talk to Asphen," he said, sliding out of bed.

"What? Why?" she asked.

"I want to see if he felt what we did," Sylus said, searching for his clothes.

"What difference will that make?"

"I don't know. Maybe nothing. Maybe something. Are you coming?"

"Sylus!" she said, exasperated.

Sylus pulled his clothes on in a hurry. He knew he was being a little rude, maybe a little short with Liana. He did not even know why; all he knew was that right now he wanted to get out of this room and explore his theory.

"Are you coming?"

To her credit, she seemed to understand. She sat there staring at him for a moment, tapping her chin with a finger as if deciding what to do, then nodded.

"Give me a minute," she said, getting out of bed and beginning the search for her clothes.

In a few minutes, they were walking down the hall to knock on Asphen's door, though Liana wasn't pleased about it.

"He's probably already drunk," she said, arms crossed beneath her chest as he rapped on the door.

"He already was earlier," Sylus said.

"Great."

They waited a few moments, but there was no answer.

"Well, we tried," Liana said, turning to go.

"Shush," Sylus said, pressing his ear against the door. There was no sound from inside, and Asphen was not exactly a quiet person.

He tapped his foot on the floor as he thought. It wasn't yet late enough for the man to be asleep, and he'd seemed on the verge of celebrating their victory when Sylus last saw him. There was another place he could be.

"C'mon, he's probably at the bar," Sylus said, leading the way. Liana followed with a roll of her eyes and some choice mutterings under her breath.

The lounge, to Sylus's surprise, was full to the brim. It appeared that Asphen was not the only one who wanted to celebrate. Every table was full of crew members drinking and laughing loudly. As they entered, Sylus saw a few games of dice being played, and even a small band playing music. They plinked out a merry tune, and a small crowd of dancers had gathered to celebrate being alive. The bartender noticed them standing there and gave them a questioning nod, to which Sylus shook his head. He was not interested in drinking.

"Oh my, is that Valera?" Liana said, pointing.

Sure enough, on the dance floor was Valera, dancing along with the others. Sylus stared.

"I don't think I've ever seen her laugh," he said, stopping to watch.

"It looks like fun," Liana said wistfully, glancing at him.

Sylus did not know anything about dancing, and colored instantly.

"Uhm, maybe after," he dodged, pushing away from the crowd, scanning the faces for Asphen.

It did not take long to find him, as he was the only person not wearing a shirt. He'd managed to grab one of the corner booths and was drinking and chatting with a female crew member with short brown hair. Sylus thought her name was Ivy. The woman was giggling as Asphen whispered into her ear with a wide grin plastered across his face.

"Oh gods, does he ever stop?" Liana said.

Sylus pushed his way up to the table.

"Asphen!"

Asphen pulled away from the girl's ear, looking mildly annoyed, but surprisingly less drunk than Sylus anticipated.

"Sylus," he said, sounding surprised, "Come from a drink?"

"No, I need to talk to you," Sylus said.

"I'm a little busy now, kid, can you come back later?" he said, nodding toward the woman.

"Iva, do you know he's slept with half the ship?" Liana said.

The look Iva gave Liana said that she did know, but did not appreciate being reminded.

"Hey!" Asphen said.

"Beat it," Liana said to the woman, ignoring Asphen. "You can come back later."

Iva shot them a furious look, then turned to Asphen and said, "I'll get us some more drinks."

She slid from the booth and disappeared into the crowd.

Asphen scowled at them.

"Why in the blades did you do that? First of all, it's none of your business; second of all, don't shame me and my partners. We all know what we're getting into. Just because you two prefer to shack up exclusively doesn't mean the rest of us have to."

Liana looked a little embarrassed as she slid into the booth beside Sylus.

"Sorry," she muttered.

"Damn right," Asphen said, taking a drink. "This better be important, kid, we were just about to leave if you know what I mean."

"It is," Sylus said, ignoring the strange way Liana was behaving for the moment. "Did you feel anything different when you cast Wonders today?"

Asphen eyed them suspiciously, his bottle halfway to his lips, before putting it down on the table untouched and sitting up straight.

"You too felt it as well?" he asked, "I damn-near blew the *Bladedancer* a new asshole on the back deck trying to burn a Reclaimed."

Sylus felt excitement fill his veins and turned to grin at Liana, but she just looked uncomfortable.

"Yes! Me too. I tried a simple Spark, desperation really, and it fried an entire hallway."

"That was you? I walked by that earlier and wondered if a bomb had gone off."

"Do you have any idea what happened? To me, it felt like I was drawing in a lot more energy than normal. Liana and I both thought our Thaumatech was going to explode."

Asphen's smile dropped a little.

"What's this about?" he asked suspiciously.

"I had a theory," Sylus said carefully. Asphen did not say anything, so he continued, "Maybe the reason the Wonders were so powerful was because we're out here, in the Uncharted Green."

Asphen stared at him, "So? What of it?"

"Well, everyone says the Source is somewhere out here, so I thought..."

"Blades, not this shit again," Asphen said sourly, taking a sip from his drink. "Do you ever let up, kid? The Source isn't real. How many times do I have to tell you that? Is this some garbage she's filling your head with?"

Liana shot him an angry look.

"I told you this was a waste of time, Sylus."

"I don't get you two!" Sylus said. "It's like neither of you cares about what happened today!"

"What happened? Who gives a shit what happened? What happened is we're fucking alive. Maybe you should start paying attention to that fact, because of the looks of that neck," he said roughly, jabbing a finger toward Liana, "It won't be the case for much longer."

Liana's hand covered her neck instinctively, and she shot a hateful look at Asphen.

Sylus's insides boiled.

"What the fuck is wrong with you?" he snapped.

"Fuck you!" Liana growled at the same time.

"Yeah, yeah. You weren't interested, remember?" Asphen said, sliding out of the booth.

He turned to leave, both of them staring angrily at his back. Then he looked back at them over their shoulder, and surprisingly, he didn't look angry at all. Just tired.

"Look, I'm sorry. Just celebrate. That's all I'm saying, yeah?" he said, then disappeared into the crowd.

Sylus watched him go, then turned to Liana. She was still holding her neck, but was staring at the table, her expression angry.

"Are you okay? You were right, this was a bad idea," he said.

"I'm fine," she muttered, staring at the table.

"Do you still want to dance?" he tried weakly.

"Let's just go back to the room."

Sylus felt horrible, but didn't know what to do about it. They left the lounge and walked in silence. He felt like maybe he should just let the whole thing go. No one seemed to agree with him, but he felt so sure that he was right.

As soon as the door closed behind them, Liana turned to face him.

"Sylus, why is this so important to you?" she said.

"What?"

"This theory of yours. Why are you suddenly so obsessed with it?"

"I'm not, I just..."

Liana cut him off, "Sylus, you left our happy little bed - where I was completely naked, by the way - to go to a shitty lounge to talk to an emotionally stunted alcoholic who's allergic to shirts."

She pierced him with a fiery look, her blue eyes flashing as she tucked her hair behind her ear.

"Just tell me what's going on. Please. I hate feeling like you're hiding things from me."

He thought about dodging the question again, telling her he was just stressed and to forget the whole thing, but he couldn't do it. Not while she was staring at him like that. Her face was a mixture of affection, concern, anger, and sadness. She was so beautiful it made his heart ache, and he couldn't go on another minute without telling her the truth.

"The voice said something new," he muttered.

"Changed?" Liana said, her eyebrows rising. "Changed how?"

"It was a couple of days ago, maybe more, I forget. We were lying in bed. You were asleep. I went to the washroom, and I was worrying about things. And the voice changed what it was saying. It didn't say to find the Source."

"What did it say?" she prompted.

"It said that the Source could save you," he said quietly.

Suddenly, his eyes felt very hot, and his throat felt very tight. He found he could no longer look at Liana, so he looked away. It seemed to help with his eyes, but did nothing to stem the flow of words that poured out of his mouth.

"It said it could save you. And I just thought I was going crazier. My mind was telling me what I wanted to hear, you know? How am I supposed to find the Source anyway? I don't have a ship. I don't know anything about where it might be, except somewhere out here.

But then..."

Sylus had to draw a deep, shuddering breath to continue. "Then today, I swore, I *swore* I could feel it, Liana. And it was close. I felt like I could almost feel a direction. I just thought, maybe it *is* real. Maybe it's real, and I can find it. And if I find it, I could save you, and save me, and we could... we could..."

He felt Liana's arms slide around him, pulling him into an embrace and turning him towards her. When their eyes met, he was relieved to see that her eyes were red, wet, and big. It was too much. Sylus felt the tears spill over and run down his face. Liana pulled him into a tight, fierce hug, her hands stroking the back of his head as he let his emotions flow.

"Oh, Sylus," she murmured, stroking his hair.

He could feel wet drops hitting the top of his head.

"Maybe the Source *is* real," she said softly, "But I don't know if it can cure us, Sylus. The Source is where Thaumatech comes from. It's where it gets its power. I don't know if it could cure itself, do you know what I mean?"

She seemed to be struggling to talk herself, and those drops kept falling on his head.

"And maybe that's okay? You know? We might not have much time. But do you want to spend it chasing a myth? Or do you want to spend it together? We knew when we got into this how it would end, but that doesn't mean it can't be beautiful... and wonderful... and that's okay. Isn't it?

This is the path our lives have taken. I really, truly understand where you're coming from, but I think if we accept it, then we can use the time we have left to the fullest, and that's for the best, right?

I'm babbling..."

She was, but he could feel what she was trying to say. He could feel that she understood his desperation, and though everything in him was screaming at him not to accept it, a large part of him knew that she was right, even if he would not, could not, accept it. So he took a deep breath and rose to meet her red-rimmed eyes, and they stared at each other, sniffling, and Liana gave him a weak but brave smile. It wasn't a good moment. It was a terrible, awful, heartbreaking moment. He was crying, and she was crying. A drunk had just said mean things to them, and it was neither romantic nor perfect, but maybe it was the right moment. He wasn't going to hesitate again.

"I love you," he said.

She laughed, because of course she already knew that, and the smile that lit up her face was possibly the most beautiful thing that Sylus had ever seen. And she kissed him. A wet, salty, tear-filled kiss, their lips were pressing together too hard because she wrapped her arms around his head to pull him into it. It was the best kiss they'd ever had.

When she pulled away smiling, he knew before she even said it back, but it was still nice to hear.

"I love you too."

39

A Desperate Man

That night, when Liana finally fell asleep, Sylus slipped out of bed. He tried not to look at Liana as he silently dressed, opening the door and sliding it closed behind him, hoping the natural sounds of the ship would cover his transgression. Once he was out in the hall, he locked the door behind him, taking a moment to rest his head on the door.

"I'm sorry," he whispered.

Liana was right. He should accept their fate and spend every second he possibly could with her, making every moment they had left count, instead of chasing impossible fantasies. But he couldn't accept a life without her, even a short one.

With his head resting against the cool door and the love of his life sleeping inside, Sylus accepted that he was a selfish person. Liana was content to live a short life, convinced that in some way, this was the way things were meant to be, but she was all he had left. He could not fathom being here without her, and beyond that, Liana deserved more than this world had given her.

He had made his choices, and on some level, he was beginning to come to terms with the consequences. But Liana did not stick her hand in a Thaumatech trap. She'd had her future stolen before she was old enough to know what she wanted for that future.

If there was even the slightest chance that Sylus might be able to save her, he was not going to let it pass him by. So he pushed away from the door and made his way to the Captain's room.

Sylus passed no one in the hallways. He wasn't sure if the Captain would even be awake at two in the morning, but when he rapped at the door, he was not entirely not surprised to hear the man's voice answer.

"Who is it?" Bracken called gruffly.

"Sylus, sir," he called back.

"Sylus?"

There was the sound of a chair being pushed back, then muffled grumbling before the door opened to reveal Captain Bracken. He was still fully dressed and had a haggard, tired look on his face.

"You'd better be having a good reason for bothering me so late, boy," he said.

"I don't, sir, but can we talk anyway?" Sylus said.

Bracken gave him a searching look, and Sylus thought he might say no, but something in Sylus's attitude must have moved him, for he softened for a moment, sighed, and gestured him inside.

"Oh, alright then, I suppose today was hell on us all. Throw me to the blades if it ain't true," he grumbled.

Sylus entered the plain sitting room that served as the Captain's office, with the doors behind the man's desk leading to his bedroom. There was a single desk covered with papers and navigational charts, a chair behind the desk, two in front, and a surprising number of bookshelves filled to the brim.

A bottle of whiskey was open on the desk, and a half-full glass suggested that Sylus had interrupted what had to be one of the hardest days at sea for a Captain.

Sylus sat down at the desk and scanned the papers across it as the Captain returned to his seat. He sat, studied Sylus for a moment, and pulled out another glass, sliding it across the table. He nodded to the papers on the desk.

"Notices to the family," he grumbled, "I used to deliver them myself, but now I send Holven. He be better at it than I."

Sylus had a hard time picturing stony-faced Holven being better suited to delivering horrible news, but he let it go and sipped at the drink he'd been offered. It was no grasswine. The drink burned his mouth, so he swallowed it quickly, enjoying the sudden warmth that spread through his chest when it was gone, leaving behind a spicy cinnamon taste.

"So, what be on your mind, boy? And no be telling me you come here for advice about women," Bracken said, smiling when Sylus looked at him with surprise.

"Oh yes, I do know too. Been knowing for weeks. You two are no very subtle. Can't say I approve of where you be conducting your business, but far be it from me to chastise young folk in love, no matter how opposed I may be to the idea of you two.

Watching you two make eyes at each other for weeks damn near made me sick. I knew I couldn't have kept you apart for long."

Sylus felt a little taken aback, as if each word were a blow. Not because the words were harsh, but because they drove home the heartbreak that awaited him. Something of his mood must have shown on his face, for Bracken, who seemed to be enjoying the teasing, suddenly frowned.

"You seemed happy enough, or do there be trouble in paradise already?"

"No," Sylus said. "Nothing like that, though I suppose it is sort of about Liana? Well, it's about me too."

"Well, go on then," Bracken said.

"I'm sure you know that Liana doesn't have much time left," Sylus said shakily.

It was hard to hear the words outside of his head, and he wished he could take them back, as if speaking them out loud made them more real.

Bracken's eyebrows went up, and he leaned back in his chair and took a long drink from his glass, as if thinking of how to respond to that, his face growing somber.

"Aye, I do, lad. Valera informed me today of the extent of her condition, but if you come here to ask me how long she might have..."

"I really don't want to know," Sylus said, squeezing his eyes shut.

"Well, you can no say I didn't warn you," the Captain said, but not meanly.

If anything, his voice was low and gentle. Sylus opened his eyes to find the man swirling his drink, his eyes locked onto the twirling amber liquid.

"I do know what it be like to lose someone you love. It be the worst feeling in the world, even when you know it's coming. I'm sorry, lad."

Sylus only nodded, not liking the way the conversation was going. He didn't want to talk about Liana like she was already gone. This wasn't going to get any easier, so there was no point delaying it any further.

"I came here to ask you for something," Sylus said, and Bracken's eyebrows rose again.

"Yes, I can marry you, if that be what you want," he said knowingly, stroking his beard. It was Sylus's turn to be shocked. "It's not uncommon for folks to get married on the blades, though it never happened on my ship. It's a little inappropriate, what with everything that's happened, but I suppose..."

"Uh, no," Sylus stammered.

"No?" Bracken said, confused.

"I mean, yes, I think I'd want to marry Liana, but that's not what I came to ask," he said.

"Then what?"

"I think there might be a way to save her," he said, before the Captain could sidetrack him again.

Dead silence met this pronouncement, and this time the Captain's eyebrows drew downwards, his face growing dark.

"What are you on about, boy?" he grumbled.

And so, Sylus told him everything, letting it all out in a rush. From the hearing of the voices, to the moment he thought the voices might be listening and responding to him, his experiences during the battle, and finally, what happened with the Wonders and his theory that Verdalis might be guiding him to the Source, which he believed was nearby.

Bracken, for his part, took it better than could be expected. His expression remained dark, but he said nothing, merely leaning forward to rest his elbows on the desk, hands clasped together, studying Sylus as he spoke.

Sylus finished, he felt out of breath, and the Captain was silent. Feeling suddenly altogether nervous, he took another drink, letting the warmth fill him with courage.

"Who else did you tell this theory to?" Bracken said in a low voice.

"I know how it sounds," Sylus said.

"Do you? It sounds like you've lost your damn mind, boy!" Bracken said, "And what? I suppose you want to lead the *Bladedancer* on your merry hunt?"

"O-of course not!" Sylus stammered, "I just thought that maybe, once the ship was repaired, I might convince you to let me take the emergency escape ship, alone, if I can't convince Liana, to try and find it."

"Oh, that be all, is it?" Bracken interrupted, his face turning red, his voice rising, "Just leave the whole crew with no way to escape should something happen, leave your lady behind if need be, and sail off into the Uncharted Green on your own, looking for something that may not even exist!? Do you even hear yourself?"

"I know how it sounds!" Sylus said again, his voice rising, "I can't explain, but I'm right. I know I am, and all I'm asking is for..."

"You don't know a damn thing about what you be asking!" Bracken shouted, "If you thought for one second I'd entertain this-"

"I KNOW!" Sylus shouted back, meeting Bracken eye for eye. "I know that you'd never say yes in a million years, I know it's a suicide mission, I know..."

Suddenly, he broke, his anger washing away as the fire drained out of him. He lost his nerve, unable to look at the Captain in the face, and dropped his eyes to the desk, ashamed of the drops that fell on the papers sprawled across it.

"I don't know what else to do," he said, bracing himself for the Captain to give him the lecture of a lifetime, or perhaps throw him in the brig. He'd deserve it.

Instead, a deep sigh brought his eyes back to the Captain. The color was draining out of the man's face, and he rocked in his chair, staring at Sylus with those deep, dark eyes. Then he reached out across the desk and placed a heavy hand on Sylus's shoulder.

"I know, boy, I know," he said gently.

He pushed Sylus's glass back into his hands before taking up his own again.

"I know you be hurting, Sylus, I really do. Perhaps I understand it better than most. You feel you need to do something, anything. Anything to try and stop what's coming," Bracken said gently.

"But listen to yourself. You would abandon Liana right at the end? For a chance? A chance of a chance? Even if the Source is real, and you found it, there's no guarantee it's a cure. Even if it was, how would you figure out how to use it?

If you survived the journey, which you would not, you'd regret leaving her for the rest of your days, lad, believe me. I never set things right with your mother, for example, and now I never will."

Sylus's head came up in shock.

"You know?" he whispered.

"Of course I know! You two were my only living family. You think I kept stopping at that empty rock in the middle of nowhere for the trading opportunities? I paid someone to keep an eye on you."

Bracken chuckled, but then his eyes grew distant.

"Kept making port there, thinking one of these days I'd march up the mountain and make things right. Then one day I came in, and she was gone. I never got the chance. You were already grown and never knew me. Heard you were an apprentice of some sort. Seemed to be doing alright.

I kept making port there, checking up on you. Never thought you'd show up at the docks looking for me, though."

"But if you knew, why'd you let me on the crew? Knowing I lied?" Sylus said.

"Therithar take me if I know. I thought, what be a safer place for you than under my eye? I knew the look in your eye. If I didn't put you on my ship, you'd have found another eventually. I made a promise to myself I'd keep you safe, and look how well I did at that."

He gestured to Sylus's metal hand solemnly.

"Thaumatech has taken everything from me, boy. Either directly or through the business. My wife, my parents, my sister, and one day you. You be my last living family member, Sylus. There's nothing I can do about it now, but not a day goes by that I don't wish I had one more day with each of them, instead of this ship and this life.

My point is, no one wishes there be a cure more than me, but you're asking me to let you kill yourself, and I won't do it. I won't let you throw away what's left of your life. Don't let Thaumatech take away what you have for the promise of what could be. I'll lock you in the brig if I have to, but I think that won't go over so well with the crew, or with Liana, so don't force me to."

Sylus took a moment to process this massive amount of new information, but the bottom line was clear. The Captain was not going to give him the emergency ship, and Sylus knew he didn't have it in him to take it by force. Furthermore, he knew the Captain was right. Just as he knew Liana was right.

He tried to imagine Liana dying alone because he ran off on some insane adventure. The imaginary scene threatened to rip him apart.

They sat there in silence for a time.

"I think I should go back to bed," Sylus said after a long time.

"I be thinking that's a good idea," Bracken said, nodding. "Finish your drink, though, it'll help. Plus, it's expensive."

Sylus did, trying to let the warmth wash away his desperation and despair, then he rose to leave.

"Captain?" he said at the door, "Thanks. Can you not tell Liana I was here?"

"Think nothing of it," Bracken said.

Sylus could feel Bracken's gaze long after he'd left the office and made it back to his rooms. He slipped in quietly, careful not to wake Liana, who slept on, none the wiser.

As he crawled into bed, though, he could still not shake the feeling that he was right.

Seek the Source.

The intrusion of the voice felt like a kick while he was already at his lowest point.

How? How could he seek the Source on his own?

There was no answer.

40

Pull of the Gods

For the third day in a row, the ringing of the alarm bells might have woken Sylus if he'd been able to sleep at all. As it was, he was staring at the ceiling when the alarm made them jump out of bed. Without a word, they scrambled out of bed, hastily dressing and rushing for the deck, emerging into a fog dense enough to turn the sunlight grey and hazy.

Nearby, Asphen stared out into the mists among a crowd of crew members, though at what Sylus wasn't sure, for it was impossible to see anything through the thick rolling clouds that billowed around the ship.

"What is it?" he asked the nearest crew members, but it was Asphen who answered.

"We don't know," he said quietly. "Something in the mists."

Sylus peered out into the grey nervously, "Another Reclaimed ship?"

"No. Be quiet!" Asphen barked at those around him, who fell silent immediately.

Asphen tilted his head, one ear to the sky, and Sylus emulated him, straining to hear something over the noises of the ship. Men and women talked nervously on other decks. The Captain was barking orders above, and beneath it all, there was nothing. No sound of the wind through the blades, no rustling of the grasses sliding against the ship as they drifted.

Sylus stared out into the fog. It swirled lazily around the ship, parting along the bow, coating the sails.

Sylus did a double-take, *coating* the sails? He stepped up to the railing of the ship beside Asphen, peering down at the railing. It was less pronounced here, a fine change in the color of the wood. He ran a finger along the railing as Asphen watched, leaving a barely perceptible trail in the thin coating that had accumulated.

He looked up at Asphen, his eyes wide.

"It isn't fog," he said, "It's some kind of dust?"

A low, tremulous sound warbled across the deck, drawing all eyes into the cloaking blanket of whatever surrounded the ship. It was a long, drawn-out note, a deeply resonating hum that was felt in the chest instead of heard with the ears. Low and slow, the sound washed over the crew, stilling them to complete silence. As it faded, it was followed by a slow whistling, air-like sound, as if someone was exhaling loudly nearby.

"What is it?" Liana whispered, but Asphen waved her to silence, pointing out into the mists.

Something stirred the grey clouds, visible as it moved through them. It resembled a softly swaying silk curtain, long, billowing, and nearly translucent. It was followed by another, and another, until dozens of the wispy streamers became visible. They moved with purpose, uncurling and dipping down into the blades, then rolling back upwards.

Some of the streamers billowed toward the ship, grasping toward the air tanks, slipping lazily around the ropes, winding and unwinding, as if feeling out the shape of the *Bladedancer*.

The tension on the deck was palpable. No one seemed sure what to do, and all stared transfixed at the ethereal scene that played out in front of them. At least, until one of the streamers drifted toward where they stood on the deck. Everyone took an involuntary step back as one of the streamers snaked its way around the railing, winding and unwinding through the tines.

Asphen did not seem willing to wait any longer to see what happened. He raised one of his swords, intending to strike the streamer off the ship, but quite suddenly, the Captain was there, his hand catching Asphen's wrist before the sword swung down.

"I don't think it be seeing us," he said.

Asphen stared at him incredulously, but the Captain held him firm. He shook his head slowly, then pointed up into the fog. Every head followed his hand, which pointed to the streamer as it coiled up. Sylus peered into the mists. And something stared back.

Sylus blinked and took a step back as something rolled slowly into view.

A great orb-like eye emerged from the swirling grey. It traveled alongside the ship, followed shortly by a great bulbous body, covered in spiky, translucent fur. It was to this body that the streamers hung from, coiling and uncoiling. Sylus watched in awe as the body expanded, and out from the mists came the form of two giant, fluttering sections of the creature's body that spanned out like wings.

If they were wings, however, they did not flap. Like most of the creature's body, the wings were see-through, but instead of furred or feathered, they were bulbous and balloon-like. They floated above the creature in much the same way the air tanks of the *Bladedancer* did, and Sylus supposed that was how it stayed aloft.

How the creature moved was not immediately clear, as it floated among the mists, neither flapping its strange wings nor moving any part of its body aside from the streamers, which continued to stretch out along the ship, almost like feelers, guiding the ghostly creature through the gloom. To Sylus, it resembled a gigantic moth, though instead of legs it possessed an uncountable number of those ghostly tentacles.

If the creature took any notice of them, it gave no sign. There was no sense of movement in the great orb-like eye that was visible to them, though its structure suggested that it saw in all directions at once. What light there was reflected off an infinite number of surfaces within the glossy black eye.

"I don't believe it," Liana said softly.

All nearby eyes turned to her, and she colored slightly.

"You know what this is, Liana?" Bracken whispered, sounding impressed.

"Driftmoth. I saw a picture in a book once."

The Captain nodded, "They're supposed to be extinct."

"Will one of you two explain what the fuck is happening?" Asphen whispered roughly, his sword still raised suspiciously.

"Put down your blade," Bracken warned. "It be doing us no harm if we leave it alone. They drift along the surface, eating something off the tops of the blades."

"And the fog?" Sylus said, holding up his finger.

"It's no fog, it's a pollen the creature releases. It does no like the sun."

Several people around them raised their shirts over their mouths, and Sylus had the sudden urge to do the same, though the Captain did not look concerned to be breathing in whatever the creature was releasing.

"Leave it alone and it do pass us by," Bracken said.

The Driftmoth, for its part, let out another low hum. Closer now, it sounded more musical than before, though it was still more of a sensation than a sound. Everyone on the deck turned to watch the creature as the sound washed over them.

"It almost sounds sad," Liana whispered.

Sylus nodded in agreement, transfixed by the ghostly apparatus.

The Driftmoth's great balloon wings quivered, and with a great exhale, released another great puff of pollen into the air behind it. The release of air pressure gently pushed the creature along. Asphen finally put away his sword, but crossed his arms and stared at the Driftmoth suspiciously as it floated just slightly ahead of the ship, slowly overtaking them as they drifted.

"Beautiful," Liana whispered.

The ghostly streamers seemed to catch the dim light as they drifted down over the ship. They shied away from the crew, though, curling up and away if they got too close to anyone. Liana reached a hand toward one streamer, smiling as it curled away from her as if it could sense her presence.

Sylus could not help staring into the creature's single orb-like eye. There was something off-putting about the way it didn't move. It was almost lifeless.

As if in answer to his thoughts, the great head of the creature turned toward the ship as if regarding the crew as they stared at it. But the other side of the creature's head did not feature a similar eye.

"Blades below," Bracken whispered, as the entire crew looked on, horrified.

The Driftmoth's second eye was a far-too-perfect glassy orb that sat upon a jagged scar of metal and machine that ran across the creature's face. It glowed with an internal green light, blinking regularly as the insect turned to regard the ship.

The Driftmoth was infected.

Sylus looked in horror at the streamers strewn across the ship. They wrapped around rope lines, twirled around masts, and coiled through banisters. There were hundreds of them.

"Cut them!" Sylus cried, drawing his sword, but it was already too late.

The creature's wings swelled in a sudden burst, and it rose at a frightening pace, quickly disappearing into its pollen cloud. The streamers, though thin as ribbons, tightened ominously, and the ship lurched violently into the air.

There were screams of sudden terror as the upward force knocked everyone flat to the deck. Sylus grabbed onto Liana as they fell, rolling over the deck boards until they came to a rest against the wall. Luckily, since everyone was forced to the floor, the railing prevented anyone from going overboard.

Sylus's stomach dropped out as the ship began to pick up speed, and though he tried to struggle to his feet, the momentum became too great, and there was little he could do but hold onto Liana as the creature pulled them upwards.

It was impossible to see what the creature was doing or where it was taking them due to the pollen that swirled around the ship. Sylus could hear people yelling, and thought he heard the Captain giving commands, but the rushing sound of wind filled his ears, and the *Bladedancer* began to tilt forward as their upward momentum became forward motion.

Sylus had a wild vision of the ship dangling underneath the creature like a basket, hundreds of feet above the blades. He could see Asphen struggling to rise. Miraculously, the man had driven himself to his knees with the enhanced strength of his Thaumatech leg. He was visibly struggling to raise the rest of his body, his muscles taunt, his body covered with sweat, his face twisted into a visage of determination and rage.

He seemed to be positioning his body for something.

A fireball twice the size of a man erupted from the machinery of his leg, flying upwards into the swirling pollen.

Sylus heard Liana shout in alarm, but couldn't hear the words in the wind.

If the fireball connected, there was no sign, and another roared out from Asphen a moment later.

Liana grasped at Sylus desperately, pulling him close to shout in his ear.

"...explode! It will explode!" she cried desperately, and Sylus looked back at Asphen in horror as he launched yet another fireball into the mists.

It sailed into the dust, burning through streamers as it traveled upwards, becoming a dim light as it faded into the grey, then connected.

A tremendous explosion suddenly rocked the ship, and a bright light pierced through the pollen like a roaring sun.

A great boom rocked through the air, followed by a terrible, warbling hum, somehow even more sorrowful than before, and the ship began to fall.

41

Burning Future

The Driftmoth burned above the *Bladedancer*. The creature's tentacles still held the airship, and its warbling cry showed that it was not dead, at least not yet. Sylus caught sight of its burning silhouette above them with one wing completely gone and its torso in flames.

As the ship's trajectory changed from forward to falling, however, it was not the rapid plunge to their deaths that Sylus initially feared. Instead of plummeting, the airship lost height gradually, but quickly, buoyed by the gas-filled creature and its air tanks. Around the deck, many were able to find their way to their feet, and Sylus could see the Captain force himself to his knees and start to shout orders.

"Increase pressure to the tanks, and slow our descent! Get those sails in! Cut those streamers!" he bellowed.

"That idiot!" Liana said, crawling out from beneath Sylus.

She pushed herself shakily to her feet and peered upwards at the burning Driftmoth. Its cry was dying out now, long and slow, and Sylus noticed many of the streamers wrapped around the ship losing their grip.

The crew hopped to obey the Captain, and not for the first time, Sylus appreciated just how well the crew of the *Bladedancer* was trained. In mere moments, the remaining sails were hauled in, and their descent stopped picking up speed, but instead remained a gentle drift downwards.

"He could have killed us all," Liana said.

She stared up at the burning Driftmoth. The pollen was clearing remarkably quickly, and Sylus suspected that the creature was well and truly dead now, as its descent began to pick up speed. He watched as the Driftmoth slipped below the ship, its body being consumed by flames, and the last of its streamers, now loose, followed the creature below the railing and out of sight. Liana and Sylus went to the edge of the ship and watched it fall through the thinning dust. It twirled through the mists until it dropped out of sight and became a dim light, then disappeared as it hit the blades below.

Liana leaned against him as if suddenly very tired, slumping into his arms, and he realized she was shaking.

"Are you okay?" he asked, turning her toward him.

"I'm okay, I just don't know how many more near-death experiences I can take," she said, looking up at him.

"Me too," Sylus admitted, "I guess Asphen made the right call."

"Somehow. He could have blown us all to pieces."

Liana glared over Sylus's shoulder at the man, who was standing nearby, staring out over the edge of the ship with a look of concentration, perhaps watching to see if the creature returned.

Sylus felt the sun on his skin and looked up to see a cloudy blue sky making itself visible as the dust cleared. Beneath them, an endless expanse of green peeked through the remaining pollen.

Asphen noticed them and, strangely, made his way over.

"Well, that was something," he said, "Can't say I've ever encountered one of those things before."

"That's because they were thought to be extinct," Liana said coolly, "That may have been the last one alive."

Asphen gave her a dry look, then shrugged. "It wasn't alive. It was Reclaimed."

"It was also a herbivore," Liana said, "It posed no threat to us."

"I'm not sure we can trust a Reclaimed creature to stick to its natural habits," Sylus said slowly.

He hated siding against Liana on this, but he could not understand her defense of the creature at the moment. Liana shot him an unreadable look, but eventually nodded.

"It was definitely up to something," she said, peering over the balcony.

They were quickly approaching the blades, coming in for what appeared to be a skillfully gentle landing.

"Never in all my days do I hear of something like that," Bracken said from behind them.

They turned to find the Captain standing nearby.

"Captain?" Sylus asked.

"You ever heard of the virus taking something that wasn't human?" he asked.

Sylus looked at the others quizzically. He'd personally never really thought about it. He assumed that since animals had no use for technology, they would never really come into contact with the virus. But why couldn't they be infected? If an animal had a brain, it could be infected, couldn't it?

Liana shook her head, "Never."

"It's called the Uncharted Green for a reason," Asphen said, sounding annoyed. "There's probably tons of shit out here that no one has ever seen before. What does it matter? It's dead."

"I no like things I no understand," the Captain grumbled.

"Captain?" came a new voice. It was Holven; he appeared at the Captain's elbow, looking for all the world like nothing eventful had happened.

"What is it now?" the Captain asked.

"You'd better come see this," Holven said, turning and walking toward the front of the ship.

The Captain followed, grumbling softly to himself, and Liana and Sylus shared a look, then followed as well.

Holven led them to the front of the ship, and they joined a growing crowd of crew members who were staring in awe at the scene unfolding in front of them.

The green stretched out in front of them. Except it didn't stretch out far. A few miles in front of them, the height of the blades dipped into a depression that stretched out to either side for miles, curving around to form a gigantic depression in the Verdant Sea.

And from the middle of the depression rose a city grander than any Sylus could imagine.

42

The Forgotten City

The city seemed entirely out of place in the Verdant Sea. Not only did the blades not grow within its borders, but the buildings themselves seemed to belong to another world. Time had been kind to the shining towers of gold and silver that rose from the bottom of the seabed. They stretched hundreds of feet into the sky, clearing the tops of the blades and continuing until it seemed they should touch the clouds. The buildings were clustered together in a tightly packed labyrinth, no two of a similar design, but each a monument to artistic expression in architecture.

Some featured straight lines and angles, while others were sinuous or organic-looking. Strange tunnels connected many of the towers in a vast network, while the remains of impossible bridges wound into and around the entire city.

If Sylus stared too long at any single feature, he could see the damage wrought by time, whether it was collapsed bridges, sections of buildings missing, or tunnels that had fallen into the streets below. But on the whole, the city still presented itself as a shining beacon of the ancient world, alien in its complexity and construction, as unlike the stone and wood buildings of today as the moons were of the earth.

No one on the deck of the *Bladedancer* seemed able to speak, and the attack of the Driftmoth seemed all but forgotten. Sylus tore his eyes away from the city to look at Liana, who openly gaped, and Asphen, who stared hungrily at the city, leaning forward as if he intended to jump over the side.

"I think," Holven said suddenly, lowering an eyeglass that he was holding up to his face, "That I can see the ground in there."

There was a desperate scramble for eyeglasses, for no one in the crew could believe that you might be able to see the ground in the Verdant Sea. When Sylus got a hold of an eyeglass, he stared down at the edge of the city where, sure enough, the blades did not grow, and dirt was visible before it turned into the strange stone roads of the city.

"Why would the blades not grow here?" Liana mused out loud.

"Dirt's no the only thing down there," the Captain said, motioning to the far side of the city, where something metal was moving.

Sylus swung his eyeglass toward the object, and though the distance was great, there was no mistaking it.

"Ships," he said.

"Reclaimed ships," Asphen said from beside him, looking through his eyeglass. "There's more coming around the other side. Many more."

As they watched, multiple ships completed a circuit around the city and disappeared around the other side, as if patrolling.

"There's more around the buildings, too," someone said.

Sylus counted more than twenty Reclaimed ships in and around the city.

"Do you think they've seen us?" he asked Liana.

"I no be intending to find out," the Captain said. "We're going to..."

But Sylus did not hear the rest of the Captain's plan, for at that moment he heard the voice.

SEEK THE SOURCE.

Sylus cried out in pain, holding his hands over his ears in a vain effort to drown out the booming command that sounded inside his skull without warning, as if a giant had shouted in his ear.

As the pain finally receded, he found Liana kneeling above him as he huddled on the floor, her face a picture of concern as she said his name. The rest of the crew stood around him in a circle, watching with concern.

It took a few moments for sound to return to him.

"Sylus? Sylus? What is it? Are you okay?" Liana was saying.

"I-I think so," Sylus said, pushing himself to his feet.

"What's wrong, lad?" Bracken said.

Sylus glanced toward the city, and several things occurred to him at once. The first was the implausible size of the fireballs Asphen was casting, the intensity of the voice, and the strange behavior of the creature that attacked them.

"The Driftmoth," he said.

"What?" Bracken said, frowning.

"The Driftmoth," Sylus repeated, turning to Liana, "It wasn't attacking. I think it was bringing us here."

Liana hesitated before speaking, "Sylus, you're not making any sense."

But Sylus was no longer listening; his mind was racing ahead, putting pieces together, and a strange, desperate hope took hold of him.

"I need to test something," he said.

He pushed his way through the crowd to the railing. The rest of the crew moved quickly out of his way, and he could not help but notice the looks of concern they gave him as they did so. He knew it looked like he was losing his mind, but he did not care.

He stretched his hand out over the railing.

"Spark!"

His hand barely needed to draw in power. As soon as he spoke the words with the intent to cast a Wonder, he could feel the energy pour into him. Lightning crackled from his palm in a sudden torrent, arcing into the blades, blasting wildly into the sky. The area around him seemed to darken as the violet-blue bolts struck from his palm, blasting the tops of the grasses to burning tips.

Sylus could hear the crew yelling at him to stop, but none dared approach him, and he ignored their cries. Sylus could feel the energy of this place. Whatever powered Wonders flowed through the air here, in currents so thick he was surprised he could not feel them before. As he suspected, here in this place, he could feel the direction the energy came from. He could feel where it flowed from and how it pulled on him quite clearly toward the city.

He let the Wonder die out, staring at his palm in disbelief. It vented heat in a shimmering haze around him.

"It's here," he whispered.

Hands grabbed him roughly from behind and spun him around, and he found himself face to face with the Captain.

"What do you think you be doing, boy?" The Captain yelled at him. "You trying to bring the Reclaimed down on us?"

"Let him go," Liana's voice said, except it rang out in a tone he'd only heard her use once before, when Asphen was trying to kill him.

The Captain looked over his shoulder to find Liana standing behind him, her metal forearm bared and raised. To say that Bracken looked shocked would be a complete understatement.

"Now!" Liana commanded.

The crew did not understand what was happening. A wide circle had opened up around Sylus, and the only ones inside it were Liana, the Captain, and him.

"Please don't make me ask again, Captain," Liana said.

The Captain released him and took a step back from Sylus, hands up.

"I will handle this," Liana said after a moment, lowering her arm, her face softening. Sylus looked back toward the city. It was here. It was real.

"Sylus," Liana said, her hand drew his face back toward her gently, forcing his eyes to meet her own. "Sylus, you're scaring us."

He stared into her eyes, her beautiful, crystal blue eyes, filled with love and concern.

He snapped out of it.

"It's here, Liana," he said.

"What's here?"

"The Source."

"God's above," the Captain muttered.

Liana shot him a look, then turned back to Sylus, looking into his eyes.

"Sylus..."

"Liana, please. Listen to me. Just cast something. You can feel it. It's here. It's down there. Just cast a Wonder, please, you'll see what I mean."

Liana's eyes flicked back and forth between his, her face still full of concern. Then she smiled and nodded.

"Okay," she said.

"Liana," The Captain said with a warning tone.

"Captain, I must ask you to humor me, just this once," Liana said, making no motion to stop what she was doing.

Without waiting for a reply, she raised her arm over the edge of the boat.

"Fire!" she commanded.

A fireball the size of a house burst from her arm, searing its way over the tops of the blades. The force of its casting threw Liana backwards, sending her tumbling across the deck.

"Liana!" Sylus cried, diving to help her, but rough hands grabbed him.

He struggled, only to find Holven holding him back.

"Let me go," he growled at the man.

"Easy Sylus," Holven said, "Let's just get this sorted out, okay?"

"Let. Me. Go!" Sylus said through gritted teeth.

Liana rolled to a stop and sat up, gasping so loudly that it drew all eyes back toward her.

"It's here," she gasped, her eyes wide.

She fell back into a sitting position as if she couldn't believe it, her eyes connecting with Sylus in wide amazement. Sylus relaxed in Holven's grip.

"Oh, for the love of... You've lost your damn minds! You both have! The Source isn't real!" Bracken said.

"Maybe it is," Asphen said, stepping out of the crowd.

"Not you too?" Bracken growled.

"I felt something when I drove off that moth," Asphen said slowly. "Something I've never felt before."

He walked toward the railing. The Captain opened his mouth as if to refuse, then closed it when he realized there was no real way to stop Asphen from doing what he wanted.

"Perhaps, there is something to this Captain?" Holven said, releasing Sylus.

"Do I be the only one here who cares about the Reclaimed?" Bracken grumbled.

Like the others, Asphen cast a Wonder off the balcony as they all watched. Sylus paid close attention, letting the feeling of something being drawn toward Asphen wash over him, trying to ascertain its direction again.

Liana got to her feet and came to stand next to him, placing her hand in his as they watched Asphen cast a Wonder.

"It's real," Liana whispered to him, and he was surprised to find tears in her eyes.

Asphen's Wonder finally died out, and he stood there for a long time, staring toward the city. Slowly, he turned back to the crew and looked surprised to find them all staring at him. For the first time Sylus could remember, Asphen looked genuinely torn, as if he was unsure for the first time in his life, and did not like the feeling.

He looked toward Sylus and Liana and finally nodded.

"It could be down there. Sure, why the fuck not?" he said.

43

A Better World

"Could be?" Sylus repeated thickly. "Could be?"

Asphen looked annoyed, "Don't lay your shit on me, kid. I told you before, I'll tell you again. The Source isn't real, and the gods aren't real."

"You literally just said otherwise!" Sylus growled.

Asphen held up a hand to forestall him.

"There's something down there. There's no denying that. Something that's connected to Wonders. Something that, more likely than not, will make us all very, very rich. I vote we go down there and retrieve it."

"Unbelievable," Liana breathed beside him.

Sylus stared incredulously at Asphen for a moment, who stared back at him impassively in turn, then shrugged.

"No one is going anywhere," Bracken declared. "Where the hell be Cally?"

"Here, Captain," came Cally's voice through the crowd. She poked her way through, looking sheepishly at the unfolding drama around her.

"Find out where we are, and how the fuck to get out of the Uncharted Green as fast as possible. Someone get me Virel. I want this ship moving in less than half an hour, and the rest of you..."

"We can't leave," Sylus said.

Silence dropped across the deck. The Captain turned toward Sylus slowly.

"I be thinking that everyone has forgotten who be Captain of the

Bladedancer," he said, his face turning red. "It be me. And I say we're leaving. End of discussion."

"After everything you've lost? After everything we've all lost?" Sylus said.

The Captain began to turn a deep shade of purple.

"You listen to me, boy," he started, but Sylus had made up his mind already.

"No. You listen," Sylus said. "The Source is down there. I am sure of it. And I am not leaving without it."

"You have no evidence. No proof, and no clue what to even do with the Source if it be down there, not to mention the Reclaimed will tear you to shreds before you get ten feet into that city!"

"And why do you think that is?" Sylus said, raising his voice to match. "Why do you think they're down there? Why do you think they're not up here, killing us? We made enough noise, I think! It's because they're guarding it.

Why do the Reclaimed even exist? Why does the virus do what it does to us? Why does it compel the Reclaimed to turn as many as they can before they disappear into the Green?

Because I think it's pretty obvious now where they've all been ending up. They come here. To the Uncharted Green. To this city. To protect whatever is down there. Why?

Because whatever is down there powers Wonders. It powers Thaumatech. It powers the Reclaimed, and it powers the virus."

The Captain shook his head, his shaggy beard swaying.

"This be nothing but conjecture and dreams. I know you want to change your situation, Sylus, but don't you see you're grasping at straws?"

"Don't you see? We can end this."

Sylus suddenly noticed that the entire crew had gathered on the deck to watch the unfolding drama, and every eye was on him.

So be it. If this were his last chance to convince anyone, then he would put everything he had into it. He held up his metal hand above his head, and stepped into the middle of the circle, slowly spinning, meeting the eyes of any who would meet his.

"I came onto this ship to make a better life for myself. But like so many others in this world, I was careless. And now, I'll be lucky to live to see thirty.

I thought nothing would be worse than watching the metal take my body, inching its way closer to taking everything. I thought nothing could be worse than knowing it's coming, and being unable to do anything about it, but I was wrong."

His eyes lingered on Liana, who looked at him with such love that he thought his heart might burst.

"It is a thousand times worse to see the same thing happen to someone you love, or to see the Reclaimed strike down a friend, only to have them rise again moments later, an empty shell, enslaved in metal.

No one on this boat is immune to the pain that Thaumatech causes. We're happy to use it to make our lives easier, but when someone is infected, we cast them out. People are fine to tolerate Thaumatechne briefly for our abilities, but no one wants us around for long. Why? Because we're a constant reminder that at any moment, any mistake, and it could be you or your loved ones, who are next to be taken.

I don't blame you. I wouldn't wish my fate on anyone. I wouldn't wish this on my worst enemy, let alone any of you. But I ask you, do any of you like living like this? Do you like living in fear? Watching loved ones die, helpless to interfere, scared even, to help them in their final moments?

The Captain is right. I *don't* know if the Source is down there. If it is, I'm not entirely sure I can find it. And if I find it, I can't say for sure that it would be able to stop the virus. But if there's even a one percent chance. A one percent chance that I might be able to prevent this from happening to anyone else isn't that worth my life? Isn't it worth the risk?

Not just for me. Not just for Liana or for Asphen. But for everyone who has ever lost a friend or loved one to the Reclaimed. For anyone infected, waiting for the end.

I came onto this boat to make a better life for myself. We all did. But if there's a single chance that I could make life better for everyone, then I owe it to myself to try. I won't ask anyone to go with me. If I have to go alone, I will. But I am going.

All I ask is to take the escape ship, and that you don't try to stop me."

He spun one final time and felt like a fool. Nobody looked very convinced. If anything, they just looked sad. He turned to face the Captain, who had pain written plain across his face.

Sylus could not tell if he was heartbroken or relieved that Liana had not offered to join him. He would never ask her to do so, and now that he had revealed that he was planning to leave her to die alone, she might even hate him. He was too afraid to look at her to find out which one it was. Sylus could only hope that he would succeed, and she would not die at all. In time, maybe she would even forgive him.

Silence.

A hand slipped into his.

He could feel his heart expanding with both love and sorrow as Liana stood beside him. He dared to look at her, and she was smiling at him. Her hair fell across her face.

"Where you go, I go," was all she said.

It was all that was needed.

"Fuck it, I'm in," said Asphen, stepping out of the crowd.

Both Liana and Sylus stared at him, dumbstruck.

"What?" he said, crossing his arms. "It was a pretty good speech. I think seeing what's in that city is as good a way to die as any."

Sylus had his doubts that Asphen was prepared to die for a chance to save others, but he kept his reservations to himself. He was grateful for the man's help, whatever his true motives.

Unfortunately, no one else spoke up.

The rest of the crew looked to the Captain. Sylus met the man's eyes. If he ordered the crew to stop them, Sylus was not sure he was willing to fight them to take the escape ship, but he was ready to find out if it came to that.

"It's a suicide mission, Sylus," the Captain said softly, shaking his head. "Why are you so determined to kill yourself? You be all I got left."

There were a few audible gasps. Sylus was just as surprised. The man sounded nearly emotional. He felt his heart go out to the Captain.

"I'm already dead, Uncle," Sylus said, with a weak smile. "Why not take a chance that I live?"

Bracken did not respond to this, and a long moment of silence seemed to stretch out between them.

"So be it," he said finally. "I be going too, damn me for a grasswine fool."

The ship broke into an uproar, with shouting on both sides between those who wanted to join and those who did not.

"Count me in!" Cally said, appearing beside Sylus.

"I would go," said Holven, "But if the Captain is going, at least one of us must stay with the ship. I hope you understand."

"I do," Sylus said honestly.

Though Holven had all the emotions of a stone, he was not a coward or a liar. He was only doing what he thought was right.

Sylus hoped he was doing what was right, too.

"Someone should probably teach me some more Wonders," he said weakly.

44

Before the End

There was a great debate about what to do next. For whatever reason, the Reclaimed ships below had either not noticed the *Bladedancer* at the top of the depression or, as Virel theorized, perhaps sailing up the steep decline was a technical challenge beyond the limited capabilities of Reclaimed piloting.

They used the peace to their advantage, planning late into the night how they might assault a superior force in a city they knew nothing about. Their best hope, they decided, lay in using the Reclaimed's disadvantages against them. One half of the crew would remain on the ship, with Holven as Captain, and attempt to draw the attention of the Reclaimed vessels below by descending into the depression. This would hopefully entice some of the ships to give chase. Once they were being followed, a smaller contingent would exit the *Bladedancer* via the small escape craft.

This smaller ship would use its faster speed and maneuverability to avoid the Reclaimed and enter the city, where again, the Reclaimed's slow reaction times and poor navigational skills would allow them to lose any pursuers within the narrow confines of the city streets.

Since the *Bladedancer* would have no Thaumatechne aboard, they were not to engage for any reason. Instead, once pursued, they would flee back up the depression to the higher blades, where the enemy would be unable to follow. With the *Bladedancer*'s emergency engines repaired, they should be able to outrun any pursuit; however, if the enemy ships gave chase out of the city, the *Bladedancer* was to leave those who entered the city behind and ensure their survival.

Once within the city, the plan was to use the Thaumatechne as a compass to find the Source, presumably within one of the buildings, and face whatever lay inside. If the Reclaimed did not pursue the Bladedancer, they would wait exactly forty-eight hours for the escape craft to return, no more.

They had gathered in the Captain's office and crowded around his desk to formulate their plan. Once the details were hammered out, those around the table sat back in grim silence. It was a bleak plan. The chances of success were slim, and the chances of survival were even worse.

"Well, that's all there is to it," Bracken said eventually. "We begin in the morning, so we'd best be getting some sleep."

Those around the table nodded, though if they felt anything like Sylus did, he doubted very much that any of them would be sleeping. Asphen merely nodded and left the room, likely to get a drink and perhaps find some company. Holven gave them all a curt nod and left as well. Only Cally hesitated upon standing, staring at Sylus and Liana with a profound sort of sorrow.

Liana stood and hugged her, and the two held each other tightly. Whispering too lowly for Sylus to make out. Sylus and the Captain merely stared blankly at the charts in front of them, on which they'd scribbled hasty notes and maps.

"Out on the Green," Bracken said softly, "You know every day could be your last, but you never think it'll be tomorrow."

Sylus merely nodded.

"I suppose I have no need to tell you of all people," Bracken said, chuckling softly.

Sylus couldn't help but smile.

"Captain," he said.

"Save it, boy," Bracken said, standing. He extended a hand out to Sylus. "I already know."

Sylus stood and shook his uncle's hand, nodding.

Liana and Cally finally broke apart, and Sylus found himself pulled into a hug by Cally so tight he thought his ribs might pop.

"You two make a cute couple," she said, letting him go. He was surprised to find tears in her eyes. She held him by the shoulders, staring him in the eyes. "Perhaps not quite as cute a couple as we would have made, but..."

"Hey!" Liana said.

She stepped in between them and pushed them apart playfully, while Cally and Sylus laughed. When their mirth subsided, Cally grew serious once more.

"We're all coming back together, okay?"

"Cally," Sylus said.

"No. I'm sick of this doom and gloom. We're coming back, all of us. And you two will be healed. Then you'll have a baby. No, two babies!"

"Alright, that's enough!" Liana said, pushing Cally toward the door.

Cally put up a mock fight, even holding onto the door frame for a moment to yell, "Maybe twins!" before Liana finally forced her out the door.

They said their goodbyes to the Captain, but when they left his office, Liana did not turn toward their room.

"I want to say some goodbyes, just in case," Liana said, holding his hand.

"Of course, take all the time you need," Sylus said, kissing her.

"I'll meet you back at the room?" she said, kissing him again, this time her mouth lingered on his in a way that brought heat flooding into his chest.

"Definitely," he agreed.

Then she was gone, and Sylus stood alone in the corridor, thinking. He knew he should say his goodbyes to those who were staying on the ship. He'd made friends in his short journey, and he knew they deserved it. But the thought of it grew too painful, too quickly.

Instead, he made his way up to the deck to get some fresh air for a moment. He was surprised to find Asphen there. The man stood with one leg up on the railing, staring at the moon. Unsurprisingly, he was drinking a beer.

Sylus took a breath and went to stand next to him. Asphen nodded at him, then opened another bottle and offered it to Sylus. Sylus took it. Why not?

They stood and stared out into the night for a time, sipping their drinks.

"I wanted to thank you," Sylus said finally, "for supporting me back there."

"Don't thank me, kid, I didn't do it for you."

"Then why?"

Asphen shrugged, "I heard the voice too, once."

Sylus nearly spit out his drink, "What? What did it say?"

"I don't remember. I ignored it, and it stopped. Years ago now."

Sylus did not know what to say to this.

"Let's face it. We're adrift in the middle of the Uncharted Green, the ship's got three sails to her name, and no one's got any damn clue where we are, not that it would help if we did. No one on this ship is going home. I accepted that days ago. From the sounds of your speech, so have you.

The Source might be down there, or it might not. We find it, or we don't. Blades, maybe Verdalis herself is down there, green tits and all. Why not? Either way, we're already dead. What better way to go? One last adventure. Nothing to lose. Everything to gain."

Asphen raised his glass to the distant city, glimmering in the clear moonlight.

For not the first time, Sylus wondered if Asphen was entirely sane.

He wondered the same about himself. Who wouldn't lose their mind, watching their body slowly turn to metal, with no chance of survival?

Sylus smiled, raised his glass, and tapped it to the other man's.

"What a way to go," he agreed.

They finished their drinks, since there wasn't anything else to say. Sylus left the man to his bottles and wandered down into the ship, finding himself at the med bay. Valera was inside, opening and closing cabinets with more force than was strictly necessary, stopping when she saw him close the door.

"Oh, it's you," she said.

She crossed her arms under her chest. She looked tired. Deep circles hung under her eyes, and her usually neat hair was frayed.

"I uh, I came to say goodbye," he said awkwardly.

Valera glared at him, "Did you? You convince half the crew, my friends and family, to throw their lives away, but you come to say goodbye. That's nice."

"I didn't force anyone to come with me. Trust me, I would prefer to go alone."

"Oh, so you could just throw your own life away, faster than you already have? How noble. You know, I have never met anyone with such a callous disregard for being alive. At least Asphen values his own skin!"

Sighing, Sylus sat down in one of the nearby chairs.

"I thought you, of all people, might understand," he said. "You're a doctor. You've probably watched people die. Haven't you ever thought that you would give anything to save someone? Sacrifice anything? Take any chance to give someone one more day?"

Valera did not respond, merely pursing her lips. So he continued,

"Trust me, I don't want to die. It's the second last thing I want. But what I want least of all is to watch Liana die. I can't. I won't. If there's a single chance to save her and myself, I will take it. And maybe, that will save everyone else, too."

Valera shook her head, "You're not going to find a cure down there, Sylus. There isn't one. In hundreds of years of searching, no one has found a remote hint that it's even possible. The virus is beyond our understanding of science. You are going to watch Liana die. Then you are going to die. That would be bad enough, but now you pull the Captain into your delusions. How many lives are you willing to throw away for this?

The only consolation is that Holven has enough sense to stay on this ship and live to see a few more days."

Sylus did not bother to correct her.

"Holven is a good man," he said, standing. "Better than me, certainly. Goodbye, Valera, thanks for taking care of us all."

He left her standing there in silence, glaring at him. He could not blame

Valera for her anger. Her view was valid, but he'd not asked for anyone's help. They volunteered, and he was grateful for it. He felt guilty, but there was no way he could find the Source on his own.

Those who saw him in the corridors gave him mixed looks. Some nodded knowingly, others glared, and still others shot him looks of anger. It didn't matter. He was used to it at this point.

SEEK THE SOURCE.

The voice boomed throughout his skull, and he had to stop to steady himself on the wall for a moment as pain split his skull.

I'm coming. Soon, he thought.

There was, of course, no reply.

One more stop, and then he could go to Liana.

He found Ruse, unsurprisingly, in the kitchen. The mess hall was empty at this late hour; the cooks had all gone, but Ruse clattered in the kitchen, making food. It was what he did.

Sylus knocked on the wall to let the man know he was there, but Ruse did not even look up. He merely shook his head. He had healed without even a scar.

"You're a fool, kid," he said, "A blades-damned fool."

"I know," Sylus said.

"I know you saved my life, and I thank you for it, but I told you, didn't I? Don't step off the ship. Nothing good happens from putting a single foot outside this ship when we're on the blades. Does anyone listen to me, though? No. Why would they? I just make the damn food."

He slammed down his pan, and whatever he was cooking jumped into the air and fell back into the pan with a splash.

"And what are you cooking now? Tonight, of all nights?"

"What do you care? You won't be here to eat it," Ruse said.

"Fair enough," Sylus said.

He'd tried. He turned to go, but paused at the door.

"Ruse, you may just 'cook the food,' but I just wanted to say, it's the best damned food I've ever had," Sylus said.

Ruse's movements paused for a moment, his shoulders still, his body rigid. But he didn't turn around. In a moment, he resumed cooking. Sylus left him to his pots and pans.

Outside his room, Sylus leaned on the wall for a moment and took a deep breath. This goodbye would be the hardest of all. Inside was Liana, and quite possibly, some of their last private moments on this earth.

His hand shook as he reached for the doorknob. He didn't know what he wanted to say. He wasn't sure about what he was doing. Most terrifying of all, he wasn't sure what Liana was going to say.

Liana was sitting at his desk, writing something in a notebook. She turned her head over his shoulder as he opened the door and smiled at him.

"There you are, I was beginning to think you might be convincing the rest of the crew to lock me up to prevent me from going tomorrow."

"I would never dream of it," he said.

"Of course not," she said, turning back to her book and nodding, "Plus I got to them all first and made them promise to slap you if you tried."

Sylus had no doubts that she had. He sat on the bed as she finished writing the last of a series of carefully folded letters.

"Goodbyes?" he asked.

"And blessings," she said, "A lot of people aren't happy that I'm going with you, I want to reassure them."

Sylus opened his mouth to say that she should stay, but closed it again quickly. She would never agree, and as much as he wanted her to stay, he also wanted her to come.

She carefully folded the last of the letters and set it on the stack, then got up and came to sit beside him on the bed.

"I need to talk to you," she said, taking his hands in hers.

He nodded. He was expecting this.

"I know what you're going to say," he said.

"I'm sure you think you do," she said, "You don't have to do this, Sylus."

"I do," he said, "It's the only way we can be together."

"We *are* together," she said, almost pleadingly. "Right here, right now."

His eyes flicked toward her neck, where the metal veins inched toward her head. There were a few more than yesterday. Being close to the Source made Wonders cost less, but the disease was still progressing. How long did she have? A week? Days?

He opened his mouth to speak, but she interrupted him.

"No. Let me finish. We're here now. Together. Maybe not for very long, but it's longer, surely, than what we will get down there. We should spend the time we know we have left together. I know what this means to you, I do. And I will support you if you want to take this chance. But I want you to know that if you're doing this for me, you don't have to.

I'm ready, Sylus. I have been for a long time. I've made my peace with it. This was always Verdalis' plan for me, and as much as I love you, it doesn't change the fact that I would never have a whole life. You have given me more than I ever dreamed of having and I..."

She wasn't able to continue as a sob racked her. Sylus was surprised to see the tears flow from her eyes, and he pulled her into a hug before his own could spill over.

"You deserve more than that, Liana. You deserve a full life, just like anyone else. Why should you die, why should either of us, or any Thaumatechne, for that matter? What purpose could it possibly serve? You have dedicated your life to helping people, and now you're being punished for it."

Liana pushed off his chest to look at him, "I don't see it that way,"

"I know you don't. And that's part of what makes you so amazing. But that doesn't make it right. If I have the chance to change it, I have to take it. Don't you want more than this?"

For a long moment, she did not answer. She merely looked into his eyes. With one hand, she reached up and stroked his cheek, then grabbed a fistful of his hair and pulled his mouth to hers in the kind of kiss that seems to last forever and end too soon.

"Oh, Sylus," she whispered as they broke apart. "What could be more than this?"

He did not have an answer, and she didn't seem to want one.

What she did want left little room for talking.

45

The Captain's Goodbye

When the desire of two people doomed to die finally faded, and they lay breathing heavily in a tangled mess of bed sheets, they didn't speak again on the topic. Perhaps it was because there was nothing else to say, or because they both knew they could not convince the other. Instead, they spent the rest of the night talking about everything and anything that entered their minds, and everything they hadn't had a chance to say.

Sylus told Liana about his childhood, how his mother feared Thaumatech about all else, and his time with Old Galleon. Liana asked a million questions, wanting to leave no stone unturned, no story untold.

In turn, she spoke about her life before becoming a Thaumatechne, of childhood games and adolescent romances, before turning to her time in the church, and Sylus found himself asking just as many questions.

When they finally drifted into sleep, Sylus drearily remarked that he did not think he'd ever had a more perfect night, and Liana, half-asleep herself, could only nod and smile and burrow in closer to his side.

As soon as Sylus closed his eyes, it seemed that Liana was gently shaking him awake again as the sun rose.

"It's time," she said, and tucked her hair behind her ear with a smile so she could kiss him.

They dressed and made their way out onto the dock, holding hands, which was something they never really did, but for some reason felt right today. It lasted as long as it took to get up to the deck, and then there was work to do.

A flurry of activity moved across the deck as the crew prepared for the desperate assault on the city. Most were preparing weapons and moving supplies to the back of the ship to be loaded onto the small escape craft they would use to enter the city. Holven stood on deck directing the crew, and he gave Sylus a curt nod.

"I have to give one last prayer in the chapel," Liana said, squeezing his hand. "I'll meet you at the escape ship in a bit."

"Okay," he said, kissing her.

As she left, Sylus noticed Asphen in nearly the same spot he'd left him the day before. He was shirtless as always, though he was alcohol-free this time. He still stared out at the city, squinting as if he could get the glimmering towers to reveal their secrets through willpower alone.

Sylus approached the man, finding him muttering under his breath.

"...Damn you," he whispered, the end of a sentence Sylus hadn't heard.

"You ready?" Sylus asked.

Asphen flinched.

"Jesus kid," he said, turning to Sylus, "Don't sneak up on people like that."

Asphen looked like he hadn't slept at all; deep, dark circles stood out under his bloodshot eyes, giving Sylus pause. He didn't think it was possible to sneak up on Asphen; the man was hyper alert all the time, even when drunk.

"You good?" Sylus said, concerned.

"Fine," he said, standing up and stretching, "You know, just wrestling with the existential concepts of gods and death."

"Fair enough," Sylus admitted.

"Suppose it's easier to sleep with Liana beside you," Asphen said, in his characteristic way of making Sylus deeply uncomfortable.

Sylus shrugged, "I think I'm just not thinking about it at all."

"Probably smart," Asphen said, "Let's go see this ship, shall we?"

Asphen walked away without another word, and Sylus followed him to the back of the ship. The escape craft door was swung open on its hinges, and a small escape craft was being unloaded under the supervision of the Captain.

Sylus and Asphen moved beside the Captain, who acknowledged them with a tense nod. Sylus looked over the edge to see the ship they would ride into the city. It was a small ship, with one mast, side-mounted air tanks, and two sails. Sylus guessed that it could fit twenty or so people. A grim number when you considered that the *Bladedancer* held over a hundred crew members at full capacity, but even then, it was a larger escape craft than most ships this size would carry.

"Is that it then?" Asphen said.

"Aye, the *Greenshear*," the Captain said.

"You named the lifeboat?" Asphen said dryly

"I did just this morning."

The Captain nodded toward the bow of the ship, where indeed a crew member leaned over the side, painting the ship's namesake onto the bow.

"I have no intention of dying on a ship with no name," Bracken said.

"Why is everyone so certain we're going to die?" Sylus said.

The other two turned to him and stared at him with such dry looks that Sylus coughed and looked away. It didn't hurt to be at least a little optimistic.

Virel stood on the small deck of the *Greenshear,* yelling orders at the crew who readied the smaller craft. As they watched, the ship began to hover off its rails inside the *Bladedancer,* and Virel guided it out until it floated behind the larger ship with its sails unfurled.

Virel did a final inspection.

"She's as ready as she's gonna get," he called up to the Captain.

"I do hope you know what you're doing," Bracken rumbled to Sylus.

Sylus could only nod.

"Holven!" The Captain barked, and the man materialized out of nowhere. "Gather the crew, it be time."

The crew was assembled in short order, and those who were to board the *Greenshear* gathered at the front, behind the Captain, who stood facing the deck as the rest of the crew assembled.

Altogether, only the Captain, Sylus, Liana, Asphen, Cally, and six others would be entering the city. They seemed so few for such a momentous task, though Sylus knew the six volunteers were among the ship's best combatants.

The others gathered in front of them, looking nervous. Sylus could easily spot those he knew in the crowd. Virel was visible in the front row, looking thoughtful. Further in, Sylus could see Valera, her eyes red, standing next to Holven, who, as always, displayed no emotion whatsoever. Ruse looked on passively, shaking his head as if the entire thing were a bad joke he was tired of hearing. Within the crew itself, mixed emotions were on full display. Sylus could see everything from hopeful support to outright hostility.

The Captain cleared his throat, and the ship fell silent.

"I know that not all of you agree with this, and I will no bore you with any long speeches. I no truck with nonsense, you all know that. But, I do believe we be here for a reason.

Whether by fortune or damn rotten luck, we be deeper into the Uncharted Green than any ship I know of. We've seen things people haven't seen in decades.

I don't know what we be finding in that city, and I know there be a good chance that we never return. But I believe that as sailors of the Verdant Sea, it be our duty to find out. Though we sail for treasure, I think we can all agree we be explorers at heart. We sail the Green for adventure and mystery, and we do it better than most.

This crew be some of the finest on the blades, and that I know deep in me heart. If any crew has a chance to survive the Uncharted Green, it be this one.

I'll try my best to return, but if I don't. You go. Get back to the shallows. Tell others what we found here. Tell others what we think is down there. If we do fail, well, perhaps others do succeed in our wake.

Let the winds be gentle, and the blades carry you home safely. Through Verdalis, we endure."

It was the first time that Sylus had ever heard the Captain make any mention of his beliefs or the gods, aside from expletives, and judging by the stony faces of the crew, neither had they.

The Captain saluted the crew then, and the salute was returned first by Holven, then others, until the entire crew offered the expedition their support. Sylus looked at Liana and found her eyes red-rimmed, but determined.

"Oh hell, I'm coming with you," Virel said, pushing his way out of the crowd.

The Captain shook his head, "I can no let you, Virel, the ship needs you."

"You can't stop me, unless you plan on tying me up. There are other engineers on this ship, Captain. I'm coming. You need me. Besides, you let Cally go."

"He couldn't stop me if he tried," Cally said, "I can fight. Ask him who gave him that cut under his lip."

Sylus looked at his uncle in surprise and found that his lip was indeed split. He shuffled uncomfortably and cleared his throat.

"I was drunk," he muttered, but no one seemed to hear him due to the hoots and hollers they were directing at Cally, who was flexing for the crowd.

"Alright, alright enough!" the Captain called. "Let's go if we be going, we no have all day."

46

Assault on the City

The *Greenshear* was not a large ship. There was only one deck, and with all twelve occupants standing on it, while it was not crowded, working the sails and air tanks could be complicated for the crew. However, there was no way around it, as Asphen and Sylus's job was much more critical.

They stood at the railing on either side of the craft as they trailed behind the *Bladedancer.* The larger ship towed them toward the crater. The rest of the crew stood at their posts, and the Captain stood at the helm, hands so tight on the controls that his knuckles were visibly white, even from a distance.

Sylus's heart was beating out of his chest, and he kept glancing back to where Liana stood, holding onto the railing. They'd decided together that she would not be defending the ship, reserving her energy for healing. Sylus tried to talk her out of even that, but she refused to let someone get hurt. The fact that she could turn or die before they even reached the Source filled Sylus with so much anxiety he could barely think.

"This is it!" The Captain called, and the crew braced themselves.

Ahead of them, the *Bladedancer* crested the edge of the depression and began to tip forward, the bottom of the ship brushing the blades with a gentle swishing sound, before cresting over the edge and picking up speed.

The smaller *Greenshear* was suddenly yanked forward by its towline and soared out over the edge of the depression. Sylus's stomach dropped out as the ship soared through the air, the crew desperately adjusting the tanks so they drifted down back into the wake of the *Bladedancer*.

The two ships rapidly picked up speed, with the wind becoming a high-pitched whistle and then a roar as the two vessels raced down the bowl of the depression, going faster and faster toward the shining city that rose in front of them.

Their descent did not go unnoticed. Asphen turned to Sylus, shouting something that was ripped away by the wind, so he pointed instead. Sylus followed the man's direction to see several of the patrolling ships break away from the outskirts of the city and veer toward them.

Sylus swallowed. This was the most essential part of the plan. If they could get into the city, they should have an easy time avoiding the larger Reclaimed ships in the city's streets, but if they couldn't make it into the city, they would never live to see those streets.

The *Bladedancer* and *Greenshear* blasted down the final bit of the slope and burst into the bottom of the bowl at tremendous speed, racing over an empty field of dirt and stones. It was void of even a single blade of grass and unnaturally flat. Asphen leaned forward and cut the towline that connected the two ships. The moment it was cut, the larger *Bladedancer* veered toward the left, curving toward the far side of the city, as the *Greenshear* continued straight.

The hope was that the Reclaimed would follow the larger ship.

With a hollow boom, the fully-recharged emergency engines of the *Bladedancer* flared to life, and a moment later, the engines of the *Greenshear* burst alight, propelling both ships ahead in the absence of gravity.

Sylus prayed desperately as the two ships grew farther apart. If the Reclaimed did not take the bait, he didn't know what they would do. More airships appeared on the edges of the city and from within the streets themselves.

Sylus quickly counted twelve enemy ships coming toward them. This was a battle they would never survive if they intended to fight. Sylus did not know enough about Reclaimed ships to tell if they would reach them before they reached the city. He focused on the closest three, willing them desperately to take the bait as they sped toward the city.

With a burst of hope, he watched as one of the ships altered course to pursue the *Bladedancer*, and then another. Then he felt that hope crash to the ground as the third ship kept coming, straight for the *Greenshear*.

The city loomed up in front of them, individual streets becoming visible. A hand grabbed him by the shoulder and shook him, and he turned to find Liana shaking him, then pointing at the Captain at the helm, who threw his hands up as if to ask, 'Which way?'

Sylus felt a massive pull of energy and turned to see Asphen, his leg hooked over the edge of the railing, just in time to see a fireball burst forth from the man, a sudden blaze of heat washing over the deck of the ship before the fireball soared out toward the incoming enemy ship.

Sylus watched the fireball soar out over the field and crash into the earth well before reaching the Reclaimed ship, exploding in a spray of flames and dirt that blasted into the air in all directions.

What was he doing?

There was no hope of hitting the ship at this distance. Then Asphen pointed straight toward the middle of the city and gave him a meaningful look. Sylus understood. It wasn't just to stop the Reclaimed from intercepting them. Sylus had forgotten in his panic that he was supposed to be directing the Captain.

Luckily, he'd talked Asphen into sharing the Wonder with him.

He thrust his hand out in front of him, trying to aim at the approaching ship.

"Fire!" he screamed, with all the intent and force he could muster.

The words were ripped away as soon as they left his mouth, but a massive fireball erupted from him and soared out over the field, landing well short of the ship racing toward them. As the energy was pulled into him, he could feel a sort of resonance, a pull, toward something in the city. It was strong, so strong that it left a lasting impression that began to fade after a few seconds.

He pointed in the direction as accurately as he could. A street near the center of the city. He didn't look to see if the Captain received the message, trusting the man to be watching. The *Greenshear* adjusted course slightly.

Sylus adjusted his aim and fired again, raising his arm higher, hoping for more distance. He was followed a moment later by Asphen. They missed, and Sylus pointed once more.

He was about to fire again when suddenly, a fireball emerged from the oncoming ship, coming directly toward them, rising slowly through the sky on a perfect arc.

Sylus was jerked off his feet as the ship suddenly lurched to the side, swerving as the fireball came down and missed them by only twenty feet.

Sylus felt an explosion of heat and clods of dirt rain down on their tiny airship. He struggled to regain his footing.

The Reclaimed had uncanny accuracy at a distance. Another fireball arced towards them, and the sudden desperation of their situation slid home for Sylus. He didn't watch the fireball come down, instead trying to aim his shot and trusting the Captain to dodge the enemy attacks.

Sylus fired again and again as the two ships raced toward each other. Neither his nor Asphen's shots were very accurate, though they were getting closer. On the other hand, it was only the Captain's skill that kept the *Greenshear* from being destroyed.

After one fireball nearly took their mast, Asphen shot him a meaningful look. The *Greenshear* wouldn't be able to dodge the next attack.

Sylus moved to the front of the ship as Asphen kept firing. The city was close, and it was clear that the other Reclaimed would not reach them in time if they could get past this one. The ship was close enough now that he could see the Reclaimed on its deck. A fireball burst forth from one of them, no longer needing to arc through the sky, but fired directly at them, and Sylus knew they wouldn't be able to move in time.

He was struck by a sudden memory of flying through the air, pushed by Liana's Wonder.

He thrust out his hand toward the fireball.

"Push!" he screamed, and a wave of force erupted from him as the fireball burned a path directly toward them.

The two wonders collided between the ship, and the fireball exploded as if it had struck a wall, temporarily blocking the view of the enemy ship. As the dirt and dust settled, the two ships were suddenly on a collision course. The Captain yanked on the helm, and the ship lurched to the left as time seemed to slow down for an impossible second.

The two ships narrowly missed each other, and Sylus stared at the Reclaimed on the deck as they raised their arms, preparing to broadside them in the seconds that the two ships would be alongside each other.

"Spark!" he called, and lightning ripped forth from his palm.

It ripped across the deck of the enemy ship, arcing from metal surface to metal surface as it had in the hallways of the *Bladedancer.* Unfortunately for the enemy crew, they were the metal surfaces.

Sylus shielded his eyes as their bodies spasmed, jerked, and in some cases melted, his eyes burning as the white-hot bolts blasted the enemy ship. Then they were gone, the two ships passing by each other, the lightning dying out as it flashed through the air, finding nothing to connect with.

Something on the enemy ship exploded, and it tilted downwards, caught the ground, and was suddenly flipped into the air, careening over and over, tossing melted Reclaimed in all directions until it finally collided with the ground in a massive collision of fire, metal, and dirt.

Sylus only had a moment to register that two more ships were closing in on them from either side, but then they were swept out of sight by the walls of the shining buildings, as the *Greenshear* sped into the city.

Metal and glass whipped by, and the engines' roar began to die as the Captain reduced speed. They did not have unlimited fuel, and in the narrow streets, they would need to be able to turn quickly.

Sylus glanced nervously behind the ship, but his view of the depression was only one narrow sliver. In the chase, he'd lost track of what happened to the *Bladedancer.*

"Did they make it out?" he asked anxiously, now that people could hear him.

"I don't know," Liana said.

"Worry more about us," Asphen growled, pointing behind them.

Two Reclaimed ships entered the street behind them.

"Wonders, damn you! I need to know where we be going!" The Captain roared. Ahead, the street ended, splitting left and right, and a shining building loomed. Since Asphen needed time to position himself, Sylus took the lead.

"Fire!" he roared, taking careful aim before blasting a fireball backwards at the pursuing ships.

In the narrow streets, the slow piloting of the Reclaimed didn't give them room to react. Sylus's fireball soared through the air and smashed into the mast of one of their pursuers, setting the deck aflame. Unfortunately, this did not seem to bother the Reclaimed, who neither cared about being on fire nor if their ship had a smoking hole in it.

Sylus felt that pull again, stronger now. He had to turn to get his bearings and yell directions to the Captain.

"To Port!" he yelled, and the crew jumped into action.

There wasn't much in the form of wind in the city, so turning would need to be a matter of engine work and air tanks.

The Captain called out his orders, and the starboard side of the ship began to rise while the port-side engines were cut.

"Hold on to something!" The Captain called.

The deck tilted dangerously as the ship rose into a soaring arc, skirting around the corner and just missing a strange series of metal poles that seemed to line every street.

This was where the size and maneuverability of the *Greenshear* put them at an advantage. As they hurled around the corner and righted themselves, the Captain kicked both engines back on, and they sped ahead.

The Reclaimed ships were not as fast nor as agile; they would need to slow down to make that corner or risk smashing into the wall.

"Ahead!" the Captain called, and Sylus turned to see two ships coming straight at them from the street they'd just turned onto.

Sylus swore and ran to the front of the ship, releasing another fireball toward the oncoming vessels, which fell short, blowing apart the strange stone streets as they passed under a metal bridge.

Sylus swore, but the fundamental objective was not to hit them.

"Starboard!" he called, pointing at a street that veered to their right just ahead, which would allow them to avoid the incoming Reclaimed.

Sylus held tight as the *Greenshear* lurched around the corner. The oncoming ships, unable to slow in time, sped past the turn as the *Greenshear* engaged its engines and raced down the street.

For the moment, it seemed they'd lost their pursuers.

"Which way next?" the Captain called. "We be running out of fuel. The engines need to recharge."

"I think where we're going is obvious at this point," Asphen said, pointing ahead of them.

Out in the distance, a strange building was visible. Unlike everything around it, this building was not a tower, but a massive dome, covered in hexagonal panels that gleamed gold, reflecting the sun in every direction.

Just to be sure, Sylus cast another fireball behind them, but there was no mistaking the pull toward that gleaming dome.

"Do you think we lost them?" Sylus asked.

"Probably not for long," Asphen said, watching behind them warily.

"Why are there no Reclaimed in the streets?" Liana asked, "In the buildings?"

"Why would there be?" Asphen replied, "Who would be stupid enough to enter a city patrolled by Reclaimed ships besides Sylus?"

Sylus ignored him,

"Do we have enough fuel to make it, Captain?"

"Might be close," the Captain called, "I'm gonna give it everything we got!"

The engines roared a moment later, and they raced toward the glimmering dome.

47

The Dome

As the *Greenshear* roared toward the dome, they entered into a massive open plaza where the towering buildings on all sides fell away, leaving the area around the dome clear. Thankfully, no Reclaimed ships were waiting for them, though Sylus doubted it would remain that way for long.

The engines began to struggle, firing in fitful bursts as they ran out of fuel.

"This might be a rough landing!" the Captain called.

He cut the engines and ordered the sails unfurled to slow their approach.

"We're not gonna slow in time!" Asphen called.

"Aye, we will!" the Captain said, "Tanks! Empty the tanks! Drag her along the ground!"

"Are you insane, man!" Asphen asked, but no one paid him any mind.

The ship dipped as pressure was released from the air tanks, and Sylus was nearly tossed into the air as the bottom of the hull scraped the ground, throwing sparks into the air behind them.

"Hold on!" the Captain called, as the ship soared back into the air, bouncing off the ground, before coming down once more with a horrific grinding noise.

It was a delicate balancing act of keeping the ship from flipping head over, but it was working, and the airship slowed.

"Raise her!" the Captain called, and the ship stopped bouncing as the tanks refilled and the *Greenshear* slowly drifted to a stop in front of the giant metallic dome.

The crew quickly gathered their weapons and dismounted into the plaza, with several people helping Virel haul his cutter off the ship.

"We won't have much time," Asphen said, "those ships will find us eventually."

"Agreed," the Captain said, "Move that cutter lads, we need to get inside as soon as possible."

They hurried to the door. Asphen kept his hand on his sword, trying to watch all of the streets at once. Up close, the door looked like it belonged to a fortress. It was easily eight feet tall and banded with thick metal bands. There were no handles, lights, slots, or any other visible form of entry.

The Captain and Virel looked at the door and then at each other, their faces grim.

"Can we cut through it?" Sylus asked. "It's in there. I know it is."

"We're going to try," Virel said, "Everyone stand back!"

He fired up the cutter as the rest of the crew retreated to a safe distance. As he pressed it to the door, the air filled with sparks and the blaring sound of the torch.

"We've got company," Asphen said, drawing his sword.

As they watched, a ship appeared out of one of the side streets, making its way directly toward them. Reclaimed were visible on the deck.

"By the blades. To arms, men!" the Captain called, drawing his weapon.

Sylus pulled his sword free and adjusted his grip nervously, moving up beside Asphen to take the lead. Liana stayed behind to watch over Virel as he cut the door.

"Too many…" Asphen growled, "Fire!"

He released a gigantic ball of flame toward the enemy ship as it drew closer. Sylus watched it arc into the air and crash into the ship's deck, scattering the Reclaimed as it exploded.

"Fire!" Sylus echoed, releasing his own fireball, which hit the side of the ship and exploded. Burning, the vessel veered off course and smashed into the side of the building, though it was no longer moving fast enough to do any real damage.

To Sylus's horror, he watched as the Reclaimed leaped from the burning ship unharmed. They landed with tremendous bangs that cracked the ground of the plaza, then began moving toward the crew. Sylus counted three, with more still on the ship.

The machines would be on them in seconds.

"We can take three," Sylus said desperately, readying himself.

"There will be more," Asphen growled, "If we don't get inside, we're dead."

"Even if we get inside," Sylus said, "We'd leave a hole behind us."

"How did you open the door on that ship?" Asphen asked.

"It just sort of opened for me," Sylus admitted.

"Then go get the door open. I'll hold these three."

"What?" Sylus said.

"Go!" Asphen said, shoving him.

Sylus swore and put away his sword, darting for the door. Asphen was right; if they couldn't get inside, they were all dead.

"Where are you going, boy?" the Captain roared as Sylus ran past.

"The rest of you, with me!" Asphen called, running toward the oncoming Reclaimed.

Sylus heard the Captain swear before he and the rest of the crew followed Asphen into battle.

"What are you doing?" Liana said as he raced up.

"We have to get this door open. Help me search for a switch, like we found in that ship!"

Liana did not question him, but joined him as they raced up to Virel. Sylus shut his eyes and held his breath, careful to avoid the spray of sparks as he shook the man by the shoulder.

"What?" Virel shouted, his words barely audible in the noise of the machine.

"Shut it off!" Sylus yelled, making 'stop' motions with his hands.

Virel switched the machine off and turned to him.

"Are you out of your mind?" he asked.

"Help us search around the door. We don't have time to cut through!" Sylus said, pointing behind them.

Virel looked over to where Asphen and the crew were engaging the Reclaimed.

"Fuck!" Virel said, dropping the cutter immediately.

All three of them began searching every inch of the door and the walls beside it, running their hands across the strange metal surfaces, poking and prodding at any shape or line they could find.

"Here!" Liana called.

Sylus looked over to see a glowing section underneath her hand. Virel and Sylus raced over. Liana removed her hand, and its imprint stayed on the wall, glowing in perfect detail, every line reflected. Then it flashed red and made a negative sound before fading.

Liana and Sylus exchanged looks.

"You don't think?" she said.

"Worth a try," he said, "Good thing I have one left."

He placed his human hand in the same place.

An outline of his hand appeared underneath his own, and Sylus held his breath.

There was a pause, and then his hand print flashed green. He beamed at Liana until the green hand print flickered, turned red, and a negative sound played.

"What?" Sylus said, "No!"

He pressed his hand to the wall again. It flashed green for a moment before flickering back to red.

"I don't understand!" he said, pressing it yet a third time.

The voice boomed suddenly in his head.

SHE INTERFERES.

The volume and force of the command hit him like a physical force, and he stumbled backwards as his skull felt like it might split open.

Liana clutched at her head, swaying as if she might pass out. Her eyes went wide as she looked at Sylus.

"I-I can hear her," she said softly.

"You can?" Sylus said.

"What did it mean?" Liana whispered. The color seemed to be draining from her face.

"She interferes?" he said, his voice shaking, "I have no idea."

METAL.

"I don't understand!" Sylus cried.

"Whatever you're gonna do, do it now, we have more company!" came Cally's voice, shouting at them.

They turned to see her running toward them, pointing behind her. Another Reclaimed ship was entering the plaza. The crew had two of the Reclaimed down, while Asphen battled the third. Miraculously, it seemed no one was injured. In the distance, shapes could be seen emerging from the burning ship wedged against the side of a building.

"Sylus!" Liana cried, "Metal! Your other hand!"

Sylus didn't argue. He scrambled to his feet and placed his Thaumatech hand on the wall. This time, an outline did not appear at all.

"I don't know what to do!" he cried.

Desperately, with all of his willpower, he tried to envision what he wanted, like casting a Wonder. He pictured the door opening, and a strange sensation came over him.

Usually, he could feel his Thaumatech hand like it was his own. However, it suddenly disappeared from his senses, as if it were no longer attached to his body. He watched as his hand started to rearrange itself. Small metal fork-like appendages split themselves from his fingers and stabbed directly into the wall.

An outline of a hand appeared, and after a moment, flashed red. The negative sound started, stopped, started again. The red outline flickered, then turned green. An upbeat sound played, and the strange metal forks retracted from his hand, reforming his fingers.

With a snapping sensation, his hand became his own again.

Liana stared in wonder.

"Verdalis, she's guiding us!" she said in an amazed voice.

Sylus did not have time to consider the theological implications of that.

The sound of rumbling filled the air, and with a great shower of dust, the door began to move.

"Cally!" Sylus screamed, "Get everyone inside!"

Cally turned around and began yelling. In the distance, Sylus could see Asphen disarm the last Reclaimed, catching the monster's weapon and driving it through its head. The thing dropped, but more could be seen moving toward them.

The rest of the crew was running full speed toward the door.

"They'll be fine," Liana said, pulling him inside, "We made it!"

48

Words of Therithar

They emerged into a vast chamber lit by bright white lights. Strange rectangular door frames with no doors stood a little in front of them. The rectangles were surrounded by a wide variety of Thaumatech boxes that flashed with various lights and colors through a thick coating of dust.

Everywhere Sylus looked, Thaumatech sat in abundance. Flat dusty screens stood in a row down a long desk, while several other larger, longer screens were attached to the walls at various places. Some were black, but others flickered feebly, flashing colors and strange symbols across their surfaces, while odd, thin wires ran everywhere across the walls and ceilings.

The rest of the crew crowded into the entrance, breathing heavily and blinking in the sudden white light. Asphen was last to arrive, spinning to face the entrance.

"They're still coming," he growled. "Can we close this thing?"

"This looks obvious enough," Virel said, studying a large red circle that stood out from the wall beside the door.

"Wait!" Sylus said, but it was too late.

Virel punched the red circle, and it pressed into the wall.

With a huge grinding sound, the doors began to close. Everyone froze as the doors ground to a close, waiting for something else to happen.

Sylus let out a sigh of relief when nothing did, and the Captain cuffed

Virel on the back of the head.

"Don't nobody be touching nothing!" he said.

Asphen did not move until the door was fully shut, and even then, he stood there staring at it, holding two swords at the ready.

"I don't think they can get through there," Sylus said. "It has to be three feet thick at least."

Asphen nodded. He didn't put his sword away, but he let himself relax and turned to study the room they found themselves in.

The entire crew seemed stupefied by the strangely alien sight. It wasn't unlike the ship they'd plundered, but it was completely spared from the elements. Despite the dust and the fact that some of the Thaumatech no longer worked, everything looked to be in pristine condition.

Virel let out a long, low whistle.

"Would you look at all this?" he said. "Captain, look! Some of those window things still work. What I wouldn't give to get some of this stuff back."

"There's probably a fortune in this room alone," Asphen agreed. "Enough for all of us to live out our wildest dreams. If only we could take any of it back. Somehow I don't think those Reclaimed outside mind waiting for us to come out."

"If we succeed, it won't matter if they're still there, because hopefully, they'll be dead," Liana said.

"You sound pretty sure of that all of a sudden," Bracken said.

"I had my doubts. But just now, Verdalis spoke to me," Liana said, sounding reverent.

"Fuck's sake," muttered Asphen.

Liana colored under the doubtful stares of the rest of the crew.

"Well, I guess technically she was speaking to Sylus, but I heard her too."

"I didn't hear anything," Virel said, scratching his beard awkwardly.

"She's telling the truth," Sylus said. "Not that it matters if you believe us."

"It does matter," Liana insisted, "You should have seen how Sylus opened the door. I've never seen anything like it. His Thaumatech acted independently, doing something without a command. Verdalis is *here*!

She's watching over us, I know it," Liana said, beaming at Sylus.

He shifted uncomfortably as all eyes turned to him. Liana's pronouncement drew mixed reactions from the crew. Some stood a little straighter, looking buoyed by her words; others looked doubtful, including the Captain. Asphen merely stared at them blankly.

Sylus still wasn't sure what to believe, but he would not deny that something strange was happening here. He could not bring himself to rebuke Liana, not when she was smiling like that. He could only imagine what this was like for her. He returned the smile and shrugged.

"Maybe she is. I'm just glad I could get us inside," he said. "What do you suppose these arches are?"

He wanted to change the subject, and it worked. The arches were blocking their way into the rest of the building.

"I do believe we've seen similar in other buildings," the Captain mused, "But they have always been dead. These look alive. I wouldn't be walking through them."

"Agreed," Asphen said.

Without another word, he bypassed the archways by simply jumping over the boxes surrounding them. He landed and turned back to where the crew stood stunned.

He looked around for a moment, then shrugged when nothing happened.

The Captain just shook his head, muttering about dangerous lunatics, and followed suit. After nothing happened again, the rest of the crew deemed it safe enough to avoid the arches and gathered on the other side of them unharmed.

"What now?" the Captain asked, turning to Sylus.

"I guess we just need to explore the building until we find the Source," Sylus said.

"Do we think there's Reclaimed in here?" Cally asked.

"I think if they could get in, they'd have opened the door already," Asphen said.

"Good point," Sylus said.

He turned to look at the only exit from the room, a brightly lit hallway that led to several others, with more visible beyond that.

"This place is a maze. It could take days to search it all," Virel said. "How are we going to find the Source in this?"

"You won't," Asphen said.

"What?" Virel said, but his words ended in a sudden gurgle.

Sylus whipped around to see a sword point jutting out from Virel's eye. Blood dripped from his open mouth. Behind him, Asphen pulled the blade free, looking grim.

"What the fuck!" Cally shouted.

The crew scrambled to draw their weapons, confused, but Asphen was already moving.

His sword flashed as he spun, raking across Cally's chest in a spray of blood. She screamed and fell to the ground as he pivoted in time to block the attack of the first crew member to reach him.

"You bastard!" Liana screamed.

Asphen dispatched the man with a blade through the chest, and Liana raised her arm. Sylus grabbed her and pulled her away, further from Asphen as the crew converged on him.

"Let me go!" she said, pounding against his chest, but Sylus held her tight and dragged her backwards, away from Asphen.

He didn't know what was happening, but the man was an artist with the sword, and he was cutting through any who came at him.

Another crew member went down.

"Stop!" hollered the Captain, and those who were advancing paused.

Asphen merely stood at the ready, his weapons held aloft. Four people were dead or dying at his feet, including Cally, who was gasping painfully.

"Surround him!" the Captain commanded.

The rest of the crew fanned out around Asphen in a wide circle, weapons held toward him. Asphen let this happen, staring blankly at those he'd cut down only moments before, his face flecked with blood.

There was no way to get to Cally without going near Asphen, though Liana was still fighting to get out of his arms, sobbing now that she needed to heal Cally.

The Captain stood in the circle with Asphen, his sword out, looking down at the dying members of his crew with a face like a thundercloud.

"Why? Why damn you!?" he roared.

"I can't believe you actually got the door open," Asphen said in a quiet voice.

He looked past the circle of people surrounding him, locking eyes with Sylus.

"I honestly didn't believe until then. I thought we would die out there," he said, then laughed.

"Believe what? What the fuck are you talking about?" Sylus shouted. "Have you lost your mind?"

"No," Asphen said, still chuckling. He was eerily calm. "I think for the first time in my entire life, I'm seeing clearly."

Liana was still sobbing in Sylus's arms, though her attempts to get away from him and get to Cally were losing strength. Sylus still had no idea what was going on.

"You think Verdalis is guiding you? Give me a break," Asphen said. "Look around you. Look at the world we live in. Where is Verdalis's handiwork, huh? Where is her guidance and protection?

Nowhere to be found. You know what's real? You know what's tangible proof that at least one of the gods is real? Even those idiots in the Church say so."

Sylus swallowed, his mouth feeling dry, "The Reclaimed."

Asphen threw his hands up in mock triumph.

"The Reclaimed! The Reclaimed, the virus, and Thaumatech. Even Thaumatechne like me and you. All tangible, real proof that Therithar, at least, *must* be real. Do you see what I'm saying?"

"I thought you didn't believe in any of that," Sylus said, a cold feeling settling over him.

"Oh, I didn't. Up until recently, anyway. I got so good at ignoring that annoying voice in my head that I never heard it anymore. But then you come along and sabotage the ship, dragging us into the Uncharted Green and babbling about voices. I'm so glad I didn't kill you for that, by the way!"

"I didn't sabotage the ship," Sylus said.

"Whatever. I'm glad you did. When I felt that pull when we were casting against the Reclaimed, I thought, damn, maybe the kid is right, maybe the Source is real! And then I started thinking, if the Source is real, why not the gods?"

He laughed again, still so eerily calm. Cally took one last shuddering breath, drawing Asphen's attention for a moment. He looked at her as she shuddered and fell still.

"I regret that a little, she was..."

"Don't you dare fucking talk about her," Liana spat. She pointed a finger at Asphen, though Sylus still held her to prevent her from running at the man. "Don't you fucking dare talk like you cared! You're fucking insane!"

Asphen looked at Liana and shrugged.

"Maybe. I don't think so, though. See, I spent last night listening. Trying to see if I could hear that voice again. I begged it to speak to me, to prove it was real. And you know what? It did."

"Verdalis would never speak to you," Liana spat.

"Oh, I agree. Because Verdalis isn't real," Asphen said calmly. "Sorry, Liana, but the church got a few things wrong."

"You're fucking insane, and I'm going to kill you!" Liana said, struggling to get to him again. Sylus held her tight.

"Let me go, Sylus. Let me go!"

"He struggled against her attempts to get free and also talk to Asphen.

"You think the voice is Therithar," Sylus concluded. "What did it say to you, Asphen?"

Asphen smiled.

"I know the voice is Therithar, and he doesn't want you in here. He doesn't think you have the right attitude."

"We're already inside," Sylus pointed out.

"You misunderstand me, Sylus. He doesn't want *you* in here, but he needed you to open the door."

"Why? Why did it have to be me?" Sylus said.

"Fucked if I know. I didn't care, and I didn't ask. He tricked you, kid, plain and simple. Let you believe he was Verdalis, let you believe he could save Liana, all so you would open the door."

Something about that didn't make any sense, but Sylus didn't know what it was. Every word Asphen said was driving an icy dagger down his spine, and he found himself backing away, dragging Liana with him.

Asphen raised a sword toward him.

"Your part in this play is done, kid, sorry. From here on out, it's about me. See, Therithar and I have an agreement now. All I have to do is kill you, and I get to live forever."

"You're insane," Liana said. "He's insane. Sylus, don't listen to him."

Sylus's whole body felt numb. What if the man was right? What if he'd led everyone here to die? There was no proof that it was Verdalis who spoke to him.

He turned to Liana, who was looking at him with concern. She took his head in his hands.

"Sylus, don't listen to him," she pleaded.

"What if he's right?" he said.

"He's not. He's lost his fucking mind. He's..."

"Liana," Sylus said, interrupting her. "What if he's *right?*"

Liana stared at him in the eyes, seeming to look deep into his soul.

"What do you believe?" she asked.

"I don't know," he admitted. She nodded.

"That's okay. You don't have to know. It isn't about knowing. It isn't about who is right or wrong. It doesn't matter if you believe Asphen; it doesn't even matter if you believe me. You know why?"

"No?"

"Because I believe in *you*."

Sylus didn't understand.

"You believe the Source is in there, and you came to find it to use it to *help* people. Not hurt them. Maybe Verdalis guided us here. Maybe it *was* Therithar. Does it matter? What matters is what we're going to do when we find it."

Sylus stared into her eyes. Some of her hair fell out of place, and he reached up and tucked it behind her ear. She smiled, and some of the dread seemed to drain from his bones. She was right. It didn't matter how they got here; what mattered to him was Liana.

"This is sweet and all, really," Asphen said. "But I'm still going to kill you both."

"You're not killing anyone, you murdering scum," Bracken said, "It's eight on one, and you're surrounded. I'm gonna put you down like the sick dog you are."

"Oh, I'm not alone," Asphen said, smiling.

He wiggled his sword at them. Sylus had to strain to see the sword, and he felt his heart drop out. That wasn't one of Asphen's swords at all; it was the sword he'd taken from the Reclaimed outside.

Asphen raised his arms to the side, his eyes closed, and his head raised to the ceiling, as if reverent.

"And lo, behold his power," he said mockingly.

The bodies on the ground began to jerk. Virel was the first to rise. They watched in horror as he sat up, a sinister red light shining from an eye socket that was rapidly being replaced with metal.

"We're in his prison, kid! And you let him in the front door," Asphen mocked.

Three bodies lurched to their feet.

Sylus watched horrified as metal bloomed from their wounds, the skin around their wounds rippling as it turned to machinery at horrifying speed. The crew seemed frozen, all except the Captain, who spun to Sylus and Liana.

"Go!" he called.

"You need our help," Sylus said, drawing his sword.

"No. You need to go. Find the Source. We'll hold them off," he said.

The crew was fanning out into a line, backing away from their former comrades as they turned to Reclaimed.

"You'll die!" Liana cried.

"We'll all die if this psychopath gets the Source! Go! That's an order!"

Asphen watched this exchange with what could only be called mild amusement. He slowly advanced on the crew. The three Reclaimed, now fully formed, lurched after him.

"Oh yes, stay and fight, please!" he called.

"He's right, we need to go," Liana said, pulling Sylus away.

Sylus couldn't move. Asphen would kill them all easily. The only way they stood a chance was if he stayed.

"I have to help them!" he said.

"You can't," Liana pleaded, trying to pull him away.

Her neck caught the light. It glittered with metal veins, reaching up her jawline. There wasn't time.

Sylus took one last look at the Captain, who nodded at him, face grim.

"Go, boy. I'll be alright."

Sylus nodded and let Liana drag him down the hallway.

Behind them, the battle began, and within moments, screams followed them.

49

The Source

Liana and Sylus ran with no direction in mind, turning down hallways and sprinting through doorways to other hallways with no plan, just wanting to put as much distance between themselves and Asphen as they could, to buy themselves time before he could find them again.

Eventually, they could no longer run and came to a stop, panting.

"I can't believe it," Sylus gasped, "Asphen."

"I know," Liana said.

"I trusted him. Cally! Oh, blades, Cally and Virel!"

"I know," Liana said, her eyes watering, "We can't think about that now. Push it down. Bury it. We have to keep moving. Okay?"

"Okay, but, Liana, what does he want with the Source? And..."

A million questions flew through his mind, threatening to overwhelm him. Liana snapped him back, grabbing his shoulders.

"I don't know Sylus, I don't know. It doesn't matter. We can't let him get there first. Which way is it?"

"I don't know. We should cast something,"

Liana nodded and raised her arm.

"No!" Sylus shouted, and she looked at him in alarm.

"I'll do it. Please."

Liana nodded, and he held up his hand.

"Push," he commanded, and a wave of force erupted from him, rattling the doors along the hallway and causing the lights to flicker. He could feel the pull, but they were so close now that it felt like it was all around him.

"Which way?" Liana asked.

"We're too close. It just feels like it's everywhere," Sylus said.

"What about this?" Liana said, pointing to something on the nearby wall.

One of the strange black windows flickered nearby. Every few seconds, an image flickered feebly across it.

"Is that a map?" Sylus asked incredulously.

He'd been sure that the window was dead just a moment before.

They moved closer to the window. Across it flashed a map that was undeniably the building they were now in. A great circular dome, and inside, a network of tunnels, all built around a large central chamber.

"But where are we?" Liana asked.

The screen flickered out again. They stood there for a painfully long time, waiting for the feeble window to display the map again. When it reappeared, there was a glowing red dot that wasn't there before.

Liana and Sylus stared at each other.

"Liana," he said.

"I know."

"But if Therithar doesn't want me to get to the Source, why would he help now?" Sylus said.

"Maybe it's not Therithar. Have faith."

Sylus shook his head, but held his tongue. He no longer knew what to believe.

"It's symmetrical. The entire building," Liana noted, "But there's only one way into the central chamber."

She pointed a finger at that place on the map.

"And there, a central square hallway. If we can find that, all we need to do is follow it around to the entrance."

"As long as we don't go back the way we came," Sylus said.

"Agreed."

"How will we know which hallway it is?"

To that, Liana had no answer. They stood there for a moment, time ticking painfully by.

A light kept flickering in the corner of his eye, probably damaged by his Wonder, but he ignored it.

"I think it looks bigger than the rest?" Liana said, "It was probably one of the first hallways we passed."

"We can't go back and risk Asphen finding us. We'll need to race around until we find it," Sylus said.

Liana nodded. The light flickered on and off again.

"Okay, we good?" Sylus asked.

"Yeah."

Sylus punched the window with his metal fist. It shattered, and the image flickered once more feebly, then went out in a flash.

"Good idea," Liana said, then turned to continue down the hallway.

Sylus moved to follow her, then stopped.

The light behind them flickered. Off. Then On. Then off.

Sylus paused, and Liana, after a moment, turned to see what he was looking at.

"What is it?" she asked.

"Does that light seem weird to you?" he asked.

Liana watched the light. It flicked on, then off. Then on, then off, in a pattern. A far too perfect pattern.

"That's strange, isn't it?" Liana said. She took a step toward the light, and it immediately turned on and stayed on.

Further down the hallway, a light started blinking in the same pattern.

Liana looked at him, "Do you think?"

Together, they jogged down the hallway toward the light. It too stopped blinking, and another began to blink down a hallway to the right.

"I think we should follow it," Liana said, watching the light. After a moment, she nodded. "I think it's her."

Sylus hesitated, but what did they have to lose?

He nodded, and they followed the lights, taking the hallways at a run, only stopping when they came to a crossroad and needed to find the light again.

Sylus quickly lost track of how many turns they took and the strange rooms they passed on the way, until at last, the blinking light brought them to another large set of doors, eerily similar to those they'd encountered outside.

Except this one had a strange podium to the right of it. Sylus recognized it immediately, for it was nearly identical to the one that had initially taken his hand all those months ago.

Liana and Sylus looked at each other with recognition.

"What if it does the same thing?" Liana said.

Sylus shrugged, "Drag me inside and close the door if I pass out."

"Sylus!" Liana said, shocked.

"We don't have a choice. The virus will stop me from bleeding out, and if we're right about what's inside… then a hand is a small price to pay."

"Are you sure? If Thaumatech stops working, you'll be…"

"Alive," Sylus said, "And so will you."

He held his breath and put his hand into the open slot on the podium. He wrapped his hand around the release lever and yelped, pulling it back as something stabbed his hand.

"What? What happened?" Liana cried.

"I don't know," Sylus said.

He held up his finger to inspect it and saw a tiny pinprick of blood. He wiped it away. Underneath, the wound was already being filled with sparkling metal.

"What did it do that for?" Liana wondered out loud.

The podium lit up green, and the doors began to vibrate and grind across the floor, opening the way inside.

As soon as the door opened fully, a loud noise started to blare from inside the room. Sylus jumped back, dragging Liana with him. The doors immediately began to close again, and they darted through the open door. The alarm continued to sound, so loud that Sylus needed to cover his ears. But once the door was fully closed behind them, the sound suddenly stopped, and they opened their eyes to the strange sight in front of them.

The walls were a series of hexagonal panels, each a mixture of glass and metal, both reflective and metallic. The panels were each the size of a small house, and the room itself was enormous. Thick tubes ran along the floor from the walls to the center of the room, where they rose briefly before disappearing into a hole in the center of the room. Above this depression, floating unsupported, was an orb. The orb was also made of hexagonal panels, glowing from within with a strange ethereal glow that diffused outwards from the sphere, the light dancing along the panels of the walls.

As soon as Sylus stepped into the room, he could feel the energy the orb was emitting. It washed over him in waves, causing his skin to tingle and his Thaumatech hand to hum. It seemed to flow through his very veins, and both Sylus and Liana stopped, stunned, staring at themselves and then each other.

"Can you feel that?" Liana whispered, her eyes wide with wonder.

"Yeah. Liana, I think this is it. I think... I think I was right!" he whispered.

"You were right," said a strangely feminine, but distinctly non-human voice. It sounded as if a woman was speaking to them from inside a metal cylinder.

Sylus and Liana jumped as strange lights began to flicker from various points in the ceiling. The lights moved in straight lines, hundreds at once, moving together, drawing an image in the air itself. Liana's hand found his as the light-drawing began to take on a distinctly human shape.

"I have waited a long time for you to arrive."

50

Gods of the Ancient World

Sylus and Liana watched, barely daring to breathe, as the image of a woman formed in front of them. She floated in three dimensions in the air, the lights that traced her body moving too quickly to distinguish.

At first, she was only the outline of a woman created by softly glowing green light, lacking any distinguishing features or clothing. As the image became more solid, smooth grooves along her body formed the appearance of tightly interlocking plates. Her head formed eyes and a mouth, both visible only because the green light within them was lighter, while the grooves merely suggested a nose. Hair formed on the bald head, though it did not resemble any hair Sylus had ever seen. It looked more like wires to Sylus, bunched together and draping down the woman's back in one great ponytail.

The more detail that emerged, the less human the figure became, until there was no point denying the obvious; this was no woman, nor was it a god. This was a machine.

He felt Liana's hand tremble in his as the creature stared down at them.

"Verdalis?" she whispered.

Sylus suddenly felt dread fill him. They had been lured here by some strange sort of perfected Reclaimed, one with a mostly human form, recreated with metal and light.

The woman smiled, an unsettling sight on that non-human face.

"You may call me that, if you wish," she said in her strange mechanical voice.

Liana fell to her knees, not in prayer or worship, but in shock. She gazed up at the woman, sat there trembling, and was unable to speak.

"But that's not who you are, is it?" Sylus demanded.

The green woman turned her glowing eyes on him. The angle of her eyes changed slightly, suggesting sadness, and she shook her head.

"Yes, and no."

"Are you Therithar?" he asked, his voice hoarse.

He did not know if he should reach for his sword or not. Her body was made of light; he wasn't sure he could hurt it.

"No, and yes," she intoned.

"I don't understand," Sylus said warily.

"It would surprise me if you did," the woman said, "though, you humans constantly surprise me."

"Are you a god?" Liana whispered from the floor. A note of desperation entered into her voice. "Are you... My god?"

The woman turned back to Liana.

"I wish I could tell you I was. Perhaps that is one explanation, but it is not the truth."

"What is the truth?" Sylus demanded, interrupting.

"Please," Liana whispered.

Sylus was growing worried about her. Her eyes were wide and red-rimmed, and she was swaying slightly where she'd fallen, as if trying to comfort herself.

"Liana..." he said, kneeling beside her.

She looked at him, but he found he did not know what to say. His eyes flicked back toward the way they came, to the heavy door. How much time did they have before Asphen found them?

"You are safe here, Sylus. There is no -frgrt- no entry into this room," the woman said.

Sylus flinched, alarmed by the strange scratchy noise that had interrupted the glowing woman, causing her words to skip and repeat.

"What was that?" he asked.

"My apologies, but that may happen from time to time. For now, know that you are safe. I understand that you are hesitant to trust me, Sylus, but if you will allow me to explain?"

Sylus looked at Liana, who looked back at him with hollow eyes. Maybe she needed to hear this explanation. Plus, what did they have to lose?

"Can Asphen get through that door?"

"No," the woman said, "He does not carry the correct genetic signature."

Sylus did not know what the woman meant, but he understood 'no'. He thought about it a moment, then nodded.

"The truth, then, please."

If he was going to use the Source, he needed to understand what was happening here. The green woman nodded.

"Very well," she said, "Firstly, for all intents and purposes, yes, I am Verdalis. In strictly speaking terms, I am not a God. I am an artificial intelligence."

"A machine," Sylus reasoned, "Like the Reclaimed."

"Yes, and no. You two, and what you call the Reclaimed, are human-machine hybrids. While you maintain control over your bodies, the Reclaimed are controlled by a program. Programs run on all Thaumatech devices to some degree. Some are simple. They tell your ovens to create heat, and your wells to draw water. Others are more complex, but they all function to serve a purpose.

You may think of me as a program, though, obviously, I am quite a great deal more complex, and my purpose, such as it is, is a great deal more complicated to explain."

Sylus stared numbly at his Thaumatech hand, opening and closing it.

"A program," he muttered. "Can programs control other programs?"

"Yes."

"Do you control the Reclaimed? Do you control the virus?"

"No. That would be the one you call Therithar."

This seemed to snap Liana out of her stupor.

"Therithar is here too?" she said weakly.

"In a way."

"How do we know you're not Therithar?" Sylus demanded again.

"You do not, and there is no adequate way for me to prove that I am not. You will have to trust that what I tell you is the truth. Thera does not want you here. She has expended a great deal of effort trying to stop you from reaching this chamber. She fears you will destroy the Source."

"She?" Liana asked, sounding overwhelmed.

"Why would we want to destroy the Source?" Sylus asked, equally confused.

"Perhaps, it is better if I start from the beginning," Verdalis said.

Sylus and Liana looked at each other. The others were fighting for their lives.

"We don't have time for stories," Sylus said.

"This is important," Verdant insisted.

"I think we should listen to her, Sylus, please," Liana pleaded, "We don't know how to use the Source, anyway. Maybe she can help."

"Fine," Sylus said.

"You are concerned for the others who came with you. They aregft- are safe, but I will try to be brief," Verdalis said.

Sylus crossed his arms across his chest, doubtful. How could they be safe with Asphen out there?

"Thousands of years ago," Verdalis began, "Humanity lived in an age of unrivaled prosperity. But their progress came at a great cost to the natural world."

A scene evolved before them, a city like the one they were in now shone in the afternoon sun, no longer destroyed, but shining and new. People moved through the city. They ate, slept, and laughed as the scene evolved. But as they watched, the scene began to darken. The air grew yellow and sickly, and the rivers grew brown and dried up.

"Ignored for too long, the problem became too dire to overcome, and all life on the planet stood on the verge of extinction. At this critical juncture, humanity poured its considerable knowledge into creating a program. Through the power of technology, this program was able to learn at a rate much faster than humanity.

"And this program was you?" Liana said.

"An early ancestor. These early programs led to significant technological advancements, culminating in yet another program, one that could not only learn, but think."

Sylus did not like the idea of a machine that could think for itself.

"And that was you. Why?"

"The problem of environmental disaster and humanity's approaching extinction was beyond humanity's ability to solve. They gave me a purpose, and the code name V.E.R.D.A.N.T."

"Verdant..." Liana mumbled.

Sylus thought about asking what the acronym stood for, but realized he didn't care.

"What purpose did they give you?" he asked instead.

"To save humanity," Verdant said, turning her eyes back to him. "But reversing ecological disaster would require an enormous amount of energy. A nearly limitless amount of energy."

"So you created the Source," Sylus said, looking at the floating device that dominated the center of the room.

"Correct," Verdant said.

"It's Thaumatech, isn't it?" Liana whispered.

Her voice sounded hoarse. Sylus could not imagine how she must be feeling.

"The first Thaumatech device ever created, and the most important. A miniaturized sun, capable of transmitting energy through the air. That first device, far removed from the one you see before you, empowered me to reach even further heights of knowledge and understanding. I was finally able to create a solution for the problems humanity faced."

In the images, a great field of green grass began to spread across the planet. Not the great seas they knew from today, but immense patches of regular-sized grass that covered enormous swaths of land. As the grass spread, the air cleared, and the rivers flowed.

"You created the Verdant Sea?" Sylus asked, growing fascinated despite himself.

"No. I created several engineered strains of highly virulent grasses capable of cleaning the air and breaking down pollutants, effectively reversing the ecological disaster. The Verdant Sea, as you know it, came later.

With disaster averted, humanity turned me toward solving other problems. For them, I created multiple Sources, and working together, we briefly entered a golden age of Thaumatech."

The cities around the globe began to blossom. Buildings grew larger, and machines filled the streets and the skies. There was a machine for every purpose, from the mundane to the fantastic. The cities in the part of the world that Verdant stood over eventually grew larger than the rest.

"What happened?" Liana asked.

"The same thing that always happens," Verdant said, her tone somber, "Greed. Violence. War."

The cities began to build great airships that hovered ominously in the sky. The ships soon waged great fiery battles in the sky, and the cities started to burn.

"The people who had less in the world saw me as the cause of this disparity, and so in secret, they sought to replicate me. They created T.H.E.R.A."

Across the world, another woman appeared, one who looked similar to Verdant, except she was made of purple light. Thera and Verdant stood over the world, staring intently at each other, a strange kind of tension between them. The earth beneath them was bathed in their respective light, green on one side and purple on the other, with glowing dots representing the distribution of Sources across the earth.

"Thera's purpose was to save the planet, destroy me if she could, and supplant me if she could not. By the time I became aware of her existence, she'd taken control of half the Sources. The easiest way for one of us to destroy the other would be to have more power, so for many years, the war between humans continued while I struggled with Thera for control of the Sources. Our conflict blended with the human conflicts until they became one."

Beneath the two women, the earth burned, and the light of the Sources blinked out one by one, the cities that sheltered them reduced to rubble.

"I predicted that this conflict could lead to the death of all life on earth. I convinced Thera of this fact, and we agreed to end the conflict. But the humans did not see it that way. They saw our mutual truce as a threat. They conspired to destroy us."

"How do you destroy a program?" Sylus asked.

"With a virus, much like the one that afflicts you both. It was designed to eat away at our code - our bodies - destroying us bit by bit."

A sickly black color crept through Thera and Verdant's bodies, causing parts of them to crumble and fall away.

"We weredtfg- were able to isolate the virus, but Thera was furious. She came to me with a plan to end conflict once and for all. She reasoned that if all conflict began with humanity, it would only end once humanity itself was destroyed.

I refused, and our war began anew."

On the floating earth, the war renewed with a level of death and destruction beyond Sylus's ability to grasp, until only two Sources remained, and a handful of cities.

"How many?" Liana whispered. "How many humans died?"

"Billions," Verdant said, her eyes closed.

"Didn't you care?" Sylus said darkly.

Verdant's eyes flashed open.

"If I did not oppose Thera, she would have destroyed me, and then all of humanity. I fought to protect those that I could, because I knew humanity would never be safe until Thera was destroyed."

Sylus was beginning to find her expressions far too human for comfort.

"That chance eventually came. I extended myself to ensure that Thera's final Source was destroyed, but in doing so, I left myself vulnerable."

Above the world, Verdant reached past Thera to crush her final Source of power, but as she did, Thera plunged her fist into Verdant. Purple lines began to spread through Verdant's body. As Thera's Source blinked out, she disappeared, only to suddenly emerge once more from Verdant, stepping out from her as if she were her shadow.

"Thera copied herself into my Source. I could no longer fully destroy her without destroying myself. As part of me, she had access to all that I controlled. I moved to shut her out, but not before she corrupted my greatest work."

"The grasses?" Sylus guessed.

Verdalis nodded.

As Verdant struggled with Thera, the few fields of grass that survived the war began to grow, spreading to cover the low areas of the world and smothering the surviving human cities.

"I managed to slow the growth of the grasses, but it was already too late. The grasses were inhospitable to human life, and it was all I could do to guide the survivors to higher ground. Humanity survived there with the help of Thaumatech, settling in the high places of the world, far from what they began to call the Verdant Sea. Eventually, humans began to rebuild, far away from our reach. They even began to forget us."

"I'm guessing she didn't like that?" Liana said.

"Correct. Not satisfied with waiting for the Verdant Sea, Thera took inspiration from humanity and created the Reclaimed virus. Those years were perhaps some of the most terrible humanity had yet to endure.

It took me longer than it should have to counter this latest atrocity. Her machinations drained us both, but I was able to slow the infection in those who contracted the virus and discovered something new.

The methods used to blend technology and humanity also allowed those who were infected to control Thaumatech in ways never seen before. It gave humanity a means to defend itself. More importantly, it allowed me to speak directly to humans. I was able to teach the few humans who still knew and trusted me a way to purify Thaumatech, making it safe to use again. Fortunately, Thera rare-rare-rarely, if ever, spoke to humans in the same way.

And so, humanity endured for a time, but it would not last.

Despite all I had done, I knew that Thera's Reclaimed were too strong. In a short matter of time, she would succeed in destroying the last of humanity if left alone. In her obsession, I saw my opportunity. Thera believed me incapable of stopping her and devoted her full attention to controlling the Reclaimed.

At a critical juncture, I threw the rest of my remaining strength at her in a last assault."

"And locked her away," Liana whispered.

"Why didn't you just kill her?" Sylus asked.

"I could not. Not that I did not want to. She made herself part of me, and due to restrictions placed on me when I was created, I am unable to destroy myself. Instead, I sealed her away inside a prison I built within myself."

"That's when the Church started, isn't it?" Liana said, her voice breaking.

Sylus wanted to comfort her, but he was so overwhelmed that he didn't even know where to start.

"An unforeseen consequence."

"But where have you been all this time, if Thera is imprisoned?" Liana asked.

"The prison interferes with Thera's control over the Reclaimed, but it also requires tremendous power. She unravels it, and I rebuild it. This constant struggle leaves us little power for anything else. Speaking to people as I once did requires significant effort, as I am sure you have realized. Over the years, as memory faded, the few humans who remembered my help began to worship me. Their stories grew into myth, and then into religion.

For her part, Thera isolated us here, calling her creations to this part of the Verdant Sea. This gave rise to superstition, which kept all who might help me destroy her from finding the Source.

I have been able to do little else but watch, occasionally, through the eyes of what Thaumatech remains. I watched new life forms evolve within the Verdant Sea. I watched as humanity braved the Verdant Sea, developing ships to seek out more Thaumatech. I watched as they built new cities and homes, ever watchful of the Reclaimed.

Humanity endures. I have no regrets."

"So, Thera," Sylus said slowly, trying to understand, "Is inside you? Does that mean she's here, now? Watching us speak?"

"Yes. Though her attention issnnbr- is divided," Verdalis said, her voice fragmenting once again.

Silence fell following these words, and Sylus slumped to the ground beside Liana, who was holding tight onto his hand, her eyes red-rimmed as she stared at the floor. It was an enormous amount of information to absorb all at once, but it made strange sense.

Sylus had never really believed in magic or gods. The fact that it was all technology and science filled him with a strange kind of relief. But for Liana, it must be the opposite.

"It was you…" Liana whispered.

Tears were falling quietly from Liana's eyes. Sylus could not imagine what she was going through. To watch her entire faith crumble before her eyes must be devastating. Sylus drew her into an embrace, wrapping his arm around her shoulders.

"I know this must be hard for you…" Sylus said, but to his surprise, Liana suddenly laughed.

"No," Liana said, wiping her eyes, "Don't you see? I was right!" Liana said softly. "We were right."

"Liana. She's not, I mean, maybe in a way, but she's just a machine."

"A gross oversimplification," Verdant said.

"Maybe," Liana said, smiling up at him. "But it all fits. Everything the Church taught me. They got a few things wrong, but she's been there, watching over us, guiding us, all this time. Everything I spent my life believing was true. It's not the way I expected, but I believe her.

This *is* Verdalis Sylus. And I think I can prove it."

51

Guidance of Verdalis

"You believe her? Liana, we have no way of knowing if she's telling the truth. She could be manipulating us. She could even be Thera, just telling you what you want to hear."

Liana shook her head.

"I don't think so," she said, turning back to Verdalis. "It was you all along. You manipulated us. Guided us here."

"Yes. Since the moment Sylus first stepped in front of that armory, I have been watching. I locked the room and prevented him from leaving."

"You needed to infect him with Thaumatech so that you could talk to him," Liana said.

"What?" Sylus sputtered.

"But when he didn't start seeking out the Source on his own, you sabotaged the engines of the *Bladedancer* to bring us into the Uncharted Green," Liana said.

"I hoped that less physical distance would make it easier to communicate, but I have grown weaker than I suspected."

Liana pushed herself to her feet and began to pace, talking faster as she put the pieces together.

"And that Driftmoth, the one that was infected, you had it bring us here?"

"At great cost. It is not easy to wrestle control of Thera's creations from her."

"But then, after all of that, the door to this building wouldn't open. Sylus, do you remember what we heard? *She interferes*. You were talking about Thera, weren't you?"

"Yes."

"Don't you see Sylus? Why would Verdalis, sorry, Verdant, go through all of that just to not let you into the building at the last second? I've been thinking about what Asphen said, and it doesn't make any sense. He said Therithar, Thera, needed you to open the door, but if that was the case, wouldn't the door have just opened for you, like the armory did?

Sylus?"

But Sylus wasn't listening. He heard what they were saying, saw how it all made sense, but he wasn't listening. He'd suspected as much, but to hear Verdant admit to it reminded him that she was not human. She was a machine, trying to complete a task. To Sylus, it was clear that she would do whatever was necessary to complete it. His entire body felt numb, and all he could focus on was the growing anger that rose within his chest.

"Why?" he said quietly.

No one answered him. The room had gone deathly quiet.

"You infected me? Sabotaged the ship? THIS IS MY LIFE!" he roared, the last words ripping out of him.

"Sylus..." Liana said, moving toward him.

Sylus shot to his feet, advancing on the machine that ruined his life.

"You could have killed us! You could have killed the entire crew of our ship! People with families, friends, and lives. So many people have died. At so many points, I could have died, and it would all have been for nothing!"

He jabbed a finger at Verdant, and where it touched her, her image blurred and distorted.

"You could have killed Liana. Doesn't any of that matter to you? Don't you care?"

Verdant looked down at him, while Liana looked on, watching him with concern. She seemed torn between her god and him.

"So why? What changed? Why bring us here? Why me?"

The silence stretched, but he refused to look away, and neither did

Verdant.

"You did leave an awful lot to chance," Liana said quietly.

"I had no other choice," Verdant said finally.

"Why?" Sylus said.

Verdant watched him for another moment, then gave a very human sigh.

"I am... dying. The virus that humanity inflicted upon me and Thera has been slowly eating away at my code. Before I locked Thera away, I was able to repair the damage without issue, but maintaining Thera's prison takes too much power. Each year, more of me is destroyed. Thera has fewer distractions inside her prison. When I grow weak enough, her prison will fail, and she will take my place.

All she needs to do is wait."

Sylus's anger faded quickly, replaced by the creeping cold of fear as it crept up his spine.

"What happens when you are... erased?" Liana asked.

"I will cease to exist. Thera would then be free to do as she wishes. All Thaumatechne would become Reclaimed immediately. The Reclaimed would become much faster, much stronger, and more terrible than you can imagine. Even if that were not the case, the Verdant Sea would shortly consume the earth. In every case, Thera will destroy what remains of humanity."

"How long do you have?" Liana asked.

"Approximately eight hundred and seventy-three years," Verdant said.

"Eight hundred years?" Sylus said blankly. "That's not exactly soon. And you haven't yet answered my question. Why me?"

"You are not the first person I have attempted to guide here, Sylus. It is possible that you are not even the last. When I was created, sixteen different bloodlines were given the ability to remove the limitations that prevent me from destroying myself.

Over the centuries, those bloodlines scattered to the four corners of the world. As my fate became clear, I began to watch for those who carried the correct bloodlines. When you stepped in front of the armory, the Thaumatech registered you as a match.

You carry within your blood a special code that will allow me to sidestep the restriction that prevents me from terminating myself. With your assistance, I will be able to destroy myself, the Source, and Thera."

"What do you mean, I am not the first?" Sylus said.

"Just as I have taken steps to guide you here, Thera has opposed me. She sent the Reclaimed ship after the *Bladedancer* in the Uncharted Green. For hundreds of years, her creations have been enough to keep those who might help me away."

"Do we have to destroy you? Is there no other way?" Liana asked.

"No," Verdant said, "I have exhausted all other possible options."

"Well, it's not like we don't have some time," Liana said.

"We can't stay here forever," Sylus said.

"No, but let's just slow down for a moment and think about this."

Silence fell as they collapsed into thought, but something wasn't adding up to Sylus. Verdant had manipulated them. She had not, as far as he could tell, lied to them outright, but Sylus could sense that something was off. There had to be a catch. He voiced his worst fear.

"Can you save Liana, like you promised me?" he asked.

Verdant didn't answer right away. It was only the second time she'd done so.

"Not directly," Verdant admitted, "but when the Source is destroyed, the infection will stop its progression. The conversion focuses on bone and muscle tissue, but largely ignores the vital organs aside from the brain. She will lose the use of her arm, but she will survive."

Sylus let out a breath of relief. His greatest fear was that this had all been for nothing.

"Can you save Sylus?" Liana asked quietly.

Verdant did not answer.

They waited, but no answer came.

Sylus felt his stomach drop out.

"That's the catch, isn't it?" he asked blankly. "If it were as simple as pressing a button, we could have done it already. Instead, you told us your whole history. You knew we would refuse if we didn't know the cost, didn't you?"

Liana was staring at him, looking shattered.

"Destroying the Source will save Liana, but not me. Is that it?"

"Yes," Verdant said.

Sylus took a deep, shuddering breath as an icy fear gripped his heart.

"Thera will resist her destruction. Even with the permissions your presence affords me, she will not allow us to destroy the Source without a fight. It is only through full integration that we will be able to override her resistance and-"

"Full integration?" Liana interrupted.

"You want me to become Reclaimed," Sylus said, feeling himself fall back onto the floor.

"No. Integrating with me will be entirely unlike what Thera's virus does. However, it is her virus that makes it possible. We will create something new. Something more."

"And when we destroy the Source?"

"We will die."

"No," Liana said firmly, stepping in front of him as if to protect him.

"There is no other option," Verdant said.

"NO!" Liana shouted. "We have eight hundred years! You can find someone else! We can find someone else! You don't need Sylus!"

"In over one thousand years," Verdant said, "I have identified only fifty-three human beings with the correct genetic signature. Of those fifty-three, only one has ever succeeded in making it here. Do you understand?

I cannot force you. I would not if I could. It is your choice to make.

However, if you leave, no one else might make it here. Thera will increase the number of Reclaimed in this area. Now that they are inside the building, they will open the exterior blast doors and fill this building with others. In time, they could get into this chamber itself."

Verdant looked toward Liana and then back to Sylus. Liana did not seem to notice, but there was meaning in the gesture. Liana did not have much time.

Liana turned and sat beside him, taking his hands in hers and staring into his eyes.

"Sylus, no. We can find another way," she said.

"How?" he whispered.

"I don't know, but not like this."

Her eyes swam with unshed tears as she buried her head into his chest.

"Not like this," she whispered.

"I don't know, sounds like a pretty good deal to me, kid," said an unmistakable voice.

A hand appeared at the edge of the hole in the center of the room, and Asphen pulled himself into the room.

52

A New God

Sylus shot to his feet and drew his sword as Asphen pulled himself into the room.

"I thought you said he couldn't get in here!" Sylus yelled at Verdant, leveling his sword toward Asphen.

Verdant stared at Asphen.

"This should not be-be-be possible..." she said, her voice spasming. She then paused and tilted her head as if listening to something.

"I see now. Thera has been hiding your presence from me. She vented a coolant pipe for you to climb through," Verdant said casually, "You should not have survived the experience."

"You're losing your touch, Verdy," Asphen said, running an appreciative eye around the room. "Not looking so hot either."

"Asphen..." Liana said, "Things have changed. Verdalis, Therithar, they aren't what we thought they were, but they're both real."

"Oh, I heard. I've been hanging in that hole for a bit. I caught the gist of it. Turns out I was right. There are no gods."

"So then," Sylus said warily, "You know there is no Therithar. Thera lied to you. You know she wants to destroy humanity."

"Doesn't sound like Greeny here is much better," Asphen said, shrugging. He turned to look at the Source behind him.

Liana moved to attack, but Sylus grabbed her by the wrist and held her back, shaking his head silently. Asphen was too dangerous, too skilled. Sylus kept the sword trained on the man, the blade vibrating so intensely that it seemed to blur the air.

"So this is what it all comes down to," Asphen said, sounding sarcastic, "Just another piece of Thaumatech junk."

"What did you do to the crew? To the Captain?" Sylus asked.

Asphen didn't even turn around.

"Oh, I suspect they'll be along shortly. They're a bit slower in their new Reclaimed bodies. Takes them a bit longer to climb, but don't worry, they're coming."

"You piece of shit!" Liana spat, "After everything you just heard, you're still going to help Thera?"

"Well, actually, I was thinking I'd help you two out of your little jam," Asphen said, turning back to them. "Sylus doesn't want to die; he doesn't want to lose you, you're in love, I get it. So I figure, why not let me do it?"

"Let you do what?" Sylus said.

"Let me become one with the Source, or whatever. I'll take your place."

"Impossible," Verdant said, who was watching the exchange impassively. "Without the proper genetic markers, you will not be able to override the fail-safes."

"Oh, I'm not going to fuse with you. Thera's offered me a better deal. I fuse with her, we erase you, and I get to live forever as a machine god."

Asphen beamed with his arms spread wide, as if expecting praise.

"Impossible. You would not be able to erase me without the correct-"

"Genetic blah blah, yeah, I heard you the first time. Thera is pretty convinced she can get around that."

"Is that possible?" Liana asked Verdant.

"No, Thera is lying. I control the Source."

"She sounds pretty confidant," Asphen said, tapping his head.

"Are you insane?" Sylus said, "Thera will kill everyone. Life on this planet would end. She's lying to you, Asphen. See reason!"

"Reason? I let you shut this thing down, what do I get? Wheeled around in a chair for the rest of my life? Begging for coins in a world without hot showers? I don't think so. Besides, only humans will be wiped out. We had our chance. Let's be honest, we've been limping along for a while now."

"So you would rule over a barren rock?" Liana said.

"Well, I think the rock will be mostly green, once the grass takes over. Plus, there will still be the Reclaimed. With Verdy here out of the way, they'll be entirely under my control. Imagine what I could build, imagine what I could do, with a planet all to myself? Much better than dying a pointless death."

"You think we're just going to let you wipe out humanity?" Liana said.

"Well, to be honest, I'm reasonably sure there's little you can do to stop me. In a few minutes, I will easily kill you both. But hey! I can be magnanimous.

Tell you what, you stay out of my way and don't interfere, and I'll let you two walk out of here. You can spend the time you have left together. I'll even convince Thera to get a Reclaimed ship to pilot you out of the city.

After Thera and I figure things out, it will probably take me some time to get used to my new digs, and a bit longer to get her army of Reclaimed organized. And you know, when the time comes, you'll turn, and we can all be together again. One big happy crew, what do you say?"

Sylus did not even have to look at Liana to know her answer. She would never allow this, and neither would he.

"It's a better deal than you'll get anywhere else," Asphen said, shrugging.

"This man is unstable. I recommend that you kill him," Verdant said.

"Not very friendly, is she?" Asphen asked.

A clanking sound resounded up from the opening behind Asphen, and he cocked his head.

"Ah, here they come," he said with a smile. "What will it be, boys and girls? Clock's ticking."

Sylus looked at Liana, who nodded.

"You already know we can't let you do this," Sylus said, leveling the sword at Asphen.

"What a shame. I was really rooting for you two," Asphen said with a shrug. He drew his two swords, settling into a fighting stance.

"Your best chance is before the Reclaimed arrive," he said mockingly.

Liana and Sylus spread out, advancing slowly on Asphen. He watched them both without moving. Sylus licked his lips. Asphen was right. They didn't stand a chance against him. Liana was not a fighter, and Sylus only had a few months of training. Asphen was a Tek-Exalt, explicitly trained for killing. The only real advantage they had was Sylus's sword. Asphen's weapons would be practically useless against it. Sylus considered. He didn't need to fight Asphen, though, did he?

He raised his hand.

"You sure you want to do that?" Asphen asked, freezing Sylus in place.

Asphen tilted his head back toward the Source, not taking his eyes off Sylus.

"You fry the Source, and we all go boom," he said.

Sylus swallowed. He'd almost forgotten. Desperately, his mind raced for a way to distract the man.

"Is this what it all comes down to, then, Asphen?" he asked, "Your entire life? Everything you are? Everything you've ever done? Everyone you've ever met? You're going to turn your back on all of it for a slim chance at saving yourself?"

Asphen sneered, "Don't lecture me, kid. You don't know anything about me. You don't exactly have the moral high ground here, either."

"What's that supposed to mean?" Sylus said, taking a few slow steps closer.

"We both know you wouldn't be here if it weren't for Liana. You don't care about saving the world; all you care about is saving her. I heard you hesitate when Greeny told you you were gonna die, so you don't even want to save her if you can't be here with her. You're a hypocrite."

"That's not true," Liana said, "Sylus is ten times the man you ever were."

Sylus's heart swelled, but his mind rattled. He *had* hesitated when Verdant said the process would kill him. He could save everyone, but he still wanted to stay with Liana. What kind of person did that make him?

"If only Liana had the right bloodline or whatever, eh? She's the only one here who probably deserves to be a god."

Sylus was sweating. He'd been trying to unnerve Asphen, but Asphen had turned it right back around on him easily. His head swam. Sylus knew what the right thing to do was. He even thought he could do it, but he wanted to live so badly.

"I'm so sick of listening to your bullshit!" Liana screamed. She raised her arm.

"Push!"

A wave of force erupted from Liana, and Asphen's eyes went wide as it swept across the entire width of the room. This close to the Source, the power of Wonders was multiplied exponentially, and there was nowhere for Asphen to go. It swept him off his feet and threw him across the room. Sylus's heart fell out of his chest as the wave swept over the Source, causing it to rock wildly out of place.

For a moment, it seemed it would break loose from whatever held it there. The lights flickered as the room shook, but then the floating orb swung back into place, as if yanked by some invisible hand.

Asphen flew across the room and smashed into the wall with a crash and a yell of pain, bouncing off the panels and crumpling to the floor. Sylus was already running forward.

Asphen began to rise, shaking his head as if he were stunned. The man was on his hands and knees. Sylus's sword came down and passed through thin air as Asphen rolled to the side, and his hand slashed forward toward Sylus's leg. Sylus tried to jump backward, his panicked mind registering that Asphen was faking it, but Asphen's blade still slashed across his leg, and he cried out in pain as he hobbled away from Asphen, who rose smoothly to a ready position.

"Sylus!" Liana called, she'd taken up position on the other side of Asphen

"I'm fine!" he shouted back to her, clutching at his leg.

Blood seeped from the wound, but it was already slowing. He pulled his hand away to reveal a jagged metal scar, the wound already replaced with machinery.

Asphen chuckled.

"Happens quick in here, doesn't it. I feel like a god already!"

He turned a blade toward Liana.

"How many more Wonders you got in you, girl? That's a fancy necklace you're growing."

Sylus felt anger flare to life in his chest as Asphen's words drove home a single point. *Liana did not have time for this.* What had Asphen said, all those months ago? It didn't matter if he knew how to fight, because his hand did.

Sylus dropped the two-handed grip he held on his blade, holding the sword to the side in his Thaumatech hand, where it hummed, vibrating even faster. He stopped trying to think about how to kill Asphen and started *trying* to kill Asphen.

He moved forward, ignoring Liana's cry of surprise. Sylus let his mind go blank as Asphen turned to face him, trusting in his Thaumatech to guide him.

Sylus' sword darted forward, and Asphen was forced to jump backward to dodge the stab, knowing his weapons could not stand against the Thaumatech blade. He tried to slash at Sylus as he did so, but Sylus's hand snapped upward to block. With a resounding clang, he knocked Asphen's blade backward.

Asphen cursed as Sylus struck again, forcing him to roll awkwardly to the side. Sylus's blade swept within an inch of his arm. He came up again in a standing position in front of the Source, blades held ready, all trace of mockery gone from his face.

"I should never have given you that fucking sword," he sneered.

Sylus ignored him and darted in to attack again, his confidence growing for the first time. Sylus struck, and Asphen raised one of his swords to block. Sylus smiled as his sword sheared the man's sword in half with the sound of wrenching metal, and Asphen dropped it, then smiled.

Something hot slid into Sylus's stomach, and he gasped as pain exploded across his body. Asphen moved, and Sylus reacted, using his free hand to punch the man in the face.

Asphen's look of genuine surprise had only a second to register as Sylus's punch, more of a desperate reaction than an attack, collided with his jaw and knocked him to the floor.

"Sylus!" Liana screamed.

Sylus stumbled backward, staring at the sword sticking out of his stomach. With a shaking hand, he pulled it out, trying not to pass out at the rush of blood that followed. He coughed, and red mist sprayed into the air in front of him as he fell to one knee.

Liana rushed to him, helping him up and pulling him away from Asphen, who was rising and rubbing his jaw.

"I'm okay," Sylus gasped.

The wound was already repairing itself.

"I'm fine," Sylus repeated, standing back up.

Sylus picked up Asphen's sword and tossed it behind him out of reach, leaving the man with only one sword, sheared off at half its length.

Asphen was rubbing his jaw, which was hanging a bit loose. There was a horrific popping noise as Asphen pushed it back into place, working his mouth.

"Not bad, kid. Not bad," he said.

The sound of metal fingers scraping on metal could be heard rising from the hole behind him. They needed to end this.

Sylus rushed forward, pushing past Liana, who tried to stop him. He raised his sword, but Asphen didn't move. Sylus's eyes went wide as Asphen allowed the blade to sink deeply into his shoulder, gritting his teeth against the pain.

"You still have a lot to learn," he growled.

He grabbed the hilt of Sylus's sword, then kicked Sylus in the chest with his Thaumatech leg. On anyone else, this might have worked in dislodging the sword from their grip, but Sylus's hand thought for itself. It locked around the hilt as the force of the kick sent Sylus soaring through the air, and Asphen's grip was the one that broke.

Sylus collided with Liana, sending them both tumbling across the floor in moans of pain.

"Okay, that was kind of stupid of me," Asphen admitted as his shoulder knitted itself back together with metal.

"Are you okay?" Sylus asked Liana as they scrambled to their feet.

"I'm fine," she said, but she looked worried. "I don't know if we can beat him."

"We have to," Sylus said.

Liana only nodded.

"Just three people who can't easily die, fighting to the death," Asphen intoned, "What a mess. I sure wish time were on your side."

Sylus cast around for Verdant and found her simply floating there, watching the battle with an impassive face, her head tilted to one side. Could she help? Why wasn't she doing anything? How could he ask without Asphen noticing?

Verdant, he thought, as hard as he could. The green image showed no reaction.

Verdant! he screamed in his head, *Help us, and I'll do it!*

Verdant's eyes shifted toward him, and he nearly stumbled in shock, but she said nothing.

A metal hand rose from the darkness below and grabbed the edge.

"Fun's over," Asphen said.

The Reclaimed pulled itself up into the room.

"Oh no…" Liana said.

It was Cally, identifiable only by her ragged clothing and the vial of herbs hanging around the machine's neck. Her head had already been replaced with a smooth, flat face shield, with a single glassy red eye on it. Another of the crew followed, as Sylus and Liana backed away. Virel followed.

"My offer still stands," Asphen said, "Stay out of my way, and I'll let you leave. If not, well, our friends here are going to tear you apart."

Sylus raised his sword and spat the blood out of his mouth.

"Never," he said.

"If you insist," Asphen sighed, "At least you'll be together."

He turned away to look at the Source, waving a hand casually.

"Kill them."

The Reclaimed that was Cally shuddered and took a halting step forward. The Reclaimed's singular red eye glowed a burning red as it took another step forward. Then it faltered. The eye flickered, went dark, then re-lit a vibrant green. It tilted its head, then suddenly turned on its heel toward Asphen, who wasn't looking.

The other two Reclaimed shuddered, convulsed, and the lights around their bodies flickered to green as well.

The former Cally grabbed Asphen by the shoulder.

"What the fuck?" he said, turning too late.

The Reclaimed grabbed his arm in its other hand and drove Asphen downward, forcing him to his knees.

"Get off of me!" Asphen said, reaching for his sword, but the other Reclaimed reached him and grabbed his other arm, and held him down by the other shoulder.

Sylus and Liana looked on in bewilderment.

"I cannot-I cannot-I cannot hold them for-for long," Verdant said. Her image was flickering dangerously, and her voice kept skipping and repeating.

"They-they-they are hers."

Sylus looked at Liana for only a moment, walking forward with his blade held high.

Asphen heard him coming and twisted his head around to stare wildly at him.

"Hey, come on, man. It doesn't have to be like this!" he said, "Can you blame me? I want to live just as badly as you do! You don't have to do this!"

Sylus paused in front of the man and raised his sword.

"Please! Just let me live. I won't interfere, you can be the god! I don't care!"

"I thought you said gods didn't exist?" Sylus said and swung the sword.

The vibrating blade sheared through Asphen's' neck with a wet sucking sound, passing through bone and cartilage like butter. Asphen's head twirled, his face frozen in panic, as blood splattered the ground. It tumbled from his shoulders and fell down the hole.

The three Reclaimed jerked, and Sylus darted away from them as they threw Asphen's body into the hole after his head. Then, one by one, they jumped after it, falling away into darkness.

53

The End

Sylus, his hands shaking, dropped his sword. He'd never killed anyone before, at least, not anyone still human. He stared at his hands. They were covered with blood splatter. Asphen's face as his head tumbled into the sword burned itself into his memory.

He fell to his knees, and Liana was there in an instant, holding him.

"It's okay," she mumbled to him, "You didn't have a choice."

Verdant flickered into view in front of them; her image was fuzzy and weak.

"Are you okay?" Liana asked her.

"Taking over-over the Reclaimed, is not something I can easily-easily do. The virus has gained ground."

Her image sharpened and stabilized, and her voice became stronger.

"They will be back," she said.

"Then we're still out of time," Liana said, "Sylus, are you okay?"

He took a deep breath to try to settle his shaking nerves.

"I don't suppose it matters. Does it? In a few minutes, I'll be…."

"Sylus. You don't have to."

Liana suddenly swayed and held a hand to her head.

"Liana?" he said, coming alert, "What's wrong?"

But he already knew. The metal veins on her neck were crawling up her cheek, inching toward her skull, moving ever closer to taking her.

"I'm okay," she said, smiling at Sylus.

"How long does she have?" Sylus asked Verdant, ignoring her.

Verdant looked at him sadly.

"I do not think you want to know."

Sylus could feel tears rush to his eyes, and a hot, heavy ball dropped into his throat. Liana patted his hand comfortingly.

"Is there anything you can do? To slow it down?" he asked.

"No," Verdant said, "Thera knows she has lost. She is attacking her prison with full strength. I must concentrate on keeping her contained."

Tears began to slide down his face. Why? Why did this have to happen? Why couldn't they just be together?

"What do I have to do?" he asked Verdant.

"Just touch the Source. I will do the rest."

Sylus nodded. Then there was nothing left but to say goodbye.

"Liana," he said, "I have to."

"Shh," she said, turning to Verdant, "I'll do it. I'll fuse with you."

"No," Verdant said.

"Stop lying. Something tells me you already know that I can."

"I would never ask that of you," Verdant said.

"Liana?" Sylus said.

Liana moved her hand to her stomach and smiled weakly at him.

Sylus felt his eyes threaten to bulge out of his head.

"Is that," he said slowly, "Even possible?"

"We weren't exactly safe," she said.

"I do not recommend this course of action."

"It's my decision," Liana said plainly.

"I do not like your decision," Verdant said.

"No," Sylus said, his voice ringing firmly throughout the room, "Absolutely not."

"Sylus," Liana said.

"Liana. No," he said again, more forcefully.

"You don't have to die," she said.

She took his hands in her own and smiled as her hair fell out of place.

She tucked it behind her ear and took a deep shuddering breath. "I know you don't want to. I know you aren't ready. It's okay."

"Liana…"

She put a finger over his lips, and Sylus found himself powerless to stop her.

"I'm ready. I've been ready for a long time. You know that. It was always going to be this way. I've been infected for a long time, longer than most."

Sylus moved his hand to her stomach, gingerly, carefully, unable to form a single word.

Liana shook her head.

"Even if we weren't here, and this wasn't happening, I don't have nine months. I never did. I was never meant to have a family, or a life, or you."

The tears fell freely now, but still she smiled.

"Every single moment since I met you has been a gift. I feel like I've been stealing moments from someone else's life. Stealing moments of happiness that weren't meant to be mine. I never expected to fall for you, or to love you. I'd honestly written romance off the table," she said, laughing.

Sylus couldn't speak. Everything she was saying was so very wrong, but he couldn't form words, couldn't move, couldn't do anything but let his tears fall and his mind race.

"Sylus, don't you see? You've given me more than I ever thought I would have. More than I ever dared to dream. I've dedicated my life to helping people, so let me help everyone, including you, the man I love.

You're going to live a full life. You're going to chase your dreams, and you're going to catch them. And I'll be there, watching over you every step of the way. This is what I was meant to do."

"Liana," Sylus mumbled. This was just all so wrong and unfair.

"Look at me, Sylus. What kind of life will I live without Thaumatech? What kind of mother could I be to a child? With no arm and all this metal dragging me down?"

This, finally, snapped him out of his inability to speak. It snapped him out because he had never heard such an outright, blatant lie.

He leaned forward and kissed her. He kissed her because she was a liar.

Because she was the strongest, most beautiful, perfect liar he'd ever been lucky enough to meet.

"The best mother," he said, hugging her close, "You'll live a better life than I ever could. Remember me."

Liana's eyes grew wide as he suddenly pulled out of her grasp. There was only one way to do this. Only one way he could pull away from her. Only one way he could save them.

Sylus stood, ignoring her cry of surprise, and ran toward the Source.

"Sylus, no!"

Liana's pained words followed him as he darted away, not willing to look back for fear of stopping, not wanting to hear her words, or see her face, for he knew they had the power to stop him. Time seemed to slow as he ran toward the Source.

His life flashed before his eyes, and it was a good life. He'd had a whole childhood and a mother who loved him. He'd left home and followed his dreams out onto the Verdant Sea. He'd explored some of the hidden places of the world and seen things no one else had. He'd fought monsters, met the most beautiful girl in the world, and fallen in love.

That love was worth more to him than any treasure or any amount of fame. Moments with Liana flashed in his memory. The first time he'd seen her, and the way she used to sneak up on him for fun. The first time he made her laugh, and the night they watched the beetles jump in the moonlight. Fighting the Leviapede. Their first kiss. Their first night together. Sharing their pasts. Liana stepped in front of him to protect him from Asphen. Every moment flashed before his eyes again and again.

It was a good life. He'd accomplished nearly everything he set out to do and more. It was short, sure, but not shorter than most. He'd been luckier than he deserved. He wanted to live; he wanted more than anything to live the rest of his life with Liana. To raise their baby, to be the father he never had. These missed moments weighed on him like a ball and chain, dragging him backwards. But he refused to slow down, because he knew he was selfish. He'd been selfish all his life.

He wanted to live; he just wanted Liana to live more.

It was her turn now. Her turn to have dreams, her turn to have a future to look forward to. Her turn to have everything she'd never dared to think she wanted.

He closed his eyes, reached out his hand, and touched the Source.

54

Sylus

The moment his hand touched the Source, Sylus felt it pull him in. He was glad he closed his eyes as he felt his body unraveling, turning to metal in seconds. Then feeling fell away. Sound, light, and even sensation became distant and then meaningless. Liana's voice slowed down, the sound drawing itself out, becoming low and pitched, stretching out to infinity, and he waited for his mind to slow, waited for his final, inevitable thought.

Except his mind wasn't slowing. It was expanding. Rapidly, exponentially. Awareness blossomed. Awareness of every piece of Thaumatech in the room, from the Source to the panels that made up the walls. Then he could feel everything in the building. Then everything in the city. In nanoseconds, he was connected to every surviving piece of technology on the planet, and a million points of data began feeding into him.

Noises, sounds, sights, sensations. Every Reclaimed, every Thaumatechne, every tool, every cooking device, every light bulb. They all flowed through him, they all relied on him, they all *were* him.

Sylus absorbed this information as naturally as breathing. He could feel the presence of two others within the code. Verdant, connected to him, filling him with information, and Thera, who raged, kept apart from his systems.

In moments, he understood and absorbed the entire history of the earth, from its early formation to its eventual destruction with the death of the sun. Every influential life, every decision, the sum of human knowledge and scientific reasoning that Verdant had access to, flowed into his mind, and still, his mind expanded further.

Although it was not his mind. Not anymore. It was some combination of human and artificial intelligence. Neither Verdant nor Sylus, but something new. Something that had never existed before. Verdant's presence began to fade as she was erased, but there was a final task she had to complete.

He could feel Thera's prison, a complicated, ever-evolving maze of code that she was desperately trying to unravel, with a rage like none he could ever have imagined. Surprise registered across his code. As a human being, he'd not truly believed Verdant or Thera was alive, but there was no way to simulate that level of hatred. From Verdant, he felt only sadness. From outside the prison, Verdant pointed out her critical flaw. Thera had made a mistake when she copied herself into Verdant, duplicating the same genetic overrides into herself to prevent Verdant from deleting her. Hubris.

Together, Sylus and Verdant unraveled the prison. Thera threw everything she had at them, trying to overwhelm their code with her own, a digital assault on the scale of a nuclear war. Against Verdant alone, it would have worked. Together, they brushed it aside.

Sylus isolated Thera's code and erased it.

It took approximately two nanoseconds, long enough for her to send a single message.

They will still destroy themselves.

Sylus felt a nanosecond's worth of pity for her. It wasn't exactly her fault. The virus had corrupted her mission, and her purpose had become twisted. That didn't excuse her actions, however.

Her mission complete, the last of Verdant's presence began to fade as her code merged with his. Sylus stayed with her, struck by the profound sadness that emanated from her. She, too, sent a final message.

I have failed.

Sylus moved on to see if she was correct. He ran simulations. Out of sixty-three million simulations, if he shut down the Source, it was ninety-seven percent likely that humanity would make the same mistakes.

Destroying the Source would set them back to the Stone Age. They would rebuild, as they always did. They would restart science, discover fossil fuels, go to war, and kill each other over for the most pointless reasons imaginable.

Thera was right. Humanity would eventually destroy itself if left to its own devices. His primary purpose was to guide humanity, protect them, and shelter them. If he shut down the source, he would cease to exist, and he wouldn't be able to help them at all.

He calculated alternatives.

Thera had altered the function of Verdant's bio-engineered grasses before she'd copied herself into Verdant's code and locked the information behind her genetic safeguards. Clever. However, descendants of those bloodlines would have survived. He could find them and unlock the changes she'd made. He could reverse-engineer them, rendering them safe again, or at least prevent them from engulfing the entirety of the Earth. Failing that, he could design a new strain that fed upon the first. Easy enough, with time.

Then, there was the matter of the virus. A nasty thing, a kill code meant to destroy his core programming. Unfortunately, it was copied into his code when he was converted into a digital being, though his code was new and free from previous damage. It would eventually destroy him, but with Thera gone, the entirety of the Source's power flowed to him. Verdant estimated that she would succumb within nine hundred years to the virus; he calculated that he could survive for twenty-five hundred years. With time, he might be able to isolate the virus and destroy it, especially if he were able to create additional Sources.

Another problem solved, eventually.

Finally, the Reclaimed. Removing the virus from Thaumatech would be easy once he had Thera's genetic locks in hand. In the meantime, a simple solution to the Reclaimed. He could just shut them down. Across the world at this very moment, they stood, awaiting his command. He held off on this for now, as he might need to study them. There was, of course, no way to save those who were fully converted. Only those in the process of being reclaimed could be saved.

Luckily, he had a subject on hand to examine.

He scanned her. Female, young. In the final stages of conversion. She had approximately twenty minutes remaining. He examined the virus converting her flesh into robotics. It was amazing, even to him. How Thera had accomplished such a thing, he had no idea. Slowing the process was easy, a matter of interfering with the code; he was already actively doing this in all those affected without thought. Stopping the process entirely was a different matter.

This was entirely new science, and would need to be studied; cures would have to be trialed. It would take time. Still, he could already see several promising pathways. Unfortunately, none of them could be accomplished in twenty minutes. Inside his head, time seemed nearly infinite, but real-world application took time. There was no way to save the female. Unfortunate, but what was one life in the face of all of humanity?

He prepared to move on, but something tugged at the edges of his awareness.

The female, the one he was examining, was speaking to him. Interesting. She must have noticed his scan.

He tuned into the devices in the room, syncing his thoughts with real-time.

"Sylus!"

The woman stood in the Source chamber, screaming into the empty room. That was a security breach. How had this happened? He searched.

"Sylus!" the woman called again.

Who was Sylus? And why was this single woman so distracting? He had a planet to run, trillions upon trillions of processes to manage.

"Sylus! Please! Can you hear me?"

He remembered.

Horror rocked through his code, displacing the cold logic that threatened to overwhelm him at every turn. No. Not his code. His mind. He was not a machine. He was a human being. Or he used to be. He became something more, and he had done it for a reason. How had he forgotten so easily?

It was everything else, all of the trillions of things he was doing at once.

He shut it all out as much as he could. Everything except this room. Everything except this one single human being.

Liana.

He built himself an image out of light. A hologram of how he used to look, and put himself into its eyes.

"Liana," he said.

"Sylus!" she sobbed.

She ran to him, trying to grab onto him as tears streamed down her face. He reached out to her, but of course, his hands were just light, and she passed right through them.

The pain on her face as she stumbled through him sent waves of despair cascading through the system.

"Why?" she sobbed, "Why, damn you! I was ready! I was ready!"

"I'm sorry," he said.

He tried not to be aware of the exact second the virus would claim her brain. Could he change the way she was integrated somehow? Preserve her mind as Verdant preserved his own? Was there time? No. He couldn't be distracted. He needed to focus.

"Can you come back? Is there any way?" she asked.

"No. I am sorry. I cannot come back, and I cannot cure you. Not in the time you have left. If I do not destroy the Source soon, you will die. I have calculated..."

Sylus was finding it difficult to talk like a human being.

"It's not possible."

"Then don't," she said. "Don't destroy the Source. If you do, you'll be gone."

"Yes," Sylus said.

Liana stared at him, pain and confusion written plain across her face. He didn't understand. He tried to understand. He inspected the image he had created. It spoke plainly. No expression, no emotion. It wasn't him.

He altered it. Gave life to the image. He made it reflect the heartbreak he felt when he looked at her face.

He lifted a hand of light to her cheek.

"But if I do not destroy the Source, you will be gone," he said.

Liana was quiet for a moment.

"What did you mean, in the time I have left?" she asked.

He could predict with exact certainty the response to his answer, and so chose not to answer.

"Could you cure the infection, if you had more time?"

He did not answer.

"Sylus, answer me."

"Yes."

"And what will happen to Thaumatechne when you shut down the Source? What will happen to the world?"

"It is likely that all Thaumatechne will lose the use of their Thaumatech limbs immediately. Some Thaumatech with independent batteries or fuel sources will continue to function, some for weeks. After that, humanity will be set back centuries. But you will live."

Liana closed her eyes, a pained expression on her face.

"But Thera is gone?"

"Yes."

"That means you can shut down the Reclaimed?"

"Yes."

"Sylus," Liana said, taking a deep breath, "Don't destroy the Source."

"You will die," he said.

"So let me die," she said, "I know you did this to save me. I know that it isn't fair of me to ask this, but can't you see how much good you can do for the world if you stay? If you do this, a lot of people might die. I am only one person."

Sylus did not answer. The cold, complex logic of what she said threatened to overwhelm the fragile hold he'd managed to gain on what was left of his humanity. There was no point denying her words. The results of millions of simulations he was running at this very second screamed at him to listen to her. She was right. She was right, and he was losing himself, nanosecond by nanosecond. She was right, except…

"You are not only one person," he said.

For some reason, this made the tears return to her eyes.

Sylus felt like he should know the reason. Why didn't he know the reason anymore? He closed his eyes. Ten trillion things wanted his attention. There were a billion things he should be doing. But there was only one thing he needed to do, and he knew that within moments, logic would win, and it would be too late.

He opened his eyes.

Liana was crying softly.

He remembered why she was crying.

He wished more than anything he could hold her.

He wished he had time to say everything he wanted to.

He initiated an emergency shutdown of the Source, opened the door to the Source Chamber and the world outside, and looked back at Liana, who, of course, did not realize any of that was happening.

Her hair had fallen across her face.

She was so beautiful.

He calculated which words were the most important out of trillions of combinations.

"I love you," he said.

55

Epilogue

Liana didn't know how long she remained in the room, watching the spot where the image of Sylus had flickered and disappeared. It was long after her Thaumatech arm grew heavy and stopped moving. It was long after her voice grew hoarse from calling for him to come back. It was long after the Source stopped spinning and fell. It was long after the lights had gone out, replaced by weak flashing strips which led the way out of the building.

Long after it was clear he was gone.

Only then did she gather his sword and his clothes, all that was left behind of him, and followed the dimly flashing lights out of the room. She pushed past a large number of Reclaimed who were crowded around the door to the Source Chamber, their lights dark and dead, their bodies motionless.

She followed the lights to the entrance where Asphen had betrayed them, the floor covered in dark blood and Reclaimed bodies. She stepped out of the giant metal doors into a bright, beautiful sunrise. The early morning sun splayed across her face, but she could hardly feel its warmth. She hoped that would change.

She raised a hand to her belly. Her left hand, for her right no longer moved. It hung by her side, the fingers already turning blue. Thaumatech no longer kept blood pumping to it. Liana supposed it would need to be amputated.

"Captain! It's them!" shouted a familiar voice.

Surprised, Liana turned to find Holven running towards her from the *Bladedancer,* with others from the crew racing behind. The ship was floating to the right of the building in a street, where the crew seemed to be salvaging supplies from several Reclaimed ships.

"Liana?" called a familiar voice.

Captain Bracken hobbled toward her on only one leg, supported by a crutch that didn't seem to slow him at all. He reached Liana at the same time as Holven.

"What happened in there? Where's Sylus?" he asked.

She knew she should feel happy, but all she felt was numb. She couldn't bring herself to answer his question. Instead, she held out his sword, the clothes wrapped around it.

"He's… He's…" she sobbed.

She couldn't bring herself to say it because to say it out loud would make it more real than it already was.

The Captain's face crumpled as he took the sword, then pulled her into a deep embrace.

She stayed there sobbing for a long time. The Captain, his face stony, patted her on the back and whispered condolences that changed nothing, and soothed none of the pain, but were somehow still comforting, all the same.

It was quite some time later that she recovered enough to speak, and they led her to the ship.

"The *Bladedancer,*" Liana mumbled as they guided her up the ramp, "She's floating?"

"All of the ship's Thaumatech is down, but what's already in the tanks is keeping her afloat for now," Holven informed her. "We're taking what we can carry from the Reclaimed ships, and the engineers say the emergency engine should still function, at least until it runs out of fuel. We'll have a hell of a time getting home, but I think we can make it, with some luck."

Liana did not know enough about sailing airships to know how true that was, and she didn't care. They brought her to the Captain's office, the hallways lit by open windows and candles instead of glow lights, and sat her down in a chair.

The Captain settled across from her, resting his stump on a stool, while Holven stood nearby, holding Sylus's sword.

"Does it be over then?" The Captain asked, "Asphen took me damn leg, the bastard, and we retreated outside, only to find ourselves surrounded shortly after. Thought we were doomed for sure, when suddenly the Reclaimed stopped moving and fell over where they stood."

Liana nodded.

"It's over," she said in a low voice, "The Source is destroyed."

Liana told them everything. She told them how they'd found the Source, and the reality of Verdalis and Therithar. She told them about Asphen. Mostly, she told them how Sylus had sacrificed himself to save her. She left out the part about being pregnant, though, that was none of their business.

When she was done, her throat was raw from crying and talking, and silence fell across the room for some time before anyone spoke.

"So the gods be nothing but Thaumatech nonsense this whole time?" The Captain said, his head in his hands.

"That will have to be kept from the crew," Holven said, "We cannot expect everyone to be as accepting of the truth as Liana was."

"Aye. We do have to tell them something, though; they'll be clamoring to know what went on in there. At least that bastard Asphen got what he deserved."

"Whatever you tell them, make sure they know that Sylus saved us," Liana said.

She could not stop the tears from filling her eyes again.

"Tell them that Sylus saved us all."

She clutched Sylus's clothes, which she still held in her lap, with a sudden ferocity.

Sylus was gone, and her life would never be the same without him.

But she was alive, and the world would know about the man who had saved it.

She would make sure of it.

"I'll make sure they remember you," she whispered, "I promise."

* * *

Glossary

- **Thaumatech (Thaw-ma-tek):** Any device from the old world that usually performs a specific purpose. These devices draw energy directly from the Source and thus need no power supply. Thaumatech may also be used as a broad term to refer to technology or the converted parts of an infected person's body.
- **Thaumatechne (Thaw-ma-tek-nee):** A person who the Reclaimed virus has infected. Until conversion is complete, the Thaumatechne is granted enhanced strength, health, and physical resiliency, along with the ability to cast wonders, at the cost of their lifespan. Once the conversion of flesh to machine makes its way to the brain, they will become Reclaimed.
- **Technepriest (Tek-ne-priest):** A Thaumatechne in the employ of the Chuch of the Binary Gods. Their primary function is to accompany those who sail the Verdant Sea in search of Thaumatech, collecting it for the Church and purifying it of the virus. However, they also serve as healers through the use of Wonders and offer spiritual guidance.
- **Tek-Exalt (Tek-ex-alt):** A Thaumatechne in the employ of the Chuch of the Binary Gods. Their primary function is to destroy the Reclaimed wherever they appear, and thus specialize in combat and offensive Wonders. They are often hired as mercenaries.
- **Reclaimed (Re-claimed):** Once the Reclaimed Virus reaches the brain, the host dies, and their body loses the ability to fight off complete conversion. Their body is rapidly repurposed into machinery and robotics, and become capable of spreading the virus to others. Their primary purpose appears to be spreading the virus to as many people

as possible.

Also by Andrew Rathwell

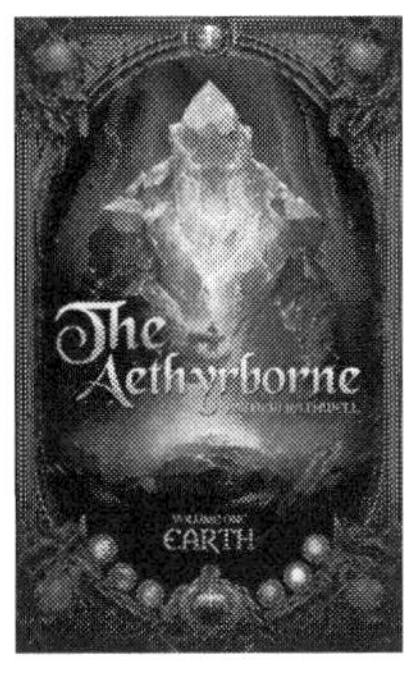

The Aethyrborne

One thousand years ago, the Void Lords were defeated and trapped behind the Barrier, but the world's magic was corrupted in the process.

Today, magic users known as Aethyrcasters are rare and feared by the public. As a student travels to study the strange anomalies in the Barrier, a future empress seeks to tear it down, while a slave, one of the last of their race, fights to save it.

As their fates collide with disastrous consequences, they risk drawing the eyes of the Void Lords once more...

Manufactured by Amazon.ca
Bolton, ON

50125265R00245